HEARTS BEGUILED

PENELOPE WILLIAMSON

AVON BOOKS ◆ NEW YORK

HEARTS BEGUILED is an original publication of Avon Books. This work has never before appeared in book form. This work is a novel. Any similarity to actual persons or events is purely coincidental.

AVON BOOKS
A division of
The Hearst Corporation
105 Madison Avenue
New York, New York 10016

Copyright © 1989 by Penelope Williamson
Published by arrangement with the author
Library of Congress Catalog Card Number: 88-92958
ISBN: 0-380-75600-5

First Avon Books Printing: July 1989

AVON TRADEMARK REG. U.S. PAT. OFF. AND IN OTHER COUNTRIES, MARCA REGISTRADA, HECHO EN U.S.A.

Printed in the U.S.A.

K-R 10 9 8 7 6 5 4 3 2 1

Prologue

1783

After twenty years of owning a pawnshop in the raucous neighborhood of the Palais Royal, Simon Prion had seen it all. Whatever they brought in to pawn—a grandmother's diamond necklace, a father's sword, the silver buckles from last year's shoes—it all came down to the same thing. They were pledging their last hope, the final piece of a broken dream.

But not this girl . . . He wanted her to be different.

He had been watching her for a good hour now. His shop was in the new Galerie de Valois, to the right of the ducal palace. Facing his front door and window were the gardens. On a fair day the gardens and arcades of the Palais Royal filled with people. Beggars and balladeers, dukes and cobblers—they all came there eventually. For the Palais Royal was the center of Paris and Paris was the center of the world, and it was there they came to broker their dreams.

But not this day. On this day the sky was a smudged gray, the color of soot. The wind was damp and cold, rustling the few withered leaves that still clung stubbornly to the branches of the chestnut trees. Occasionally the wind gusted against the sign above his shop—the three golden balls of the pawnbroker—making it groan. Although it was only November, ice ringed the edges of the puddles that formed in the depressions of the dirt paths and cobbled streets.

1

And there was no one in the gardens but the girl.

She paced the path directly across from his shop. Occasionally she would pause and glance his way, and Simon would think that at last she was coming, but instead she would resume her pacing. Whatever dream she was being forced to sell, she was finding it hard to part with.

Curiosity brought Simon to his cluttered window where he could see her better. Her tall, slight frame, enveloped by a large black *manteau,* appeared vulnerable, fragile. Yet this was no provincial shopkeeper's daughter or peasant girl. She had a certain way of standing, a proud way of holding her head, that could only have been acquired through centuries of noble breeding. And the style and flair of her cloak, her self-contained yet purposeful movements—she was, without doubt, Paris born and raised.

From this distance her face looked pale and unmarked by the pox. The bones were boldly sculptured, with a strong chin, broad forehead, and dark, flaring brows. As he stared at her, the wind pulled a tendril of hair from the hood of her cloak, plastering it against her cheek. It was the color of a flame.

She stopped pacing suddenly and turned to stare boldly at the shop.

Simon stumbled away from the window, almost knocking an Oriental vase priced at twenty livres off its stand. His face felt warm. He was acutely aware of how he must appear—a man well past middle age with too much flesh and too little hair, caught peeping out the window at a pretty girl.

He sucked in a sharp breath. She was coming.

But at the last moment she veered to the left, toward the palace gates. Simon stood in the gloomy shadows within his shop and watched her figure pass the window and disappear. She was not coming after all, and he felt an inexplicably fierce ache of disappointment.

Without looking, without really thinking, Simon pulled off his smock and snatched a coat from the racks that lined one wall of his shop. His left arm was through one sleeve and his right hand was reaching for the latch when the door was flung open in his face, cracking him hard across the bridge of his nose.

"Oh, I beg your pardon!"

A black, blurred figure loomed before him. Simon blinked back tears of pain and his eyes refocused. It was the girl.

"I'm sorry," he mumbled. "I wasn't watching where I . . ."

He lifted his hand to his throbbing nose and noticed a strange and distastefully gaudy coat dangling from the end of his arm.

"I thought I would go out for . . ."

He tried to cram the considerable rest of himself into the coat, then realized that in his hurry he had grabbed one that was at least two sizes too small.

"That is, I don't really need to go out just now . . ."

His words trailed off. He stood before her, half in and half out of the ugly coat, and his nose hurt and his cheeks burned.

But she wasn't looking at him; she was looking slowly around the shop. "Where is Monsieur Prion?" she said after a moment.

He started. "I'm Prion. But how did you know my name?"

She turned to face him and he found himself looking into strange, mesmerizing eyes of so dark a blue they were purple. Though she was very young those eyes held a bitter wisdom far beyond her years.

She smiled then. It was sweet but strained, as if she hadn't smiled in a long, long time. "Your sign above the door. It says: Simon Prion, Proprietor."

He laughed shakily. "Oh, of course. How stupid . . ." He knew he was mumbling and blushing again. He felt foolish, and normally he didn't like to be made to feel foolish. But he wasn't angry; the girl intrigued him.

He peeled off the ridiculous coat and flung it into a corner, then made a graceful bow. "I trust I may be of some small assistance, mademoiselle."

She stared at him. "I have something to pawn . . ."

She paused, but Simon said nothing. He hoped she wasn't going to pledge her *manteau*. He wouldn't be able to offer her a good price for that. He had too many coats and cloaks as it was, and besides, winter was only just starting and already it was cold. She would need her *manteau*.

"Tell me, Monsieur Prion," she said. Her voice was soft and, unlike her eyes, innocent. "Do many of your customers come back later to redeem the things they have sold?"

"But of course," he lied. "All the time. You wouldn't actually be selling your, er, the item, you understand. Merely pledging it as collateral against a loan equal to its value." To half its value, he amended silently. And not counting, of course, the interest.

She drew in a deep breath, as if making a decision. Then with an impatient gesture, she pushed the hood of her cloak off her head. Her hair fell down her back. It was thick and long, almost to her waist. Simon had heard of hair of such a color—*blond vénitien*, they called it. It was the color of young strawberries, just barely ripened.

She wrenched at a large ring on the middle finger of her left hand. It stuck a moment on the knuckle, for her fingers were slightly swollen, no doubt from the cold. Finally it came off, and she thrust it at him as if suddenly she couldn't get rid of it fast enough.

He took it and went behind a broad, low desk to examine it by the flickering light of a silver candelabra. He fixed a magnifying lens into his eye.

"It's gold," she stated.

Simon grunted.

"And the jewels are genuine. A sapphire and rubies."

Simon sighed.

It was an antique piece, at least a hundred and fifty, perhaps two hundred, years old. A two-carat sapphire mounted in a bed of half-carat rubies in a setting of filigreed gold. Very recently an inscription had been etched on the inside of the worn band. *For G, Love M.* Who was M? he wondered—her lover, her husband? Perhaps the ring was a family heirloom, passed down from mother to daughter. Or perhaps she had stolen it, or bought it from another pawnshop during a happier, richer time. He sighed because he would never know.

"How much will you give me for it?" she asked.

He looked up, expecting her face to be sad, but it was hard. Beautiful and young, but hard.

"Fifteen louis d'or, at twenty percent interest," he said.

She reached for the ring, but his fist closed over it. "Anywhere else, you would only get ten."

"But it's worth twice that much!"

"Sentimentally, perhaps. The gold is of inferior quality and the sapphire is flawed. Even as an antique it's worth twenty louis at the most. And a loan on fifty percent of the value is standard."

Her eyes flickered away from his. She knows that, he thought. She has done this many times before.

"I'll give you fifteen louis for it. Anyone else would only give you ten," he repeated gently, pretending to believe in her innocence because he wanted to. "If you can't pay off the loan to redeem the ring, I'll be forced to sell it. And we pawnbrokers must live, too; we must show a profit, however small. I have a wife and children to feed," he added. Another lie.

Her soaring brows drew together over those worldly violet eyes. "Then why are you being so generous with me?"

"Because . . ." He shrugged, smiled. "Because you are young. And pretty."

Her face revealed nothing, but she pulled her hand off the desk top. "How long do I have to redeem it?"

"Six months."

She smiled then, that fleeting, strained smile. "Six months is a long time, monsieur. You are indeed very generous."

Simon Prion shrugged and blushed again. What could he tell her? That she reminded him of his daughter, except that he had never had a daughter, never married. That if she had been his daughter, he would have cared for her so that she wouldn't need to pledge any broken dreams.

But since she wasn't his daughter, he pulled out a battered strongbox, opened it with a key, and began to count out fif-

teen louis. She took a step toward him, and he glanced up.
The front fold of her cloak caught on the corner of the desk,
pulling the heavy material aside. Simon's eyes widened with
shock.

For beneath stiff black taffeta skirts, the girl's stomach
bulged with a pregnancy near the end of its term.

An icy gust scattered raindrops among the dead chestnut
leaves in the gardens of the Palais Royal. Gabrielle de Vauclair de Nevers clutched at the folds of her long woolen coat
and bent into the wind. There was a dull, throbbing pain in
the small of her back. She was aware of it, but she didn't
really feel it.

The purse was heavy in her hand. For weeks it had been
empty, but now she had fifteen gold louis. If she lived fru-
gally, the money would last a long time. It would have to.

She did not think about what she had done to get the fifteen
louis, or of what she would do when the money ran out. She
had nothing more to pledge. She didn't pretend to herself that
in six months she would redeem the ring. The ring was gone
forever. Just as the man who had given it to her was gone.

Forever.

She crossed the wide-open square of the Place du Carrousel. The wind tugged at her skirts and blew dust in her eyes.
Soon the rain would turn the dust to black, sticky mud.

The wind brought with it the odor of crêpes frying on a
hot griddle, and her stomach cramped with hunger. She hadn't
eaten in two days. Her steps faltered a moment, but then she
saw that the crêpe vendor was already buttoning down his
stall against the weather, and she went on.

She walked along the quay toward the Pont Neuf. Below
her churned the murky waters of the river Seine. The fires of
beggars and vagabonds flickered in the shadowy darkness beneath the stone parapets.

There wasn't much traffic on the bridge. The mountebanks
and toothdrawers had sought shelter from the rain. Most of
the shops and stalls, even the shooting galleries, had closed
for the day for lack of customers. She had almost reached the

opposite bank when she heard the rattle of iron wheels on cobblestones. Automatically she drew aside to avoid being splattered with mud thrown up by the coming carriage.

She glanced behind her. It was a ponderous, slow-moving berlin, finished a dull black and pulled by four dark horses. She felt a sudden, sharp quiver of fear.

Silly fool, she berated herself. There were a hundred such vehicles in Paris.

Still, she quickened her pace. The berlin drew abreast of her and seemed to slow. The postilions, she saw, were liveried in black and gold. Reluctantly, as if pulled by invisible reins, she turned her head.

A long, slack hand pushed open the leather curtain on the carriage window. For a moment Gabrielle stood frozen, staring into dark, protruding eyes magnified by thick spectacles and a pale face marred by a raw scar on one cheek. The man's eyes blinked, and then his thin mouth stretched into a smile of recognition. And triumph.

Gabrielle ran.

"Gabrielle!" the man in the carriage shouted. "Wait! I only want to talk with you!"

She ran harder. She heard more shouts, the jangle of harness, the clatter of hooves on stone. Driven by panic, she flew across the quay and plunged into the warren of narrow streets, alleys, and courtyards that was the *quartier* of the butchers.

Her heavy belly made her clumsy, and several times she almost fell. The rain came down harder now, but away from the river the wind was less fierce. She ducked into a dark, narrow passage and almost gagged from the smell. Her feet squished on something soggy as she ran. She told herself it was only piles of entrails thrown out the door of one of the butcher shops.

The end of the passage opened onto steep stairs that led to another street below. Gabrielle paused, her breath sawing painfully in her throat. The stone steps, slippery from the rain, looked treacherous.

"This way!" she heard someone call out, followed by the

pounding of running feet. The streets were too narrow for the heavy berlin, but he had sent his lackeys after her on foot.

Gabrielle plunged recklessly down the stairs.

Her feet flew out from under her. Stifling a cry, she grabbed desperately at the stones with her fingers. Her nails ripped and pain shot up her arms, but she managed to regain her balance. Down she plunged, into unknown blackness below.

The stairs ended in the yard of a posting house. Skirting a pile of steaming manure, Gabrielle pushed through a threesome of foraging pigs and slipped into the back door of a nearby shop. The pungent, acrid odor of wine filled her nostrils.

She walked quickly past towering rows of casks and pyramided bottles and out the front door. Nobody had seen her.

Outside, she leaned against the wall, struggling to catch her breath. The sounds of pursuit had faded. There was a sharp, stabbing pain in her side; her heart pounded heavily in her chest. She shut her eyes for a few precious seconds, fighting waves of dizziness.

Louvois. She said his name to herself, hating him.

He had said he only wanted to talk with her, but he lied. She pressed her hand against the child within her. She knew what he would do to her, to them both, if he caught her.

And he wouldn't give up easily.

She looked around, trying to get her bearings. Across the street a light flickered deep within the cavernous doors of a print shop. Water poured from the open gutter spouts and lanterns creaked overhead; they hung from ropes and wires, strung between the leaning tenement roofs. Although it was late afternoon and growing dark, few of the candles were lit.

She knew where she was. Weaving with exhaustion, she ran two more blocks and turned onto the Rue de la Huchette. The lackeys, in their fancy black and gold livery, wouldn't dare follow her here.

Dark figures flitted restlessly in the shadows of the doorways and abutments. Gabrielle's fingers wrapped tighter around her purse and she pulled her *manteau* close to her, but it was done more out of prudence than fear. Five months before, in her old life, she would have been terrified of the thieves, cutpurses, and cloak-snatchers who haunted this narrow, mean street. Now she was one of them.

The driving rain sent the day's accumulated refuse swirling down the central gutter in the street to clog the drains. Wide pools of stinking, dirty water began to form. At the corner of the Rue Saint-Jacques, one enterprising young man had fashioned a small portable bridge on wheels.

"Dry crossing!" he called out. "Two sous!"

He saw Gabrielle. Removing a battered, dripping tricorne, he bowed low, grinning. "For you, my sweetness, I will charge but a kiss."

Gabrielle ignored him, stepping almost indifferently into the filthy rushing water.

"Snooty bitch!" the young man called after her. "I hope you drown!"

When she reached the church of Saint-Séverin, she stopped, pressing into the doorway to get out of the worst of the rain. Her woolen *manteau* was soaked through. It was very cold.

She fumbled beneath her skirts with numbed, bleeding fingers and ripped off a piece of petticoat. She removed all but two of the coins from her purse and wrapped them in the piece of cloth. Pulling aside her *manteau* and fichu, she shoved this makeshift package down her bodice into the hollow between her breasts. She smiled to herself at the irony: a year ago she had bewailed her small size. Now it was a blessing.

Martin had said—on the night she had first shown him her naked body—that her breasts were just the right size. With wonder on his face, he had reached out and touched them, caressed them until her nipples grew hard beneath his probing fingers, and—

No, she thought. I can't think of that. Maybe later, when I'm stronger, when I'm safe, but not yet . . .

The stitch in her side was gone now, but the pain in her back was much worse. She thought the baby must be pressing against her spine. Her stomach felt huge, distended beyond all the laws of nature. Above her, the bell in the tower began

to toll the hour for vespers. For a moment she leaned against
the church door and shut her eyes. But it was too cold and
wet. More than anything she wanted to lie down.

The door to the church creaked open, and a priest, crooked
with age, emerged. He paused when he saw her.

"Are you ill, my child?" he asked kindly.

"No, Father."

"It's cold. You should be home before the fire on an evening such as this one."

"*Ça ira*, Father," Gabrielle said, and forced a smile.

The priest nodded and raised a bent hand in a blessing
before making his slow, doddering way down the shallow
steps.

It will be all right, Gabrielle repeated to herself, using the
words as a talisman.

The signboard above the inn proclaimed it to be The Brass
Pot and showed a fat pot roasting over a fire. At one time
the pot had been gilded gold, but the paint had long ago
chipped away, so now it was a tarnished muddy brown. The
sign hung from a rusty chain, creaking in the wind.

As Gabrielle pushed open the door, a small bell fastened
above the lintel tinkled with false merriness.

Madame Falour, who had been halfheartedly wiping the
worst of the smudges off the glasses in the taproom, waddled
into the hall. She was a large woman with a plump, mushy
figure, like an overripe pear. Her face bore the ravages of
smallpox, and she wore a cheap, old-fashioned wig made of
horsehair that was too small for her large head.

She placed her hands on her ample hips and glared at Gabrielle. "Well, if it isn't Madame High and Mighty, and it's
back you've come, is it? I thought you'd scampered off."

For a moment Gabrielle felt tears fill her eyes. She couldn't
understand the reason for Madame Falour's hatred. She had
hardly exchanged a dozen words with the old woman in the
months she had been here. She hadn't really cared before, but
now . . . It's only because I'm tired, she thought. So tired.

"I told you this morning I would be back," Gabrielle said, forcing a strength she didn't feel into her voice.

The old woman sniffed. "And I told you, *madame*"—she sneered the appellation, implying that it was unearned—"you'll either come up with the ready or I'll toss you out the door on your haughty backside. Pregnant or not. This is an inn I'm running here, not an almshouse."

Gabrielle opened her purse.

At the sight of it, Madame Falour shoved her bulk forward. "You owe me for three weeks," she said, thrusting out a grimy palm. "Forty livres."

Gabrielle removed one of the louis and put it in the old woman's hand.

Madame's eyes gleamed at the sight of the gold coin, but she left her hand out. "You owe me more."

Gabrielle sighed, pretending to hesitate. Then she took out the second coin and gave it to the old woman. She made sure madame could see the purse was now empty before she pulled the strings shut.

"That settles the reckoning," Gabrielle said.

Madame grunted.

"And then some," Gabrielle added.

"Well . . ."

"Yes." Gabrielle stared the old woman down, forcing her to look away. "And I should like some hot broth brought up to my room."

Madame Falour gaped at this girl who dared to issue orders like a duchesse and then push past without so much as a by-your-leave—as if she had just bought the place with her two louis d'or.

"If you want hot broth, Madame High and Mighty," she shouted to Gabrielle's stiff back as it moved up the stairs, "you can bloody well get it yourself!"

Gabrielle didn't answer. She didn't even pause.

Her room was five flights up, under the slopping mansard roof. At one end of it, by the tiny window, the ceiling was so low she couldn't stand straight up. During the first month she lived there, Gabrielle had walked around with a permanent bruise across her forehead. Now she remembered to duck her head.

The room had no fireplace, but heat from the room below rose up between the cracks in the floor, and before long Gabrielle felt warmed enough to remove her sodden *manteau*. She draped it to dry over the ladder back of the room's only chair, then lit the stub of a tallow candle stuck into a bracket in the wall.

She arched her back, trying to stretch out the pain along with the stiffness, but the dull ache remained. Groaning, she lay down on the narrow, lumpy bed. Her monstrous stomach rose up before her eyes, like a mountain. She made a face at it.

She realized she was sweating. The ache in her back was suddenly very bad. She sucked in a deep breath just as the inner muscles of her stomach contracted in an involuntary spasm. A few seconds later the spasm was gone, and with it the pain. Gabrielle sighed aloud with relief. And then she realized what it must mean.

Oh, God, no, she thought. Not yet . . . and she was suddenly very much afraid. Even more afraid than before, when Louvois's lackeys had chased her through the streets and almost caught her.

She bit her lip hard to stifle a cry as a fresh cramp seized her. Oh, God . . . She had wanted this child, Martin's child. She had risked everything for this child. But now, God help her, she was so afraid.

She didn't want to die.

An hour later Madame Falour laboriously climbed the five flights of stairs to Gabrielle's room, carrying a steaming bowl of beef broth and muttering to herself about hoity-toity misses who put on the airs of duchesses, and *called* themselves madame and *claimed* to be widowed, when anyone who believed that tale would also buy a piece of the True Cross from the souvenir stand at the foot of Notre Dame, because if that babe wasn't born to be a bastard, then . . .

She set the tray down on the floor in the hall and raised

one small plump finger to scratch on the door when she heard the muffled cries and harsh panting of a woman in labor.

Madame stood, her finger poised in midair, undecided. She ought to send for the midwife, but she was thinking of the empty purse. If the damned girl died, the midwife would stick *her* with the bill. She thought of tending to the girl herself, and immediately discarded the idea. If the damned girl died and she was involved, she'd have the police descending on her, asking all sorts of prying questions, the way they had done when the body of that candlemaker had been found cut up and dumped in her midden last year.

No, the girl was going to have to fend for herself. If *Madame* High and Mighty hadn't eaten of the forbidden fruit, then she wouldn't be in this predicament in the first place, now would she?

The old woman started down the stairs, then turned back for the tray. It wasn't decent to let good food go to waste.

Behind the door came a harsh, strangled cry.

"Martin! Oh, God, Martin. Help me.''

Madame Falour sniffed and shook her head. ''He won't help you now, girl. There's nobody going to help you now.''

And so it was that Gabrielle de Vauclair de Nevers brought her child into the world alone. Arms shaking with exhaustion, eyes blurred with tears of pain and joy, she clutched his tiny, squawking, and bloody body to her breast.

The rain had gone with the night, and the sun was just coming up on a new morning. Her son was but minutes old. In three days, Gabrielle de Vauclair de Nevers would be seventeen.

Part One

1787

Chapter 1

Simon Prion stood in the garden of the Palais Royal and looked at the front of his shop. The sign, with its three golden balls, shone brightly in the summer sun. He nodded with satisfaction and then, because he was so happy, he laughed out loud.

He hadn't realized how lonely he had been all those years, those years before the miracle had occurred and he had found the girl again. With her he had acquired Agnes—whom he could probably live without if he thought about it—and the little boy, Dominique—whom he could not live without at all.

We are a family, he thought with another nod of satisfaction. She and I, Agnes and the boy. Yes, a family.

Because of the heat, the door to the shop was propped open with a brass stopper. Simon paused on the threshold to look inside, and his face softened.

She sat behind the counter on a tall stool with her feet hooked around its legs, polishing a set of silver teaspoons. A curtain of red-gold hair obscured her profile. Turning, she looked up, and when she saw who it was, she smiled.

"Gabrielle," he said.

"How does the new sign look?" she asked him.

"Magnificent!" he exclaimed, striding inside. "That

painter did a good job for a change.'' He grinned at her. ''I think he was trying to make an impression on you.''

''Hunh. We'll see how impressed I am when we get the bill.''

A head of tousled blond curls poked out from among the rack of coats, grinning up at them.

Simon winked at Gabrielle. ''I see that little mouse is back among my coats again. I'll have to fetch a broom and chase it out.''

There was a loud squeal and a giggle, and the head disappeared. Then a small boy came hurtling out of the coats and threw himself at Simon's legs.

''Dominique,'' Gabrielle said sharply, ''how many times must I ask you not to run in the shop?''

Simon scooped the boy into his arms. ''Don't scold him. You're too strict with him.''

''Someone must be. The way you and Agnes spoil him, he's—''

Gabrielle broke off as a young girl banged through the door, her thin arms loaded with bundles of food. Her head was uncovered, and her ash-brown hair stuck out in short, wispy tufts around her head. She had a small upper lip that was always partly lifted, giving her face a look of perpetual surprise.

''By Saint Winifred's pocket!'' she exclaimed, huffing for breath. ''That bloody ass of a baker is asking ten sous for a loaf of bread!''

Gabrielle sighed, but she couldn't help smiling. ''Agnes, don't curse.''

Until a year ago Agnes had been a child whore and pickpocket. But that was before Gabrielle had saved her, or she had saved Gabrielle; they still argued over who exactly had saved whom. Since then, Agnes had been able to give up most of the trappings of her former life, but not the cursing.

''I wasn't cursing,'' Agnes said automatically. ''Ten sous! I told that bastard just where he could put his loaves of bread.'' Dumping the packages on the counter next to Gabrielle, she made a rude gesture with her fist.

Simon set Dominique back on his feet, and the little boy ran up to Agnes to tug on her skirts.

"Agnes, explain to Maman how I'm not spoiled—"

"Of course you aren't, *petit ange,*" the girl said, pressing a piece of dark, sticky cake into the little boy's hand. "Look, I've brought you some gingerbread. And some for myself," she added, laughing and popping a piece into her own mouth. Agnes had the ability to act simultaneously both thirty and three. She was in fact fifteen and quite small, though lately Gabrielle noticed the girl had begun to develop curves in places that turned men's heads.

"Look, Maman!" Dominique said, showing his mother the treat.

Gabrielle smiled at her son and shook her head. "Oh, Agnes, I wish you hadn't. Now he'll have no appetite for dinner."

"Dinner!" Simon suddenly exclaimed. "Good God, I promised the vicomte de Saint-Romain I would pick up that engraving today before dinner."

Gabrielle pushed back the stool, standing up. She pulled her smock over her head and tossed it on the counter, then smoothed the skirt of her cheap gray dimity dress. "I'll get it for you now. Where does he live?"

"No!" he exclaimed so loudly his voice echoed in the small shop.

They all looked at him in stunned silence. "Why not?" Gabrielle finally asked.

"Why not? Why not?" Dominique parroted, before shoving the entire piece of gingerbread into his mouth.

"Because . . . it wouldn't be, uh, right."

"Why not?" Agnes asked.

Simon blushed and began to mumble. "Because of the nature . . . The engraving is by Arentino, you understand, otherwise I wouldn't . . . It's quite valuable really, but it's a trifle . . . odd."

"So?" Gabrielle prompted.

Simon sighed, his blush deepening. "The title of it is . . . *Fornication.*"

"Fornication!" Agnes hooted. "Oh-ho, Monsieur Simon, are you buying dirty pictures now?"

Simon drew himself up to his full height. "It happens to be a very important work of art even if it is a trifle, er . . ."

Agnes hooted again.

"Never mind, Simon," Gabrielle said, laughing. "I'm hardly an innocent. But if it makes you feel better, I promise not to look at it." She laughed again. *"Too* closely." She stooped to kiss Dominique's bulging cheeks. "Be good, *mon petit.* I'll be back in a bit."

"The vicomte de Saint-Romain," Simon called out with an uneasy frown. "He lives above the Café de Foy. And I've already paid for it, so don't let him tell you differently."

As Gabrielle left, she heard Dominique's piping voice exclaim, "Agnes, what is a fordicashun?" She repressed a shudder at the thought of the numerous ribald definitions that could emerge from Agnes's mouth.

The sun beat down hot on the garden paths. Gabrielle thought about going back for a bonnet, then decided against it. Simon was probably already having second thoughts about sending her to the libertine vicomte to fetch his naughty engraving. He was only trying to protect her, she knew, but the things she needed protecting from he didn't even know existed.

She had never told Simon about any of it, about what had brought her into his shop to pawn a ring that cold November afternoon—the day Dominique had been born. She supposed he could probably guess at all that she had lived through in the long months afterward, until that day a year ago when fate in the form of a child whore called Agnes had brought her across Simon Prion's path again.

He had told everyone she was a relative by marriage, the widow of a fictitious nephew who was supposed to have been a wigmaker's apprentice at Versailles. He even encouraged her to use the name of Prion—"to quiet the gossips," he had said. In the beginning she had expected he would want her to sleep with him, but he had never so much as touched her. Then one night he had gotten slightly drunk on wine and confessed that, though he'd never really been interested in marriage, he had always wanted a daughter, and now that she had come into his life he wanted to believe he had his daughter at last. Gabrielle had listened to him with tear-filled eyes and an absurdly big lump in her throat, but even then she hadn't dared tell him about her past, not about Martin or Monsieur le Duc, and especially not about the hateful Louvois. Not even her real name. All Simon knew was that one cold and empty day four years ago she had come into his shop and pawned a ring. One cold and empty November day . . .

But now it was summer and the Palais Royal was a carnival of activity. Brightly dressed courtesans strolled along the paths, flaunting their charms before gawk-eyed provincials, who would be fleeced of their money before the night was through. A pair of political orators stood on benches and tried to outshout each other, while a mountebank hawking a cure for the English pox managed to drown out them both. A prosperous bourgeois, taking his dog for a walk, paused to buy licorice water from a stall set up beneath the leafy shade of a chestnut tree.

Gabrielle strolled past the wooden and stone arcades. Several years before, the duc d'Orleans—the king's cousin and one of the richest men in France—had thought of a way to make even more money by turning three of the wings of his palace into galleries of shops and rented apartments. Now the Palais Royal was a pleasure trove of casinos and brothels, restaurants and cafés, bookstalls, bathhouses, and, of course, pawnshops.

A barker who stood in front of a gaming club called out to Gabrielle, teasing, asking if she wanted to try her luck. She laughed and blew him a kiss.

At the Café de Foy she stopped a waiter bearing a tray loaded with cups of mocha and asked him where she could find the vicomte de Saint-Romain.

The waiter thought a moment, then pointed above his head. "Two floors up, I think. In the apartment facing the gardens."

The stairway stank of stale perfume. As she passed an open door, Gabrielle heard a woman's laughter and the rattle of a dice box.

She scratched politely on the door of the apartment facing the gardens. There was no answer. She scratched louder.

"Damnation!" swore a low-timbered voice. "Go away."

Gabrielle hesitated, then pounded rudely on the door with her fist.

"Christ."

She heard footsteps; the door flew open. "What do you want? I'm— Sweet heavenly Jesus! Who are you?"

Gabrielle looked up . . . and the world stopped.

"Uh," she said, unaware that her mouth had fallen open as they stared at each other. Her breath had left her in a rush, as if someone had thumped her hard in the back, knocking the air from her lungs.

He was tall. It was the first thing she noticed about him, for she had to tilt her head up to see his face. It was a stunningly handsome face, though hard, with a cruel-looking mouth and hooded gray eyes. He had a thin patrician nose, and his skin was pulled smooth and taut over high cheekbones. His dark brown hair was unpowdered and held back by a narrow riband.

"What do you want?" he said again, softer this time. His voice was low, caressing. Heavy, long-lashed lids lowered over his eyes until they were almost shut.

Gabrielle's throat felt dry, her chest tight. She sucked in a gasping breath and swallowed. "Monsieur Prion sent me."

"Did he? How generous of him."

"Yes, monsieur," she answered, flushing at the sexual innuendo, though at least she was breathing normally again. They were all alike, she thought with an odd twinge of disappointment that was mixed with relief; these bored aristocrats with nothing to do and nothing to think about but gratifying the appendage that hung between their legs. Why should she expect this libertine vicomte with his pornographic engraving to be any different?

She tried to take a step sideways, across the threshold, but he continued to block the doorway, staring at her with an arrogant insolence that set her pride on edge.

Pride prompted her to smile at him, a friendly smile that held a promise she had no intention of fulfilling. She had used that smile before, in her old life, and she knew its power.

He smiled back at her, mockingly.

"Do come in," he said, and opened the door wide.

Gabrielle walked into the room and looked around her. For the second time in the space of a minute she gasped in surprise.

It was a laboratory. Bottles, alembics, and beakers—some empty and some filled with mysterious liquids—stood on every flat surface. A microscope sat on a table among a pile of books; a huge telescope pointed out the window toward the sky. Although it was the middle of the day, dozens of candles blazed, reflecting brightly in the many glass containers and in the mirrors that lined the walls.

But the most astonishing thing stood in the middle of the room. It looked to be a miniature *montgolfier*—a balloon. It was two feet in diameter, made of thin linen or silk, and it floated above a metal canister that hissed a blue flame. As she watched it, the balloon seemed to swell in size.

"Why?" he said.

Gabrielle started, whipping around. He was standing very close to her, too close for her comfortably to meet his eyes, and so she looked down. His white linen shirt was unfastened at the neck, and sweat sheened on the smooth, brown skin of his broad chest. Her eyes traveled downward over a trim waist and hips to tight knee breeches that revealed every muscle and sinew. She thought he was probably very beautiful naked.

Startling herself this time, Gabrielle flung her head up to meet a pair of gray eyes that glinted with a knowing mockery. Blushing, she looked away. She couldn't imagine what had possessed her to think such a thing. *Dieu,* she was getting to be as bad as Agnes, who couldn't look at a man without cataloging his attributes for the bedroom.

"Why?" he said again, patiently.

"Why what? Oh, you mean why am I here."

Amusement flickered across his face, softening its harshness. "Yes, that's what I mean. You are going to tell me, I hope. Eventually?"

Her eyes flitted back and forth uneasily between the vicomte and the swelling balloon. It was definitely getting larger. In the few seconds she'd been here it seemed to have doubled in size. "I've, uh, I've come for *Fornication*," she said unthinkingly, her mind distracted by the man's imposing presence as much as by the growing balloon.

"Forni—" He laughed suddenly, warm and husky. "God bless Monsieur Prion, whoever he is. I must admit I've never been propositioned quite so boldly before," he said, slow and soft. "I find I rather like it." He slipped an arm around her waist and started to pull her against him.

Caught off balance, Gabrielle stumbled and had to clutch his sleeves to keep from falling. The muscles of his arms clenched beneath her hands as he pulled her closer. He molded her against the length of him, tight enough for her to feel the corded ridges of his chest, his flat stomach; tight enough to feel . . . *everything*—even through the bulky padding of her skirt and petticoat.

Her face was pressed close to his throat, so close she could have kissed that smooth brown skin. Her lips parted—

"Oh, don't be such a stupid fool!" Gabrielle snapped breathlessly, pushing away from his chest with more force than was necessary. "I've no desire to indulge you in your silly games."

The heavy lids lowered over his eyes again. It gave him a dangerous look. "And I don't think I want to play at yours. Who sent you?"

"I told you. Monsieur Prion. Do you always do this—ask the same questions over and over again? It's very rude."

He laughed. "And do you always answer questions with statements that make no sense? It's very rude."

Disconcerted by the strange way the vicomte was acting, Gabrielle didn't know what to say. Conscious of his eyes on her, she lifted the heavy fall of her hair off her neck. It's much too warm in here, she thought. And was it necessary for him to stand so close to her? He was making it difficult to breathe. She wondered if the man was mad. It would be a pity, for he was very handsome. *Dieu,* but it was hot. All these candles. And the balloon . . . The balloon was getting quite large, the skin now stretched so tautly it was almost transparent. So tautly it looked about ready to—

"Monsieur," she said suddenly, "I believe your *montgolfier* is about to burst."

Without bothering to look at it, he kept his eyes fastened on her flushed face. "It isn't a *montgolfier*. *Montgolfiers* are inflated with hot air. This one is inflating with hydrogen. Inflammable air. I call it an aerostat."

Inflammable air? The man was most definitely mad.

A draft of air made the candles flicker, and the balloon swayed gently as it grew, still steadily swelling, getting bigger and bigger . . .

Gabrielle started to back toward the door. "Whatever you call it, monsieur, it is about to burst."

He finally glanced at it. Then his eyes met hers and his lips twisted into a tough, damn-the-world smile. "You know, mademoiselle, I believe you are right."

He threw himself at her, knocking her to the floor just as a tremendous explosion shook the building.

The glass that was everywhere in the room shattered into a thousand shards. The walls rattled and the floor shivered. There was an echoing rumble, a final tinkle of a falling mirror, then silence.

Gabrielle opened her eyes. The ceiling floated high above her. Clouds of plaster drifted lazily in the air. She felt a muffled pressure against her ears, as if she were swimming under water.

He lay on her, the full length of him covering the full length of her. His chest flattened her breasts; his stomach pressed against hers. One of his thighs was braced between her legs. His face was very close. She could see the fans of tiny wrinkles around his eyes, the incredibly long lashes that brushed against his cheekbones when he blinked, the lines at the corners of his mouth which no longer looked so hard and cruel. She marked the pulse beats in his lean throat, saw them quicken.

"Monsieur, you are lying on me," she said, then wished she hadn't. It would give him ideas. It was giving *her* ideas.

He said nothing. His dark gray eyes regarded her seriously. He shifted his weight a little, easing it. The movement caused his thigh to press briefly into the cleft between her legs, and Gabrielle felt the muscles low in her stomach flutter.

He lightly brushed her cheek with his fingertips. "You're bleeding a little. It's only a scratch."

Gabrielle had to smile. He had said it so matter-of-factly. Only a scratch. As if they both hadn't almost been killed. She decided he probably was a little mad. Perhaps that was what made him so exciting.

His fingers had drifted over her cheekbones, across her forehead, then down along her chin, tracing the contours of her face. The skin of his hand was rough and callused; it sent odd chills rippling down her spine.

"Your experiment seems to have been something of a disaster, monsieur," she said, mainly to stop the fluttering in her stomach. But her words sounded shaky and breathless to her ears.

"On the contrary . . ." He lowered his face until it was only inches from hers. She thought he was going to kiss her. She wanted him to kiss her. "It was"—his voice drifted into a low, silky purr—"a shattering success."

Gabrielle closed her eyes, and her mouth parted open with a soft sigh. His lips touched hers—

"The devil take you, Max you scoundrel! Are you trying to kill us all?"

Gabrielle's eyes flew open. The face above hers turned slightly and, from beneath lazy, slitted lids, regarded the woman who had just barged into the room.

"Go away, Sophie. Can't you see I'm busy?"

The woman stood above them with her hands on her hips. "Really, Max, you are incorrigible. Now is no time to be doing *that.*" She looked at the shambles around her. "*Merde,* you've broken all my windows and frightened my cust— guests half out of their wits!''

Gabrielle struggled against his hard chest. "Get off me, you oaf!''

Laughing, he rose to his feet, pulling her up with him in one smooth movement. She felt the rugged strength of him in the tingly pressure of his fingers clasping her wrist, long after he had let it go.

The woman looked Gabrielle up and down, while Gabrielle struggled to gather herself together. Her fichu had pulled half out of her bodice. Plaster dust coated her clothes and hair. Somehow one of her heels had broken off her shoe; it made her feel decidedly lopsided.

Although they had never been introduced, Gabrielle had seen the woman before, for Sophie Restonne was a well-known figure in the Palais Royal. She was at the tail end of her youth and beauty, but hiding it well, with an expertly made-up face and an elaborate, heavily powdered coiffure. Her dresses were always panniered, beribboned, flounced, and expensive. She resided in one of the apartments above the Café de Foy with several "sisters," running an establishment where one could play at any hour of the day or night— at *rouge-et-noire* or blond and brunette.

"I haven't seen this one before, Max," Sophie said, falsely sweet. "Who is she?''

He shrugged and looked at Gabrielle with cool gray eyes. "I really haven't the vaguest idea.''

"Oh, this is too much!'' Gabrielle exclaimed, angrily slapping the dust from her skirts. "I swear you must be mad. You sell Monsieur Prion an engraving and then pretend not to know him. You allow that aero— that *thing*—''

"Aerostat.''

"—to blow up in my face—''

"What engraving?'' Sophie said.

"Yes, what—'' he began, but Gabrielle had merely paused for breath.

"Then you hurl me to the floor and proceed to . . . to *assault* me—''

"I didn't notice you resisting—"

"I was going to . . . I would have if you had . . . oooh! As far as I'm concerned, Monsieur le Vicomte, you can go to hell. And you can take your nasty engraving with you, where it will no doubt go very well with the decor!"

"Vicomte!" Sophie shrieked. "For shame, Max. Since when did you have to stoop to telling lies to get a girl into your bed—"

Gabrielle had started to stalk past him, limping on her heel-less shoe, but he put out a hand, stopping her. "Wait," he said softly, but there was a hard edge to his voice, and the hand that grasped her arm tightened.

Gabrielle began to feel a horrible premonition. "You . . . you are not the vicomte?"

He studied her for a long moment, then his mouth thinned into a tight smile. "My brother is a vicomte. I am a mere monsieur."

"Monsieur de Saint-Romain?"

He shook his head. "Maximilien de Saint-Just."

"Max, you rogue," Sophie said, laughing, "you really should exchange names before you—"

"Go away, Sophie," he said abruptly, and her musical laughter cut off in mid-chord.

Her rouged cheeks flushed, then whitened. "And what about the damage to my windows? The police will be here soon, you mark my words, and . . ."

He didn't answer her. She hesitated a moment longer. "Well, really!" she said, then stormed from the room with an angry swish of her skirts.

They didn't notice. Max's hooded gray eyes were fixed on Gabrielle's face. She felt the compelling force of them, piercing her with an intensity that was as intimate as a kiss. The weight of his fingers on her arm seemed to press heavily, burning through the material of her sleeve. She heard her own breathing, then his. Then they seemed to be breathing together—

She pulled away from him and began backing slowly out of the room. "I—I seem to have made a silly mistake."

"Did you?" He took a step after her.

She bumped into the door. Her fingers gripped the edge, pulling it open. "I was looking for someone else."

"And you found me."

"No . . ." She whirled and ran down the hall for the stairs.

A crowd of people had gathered in front of the Café de Foy. One man tugged at Gabrielle's arm as she came out.

"What was it, mademoiselle? What's happened?"

Gabrielle pressed through them, ignoring their questions. Let *him* try to explain what he had been doing, blowing up aero-things—aerostats—with inflammable air. It ought to be outlawed. Maybe the king would find out about it and have him arrested and thrown into a cell in the Bastille. It would serve him right for trying to kiss her. *I didn't notice you resisting,* she quoted him to herself, exaggerating the sarcasm in his voice. Hunh! Just let him try to kiss her again. She would show him resistance . . .

"Did you hear the explosion?" Agnes asked breathlessly as soon as Gabrielle set foot in the shop. "They say it was caused by some crazy aristocrat experimenting with gunpowder. He killed himself and some whore he was— Jesu! You're bleeding."

Gabrielle pressed the back of her hand against her cheek. "It's only a scratch. Where's Dominique?"

"He went with Monsieur Simon to take that bag of old clothes we couldn't sell to the ragpickers. They just left. I'm surprised you didn't see them. What happened to you? You look as if you've been rolling in the dirt."

"I, uh, tripped on a loose stone."

Gabrielle glanced uneasily out the window, trying to quell an impulse to rush after her son. She knew it wasn't good for the boy to have her hovering over him constantly. Besides, Dominique looked no different than any other little boy. Nobody could possibly guess . . . Certainly he was safer in Simon's company than hers. He could be Simon's grandson.

She realized that Agnes had spoken. "I'm sorry?"

"I said let's have a look at Monsieur Simon's dirty picture while he's gone." She stared expectantly at Gabrielle, as if she was suddenly going to produce the engraving out of her pocket. "Well, where is it?"

Gabrielle started guiltily. "What? Oh. I never got it. Simon must have sent me to the wrong apartment."

Before long, Simon and Dominique returned, minus the bundle of old clothes, but Dominique now sported a strange felt hat with a dirty, broken plume stuck through the band. The hat's floppy brim fell to the bridge of the boy's nose, and the drooping plume curled over one eye. Agnes and Gabrielle both burst out laughing at the sight of him.

Simon met Gabrielle's brimming eyes and shrugged. "Once he saw the thing, he had to have it."

"A donkey was wearing it, Maman," Dominique proclaimed. "But the nice man said we could have it for a livre—"

Gabrielle snatched the hat off her son's head, ignoring his yowl of protest. "Jesu and all his saints! It's probably full of ticks and lice!" Holding it with the tips of her fingers, she handed it to Agnes. "Go take it into the kitchen, Agnes, and roast it over the fire. Perhaps you can smoke the pests out."

"Where did you put the, er, uh . . . you know?" Simon asked, once Agnes and the boy had left the front of the shop.

Gabrielle pushed the damp hair off her flushed forehead. "Simon, you wretch, you are so absentminded. You sent me to the wrong apartment. It was very embarrassing. Thanks to you, I made an utter fool—"

"The apartment above the Café de Foy?"

Gabrielle nodded.

"The vicomte de Sainte-Romain, he wasn't there?"

"No. Instead I found this arrogant scientist who blows up things and throws people about and then tries to kiss—"

But Simon had rushed out of the shop.

He came back half an hour later, mumbling to himself, his face red. The vicomte de Saint-Romain had been gone for two weeks, leaving behind only a pile of gambling debts.

"Five hundred livres!" Simon moaned, pulling at his hair. "I should have taken that engraving with me the day I bought it, but I had my arms full with an escritoire and a heavy

marble chess set. *Mon Dieu, mon Dieu,* five hundred livres
. . . 'I'm off to Versailles immediately to see the king,' he
says, 'but come back in two weeks and I'll give you the
engraving then.' Bah! What a fool I was to trust him simply
because of his noble manners and connections. Those cursed
aristocrats. I tell you, Gabrielle, they think nothing of stealing from the rest of us. It's as if we aren't *human* so it doesn't
count. He must have left the day after I bought the engraving.
Cleared the apartment out down to the bare walls. Someone
else is already renting there. *Mon Dieu,* five hundred livres.''
Simon sighed.

''Did you speak to him?'' Gabrielle asked, trying to sound
casual. ''The man who lives there now? Perhaps he knows
where this thieving vicomte has gone.''

''Speak to whom? Oh, you mean the man who blows up
things. No, no, he wasn't there. I spoke with Sophie Restonne. She confirmed what I'd already feared. That scoundrel
Saint-Romain. I'll never see that engraving, or my five hundred livres, again.''

Later that night, after she had tucked Dominique into his
trundle bed in their tiny room above the shop and then crawled
between the sheets next to Agnes, Gabrielle allowed herself
to think about *him*—Monsieur Maximilien de Saint-Just.

He was an aristocrat, for he had said his brother was a
vicomte. She'd heard of a comte de Saint-Just, who was
probably his father—a *maréchal* in the French army and re-
nowned for his bravery and battle lust. It would explain where
Maximilien de Saint-Just had acquired that arrogant, aristocratic nose. Yet he didn't have the pale complexion or the
languid, effeminate manners so many courtiers affected. His
brown skin and muscular physique belonged more to the
rough men who worked the river docks than to a haughty
nobleman.

Once Gabrielle had lived among the gilded, pampered
courtiers who graced the salons, men who lisped and rouged
their cheeks. Later she had survived among the dregs in the
streets, the violent, rough men who would kill for a handful
of sous and slaked their hunger with cheap wine and cheaper

whores. But this man, this Maximilien de Saint-Just, with his callused, scarred hands and handsome, patrician face, he was from neither world, yet he was of both.

He was obviously educated, for he was a scientist. She smiled—a rather reckless scientist. An aristocrat with rough manners and a reckless scientist who happened to be very handsome and who probably had scores of women parading in and out of his apartment, so he could hardly be interested in her, and why was she thinking about such things all of a sudden anyway?

Gabrielle stifled a sigh. She might as well admit it, if only to herself. One look at him and she had been stricken with love—or with that ridiculous affliction of the heart that passed for love.

Love. Gabrielle sneered at herself. You'd think she would have learned. Love didn't exist except in novels and the dreams of fools. In real life, he dies and you are left alone and pregnant and *hunted*—

She pushed those haunting memories away, rolling over and getting her legs tangled in the bedclothes. Beside her, Agnes mumbled in her sleep and stirred.

Or even if he doesn't die, she thought, then the years pass and you discover that he is weak or lazy or cruel. You have babies and he takes mistresses. Before long, you turn your back on him in bed at night and you look at his slack, unshaven face in the morning light and wonder what you saw in this man to make your blood run hot and your flesh melt at his touch . . .

Gabrielle smiled bitterly in the dark. That was the way love ended, no matter how wonderful the beginning. So why, knowing the truth about love, couldn't she stop the pounding of her heart at the memory of those firm lips descending toward hers? Was knowing the truth about love going to ease the sharp, hollow hunger that even now—

"Agnes?" she whispered, shaking the girl's shoulder.

Agnes burrowed deeper under the covers. "By the snores of Saint Peter! I'm trying to sleep."

"Do you think it's true what they say about men, that they cannot go for long without a woman?"

"Hunh?" Agnes snorted and flopped over onto her back. She waved a hand toward the window and the streets of Paris outside. "Look at all the whores who make a living soothing that particular itch and then tell me what you think."

"But do you think it's the same the other way around? For a woman. If she's known love once, does she get to . . . ?"

"Wanting it after she's gone without it for a while? It depends, I suppose, on the woman. On how good her lover was in the first place. If he—oh-ho!" Agnes sat up abruptly, laughing gleefully. "Do you have the itch, Gabrielle?"

"Don't be ridiculous."

"You do, you do!" Agnes crowed. "And what's more, you've found a man to scratch it for you, haven't you? Admit it!"

"I will not admit any such thing." Gabrielle pulled the covers up over her head. "Shut up and go to sleep, Agnes."

"Who is he? Have you done it yet?"

Gabrielle groaned. She wished fervently she had never started this conversation. "There isn't anyone, I swear it."

Agnes sighed dolefully. "Poor soul."

"My soul isn't in the least danger, I assure you."

"I didn't mean yours. I meant his. You want him, and if you want him then he doesn't stand a chance. May the devil carry me off to hell on the end of a broom if you aren't the strongest person I know, and once you've decided—"

"Don't curse."

"May the Virgin Mary preserve us both, I wasn't cursing. I was merely saying that I've never known anyone as determined as you once you set your teeth into something. You stop at nothing to get what you want. Nothing."

"Go to sleep, Agnes."

As the girl snuggled beneath the covers, Gabrielle heard muffled chuckles and she grit her teeth on a curse that would have rivaled any of Agnes's.

The minutes drifted by and she lay in the dark listening to Agnes's rhythmic breathing. Was Agnes right? Was she so determined she would stop at nothing to get what she wanted? She thought of Martin. He had been the one to declare his love first, but once she'd decided she wanted him . . . She had let Martin ruin his life for her. All because she had wanted him. Love—it had ended by destroying them both.

She pressed her eyes shut, trying to conjure Martin's image, but it was blurred, like a reflection in a muddy pond. The pain of his loss was still there, but it, too, was blurred. It was as if it had happened a long time ago, and to someone else, a woman she had once known intimately but had not seen for a long, long time.

"Martin." She whispered his name in the dark, but when she shut her eyes it was not his face she saw. It was a pair of smoldering gray eyes and a mocking smile.

At that same moment, ten miles from Paris in the town of Versailles, a small man descended from a black berlin and climbed the steps of an elegant townhouse next door to the royal palace. He had been expected, for the door opened without his having to knock. As he turned to give his hat and cane to a porter in black and gold livery, light from the *flambeaux* in the great hall flashed off the thick lenses of his spectacles. Unconsciously he touched the puckered scar that disfigured his face.

"Monsieur Louvois," the porter said, "Monsieur le Duc awaits you in his bedchamber."

The heels of Louvois's shoes clicked loudly on the marble floor as he walked across the hall toward the stairs. There was no need for anyone to show him the way. He had been the duc de Nevers's procurator, his lawyer, and his most trusted and intimate adviser for over ten years.

With the assistance of his valet and two servants, the duc de Nevers was getting ready for bed. When Louvois entered the room, he found the duc naked and scratching his genitals. The duc's belly sagged like a half-loaded sack over twig-thin legs. His chest was white and hairless. He was sixty-three and looked every day of it.

"You're late, Louvois," the duc said.

Louvois's bulging eyes blinked once behind his spectacles. "Your pardon, monseigneur."

Privately Louvois thought the duc's naked body resembled a slug that had crawled from beneath some rock. No wonder the duchesse shunned his bed, preferring to shut herself away in the Nevers country estate in Burgundy. But Louvois kept these thoughts off his face and instead gave his master his most respectful attention.

The duc had just returned from the palace where he had been attending King Louis XVI's *coucher*. It was a special privilege, this putting of the king to bed. Only nobles whose titles could be traced back four generations were allowed to remove the king's wig, hand him his nightshirt, and empty out the contents of the mother-of-pearl chamber pot. Louvois thought the whole ritual of the *coucher* degrading—and he would have bartered with the devil to exchange his salvation for the privilege of attending it.

Such a thing would never be, of course. He could amass a fortune, even buy a title, but he could never acquire two hundred years' worth of the proper ancestors.

Louvois took the folded nightshirt from the arms of the valet and presented it to the duc. This is my destiny, he thought with a sudden bitterness he could taste. To hand the nightshirt to the man who hands the nightshirt to the king.

The duc spat out his teeth into the cupped palms of his valet, and Louvois turned his face aside to hide his disgust. The teeth were real, not wooden, pulled out of the mouth of some redcoat slain in battle during the American Revolutionary War and wired back together later. They didn't fit well, causing the duc's gums to bleed, and he had to numb the pain every night with a glass of brandy.

Crawling into bed, the duc settled between satin sheets. He sipped the brandy while Louvois stood beside the bed and they spoke of the day's business accomplished and the work to be done tomorrow. The duc was closer to Louvois than to any other man, yet it never occurred to him to ask Louvois to sit down or to offer him some of the brandy.

As the conversation dwindled, Louvois noticed the duc's

eyes straying to the portrait of his only son that hung above the mantel. The face in the portrait was asthetically handsome—soft chestnut curls, moody hazel eyes—but it lacked character. It had been painted when the boy was seventeen, the year before he died.

Louvois knew what the duc would say, for they had had this conversation many times before.

"Any news?" the duc said.

"Nothing, monseigneur."

"Perhaps the child is dead."

"Perhaps," Louvois acknowledged.

"He must be dead or you would have found him by now. He could have died at birth and taken the bitch with him."

Not her, Louvois thought, fingering the scar on his cheek. It would take more than childbirth to kill that particular bitch.

"He'll be four now," the duc said. "My grandson . . . if he lives."

"Yes . . . almost four."

For four years Louvois had been searching for her. Once he'd almost had her. She had been so close he could have reached out of the carriage window and touched her face. But she had taken off, running into the *quartier des boucheries,* and the stupid lackeys had lost her. He hadn't been discouraged though, not then. For he still believed she couldn't elude him forever. Her looks were too striking. People, men especially, noticed her. And once noticed, she was not forgotten. He had all the Nevers power and wealth at his command. She had nothing. No money, no family, nothing.

Yet she *had* eluded him. Oh, she wasn't dead. He was sure of that. She had survived, though he hoped the surviving had not been easy. He hoped she had suffered, was suffering now. He hoped she was out on the streets, selling her body for a few sous to rough men—tanners, cobblers, chimney sweepers—men with filthy hands and foul mouths who would use her cruelly, humble her, break her—

Louvois felt a sharp pain in his arm. Looking down, he saw he had clenched his fist so tightly he had given himself a cramp.

Gabrielle . . . I will find you yet, he vowed. If it takes years.

He would find them both. The child he would give to monseigneur, as a gift. But Gabrielle . . . Gabrielle he would keep for himself. He would kill her. But only after he was finished with her.

Chapter 2

Agnes sent the hoop rolling with a slight push, and Dominique chased after it, poking at it with a stick. The hoop teetered, wobbled, and fell.

"No, *petit,*" Agnes said, laughing. "Don't push it so hard. Gently, see. Like this."

Gabrielle stood beneath the shade of the canvas awning that stretched over the door to the pawnshop and watched her son at play. Agnes's words of the other night came back to her—*You stop at nothing to get what you want.*

Sometimes—especially during the dark and terrible months after his birth, when the money from the ring had all been spent—Gabrielle had wondered if she had done the right thing. Not for herself, but for Dominique. She had wanted her son, and so she had stopped at nothing to keep him. But as the duc de Never's grandchild, he could be wearing satin breeches now, not rough pantaloons with patches on the knees. He could be dining on partridges or capon this afternoon, not the stewed mutton that now simmered over the hearth in the kitchen. He could be *Monsieur* Dominique with a mansion full of servants at his beck and call to gratify his every wish.

But he would not have her. And when she thought of that, then she knew she had done the right thing after all.

"Look, Maman!"

The hoop was rolling smartly now, and Dominique ran

38

beside it, laughing, his thin legs pumping hard. Then he accidentally nudged the hoop with his knee and it clattered to the hard-packed ground. He stared down at the fallen hoop, and his lower lip began to tremble.

"Don't cry, Dominique," she called out to him. "Pick it up and try again."

Agnes helped him to get the hoop rolling again and soon he was running, sending it spinning up and down the garden paths, and passersby paused to share in his laughter.

A customer came to redeem an ivory jewel box pledged last month, and Gabrielle went with him into the coolness of the shop. Simon wasn't there, having slipped off to his favorite café that afternoon for a game of chess.

After the customer left, Gabrielle sat down behind the desk and opened the book she had been reading. It was a fascinating political satire by an English author called Jonathan Swift, about a man named Gulliver who traveled to exotic lands.

But today the story couldn't hold her attention. The face of Maximilien de Saint-Just kept appearing on the pages; the printed words spoke to her in his soft, drawling voice. It had been two days since he had almost blown her across the river Seine with his crazy experiments with inflammable air, and she couldn't stop thinking about him.

She had contemplated and discarded a hundred implausible excuses to seek him out again. But he would never be fooled and she absolutely couldn't, wouldn't make such a fool of herself. Still, this morning she had found herself dressing in her best gown—a violet muslin that matched her eyes, with a ladder of stiff rose bows on the bodice—and strolling by the Café de Foy for no justifiable reason at all except that he might be coming or going at that precise moment, might see her, might pause to talk . . . It made her breathless with excitement just to think of it.

It's a simple infatuation, she thought, giving herself a mental shake. It was hardly to be wondered at—the man was handsome, worldly, and just different enough to be interesting. She had felt this way once before, about a dancing mas-

ter her maman had hired during one flush summer when she
was twelve.

When she realized she was tracing the letters MAX with
her fingernail in the margin of the book, she slammed the
cover shut with a snort of self-disgust and pushed away from
the desk. This time she didn't have the excuse of being
twelve.

Gabrielle began to wander aimlessly around the shop. The
small lap escritoire that Simon had bought from the thieving
vicomte de Saint-Romain was displayed on a table in back.
Yesterday, while showing it to a potential customer, Gabrielle had found it to be filled with paper and a set of pens and
charcoal sticks. She went to get it now, hoping for some other
diversion to take her mind off that mad scientist.

Gabrielle's mother had been a *salonière*. Her elegant townhouse on the Rue de Grenelle had been visited almost nightly
by a coterie of the elite of the literary world. Novelists, poets,
philosophes, or free-thinkers—some of the greatest minds of
the day—had gathered at Madame Marie-Rose de Vauclair's
to read their works aloud and discourse on life, religion, and
politics.

Even as a young child, Gabrielle had been a part of these
soirées and sometimes, to amuse her maman's guests, she
would take charcoal and paper and draw caricatures lampooning the famous personages at court. A favorite target
was the haughty and frivolous queen, Marie Antoinette,
whom the *philosophes* called "the Austrian bitch." Gabrielle
would exaggerate the queen's features until her face resembled a greedy weasel's, and everyone would laugh.

Now she resumed her seat behind Simon's desk, intending
to draw the queen going masked and dressed as an angel to
a theater where the players were all devils, but her fingers
began to sketch a balloon instead. She made it quite large,
with a boat-shaped basket swinging by ropes underneath. She
added oars and a fanciful sail. Then, with her tongue tucked
into her cheek, she drew a man hanging upside down by one
foot from the rim of the basket. She exaggerated his aristocratic nose and sharp cheekbones. She laughed softly to her-

self as she made his eyes wide and filled with comical terror, his mouth open in a huge scream—

A shadow fell across the paper. Gabrielle's head jerked up. She looked into a pair of sardonic gray eyes and felt the flush of hot color surge slowly up her neck to flood her face.

Surreptitiously she tried to cover the paper with her hand, but he slipped it out from under her fingers and turned slightly, holding it up to the sunlight streaming from the open door and window.

A smile flitted across his arrogant mouth. "Not a very good likeness, *ma mie*. You've made the nose a trifle long, and the chin is much too weak."

Gabrielle bit her lip to hide a smile. She assumed her haughty look. "An art critic as well as a scientist—there seems to be no end to your accomplishments, Monsieur de Saint-Just—"

"Max. Please call me Max, *ma mie*."

"Monsieur de Saint-Just. And I am not your lady-love." *Although I want to be, God help me.*

"I insist you call me Max." He gave her that maddeningly mocking smile. "After all, we faced death together . . . Gabrielle."

His silky voice made her name sound like the notes of a song. No one had ever said her name like that before. It gave her a warm feeling.

Blushing again, she lowered her eyes. She saw that her fingers were wrapped tightly around the charcoal stick. She let it go and lifted her head. "How do you know my name? How did you even find out where I—" She cut off the words, furious with herself. What had made her automatically assume he was here because of her?

"I found you by searching for a mysterious Monsieur Prion," he said, drawling the words in the fashion of the king's courtiers at Versailles. "A mysterious Monsieur Prion who turned out, to my considerable disappointment, to be nothing more exotic than a pawnshop owner."

He walked around, gazing idly at the racks and display cases. He was dressed formally today, in a suit of black velvet with silver lacing. His shirt spilled out in heavy frills at his wrists and throat, enhancing his dark coloring. Oddly, the dainty elegance of these clothes seemed to emphasize his raw masculinity that had so intrigued her the first time she had seen him.

"I discovered your name by having a bit of a gossip with the baker's wife," he was saying in his teasing drawl. "Veritable founts of information are bakers' wives. She told me, for instance, that you are widowed with one child, a boy of four. That you are Monsieur Prion's niece by marriage and a blessing to him. And that he needs all the blessings he can get since he seems to have afflicted himself with the care of a foulmouthed urchin by the name of Agnes. Who, if the baker's wife ever has her wish, will be put in the stocks for her impertinence."

Gabrielle was laughing. She suddenly felt very happy. He had wanted to see her again, wanted to see her badly enough to go to the trouble of finding out her name and where she lived.

He smiled back at her, with genuine feeling this time, not cruel and not mocking. It eased the harsh lines around his mouth and dimmed for a moment the cynical gleam in his eyes.

He picked up an ivory fan and unfurled it with long brown fingers, and she noticed that, contrary to fashion, he wore no jewelry, nor adornment of any kind except for the plain silver buckles on his shoes. If it weren't for the patrician bones in his face, he might have been a peasant dressed up in his lord's clothes. Everything about him was a strange mixture of elegance and roughness. She could just as easily picture him brawling with his fists as fighting with a sword.

The painting on the fan was a pastoral scene, a shepherdess with her cavorting flock. He made a face at it and tossed the fan aside. "I thought that while I'm here I might as well buy something," he said casually. "A gift. For my mistress."

Gabrielle stood up, her happiness slowly disappearing like smoke out an open window. She should have known he would have a mistress. He probably had hundreds of them. "If you give me an idea of her tastes," she said stiffly, "perhaps I can help you."

"She has expensive tastes, of course. What woman doesn't?" Another smile, once again mocking. "It should be something intimate, I think, but not too extravagant. I intend to give it to her tonight . . ." He paused, and his dark gray eyes fastened onto Gabrielle's. "After I tell her goodbye."

There was no mistaking his meaning, not in his words and not in his eyes. Gabrielle stood before him, feeling joy and terror, excitement and guilt. She realized that one word, one movement on her part, would give him an answer. Yes or no, stay or go.

Unsure, she did nothing.

There was a large glass case resting on the counter in back of the shop. It contained small valuable items, such as snuff-boxes, cameos, and jewelry. He went to it and leaned over to examine its contents. Gabrielle made a small movement as if to stop him, barely quelling it in time.

"Perhaps a ring," he said, turning, and Gabrielle's breath caught in her throat.

For the ring, the sapphire ring that she had sold to Simon Prion four years ago, the ring that a duc's son had once placed on her finger, still rested on the velvet lining of the case. Simon had many times tried to give it back to her, but she had always refused. She would redeem it, she had said with pride, when she had worked off her debt.

But there were other rings for sale, she told herself. Prettier, more valuable.

Max had turned back to the case. "This one," he said, and pointed to a ring—a ruby ring. Gabrielle slowly let out her breath.

She took a small key from the desk and unlocked the case. Her fingers were shaking so badly she was sure he would notice.

He slipped the ruby ring on the little finger of his left hand. He blew on the jewel, rubbed it with the lace at his cuff, then held his hand out to study it.

"What do you think?"

Gabrielle swallowed and forced a smile. "It's very pretty, monsieur . . . and only five hundred livres."

"I don't know." He looked at the ring again, then set it aside. "I've never fancied rubies."

His eyes roamed slowly over the contents of the case. Gabrielle's hands pressed so hard onto the countertop that her knuckles whitened.

He picked up one of a pair of earrings, a cluster of pearls dangling from a tiny gold chain. He regarded it for a moment, glanced at her, then tossed it back into the case. He ran his fingers over the enameled top of a snuffbox, fondled a diamond-chip bracelet, picked up a ring. Her ring.

Gabrielle visibly stiffened. He looked at her again, smiled.

He held the ring up to the light, and the sun shining through the window bounced off the facets of the sapphire, making rainbow reflections on the wall.

"Perhaps I'll take this one."

"No!" Gabrielle exclaimed on a hiss of breath.

He stared at her. "Why not? Don't you like it?"

"No . . . yes." She snatched it from his hand. "It isn't for sale."

He raised one dark brow, challenging her. "Then why display it?"

Gabrielle shrugged with feigned indifference. "You'll have to ask Monsieur Prion." She ran her tongue over her dry lips. "I really do prefer the ruby myself, monsieur . . . Max."

He smiled slowly. Then his heavy lids lowered over his eyes until they were almost shut. "Do you? I wouldn't have thought it. Sapphires seem more your style. That one in particular. Did you notice, it matches the color of your eyes."

Gabrielle shrugged again, clutching the ring tighter in her fist. "I really hadn't noticed."

He reached into the deep pocket of his velvet coat and pulled out a heavy purse. "I'll have the ruby then. Since the sapphire isn't for sale."

He dumped out a handful of gold coins, stacking them in a pile on the counter with those long brown fingers. She remembered the rough feel of them brushing her face and again felt the chills rippling down her spine.

"Shall I . . ." She cleared her throat. "Shall I wrap the ring for you, monsieur?"

"That won't be necessary." He picked it up and slipped it into his waistcoat pocket.

"Then I owe you ten livres in change, monsieur," Gabrielle said, pleased to hear her voice sounding so brisk and businesslike.

She left the counter, going to the desk where Simon kept the strongbox. But when she went to open the drawer to get the key, she realized she was still clutching Martin's ring tightly in her fist. She set it down carefully, next to the charcoal stick and the caricature. The ring had left small indentations in her palm.

Max had followed her over to the desk to stand close beside her. His presence seemed to fill the shop, and with every breath she took the tangy, masculine scent of him filled her head. She could feel his hooded eyes watching her.

Her hands trembled as she opened the strongbox and counted out ten livres. Without looking up, she held the money out to him. His fingers brushed hers as he took the coins, and the muscles low in Gabrielle's stomach tightened and her breath caught.

Dieu, she thought. What is there about him that does this to me?

"Gabrielle . . ."

She sighed. Looking up, she searched his face. It was relaxed, smiling.

"Tomorrow is Sunday. Will you come with me to the Jardin des Plantes? I want to show you another aerostat that I'm building. A full-sized one." His lips twitched. "I promise I won't let it blow up in your face."

"Well . . . I don't think . . . My son. I must take him to Mass."

"After Mass then. We'll bring the boy with us. He'll love the Jardin des Plantes." His voice took on the silky purr that seemed to imbue even the simplest words with a deep, significant meaning. "Say yes, Gabrielle. Please."

Her face broke into a smile and her heart soared.

"Yes," she said.

"Maman!" Dominique cried, bursting into the shop a few minutes behind the departing figure of Maximilien de Saint-Just. "I rolled the hoop all the way to the Place du Carrousel. There was a bear there. A dancing bear! I rode on its back."

Agnes laughed at the appalled look on Gabrielle's face. "It was a very old bear. And toothless, too. Look," she said, unwrapping a small package bound with twine. "We stopped by Madame Tussard's. I got us some new fichus." She held up one of the thin muslin kerchiefs. "See. She was practically giving them away."

Gabrielle exclaimed over Agnes's bargain. "I can wear it tomorrow," she said. "When I go—when I go to Mass."

Agnes's eyes opened wide. "Ah-hah! So *he's* going to be in church tomorrow, is he?"

"I don't know what you're talking about, Agnes. Unlike you, I go to church to worship our savior, not to ogle the neighborhood rakes."

Agnes laughed. "Since when do the neighborhood rakes go to Mass? And you aren't going to change the subject that easily, Gabrielle. I happen to remember a little talk we had the other night . . ."

Bored with this conversation, Dominique drifted to the back of the shop. He burrowed under the rack of coats, pretending to be a mouse. But since Monsieur Simon wasn't there to chase him out with a broom, this game soon palled. He saw that there was some paper and a charcoal stick on the desk and thought he might draw a picture of the bear so Maman could see how brave he was to ride it, for it had been a very big bear.

He was reaching for the charcoal stick when he saw a shiny blue rock in a ring. He snatched this prize up eagerly. He had started collecting rocks that week. Monsieur Simon had given him a round, smooth one that was good for skipping across the pond in the Tuileries, and yesterday he had found a red one with yellow stripes. He had collected a few more this morning in the garden, but this blue one was the prettiest yet. He dropped it into his pocket with the others.

Dominique's stomach rumbled. How long would it be before dinner? He ambled over to his mother, who was holding her new fichu up to the light of the window, examining the stitching.

"We'll have to dress your hair for Mass tomorrow morning," Agnes was saying, her brown eyes twinkling mischievously. "We'll crimp it with the iron and perhaps lighten it with a bit of flour . . ."

Dominique stared up at his mother's preoccupied face. "Maman, may I have some bread and jam?"

"Of course, *petit,*" Gabrielle replied absently, and Dominique dashed into the kitchen before she could change her mind.

Gabrielle cut off Agnes's teasing suggestions as to which dress she should wear to church tomorrow, saying she wanted to straighten the shop before Simon returned. She locked the strongbox and replaced it in the desk. She picked up the drawing she had made, smiling at the memory of Max's teasing voice and mocking smile. Folding the paper in half, she stuffed it into the pocket of her skirt. Then her smile faded.

Hadn't she set Martin's ring down here?

She searched the row of cubbyholes along the top of the desk, then bent over to scan the floor. She unlocked the strongbox and looked through the coins and bank notes. She shut her eyes.

She could picture herself walking to the desk, Max beside her. Hadn't she set the ring down then, beside the caricature and charcoal stick? No, she must have put it back in the case. She hurried over to the counter—

"Why, the thieving bastard!" Gabrielle cried.

Agnes, on her way back to the kitchen, whirled around. "What's happened?"

"He's stolen it! My ring."

"Which ring?"

"*My* ring."

Agnes flew over to the case to see for herself. She had heard at least a dozen times Simon's strange story of the day Gabrielle had come into his shop to pawn a sapphire ring.

"Well!" she huffed. "That'll teach you to leave it lying about where just anyone can steal it. How could you allow this to happen?"

"I didn't *allow* it to happen. That—that wretch plucked it right out from under my nose." My stupid, infatuated nose, she thought, feeling a tight ache in her chest.

"What wretch?" asked Agnes. "Who stole it?"

"A man," Gabrielle hedged, unable to admit the awful truth of her gullibility, even to herself.

Agnes waved her hand as if shooing away a bothersome fly. "Oh, of course. A man. Well, what could be easier? We'll simply search all of Paris for a man, and when we find one we'll summon the *gendarmes* and demand they arrest him for a thief."

"I know who he is," Gabrielle said between clenched teeth. "His name is Maximilien de Saint-Just. He's that mad, insufferably arrogant scientist who lives above the Café de Foy. He came in here to . . . to buy a gift for one of his light-of-loves and he walked out with my ring."

Agnes glanced again at the glass case. "Oh, but this is awful, Gabrielle. Think of Monsieur Simon, how hurt he's going to be when he hears of it. You know how much that ring means to him."

Gabrielle felt a stab of guilt. She hadn't thought at all of Simon. She'd been too busy wondering why Maximilien de Saint-Just had taken her ring. He didn't strike her as a common thief. Was it possible he had recognized the ring as once belonging to the duchesse de Nevers? She prayed to God that was not the case, for if it was, she and Dominique were already doomed.

No, no, he'd only fancied it—hadn't he admitted as much? And since she wouldn't sell it, he had simply taken it. He wanted to give it to one of his women. She imagined a beautiful courtesan with expensive tastes wearing the sapphire

ring, perhaps to a rout or ball in the ducal palace, and someone—someone who knew the noble family Nevers, who had
once seen the ring on the old duchesse's finger—recognizing,
exclaiming, pointing it out. And Louvois would hear of it;
his spies were everywhere. He would question the courtesan,
and then he would question Maximilien de Saint-Just, and
then—

She would have to get it back. Get it back this instant or
take Dominique and disappear. Leave Simon and Agnes and
her home here above the pawnshop in the Palais Royal and
start running again.

"I must get it back," she said aloud, desperation making
her voice fierce and hard.

Agnes gave her a strange look. "Gabrielle . . . how ever
are you going to get it back?"

"He stole it from me. I'm going to steal it back."

Agnes snorted. *"You* steal? This I should like to see."

"I've stolen before. When I had to. But this time it won't
really be stealing. I'll merely be recovering my own—or
rather, Simon's—property."

"This time! By the wounds of Saint Sébastien, do you
mean to tell me you really have stolen before?" Agnes looked
astounded. It had always amused Gabrielle that Agnes believed she possessed virtue something on the order of the
saints Agnes frequently called upon.

"Don't curse . . . I have a plan," Gabrielle said.

Agnes rolled her eyes in mock horror.

"It's very simple," Gabrielle explained. "We'll watch his
apartment this afternoon and the next time he leaves, you'll
waylay him and borrow the key—"

"Borrow!"

"Pick the key out of his pocket, damn you . . . Then you
give the key to me and I'll run up and get the ring." Unless
he takes it with him. *Dieu,* she thought, what if he takes it
with him?

"I don't like it," Agnes said.

"I'm not asking you to like it and, besides, what's wrong
with it?"

"What if he catches me trying to pick his pocket? I could wind up at the whipping post in the Place de la Grève." Agnes spread her fingers in front of her face, flexing them and frowning. "I haven't had much practice lately."

Gabrielle gave her a skeptical look.

Placing her hand over her heart, Agnes made her eyes look round and innocent. "I swear by my virginity—"

"What kind of a lying oath is that?"

"May a brace of devils broil me over an open pit if I've stolen so much as a single sou since that day I saved your ungrateful life."

Gabrielle seized the girl's hands. "Then you'll do it for me, Agnes?"

Agnes's lips quirked up into a mischievous smile. "Will I do it? By Saint Bartholomew's tit, I wouldn't miss this for the world—" Her eyes suddenly opened wide and her mouth fell open. "This thief of yours, he wouldn't by any chance be the man who's managed to put you into such a fever these last two days?"

Gabrielle assumed a mystified look. "Really, Agnes, I haven't any idea what you're talking about. I've never felt better."

Gabrielle hovered around the newspaper vendor across from the Café de Foy, pretending to be engrossed in a pamphlet expounding the virtues of peasant life. Every few seconds she peeked over the row of papers displayed for sale—clipped with clothespins on a long string—to study the entrance to Maximilien de Saint-Just's apartment.

She was so tense that when he finally did come out she almost yelped aloud with the shock of it. She whirled around, bumping into Agnes, who hovered at her elbow.

"There he is," she said breathlessly.

Agnes stood on tiptoe to peer over the string of papers. "Jesu. You forgot to tell me he is such a handsome devil. I have a better idea. Instead of picking his pocket, why don't I go with him up to his rooms? Then I can search for the ring afterward, while he's asleep."

Gabrielle shoved her in the small of the back. "Quit acting like a Saint-Denis whore. Hurry up. He's getting away."

Agnes fluffed her short, wispy curls and loosened her fichu, exposing an expanse of white bosom that made Gabrielle feel a decided twinge of envy. Then Agnes picked up the basket at her feet—it was filled with withered violet posies—and joined the flow of traffic in front of the Café de Foy, her hips swaying saucily.

Max was walking fast, a look of intense concentration on his face. When Agnes was but a few feet away from him, she turned abruptly and took two steps backward while gesticulating with her fist and shouting at a mysterious someone behind her, calling him a cuckoldy, cow-hearted mongrel—

Max slammed into her.

The basket flew out of Agnes's arms, dumping posies into the dirt. Agnes began to wail.

"Ow! And look what you've done, you gouty lummox. Who taught you to walk, a blind man with no feet? You've ruined my flowers, you cursed son of a poxed whore!"

"A thousand pardons, mademoiselle," Max said politely as he bent to gather the posies back into the basket.

"And may a thousand devils carry you off to hell, you're trampling all over them with your big feet!" Agnes exclaimed. She jerked the basket out of his hands, lurching into him.

Max steadied her. "And I think you're a little drunk," he said, laughing and casting an appreciative eye at the girl's heaving and half-bare breasts.

"I most certainly am not!" Agnes huffed with indignation, her bosom swelling provocatively.

Then she spoiled the effect by belching and swiping at her mouth with the back of her hand. She began to sidle away from him. Max watched her a moment, his face relaxed with amusement, before he shook his head and, turning, went on his way.

Gabrielle had moved to a nearby bench in the gardens to wait for Agnes because the newspaper vendor had started to eye her suspiciously. She felt sick with disappointment. Why couldn't she fall in love with a simple man—a farmer or a shopkeeper? Instead first she had chosen Martin de Nevers, a duc's only son and heir to one of the most powerful houses in the kingdom. And now this Maximilien de Saint-Just . . . At best he was a thief. And at worst—

She almost shouted with relief at the sight of Agnes running through the trees.

Agnes pressed a heavy black key into Gabrielle's hand. "Here it is," she said breathlessly, glancing back over her shoulder. "I think he suspects something."

"Why should he suspect anything?"

"I don't know . . ." Agnes gave her a worried look. "Don't dawdle, Gabrielle. Get the ring and get out. He could return at any moment and, well, he has a look about him, around the eyes. I think he's a man who could be very, very dangerous if crossed."

Gabrielle nodded once and swallowed hard. "You should go back to the shop, Agnes, in case Simon and Dominique come back early and wonder where we are." She had gotten them out of the way that afternoon by sending them off with a pair of poles to do some fishing at the river, ushering them quickly out the door after dinner before Simon could notice the empty space in the jewelry case.

Squaring her shoulders, Gabrielle stood and began to walk with jerky movements toward the apartments above the Café de Foy.

The stairway still smelled of the same perfume, but this afternoon there was no rattle of a dice box and no woman's laughter. The building seemed strangely empty, although she could hear snatches of conversation and voices raised in argument from the café below.

Her hands shook so badly trying to fit the key into the lock that for one heart-stopping moment she thought he must carry more than one key and Agnes had picked the wrong pocket. Then suddenly it slid smoothly into the hole, the lock turned, and the door clicked open. Gabrielle darted inside and quickly shut the door behind her.

She didn't feel so nervous once inside his apartment, perhaps because there was already a familiarity about it. The broken glass from the windows and mirrors had been swept into one corner, but all his scientific paraphernalia—what hadn't been shattered by the explosion—still littered the shelves and tables of the large room.

She peered through the microscope, first with one eye and then with the other, but could make nothing out. She looked through the telescope and saw a square of blue sky. She tilted the instrument toward the galleries across the way, focusing on the newspaper vendor. His seamed and pitted face jumped before her, startlingly close, and she watched for a moment, fascinated, while he dug the wax out of his ear with a twig.

One end of the room was dominated by a large fireplace equipped with a spit and trivet for cooking, but there were no ashes in the grate. He probably eats all his meals in the café downstairs, she thought, and felt strangely sad to realize he had no one to cook for him.

A set of heavy mahogany bookcases lined the wall beside the door. He had, she saw, every single one of the thirty-six volumes of Buffon's *Histoire Naturelle,* as well as a complete set of Diderot's *Encyclopédie.* Most of his books were scientific tomes, or treatises on travel and geography. But here and there she spotted a novel, mostly untranslated English titles, and she was pleased to see her favorites by Fielding and Defoe. Next to the bookcases, maps of the stars and constellations had been tacked onto the wall. She saw that the charts had been corrected where he had made discoveries of his own.

The slam of a door downstairs startled her, making her suddenly aware of the passage of time. She looked around the cluttered room with despair; if the ring was in here she would never find it.

She decided to look for it in the bedroom first.

His bed was a large but plain, uncurtained affair, fashioned simply with a bolster and a good feather quilt. An impressive, classically styled armoire filled one wall. Opposite squatted a marble-topped commode table with two drawers faced with mother-of-pearl marquetry. The top of the commode was empty but for a large silver candelabra. The only incongruous note in the room was a stuffed owl on a perch near the window facing the gardens. In contrast to the laboratory, this room was sparse and neat.

She laid the door key on top of the commode and pulled open one of the drawers—

Oooooh.

Gabrielle whipped around, so startled by the strange noise that she emitted a tiny, high-pitched shriek. She pressed a shaking hand to her chest in case her heart decided to burst right out of it, but the room was empty and now utterly silent.

"Who's there?" she called tentatively, then cursed herself for a fool. After all, *she* was the intruder here.

A breeze drifted through the broken panes of the window, cooling Gabrielle's sweating face. The feathers stirred on the neck of the stuffed owl. Then, slowly, his two glazed yellow eyes blinked at her.

Warily she approached the bird. She started to reach out to touch him, to see if he was real, when he blinked again.

Gabrielle snatched back her hand, then began to laugh. It was just like the man, she thought, to keep an owl for a pet. Like a wizard straight out of English folklore. She pressed the back of her wrist against her mouth to stop the laughter, sure she was getting hysterical. Resolutely she turned her back on the bird and began to search the drawers of the commode, although it was difficult to do with an owl watching her, well . . . owlishly, she thought with another warbling, nervous giggle.

Her ring was not in the top drawer, but she did find something that made her pause. It was a case filled with mercury molds used to make copies of the red wax seals which closed letters. She wondered whose secret correspondence Maximilien de Saint-Just had been steaming open and then resealing.

In the second drawer she found a large Chinese wooden casket elaborately carved with warriors in strange armor fighting with swords. She lifted the hinged lid. Inside was a heavy black pistol gleaming with oil. It looked well cared for, and used. She hefted it. Was it loaded?

A small velvet bag lay in the casket with the pistol. She emptied the contents on top of the commode. A scattering of foreign coins, a man's diamond stock pin, a miniature of a young woman. And a single ring—the ruby ring he bought that morning.

She picked up the miniature.

It was of a girl at the first bloom of womanhood. Her hair was very pale, powdered probably, for her eyes were a deep rich hazel. She had a round, full mouth that quirked up at the corners, dimpling one cheek. There was something familiar about the girl, but Gabrielle couldn't place her. She wondered if this was the girl destined to receive the ring, or if she was an old love; if she, perhaps, was the reason for the cynical glint in Max's sooty gray eyes.

She stared at the miniature a moment longer, then gently slipped it back inside the velvet bag. Her fingers closed around the ruby ring—

"Looking for something?"

Chapter 3

A ny other woman in the world, thought Maximilien de Saint-Just, would have screamed. Any other woman . . . but not this one.

She slammed shut the drawer to his commode table and whirled to demand of him indignantly, "Jesu! What are *you* doing here?"

Her words surprised a laugh out of him. "Silly me," he drawled in his mocking way. "I thought I lived here."

He leaned against the doorjamb, his long legs crossed at the ankles, his hands shoved deep into the pockets of his tight breeches. He watched her from beneath lowered lids. Her fiery hair blazed in the afternoon sunlight streaming through the window. Her skin was so translucent it seemed illuminated from within. Dark violet eyes, purple like a mountain range at dusk, glowered at him.

Damn, but she was beautiful, he thought. But then, the most treacherous ones usually were.

"If you're looking for money," he said, "you won't find any in there."

Her lips curled with pure scorn. "You're a fine one to be calling me a thief after what you've done."

Max thought of the many crimes he had committed over the years, wondering which one had managed to touch on this intriguing girl. He was sure that, until two days ago, he had never seen or spoken to her before, although she had managed to haunt his thoughts every moment since.

He straightened and took a step toward her. Her back stiffened, but she didn't turn away or shift her eyes from his face. He stopped when he was standing right in front of her. He saw the movement in her throat as she swallowed, and the muscle in her jaw tense as she lifted her chin to look at him.

"Gabrielle." He stared down into a pair of mesmerizing, purple eyes . . . and forgot what he was going to say.

He slid his hand along her neck, under the heavy fall of her hair. Her skin trembled beneath his palm and he heard her breath catch. Splaying his thumb along her jawline, he tilted her face up. She started to turn her head away, then stopped as he brought his lips down over hers.

Her mouth was warm and moist, opening and moving easily beneath his. He increased the pressure of his lips, forcing her head back as he slid his tongue along the sharp edge of her teeth, probing the wet, silken cavity of her mouth. She made a small sound in the back of her throat—of protest or perhaps of surrender.

He had expected anger, resistance, fear—but not this. The depth and uninhibited warmth of her response fired an answering and unexpected hunger deep within him. Surprised, he tried to repress those feelings, shuddering with the strength of will it took.

Swaying into him, she reached up and clasped the lapels on his coat. Her tongue met his, curled around it, drew it deeper into her mouth.

Max felt himself surrendering to the hot, hard need that surged through him. He wanted this woman, would have her, but first . . . Keeping his lips locked on hers, he moved his hand down the column of her neck and along her shoulder, following the length of her arm. The material of her dress was thin and soft with wear and repeated washings, and he could feel her skin quivering underneath it. Her flesh gave off a warmth, a vital heat, and she smelled of sunlight and summer flowers. His strong fingers encircled her wrist, around bones that were light and impossibly fragile—

He tore his mouth from hers and jerked her curled fist up between their faces. "Open your hand," he said, his voice silken, dangerous, and more than a little breathless.

She clenched her fist tighter. "No," she said. Her lips were reddened and slightly swollen from his kiss, but her eyes were hard and defiant. "Give me the other one first, then you can have this one back."

"Other what? What in bloody hell are you talking about?" He increased the pressure of his fingers around her wrist, saw the pain of it register in the tightening of her mouth, but she didn't make a sound, and he felt a sudden, and unusual, stab of self-disgust that he was deliberately hurting her.

He relaxed his grip, although he didn't let go.

"Open your hand or I'll snap the bone in two," he said, for the first time in his life making a threat he had no intention of carrying through. Still, his voice had lost its courtly inflections. Now it was the rough street French of cutpurses and pimps, and harsh enough to convince her he meant what he said.

Her eyes were on his face, measuring his strength even as he measured hers. Max knew she could read nothing in his expression, but the maddening thing to him was that he could read nothing in hers. He had never before encountered such a strong will in a woman.

Then she surprised him again by smiling suddenly, deliberately teasing and tantalizing.

"Very well, Monsieur de Saint-Just," she said, mimicking his former mocking tone. "Since you've asked me so politely." She relaxed, uncurling her fingers.

The ring he had bought in the pawnshop that morning lay in her palm. He was surprised, surprised especially at his disappointment that she had come to his rooms simply to steal from him. It had been a long time since Maximilien de Saint-Just had been disappointed by anyone or anything. For to be disappointed, you first had to care.

Max had spotted the little pickpocket's ploy right away. Noticing things like that had helped to keep him alive during his twenty-eight years, and he was good at staying alive.

Curious as to what the voluptuous urchin was after—once he realized she was lifting his key and not his purse—he had let her play the trick through, allowing enough time for her, or an accomplice, to make it up to his rooms with the key before following.

Years of practice had taught Max how to move through a house without making a sound. It was especially easy to enter and walk silently through his own apartment where he knew every loose board and squeaky hinge. He had paused in the doorway to his bedroom, waiting while the girl he knew as Gabrielle searched his drawers, hesitating until he was sure she had found what she had come for.

Sighing now, he plucked the ring from her hand and tossed it on the marble top of the commode. They watched together as it rolled across the smooth surface to nestle against the velvet bag.

"And how many times has this particular ring been sold?" he asked, hard weariness in his voice.

She blinked in confusion. "What?"

He flashed his mocking smile. "Come now, Gabrielle, the game is hardly an original one, although I'm sure it's consistently profitable. You sell the ring and then steal it back again. Over and over—"

"How dare you accuse me of such a thing when you're the one who—oooh!" She tossed a clump of copper curls over her shoulder and glared at him. "I know what you're trying to do and it won't work!"

He laughed. "You'll have to rid yourself of those haughty airs if you expect to play the part of the falsely accused innocent, Gabrielle. Or whatever your name really is."

"I *am* innocent! You're the one who's a thief!"

He shrugged and made a movement toward the door. "In that case, perhaps we should summon the police . . ."

"No!" She grabbed his arm, desperation in her face and in the strength of her fingers that grasped his sleeve. She forced out a smile. "Surely we can settle this matter without involving the police. I didn't come here to steal from you, I swear, monsieur. Please . . ." Her lips trembled and tears filled her eyes. He watched, amused, as she squeezed her lids shut to keep the tears from spilling over. "I only want back what is mine," she said, her voice low and husky.

Max couldn't help himself. His hand came up and touched her face, his palm cupping her cheek and tilting her head up. "Ah, Christ, Gabrielle—" He cut himself off and pulled away from her, removing her fingers from his arm. "What am I supposed to have that is yours?"

"My ring!"

His brows drew together in a frown. "But I paid for that ring. Five hundred livres. You offered to wrap it for me, remember?"

"Not *that* ring, you fool. The other one."

"Which other one?"

"But you . . ."

She searched his face. He watched her thoughts revealed in the purple pools of her eyes. Thoughts that changed from fear and righteous anger to confusion and doubt.

"Mon Dieu. Is it possible it wasn't you who stole it after all?" she said, more to herself than to him. She sucked on her lower lip in consternation, which made her look like a pouting child, and to Max's eyes quite adorable. "I think perhaps it's all been another silly mistake, monsieur . . ." She began to scuttle sideways like a crab, trying to get around him.

"No, you don't, *ma mie.*" His hand snaked out, grabbing her. He swung her around, flinging her onto the end of the bed. She stared up at him, and he saw fear darken her eyes and the pulse jump in her throat. Or perhaps she wasn't afraid at all; perhaps it was something else that he didn't want to put a name to.

"Oh, to hell with it," he said aloud, taking a step toward her with some vague idea of taking her in his arms and kissing that pouting mouth. It was, he decided, the only thing to do with her that so far made any sense.

She misunderstood the determined expression on his face and cringed away from him. "Please, monsieur . . . don't. I can explain."

He stopped. "All right then . . ." Leaning against the bureau, he folded his arms across his chest. "Explain."

He didn't expect to believe much of what she told him, but one valuable lesson he had learned over the years was that the lies one told often revealed as much, if not more, than the truth.

"It was the sapphire ring, monsieur," she said. "The one you so admired this morning. I noticed it was missing shortly after you left the shop, so naturally I assumed . . ."

"That I had stolen it."

Splashes of bright red dotted her cheeks like rouge and she lowered her eyes. "Yes. I'm sorry."

"Never mind. I've been accused of worse." And done *far* worse, he thought.

"It's just that the ring was given to me by my husband," she babbled on, desperate now to atone for her mistake. He studied her face while she told him a tale he didn't believe, about a husband who had been a wigmaker's apprentice at Versailles before his untimely death, who had given her the ring during the first and only year of their marriage.

"He left me destitute, monsieur. There were debts—he had his professional image to maintain, you understand—but then he died, and with a little one on the way . . . what could I do?" she finished with a shrug. "I borrowed some money from his uncle, Simon Prion, and in return I gave Monsieur Prion the ring. I never really meant to sell it, you see. It was only out of foolish pride that I insisted it be displayed in the case until I could redeem it, and now that it's turned up missing . . ."

Her voice trailed off and she licked her lips nervously. Max thought about those lips, about how sweet they had tasted. He didn't want to question her any more, didn't want to hear any more lies from those lips. He wanted to kiss them.

"Your wigmaker's apprentice must have had a generous master," he said instead, "to afford such a ring."

"It was given to him as a gift by a rich patron at court. He invented a new wig style that was full but weighed little and he had a light touch with the powder paste. The patron was pleased, and he wanted to show it with a small token, you understand. Such a thing happens all the time.'' She clenched her hands together in an unconscious supplicating gesture that moved Max more than her words ever would. ''Oh, why can't you believe me?''

''But I do believe you,'' Max lied. ''You plead your case so convincingly.'' He took her hands in his, drawing her to her feet to face him, and his mouth curved into a soft, teasing smile. ''I'm sorry you lost your ring, but you didn't need to go to this elaborate ruse of picking my pocket for a chance to rifle through my drawers, *ma mie*. There would have been plenty of opportunity during the coming days. And nights.''

The bright color that stained her cheekbones deepened. ''I . . . I don't understand.''

He brushed the back of his knuckles across the blush on her cheek. ''You do understand. You could have searched my rooms to your heart's content. After we become lovers.''

She jerked away from him so fast she stumbled backward and had to clutch the bedpost to keep from falling. Then, when she saw what she was grasping, she let go as if the wood were a burning torch singeing her flesh. He almost laughed.

She threw up her head, tossing back her hair. ''I don't know what has provoked this delusion of yours, monsieur, that I desire to become your lover—''

He did laugh then. ''You know damned well what provoked it. This—''

He pulled her against him, wrapping his hand in her hair and pulling her head back, crushing his mouth down hard over hers. She resisted him for a moment, pressing against his chest with her clenched fists. Then her lips parted under his with a long, shuddering sigh.

He had meant to take possession of her with that kiss, to claim her mouth the way he later intended to claim her body. But what began as an act of conquest became one of surrender, as her lips moved beneath his with such exquisite tenderness it brought a tightness to his throat so that he couldn't breathe.

Breaking the kiss, he pushed her away from him, holding

her at arm's length. He drew in a deep, decisive breath and briefly closed his eyes.

"Gabrielle . . ." he began.

Whirling, she fled from the room.

"Wait, Gabrielle!" He bounded after her, slamming his palm against the front door before she could pull it open. "What about tomorrow? The Jardin des Plantes. I still want to see you again."

"I don't want to see you."

"You do."

"Please." She begged him with wide violet eyes. "Please . . . let me go."

And he saw in her face that what he was feeling, she felt as well. And that it frightened her as much as it did him.

His arm fell to his side and he stepped back.

She pulled open the door and, without looking back, ran along the hall and turned down the stairs. He shut the door and crossed the room, went to stand by the window so that he could see her when she emerged into the gardens. Her head, flashing red-gold in the setting sun, reminded him of piles of autumn leaves blown into fiery swirls by the wind. He watched her weave in and out among the tables and chairs of the Café de Foy, scurry along the garden path around trees and benches, to disappear . . .

"But not forever," he said aloud to the empty room. "Whatever or whoever you are, Gabrielle, I am going to have you in my arms, in my bed. Gabrielle, *ma mie*. My lady-love."

Gabrielle leaned against the gnarled trunk of a chestnut tree, gasping for breath as if she had just run the sixteen miles around the city walls instead of the few yards across the Palais Royal gardens. She pressed trembling fingers against lips that felt bruised and swollen. Never, not even in dreams, had she been kissed like that.

Glare from the setting sun dazzled her eyes and she squeezed them shut, then opened them immediately because the image of Maximilien de Saint-Just's face seemed to sear through her closed lids.

Her face burned at the memory of the way she had kissed him back. She, Gabrielle de Vauclair de Nevers, who prided herself on her hardheaded approach to life, had allowed herself to become infatuated with a complete stranger. When it came to Maximilien de Saint-Just, it was as if she had no control, not over her head, and certainly not over her heart. In her present weakened state, he could convince her of, get her to do, anything.

Just keep away from him, she told herself, pushing away from the tree trunk and resolutely squaring her shoulders. You'll be all right as long as you keep away from him.

But she knew that already it was too late. She was being drawn to Maximilien de Saint-Just by a force beyond her control to resist, the way a leaf, floating down river, can be sucked helplessly into swirling rapids.

Agnes pounced on her the minute Gabrielle set foot in the shop. "Did you find it?" she asked in a stage whisper, casting an anxious glance toward the kitchen.

Gabrielle bit her lip. "Has Simon—?"

"No, no, he didn't notice," Agnes said quickly, guessing at Gabrielle's worst fear. "He's in the kitchen, having his glass of wine. Dominique's with him. There will be fish for supper. Hurry and put the ring back before he notices."

"It wasn't—I couldn't find it," Gabrielle said evasively. Already, once out of Maximilien de Saint-Just's mesmerizing presence, she was beginning to doubt his innocence. After all, if he didn't take the ring, then who did? And if somehow, some way . . .

Louvois.

Gabrielle suppressed a shiver of fear. If Louvois saw the ring, even heard of it, he would be able to trace her and Dominique to Simon's shop. The risk of discovery was now too great; they were going to have to disappear again, yet she couldn't bear the thought. She had been so happy here in the pawnshop with Simon and Agnes. Happier than she had ever been in her life.

Not tonight, she thought. I can't do it tonight. Tomorrow. We'll leave tomorrow.

"What do you mean you couldn't find it?" Agnes was whispering frantically. "By the toes of Saint Hubert, what are you going to do now?" Gabrielle hurried into the kitchen before Agnes could question her further.

Simon, she saw, was dozing before the banked fire grate, an empty wineglass in his lax hand. His face, flushed from drink and the afternoon fishing in the hot sun, glowed ruddy in the fading daylight. An occasional soft snore puffed his lips.

Dominique stood on a stool before the table, wielding a bloody knife. A pile of fish lay in a gory mess in front of him. "Look, Maman," he exclaimed, waving the knife. "I gutted all the fishes all by myself."

Gabrielle snatched the deadly instrument from her son's hand before he could slice off his own nose. He was covered in slime and scales and fish blood, from his bare feet to his tangled flaxen curls.

"Jesu, child, you reek like a two-day-old mackerel."

Dominique wrinkled his nose. "I don't smell anything."

"Hunh. They can smell you clear out at Versailles. Fat old King Louis is probably shouting at his ministers at this very moment." She lowered her voice into a rough baritone. " 'Who is responsible for that horrible stink that is assaulting my royal nostrils? Find the culprit and have him tossed into the Bastille.' "

Dominique giggled, but his laughter died when he saw that his mother had opened the kitchen door and now struggled to drag a heavy wooden barrel inside.

Directly out the back door, which opened onto an alley, stood a rain barrel made of half a wine cask to collect water for bathing. It had been several weeks since Paris had had a good rain, but for the past three days Gabrielle had been buying an extra bucket or two from the water vendor, intending to treat herself to the luxury of a long, soaking bath. Now she would have to sponge off in a hand bowl and use the precious water on Dominique instead.

"But, Maman, I don't need a bath," Dominique protested.

"Off with your clothes, young man," Gabrielle ordered in a tone of voice Dominique knew demanded instant obedience. Sighing loudly, he began to untie the knot of the cord that held up his pantaloons.

Gabrielle waited by the barrel while Dominique slowly shed his clothes. Eventually he was naked, and the inevitable could be delayed no longer.

Gabrielle lifted him into the tub, and he howled as the water lapped over his bare flesh. "Jesu and all his saints! It's freezing!"

From his chair by the fire, Simon grunted and opened one eye, then drifted back to sleep.

"Don't curse, and it can't be freezing," Gabrielle said. "That barrel's been sitting in the sun all day." She handed the boy a sliver of lye soap and a brush. "Scrub, or I'll do it for you." Dominique quickly snatched the brush from his mother's hand before she could make good on her threat.

Gabrielle picked the grimy pantaloons off the floor with the tips of her fingers. She was surprised at how heavy they felt. She shook them, and the pockets rattled. "What have you got in here, rocks?"

"Don't throw them out, Maman. That's my collection."

She emptied the pockets onto the table. Rocks and stones rolled across the scarred, pitted wood. Just then the setting sun dipped below the sill of the window and something blue caught the dying rays, flashing in Gabrielle's eyes.

Laughter bubbled up in her throat at the same time that tears crowded her eyes. She snatched up Martin's sapphire ring, clutching it to her breast. He *is* innocent, she thought, her heart singing. Max is innocent, and the ring was never missing at all. We won't have to run away again and, *Dieu*, but I made such a fool of myself. But that doesn't matter because tomorrow I can explain everything. She could almost hear Max's teasing, mocking laughter as she told him what had happened. She laughed out loud herself, whirling around and hugging her arms.

She stopped when she saw that Dominique was watching

her, openmouthed, from over the rim of the barrel. Agnes stood in the doorway staring at Gabrielle with startled eyes, and Simon was sitting up and gaping at her.

"Gabrielle, what . . ."

Gabrielle slipped the ring over her finger and held her hand out to him. "Simon, I've decided that from now on I'm going to wear my ring. It seems silly, don't you think, to leave it lying in the case where anyone might see it and want to buy it? Mind you, I'll still pay you back those fifteen louis someday."

"My dear girl . . ." Simon beamed at her, and his eyes were moist. "You've earned back the price of the ring a thousand times, just by being here."

"But, Gabrielle," Agnes said, "I thought you told me you couldn't find the—" At Gabrielle's fierce glare, she clapped her hand over her mouth to shut off the spill of words, swallowing hard. "Uh . . . oh," she said weakly.

"But, Maman," Dominique protested loudly, "you can't wear *that*. It's my most favorite rock!"

Later that evening, a man by the name of Abel Hachette sat at his desk in his library, reading the day's stock quotations. Of the twenty-three rooms that comprised his mansion in the exclusive neighborhood of the Faubourg Saint-Honoré, Abel Hachette loved his library the best. It was in this room— with its musical-instrument motif, its gold marquetry, its pilasters of white marble with bronze capitals—that he most felt the contrast between what he had been and what he was now.

He had been born a peasant in a sod hut in Brittany, the grandson of a serf. Now he was a banker, an investor, a financier. He headed a cabal of Parisian businessmen who were wealthy enough to buy the kingdom of France and not even feel the pinch. And the source of the cabal's power and wealth, the secret to its success, was knowledge.

For there wasn't a conversation of any importance uttered in any capital in the European world that Abel Hachette didn't hear of verbatim. If the price of bread in Paris was going to fall next week, he would know about it in time to hoard his grain stores until prices went back up. If French tuckers were going to be all the rage at the London court next month, he would hear of it in time to buy stock in the lace factories of Lyons. His rivals often accused him of having a crystal ball; in fact, he had a whole net fastened with crystal balls, a net he cast over Europe in the form of his spies.

Knowledge, Abel Hachette told himself as he sat this evening behind his rosewood desk, alone in his magnificent library in the growing twilight, knowledge was the key to making money. And someday . . . someday it would be the foundation to far more. It would buy success in the secret cause toward which he and the cabal had been working for these last eight years and more.

The cause of revolution.

Someday, and soon, intelligent and wealthy men, men who *earned* their way, would not have to sit back and allow their country, their lives, to be run by a stupid old fool who was king only because he was born to it. Someday a man raised in a sod hut would be considered the equal of a man brought up in a palace. Someday a man wouldn't have to bow down before a title or a name. Someday—

"Onions! Fresh and strong! Onions!"

The harsh voice of the vegetable vendor carried over the rest of the street noise that drifted with the evening breeze through the open window. Sighing, Hachette laid down his newspaper and reached for the bell at his elbow, then thought better of it and rose, going to the window himself.

Below him, in the Rue Royal, a parade of elegant carriages clattered slowly through the pedestrian traffic going to and from the bustling Place Louis XV. If he leaned out the window and craned his head, he knew he would be able to see the new, huge bronze statue of the previous king on horseback that stood in the center of the place. But he would never do something so vulgar, so *peasantlike,* as to lean out his window to look at anything.

He could, however, without bending or leaning in the slightest, glance out the window at the traffic in the street directly below him. The lamplighters were just now making their rounds. Oil lamps had recently been installed on the corners of all the buildings in this fashionable district, replacing the old candle lanterns and giving the street a decidedly modern air that pleased him.

Hachette sucked in a deep breath, then brought a scented handkerchief to his nose to stifle a sneeze. The air was heavy this evening with the smell of soot and old dust. You could often smell the city of Paris long before you could see it, and that must certainly be true this evening. We need a good rain to wash things down, he thought. A good rain would—

He spotted a familiar figure turning the corner from the Rue Saint-Honoré and emitted a small grunt of satisfaction. It was a young man with a lithe, muscular build and unpowdered dark hair, and he walked jauntily through the stalled traffic of cabriolets and coaches. Hachette even smiled slightly as the young man paused to tip his cocked hat flirtatiously at a richly dressed matron in a sedan chair.

"There you are at last," Abel Hachette said softly to himself, and his smile broadened. Mon Ange Noir. My Black Angel.

Hachette latched the window, shutting out the noise. As he turned, he caught sight of himself reflected along with the many candles of the room's crystal chandeliers in the mirrors that lined the opposite wall. He saw a tall, thin man nearing sixty, with a pale complexion, wearing a suit of silver satin embroidered with gold and a powdered wig in the sedate hedgehog style. For a moment this image startled him, as if a stranger had suddenly entered his beloved sanctuary.

Hachette shuddered and blinked once, trying to get a grip on himself. The boy—and he *was* a boy, damn him; he was still in his twenties, after all—always had this disconcerting affect on Hachette. His Black Angel. Hachette had constantly to remind himself that the young man, the *boy,* worked for him. Yet even as he thought this he knew it for a lie. Whatever his Black Angel did, it was for his own purposes, and he, Hachette, merely paid the bills.

Both sides of the double doors swung wide behind the hand

of a lackey just as the gold-plated clock on the richly orna-mented lapis lazuli mantel chimed nine o'clock.

"You're late," Hachette said, determined to establish his authority at the beginning for a change.

Maximilien de Saint-Just flashed his cocky smile. "My dear Abel, when are you going to learn to be grateful that I've come at all?"

Without waiting to be invited, Max slouched down in a gilded armchair. He shoved his hands into his pockets and stretched his long legs straight out before him, closing his eyes.

Hachette realized he had been left standing awkwardly in the middle of the room, and a warm blush spread over his cheeks. This attitude the boy projected, a sort of aloof disdain for the rest of the world, annoyed Hachette, for it never failed to remind him which of them had been born the son of a peasant, and which a son of the comte de Saint-Just.

He cleared his throat, pressing a handkerchief against his lips. "I thought I would have a cup of chocolate," he said, somehow sounding gauche to his own ears. "Would you care for some?"

Max opened one eye. "No, I would not care for some chocolate. I'll have a glass of that brandy you've got hidden deep in your cellar. The stuff you didn't pay tax on."

Hachette went to the desk and rang the bell. A servant had been hovering outside the door, expecting the summons, and he entered immediately. The order was given, the servant left, and silence descended as Hachette resumed his seat, safely barricaded behind his rosewood desk.

"Your message said you had something important for me," Hachette said when he realized that since the boy seemed to be falling asleep in the chair, he was going to have to initiate the conversation. "Whatever it is, it must have kept you up all of last night."

Max smiled, although his eyes remained shut. "Getting it certainly did."

Hachette felt a quiver of excitement. Ah, my Black Angel, he thought, what do you have for me this time?

In the early days, when the cabal had first begun to use agents to gather the information so necessary to making their investments and financing their schemes, they had referred to their spies by the code word of ''angels'' in any correspondence that might have inadvertently fallen into the wrong hands. They did not resort to such childish games any longer, but privately Hachette still thought of the dark and dangerous Maximilien de Saint-Just as his Black Angel.

The servant entered bearing brandy in a Baccarat decanter with a matching snifter, and chocolate in a Sèvres porcelain cup.

Max roused himself enough to take the glass of brandy. He swirled the liquid around the sides of the crystal, then held it up to his aristocratic nose before disposing of the contents in two swallows. When the door had closed behind the servant, he went to the marble-topped sideboard and refilled his glass from the decanter.

Turning, he tossed a packet of papers tied together with a riband between Hachette's open hands, which rested placidly on the glowing polished wood of his desk.

''What is it?'' Hachette asked, unable to keep the excitement from his voice as he reached for the papers.

''Read and see. Although some of it may be illegible. There was a lot to copy and I didn't have much time.''

While Hatchette read over the documents, squinting through a quizzing glass, Max sat down again. He leaned his head over the back of the chair, seemingly engrossed in the cupids and cherubs that cavorted on the frescoed ceiling.

''But this is incredible, Max!'' Hachette exclaimed. With the information in these papers he would be able to underbid all other contenders for the lucrative concession of supplying fodder and uniforms for his majesty's army. ''This is incredible. Where on earth did you ever get your hands on it?''

Max's lips curled and his head lowered until he had Abel Hachette fixed with his steely gray gaze. ''The papers—or at least the originals—are in the possession of a Monsieur Voltiere, who is first secretary to the minister of war. Monsieur Voltiere, you'll be relieved to know, is a very careful man.

They were sealed and put in a locked box within a secret drawer of a locked chest within his locked library.''

"But how . . . ?''

Max's eyes were filled with amused cynicism. "How do you think, Abel? Monsieur Voltiere was not at home last night, but the charming, and very lonely, Madame Voltiere was.'' He shrugged. "Seals can be loosened, locks can be picked.''

And wives can be seduced, Hachette thought. He himself didn't have a wife, but he nevertheless made a mental note never again to leave even the most innocuous documents locked in his desk drawer.

"Last night's work could turn out to be quite profitable, Max,'' he said, tapping the sheaf of papers against his chin. "You are to be complimented—''

Max's mocking laughter shattered the quiet of the room. "I don't need your compliments, Abel. Just don't fail to give me my twenty percent when the deal goes through.''

"But of course, my dear boy. That goes without saying.''

Hachette looked fondly at the young man. In return, Max watched the older man from beneath sleepy lids.

"Now, who's the girl, you pimping bastard?'' Max asked abruptly in rough street French.

Hachette started. "What girl? I don't understand.''

"Don't try to bugger me, Hachette. I'm talking about that delectable little morsel you sent to bedevil me these last two days.''

"I don't use women, Max, you know that. They're unreliable.'' He tried to look wounded. "And I never spy on my own men.''

"The hell you don't, when it suits your purposes. And you use women, too. When it suits your purposes. Who is she?''

Hachette regarded him squarely. His pale face, only lightly scored by his sixty years, showed curiosity, perhaps a bit of annoyance, nothing more. "I swear to you, I know nothing about a girl. What's more, my boy, I don't appreciate being called a pimp.''

For a moment Hachette saw genuine anguish darken the

young man's eyes. "But isn't that precisely what you are, Hachette? Doesn't a pimp profit from the work of his whore? What do you think I did for you last night to get those papers?"

"That's not the same thing."

"Isn't it?" Max stared at him for a long time, then shrugged wearily. "It doesn't matter. The girl calls herself Gabrielle Prion. I caught her searching my rooms this afternoon."

Hachette paled. He thought of the many enemies he had made within the various government ministries over the years. King Louis XVI's spy apparatus was not nearly of the caliber of his grandfather's, but still . . . And there was the secret side to the cabal, the political side. If any of *that* ever came out they'd all wind up broken on the wheel at the Place de la Grève.

He fingered the sheaf of papers covered with Max's bold scrawl. "My God, did she see these?"

Max said nothing, only gave him a look of pure contempt.

"But this is worrisome, Max. Perhaps she works for the king."

"I doubt it. Whoever she is, she's a bloody amateur."

Hachette thought a moment, then shrugged. "The name— Gabrielle Prion. It means nothing to me. Describe her."

"Young, about twenty. Pale-skinned with striking red-gold hair. Very dark blue eyes. Purple actually."

"Is she beautiful?"

"Breathtakingly so."

Hachette's eyes flickered away, and there was a faint hollow note to his laughter. "My dear boy, I can scarcely credit it. Has your breath been taken?"

"You do know her," Max said.

"There is something . . ."

Hachette did a mental thumbing through his memory. Once he received a piece of information, no matter how seemingly insignificant, he stored it away in the repository of his mind in case it turned out to be useful to him later. Hachette's memory was legendary, and more than one enemy and rival had come to suffer by it.

"I might have heard of her," Hachette finally said. "I seem to recall the minister of the Paris police was asking about a girl of that description, oh, three, maybe four, years ago."

"Why?"

Again Hachette was lost in thought for a moment. "I don't think he ever said specifically. But I had the impression the inquiry wasn't being made on the minister's behalf, but on someone else's. Somebody important. You haven't really fallen in love with her, have you, Max?"

Max ignored the question. "Could you find out about this girl the police were asking after, Abel? Discreetly."

"Of course. But you could just as easily—"

Max shook his head, standing up. "If it's the same girl and she has enemies, I don't want them finding her through me."

"And if it turns out that *she* is the enemy?"

"Why, Abel," drawled Max, and a familiar smile of self-mockery flitted across his lips, "since you know my talents for seducing the fair sex, I'm surprised you even need to ask."

Hachette's return smile was a mask that hid his worry. He would have to find out about this Gabrielle Prion. If she turned out to be a threat, she would have to be dealt with. Dealt with and even eliminated if necessary.

For the sake of the cabal. And for France and the revolution.

Chapter 4

Gabrielle dreamed it was raining. They had gone for a picnic in the Bois de Boulogne, she and Maman. That morning, when they had set out in the carriage, the sun shone brightly and Gabrielle wore her new hat, the straw one with the big pink silk bow. Then black, heavy clouds covered the sun, and big fat drops began to fall, pattering on the leaves of the trees and flattening the grass.

"*Dieu,* but we'll be soaked!" Maman exclaimed, seizing her hand, and they began to run.

But when Gabrielle looked down she saw that it was Dominique's hand she held, and he was laughing up at her. "Maman, we're getting wet!"

It began to hail. It rattled on the ground like acorns falling from oak trees. They ran faster, and the wind began to croon, calling her name. The hail clattered louder, sounding now like stones thrown against a window—

"Gabrielle!"

Gabrielle jerked upright in bed. More pebbles rattled the windowpanes, and a voice, decidedly masculine, bellowed her name.

"Fiend seize you, Gabrielle, I know you're up there!"

She slid from the bed, and feeling her way in the dark to the window, carefully pulled the shutters open, wincing as the hinges squeaked. She leaned out to peer into the gardens below.

He stepped from under the trees, a blacker shape among the shadows. As he tilted his head back to look up at her, the pale light from the flickering street lanterns highlighted the sharp bones of his face.

"Ga—"

"Be quiet!" she hissed. "Jesu, what are you—it's past midnight, you fool!"

"Come down," he said.

"No!"

"Come down or I'll serenade you. With a Russian love song. A *loud* Russian love song with lots of clapping and stamping of feet."

"You wouldn't dare."

He started to sing.

"Dieu . . . All right, all right, I'm coming down."

She turned from the window and stumbled over the chest at the end of the bed, stubbing her bare toes. Stifling a cry, she flopped down on the chest to massage her throbbing foot.

"By the patience of poor Job." Agnes sat up in bed, rubbing a hand through her wispy spikes of hair. "What are you doing up at this time of night, rattling around the room like a centime in a beggar's cup?"

"He's here," Gabrielle said through teeth gritted with pain. "The madman."

"Who? Here? Why?"

"To torment me. Why else?"

"Ah."

Gabrielle let go of her foot and twisted around, squinting to make out Agnes's face in the darkness. "And what does that mean?"

"What does what mean?"

"That sound you made. It matches the self-satisfied smirk on your face."

"How can you see my face? It's as black as a privy hole in here tonight. And I said nothing. I was only yawning."

"Hunh."

"The poor soul," Agnes said. "You see what you've reduced him to already. First stealing things and then putting them back, and then wandering around the gardens and singing in the middle of the night. No wonder he's a madman. Why not be charitable and put him out of his misery? You know you want to."

"Which shows," Gabrielle hissed indignantly, "how little you know about anything!"

Dominique stirred, mumbling softly in his sleep. Agnes got up and shuffled over to the trundle bed.

"Hush, *petit.*" She gathered the little boy in her arms and carried him back to the big bed. "You come sleep with Agnes now, while your maman goes out to meet her lover."

Gabrielle opened her mouth, then shut it. She slipped her bare feet into a pair of sabots and lifted her *manteau* from the hook by the door, draping it over her nightclothes.

In the hall she could hear Simon's snores coming from behind his closed door. Luckily his window opened not onto the gardens but onto the alley out back. He was a heavy sleeper anyway. Sometimes, when he fell asleep in his chair before the kitchen fire, neither she nor Agnes could rouse him to take him to bed.

The garden was empty when she stepped out the front door of the shop. He's gone then, she thought, but instead of feeling relief, she experienced a terrible disappointment.

"I thought you had changed your mind."

Gabrielle jumped, emitting a small cry. She turned around, pulling her *manteau* tight under her chin. Maximilien de Saint-Just leaned nonchalantly against the wall, his arms folded across his chest. His cocked hat slashed a band of shadow across his face, obscuring his expression.

They stood in the soft, dark night, looking at each other, until Gabrielle began to feel the beating of her heart and the soft bellows motion of her breathing lungs, the way one suddenly becomes aware of a clock ticking in a quiet room.

"You were caterwauling loud enough to wake all of Paris," she said finally, breaking the spell and sounding an-

grier than she had meant to because she was afraid he would
guess at what his presence was doing to her.

"Caterwauling?" He laughed. "How unflattering." He
stepped forward and took her hand. Bowing, he brought it to
his lips.

"Hello," he said.

The kiss he brushed against the back of her fingers was
cool and light. Yet the sensation it produced lingered, warm
as morning sunlight.

"What do you want with me?" she asked, her voice breaking huskily.

"Gabrielle, Gabrielle," he sang her name. "Let me show
you the stars."

Though it was well past midnight, the streets of Paris
weren't empty. Hackney cabs burst out of black shadows,
swaying past pools of yellow lantern light before disappearing into darkness again. The laughter and shouts of revelers
in the *guinguettes*—the open-air cafés and dance halls that
stayed open all night—drifted past them on the soft breeze.
Somewhere a dog bayed and a cat answered with a high-
pitched yowl.

Gabrielle's sabots clattered loudly on the cobblestones. She
pulled her *manteau* tightly across her chest, conscious suddenly that she wore only a thin cotton nightdress underneath.
She couldn't believe she was doing this, following a man, a
stranger, into a dark and unknown night.

Yet the hand that clasped hers felt strong and comforting,
and, irrationally, because it was his hand she was not afraid.

He led her into the Jardin des Tuileries. The park, which
had once been the gardens of the royal palace before the kings
of France had moved to Versailles, was now a fashionable
parade ground by day. Children sailed their toy boats in the
pond; fountains shimmered in the thick shade of ancient trees;
lovers embraced beneath the statue of Mars, the god of war.

But tonight the park was dark and deserted.

Max stopped when they reached the esplanade that over-
looked the river Seine. He turned her so that she faced the

wide-open expanse of water and, cupping her head with his hands, tilted her face up.

"Look," he said softly.

Gabrielle gasped. The stars! They filled the sky, shimmering, glittering, like thousands of diamond flakes scattered over a swatch of the blackest velvet. And they were so close. It seemed all she need do was reach out and scoop them into her hand. She had spent her life, all the nights of her life, in buildings packed along narrow streets, and though surely she must have glanced up countless times and noticed the stars, never, never once had she seen *this*. The beauty of it brought tears to her eyes.

"Max!" She laughed, clutching his hands in her excitement. "Oh, Max, it's so beautiful!"

"It's one of the better nights to stargaze. Unusual really, because there's no moon to dim their brilliance and the sky is free of mist and clouds."

His face was in shadow, yet she knew he was smiling at her. Suddenly aware of the warm, rough feel of his hands in hers, she let them go and looked up again. She sighed, at the mystery of him, at what she felt for him.

"There must be millions of them," she said, speaking to fill the sudden silence between them, afraid of what lay beneath it.

He came to stand behind her.

She felt the power of him that was a heat in the night, and she was drawn to that heat the way one would hold out cold hands to a flame. *Hold me,* she willed to him, and as if in answer to her silent plea, his hands lightly encircled her waist. She felt his breath rustle her hair, and as he spoke his silken voice caressed her ear.

"The ancients saw patterns in the stars, configurations of their gods, and so they gave them names. That one"—he pointed to a particularly bright star with a reddish tinge, and Gabrielle followed the path of his finger into the diamond-studded blackness—"the Babylonians called Sibzianna. The star of the shepherds and the heavenly herds."

He pointed to others, and their names, the way he said

them, formed the notes of a song. Andromeda, Delphinus, Perseus . . . His seductive voice wove the song around her like a net, catching her fast within its silken threads.

"Perseus," she whispered, her throat closing tightly. Unconsciously she nestled deeper within his embrace, pressing her shoulders against the reassuring hardness and warmth of his chest. "Perseus . . . How beautiful."

One of the hands left her waist and moved slowly up her arm to her shoulder. He pushed the fall of her hair aside, exposing her neck. He started to bend his head, to press his lips onto the bare white flesh, and she waited, no longer breathing, waited until even her heart seemed to pause in anticipation of his lips on her skin.

But he spoke instead, and though his breath, moist and laden with the exotic scent of brandy, stirred against her neck, it was not what she had expected, hoped for. She pressed her eyes shut against a sudden plunge of disappointment.

"Have you not heard the story of Perseus?" he said. "He was a Greek warrior, sent on a quest to slay the Gorgon Medusa. He was very brave, and so he succeeded, cutting off the Gorgon's head. She had snakes for hair and was so ugly anyone who looked at her was instantly turned to stone."

Gabrielle tilted her head around to gaze up at his face, still shadowed and dark with mystery. "How did this Greek warrior manage to kill her then, without looking at her?"

Max smiled and his eyes glinted brightly, a flash of silver, quickly extinguished. "Don't be so fiercely practical. I don't know how he did it. I think he had the help of some woman." Gabrielle sniffed, and he squeezed her shoulder playfully. "Quit interrupting the story."

She turned back within the bowl of his arms. Laying her head against his shoulder, she looked up at the configuration of stars that Max had said was the Greek warrior Perseus. "What happened then, after he killed that woman with snakes for hair?"

"He was on his way home with Medusa's head when he saw a beautiful girl chained to a rock on a seashore. She was to be a sacrifice to appease some wicked sea monster. Her name was Andromeda, and he fell instantly and hopelessly in love with her. With his sword he broke the chains that bound her, and then he turned the monster to stone by showing it Medusa's head. He offered Andromeda the gift of either freedom or his love, one or the other but not both.''

Tears welled up in Gabrielle's eyes and her throat seemed to swell, making it difficult to swallow. Irrational anger filled her, and she pulled out of his arms, going to the stone wall that defined the esplanade. The placid water of the Seine was a black mirror that reflected the star-emblazoned sky above.

She heard his step on the gravel behind her.

She whirled to face him. ''Why couldn't she have both?''

His hands closed over her upper arms, then moved up her shoulders to cup her neck. ''It wasn't possible to have both. Perhaps it wasn't necessary.''

''Then which did she choose?''

Her mouth was set in anger. He traced the contour of her lips until they softened and parted, and he saw her tremble. ''Love, of course. Was there ever any doubt?''

She averted her eyes. ''It isn't a true story. It's only a myth.''

''But the Greeks,'' he said softly, ''believed. And Perseus and Andromeda, and the love they shared, live forever. In the stars.''

His fingers played along the flesh of her neck to become entwined in her hair, and he tipped her head back for his kiss.

His mouth closed over hers, claiming her. Her lips, cold from the night air, warmed and parted with a soft, gentle sigh. Her hands cupped his neck, pulling him closer, and she flattened her breasts tight against his chest, molding herself to the hard planes and angles of his body. He slid his tongue over her lips, and she opened her mouth, giving herself to him with the same sweet abandon as she had shown that afternoon.

Nothing mattered but this moment, with this man. The past was insignificant, the future uncertain. Nothing mattered but the night and the stars and the memory of the way his voice had woven a mythical song of love, offering it as a gift meant only for her.

But the kiss, the moment, couldn't last forever. His lips parted from hers, and his fingers released her hair. She let go of him as well, backing up a step, so that they no longer touched. They stood apart, and it wouldn't have surprised her if he had left her then, abandoned her alone in the middle of the dark Tuileries park without another word.

But he didn't leave her. "Let's find a café," he said, and the lilting happiness in his voice infected her so that she smiled. "Somewhere cozy and crowded where we can share a glass of brandy and tell each other our life stories."

They did not, after all, tell each other their life stories. Their secrets were too dark and deep, what they felt for each other too new and fragile, to risk such intimacy.

The café, a neighborhood gathering place in a narrow alley off the Rue de Rivoli, was crowded and noisy even at this hour of the night. A group of richly dressed university students was holding a political debate, and the words "liberty" and "revolution" echoed loudly in the high-ceilinged room.

They had to shove their way through the crowd to the back where a small marble-topped table stood on iron legs. There was only one empty chair, but Max stole another from a man who had leaped onto a nearby table to add his opinion to the din. Evidently it wasn't a popular opinion, for someone heaved a bowl at his head. The man ducked and the crockery shattered against the wall behind him. Unfortunately the bowl had been full of a lumpy *potage*, and the table orator howled as he was splattered with hot clumps of the brown, greasy gravy.

Max and Gabrielle looked at each other and laughed.

It was warm in the café, and Gabrielle started to take off her *manteau*, remembering just in time that she was wearing nothing but her nightdress underneath. She felt Max's eyes on her and looked up, blushing when she realized that he, too, was aware of her disgraceful state of deshabille.

A waiter shuffled up and glared insolently at Max. *"Oui, monsieur."*

"Brandy." Max raised a brow at Gabrielle.

"Thé à l'anglaise," she said, which caused the waiter to curl his lip with disdain before he shuffled away again.

The students had taken their argument outside, and the noise around them lessened. Gabrielle looked at the man across from her. The first time she had seen Maximilien de Saint-Just she had thought there was a harshness, a cruelty, about him. The harshness was still there, in the lines at the corners of his mouth, although it was relaxed and smiling now. And although there was laughter in the sooty gray eyes that regarded her so carefully, they still betrayed the bitter disillusionment he tried to disguise with his mocking ways.

She wondered who or what had hurt him so badly.

"How did you learn so much about the stars?" she asked him.

"Necessity. I once sailed a ship between France and America. The Atlantic Ocean is a very big place, and the captain had better be able to read the stars if he's going to make his way safely across it."

"America!" Gabrielle exclaimed softly. "How I've always wanted to see America. I've never even been outside of Paris. Except once, when I was a girl and Maman took me on the old chamber pot to Versailles to see the king and queen eat supper."

She remembered that day vividly, although she had been only five or six. She and Maman had crowded into one of the special tourist coaches that were called chamber pots, no doubt because of the stink of so many unwashed bodies packed together. Once at Versailles, they had all marched in a long line past the royal table, in one door and out another. The king, she remembered, who was fat even then, had shoveled the food into his mouth so fast he barely chewed before swallowing. But the queen, looking miserably unhappy to be on display like an animal in a menagerie, hadn't eaten at all. It was the only time her maman had taken Gabrielle to Versailles, although Marie-Rose de Servien de Vauclair, if she'd so desired, could have been a lady-in-waiting to the queen.

Gabrielle realized Max must think of her as the wife of a mere wigmaker's apprentice and unused to such grandeur. "That must have been a rather edifying experience," he said, mockery in his voice.

The waiter appeared at Max's elbow. *"Thé à l'anglaise,"* he said with a sneer, and plopped the cup of tea and milk down in front of Gabrielle, so hard that some of the liquid slopped into the saucer. The glass of brandy he set down with care, almost with reverence, clearly showing his patriotic inclinations and his disgust of all things English.

Max paid the waiter and waved him away. He took a sip of the brandy and grimaced. "God. This is vile stuff. It's probably made right here in the cellar."

Gabrielle laughed softly, and he smiled back at her. Her eyes still on his face, she reached for the teaspoon that lay catty-cornered across the saucer.

Max's smile vanished abruptly. He grabbed her wrist, slamming her hand down flat on the table. The sapphire ring winked in the light cast by the girandoles on the wall.

His heavy lids lowered until they all but obscured his hard gray eyes. "Is this the ring I'm supposed to have stolen? The precious ring your *husband* gave to you?"

Gabrielle swallowed hard, but she didn't look away. "It was all a silly mistake. My son took it. He thought it was a rock."

As she told him the story she tried to make a joke of it, though she could hear the nervous quiver in her voice. Slowly, Max relaxed, and the dangerous look left his face. By the end of it, he even managed to laugh with her, although she knew by the wary look in his eyes that he still did not quite believe her.

The fingers that had clasped her wrist so cruelly now gently rubbed circles on her bruised skin, and his touch warmed the blood in her veins until she burned inside.

I want him, she thought. God, how I want him. And if wanting is love, then I am, God help me, in love.

He released her wrist, and a long silence stretched between them.

"Tell me about America," she said.

"It's big and wild and raw. Everything is new there. New and clean."

"The cradle of liberty . . ."

He smiled cynically. "So they claim."

"Is that why you sailed to America, to fight in their revolution?"

"Not exactly. I ran muskets past the English warships, but I did it for money, not liberty." He gave her his tough, damn-the-world smile, and she thought it was probably that expression that made her fall in love with him. "I will do anything for money," he said.

Then his grin faded. He reached across the table to touch her hand, which had been nervously toying with her teaspoon. "You know what's going to happen, don't you, Gabrielle?"

She shook her head, unable to look at him, but the word that came out of her mouth was "Yes."

"I want you, *ma mie,* and I mean to have you. But don't go weaving myths around me because I'm a bastard and I've no desire to be reformed. I'll lie to you and I'll probably use you, and I'll most definitely end up hurting you, so if you have any sense at all you'll—"

"I don't care what you are!" she cried, unconcerned that he knew exactly what she had come to feel for him. "Besides, I don't believe you're . . . you're really like that."

He shook his head, placing his fingers against her lips. "You can't know what I've done."

She took his wrist, turning his hand to touch her lips to his palm. It seemed a strangely intimate gesture, more so than the kisses they had shared. "I know what you've done," she said to him, and she believed it, for in that moment she knew him, understood him, better than she knew and understood herself. "There are things one must do to survive. And afterward . . . afterward they don't matter. I know," she said again, "for I've probably done most of them myself."

His lips twisted into a skeptical smile. "That would be impossible."

She let go of his hand and picked up her teacup. "I was once a letter writer in the Cemetery des Innocents. I sat on a tombstone with paper and pen and earned ten sous writing love notes for those poor rustics who come to Paris to find a fortune and lose their hearts instead. I'll wager you've never done *that.*"

He laughed. "No, I can't say I have."

He chuckled again and she laughed with him, dissolving the last vestiges of the strange intimacy that had developed so suddenly and mysteriously between them. Gabrielle knew the chance had been there, in that moment, to tell him the truth about herself and her past. But it was too soon.

Chapter 5

Gabrielle grimaced at her reflection in the mildew-spotted mirror that hung above her rickety dressing table. All this primping and fussing over her appearance was making her feel ridiculous.

"Aren't you done yet?" she complained, squirming on the hard wooden stool.

Agnes unwrapped a fiery gold curl from around the hot iron and tucked it into the arrangement of crimped coils and loops atop Gabrielle's head, securing it in place with a pair of wire pins. "It's a pity we can't afford the pomatum and flour to powder your coiffure," she said, tucking a final stray wisp of hair into place. "Otherwise you would be absolutely *le dernier cri.*"

Gabrielle gingerly patted Agnes's elaborate masterpiece. "I feel like a ship under full sail."

Then she laughed suddenly, and Agnes smiled at Gabrielle's infectious happiness. "Whatever you do, don't sneeze or you will be completely undone."

Gabrielle laughed again, then stood up carefully, holding her head stiff. With Agnes's help, she pulled on her dress, arranging its full skirt over the small pads fastened to her hips that were now often taking the place of the more old-fashioned panniers. The dress was a cheap version of the thin, white muslin gown known as a *gaulle,* which the queen had introduced into fashion last summer, and the décolletage of its tight square bodice was cut so low she feared to bend over.

Agnes clucked in dismay as Gabrielle picked her new fichu from the end of the bed. "You will never capture him by hiding your charms, Gabrielle. Like the peacock, you should be flaunting your plumage."

Gabrielle arranged the folds of the fichu so that her plumage was modestly covered. "It just so happens it's the *male* peacock that struts about with his tail feathers on display. And I have no desire to 'capture' Monsieur de Saint-Just. Dominique and I are merely accompanying him on an outing to the Jardin des Plantes."

Agnes shrugged at this obvious prevarication. "He's practically yours anyway, Gabrielle. It's obvious the poor soul is madly in love with you."

Gabrielle almost snorted. "Don't be ridiculous."

"Jesu, but he's a gorgeous man. He would make a fine lover, and more's the pity, because"—Agnes lowered her voice conspiratorially—"I fear his intentions are strictly honorable."

Gabrielle did snort then. "Strictly lustful, you mean."

"I think you do him an injustice, Gabrielle. Otherwise why would he have bothered to spend the last hour charming your son and Monsieur Simon?"

"He *what?*"

Gabrielle whipped around so fast that Agnes stumbled backward in alarm. "Please, Gabrielle, your hair! Be careful or you'll—"

"Agnes, you wretch! I can't believe he's been here a whole *hour* and this is the first I hear of it!"

"By the ears of Saint Steven, I'm telling you now, aren't I? Jesu, I've never seen you so excitable. He came early and you weren't ready. He brought Dominique a toy, and he and the boy and Monsieur Simon have all gone out into the gardens to play with it."

Gabrielle slipped hurriedly into her best leather slippers, searching the disordered room for her hat. "He brought

Dominique a toy? What sort of toy? Agnes, where in heaven's name is my hat?''

''Right here under your nose.'' Agnes anchored the hat—it was boat-shaped, made of straw, and adorned with pink feathers—atop Gabrielle's head. ''It was an interesting object, this toy your handsome scientist brought Dominique. It looked like a miniature *montgolfier,* but he called it something strange . . . an aero— Gabrielle! Where are you— I haven't finished yet!''

Gabrielle tore down the stairs so fast she almost tripped over her skirts. She held her breath, expecting at any moment to hear an explosion coming from the gardens. The man was absolutely, impossibly, completely mad.

She spotted the balloon first. A bright yellow ball, it floated among the chestnut leaves like a bouncing sun. Then she saw the flash of her son's hair, almost as golden. He was tethered to the balloon by a piece of twine wrapped around his wrist. Simon and Maximilien de Saint-Just stood beside the boy, all three standing beneath the bright red and white striped awning of a lemonade and licorice stand, their heads tilted back, watching the balloon ride the air currents.

Gabrielle snatched Dominique off his feet, jerking the string from his wrist. The balloon, free of its moorings, sailed up and over the rooftops of the Palais Royal.

Dominique screamed. ''Maman! You've lost my 'stat! Bring it back! I want it back!''

''Gabrielle!'' Simon exclaimed in surprise.

She turned on Max in fury. ''How dare you endanger my son!''

''It was only a toy, Gabrielle.'' He had to shout to be heard over Dominique's wails.

''Do you deny that that *thing* was filled with inflammable air?''

''It was inflated with hydrogen, yes, but—''

She turned away from him, stalking back toward the pawnshop with Dominique twisting and screaming in her arms.

Max had to trot to catch up with her, taking her elbow and

halting her by force. "Gabrielle, dammit, will you listen? It was perfectly safe. It wouldn't have exploded—"

"It exploded before!"

"Only because I meant it to. I was testing the strength of a new gummed-silk envelope I've invented by applying heat. A lot of heat."

Gabrielle's anger left her so suddenly that she felt like one of his deflated aerostats. Hot embarrassment flooded over her, burning her cheeks. *Dieu,* she had done it again, made an utter and complete fool of herself in front of this man. She hoped a giant crack would open right here in the gardens of the Palais Royal and swallow her up.

Dominique's cries had quieted to choking, muffled sobs. "I want it back," he kept pleading over and over. "I want it back, Maman. Bring it back."

Gabrielle was now near tears herself. "Oh, Dominique . . . I'm so sorry."

Max cupped the golden head in his hand, tilting the boy's face up. "I can make you another," he said softly. "A bigger and better one."

Dominique sniffled, wiping his nose with the back of his wrist. "I want a red one."

"Then a red one you shall have." Max captured Gabrielle's eyes and smiled. An answering, tentative smile quivered around her mouth.

Dominique pushed against her chest, demanding to be let down. She set him on his feet and he immediately ran back to Simon, who hovered at a discreet distance, shouting to him about the new red 'stat he was going to have.

Gabrielle watched the boy for a moment before her gaze returned to Max. "Thank you," she said.

"My pleasure."

His sooty eyes moved over her face, as intimately as a caress, and the constant noise in the crowded gardens seemed suddenly to still. A hot summer breeze stroked her cheek, bringing with it a smell of cut lemons and dust and crushed chestnuts.

"Good morning, Gabrielle," he said, and her throat tightened. How she loved to hear him say her name.

Embarrassed, she brushed a loose curl from her flushed forehead, then plucked nervously at her hat, which had tilted askew during her mad rush down the stairs.

He stilled her hand. "Don't . . . I like you looking a bit disheveled."

She laughed nervously. "You've never seen me looking any other way."

A slow, lazy smile stretched across his wide mouth, transforming his face, brightening his eyes until they glinted like quicksilver. She lost herself in those eyes, that smile, lost herself in him, until the world faded away and there was just the two of them, consumed in each other.

So absorbed were they that Simon had to speak twice to make himself heard.

"Monsieur de Saint-Just? The hackney you ordered, it's here."

The hackney swayed as it jostled through the traffic on the Pont Neuf. Gabrielle stared out the window, pretending to be engrossed in a scene she had seen on countless occasions, although from time to time she would steal glances at the man who sat across from her.

At her feet was wedged a wicker basket with the neck of a champagne bottle poking out the top. Dominique sat beside Max and kept up a constant stream of chatter, about balloons and rock collections and dancing bears, pausing only long enough for Max to contribute a comment or two before moving on to a new topic.

"He'll talk your ear off if you encourage him," she said apologetically.

"I don't mind," he answered with a grin that put a dimple in his cheek, making him appear boyishly young.

He looked breathtakingly handsome that morning, in a white waistcoat and a green dress jacket cut in the English country style, the white stock at his neck setting off his sun-browned skin. His suede breeches stretched tightly over the corded muscles of his thighs, and his tall, polished black boots emphasized the hard length of his calves. He was too beautiful not to look at, too beautiful not to want.

The hackney lurched around a corner, and Gabrielle grasped the strap to keep from falling off the seat. A wave of dizzy exhaustion engulfed her and she pressed her eyes shut. It serves you right, she told herself, for getting up in the middle of the night to chase after the stars, and drinking tea in a café until the early morning hours. Yet when she was with him time ceased to have meaning. Reality was only his smile, his eyes, the silky echo of his voice.

Last night, as they had left the café, she hadn't even realized he was leading her to his end of the Palais Royal until they were almost outside his apartment door.

"We have hours yet before the sun fades away our stars," he had said in that impossibly seductive voice. "Will you spend them with me, Gabrielle?"

"No, I can't," she had protested, denying him, denying herself, though in truth a part of her had wanted him to take her in his arms and carry her up those stairs, to his bed.

She had tried to run from him then, from herself, but he had caught her hands fast in his, bringing them to his lips. "Tomorrow, *ma mie*," was all he had said.

Then he had escorted her back across the garden to the pawnshop and kissed her goodbye. But not on the mouth, as she had secretly wanted him to, but on the inside of her wrist. The feel of his lips, cool and firm, pressing against her sensitive flesh, had somehow left her feeling plundered, ravished.

Oh, but you are clever, she told him silently now. So clever to arouse her hunger and then leave her unsatisfied. It was a woman's trick, a seducer's ploy. *I'll lie to you and I'll probably use you,* he had said. She would do well to remember that.

The hackney pulled up before an imposing stone building. The driver opened the carriage door and let down the step. Max descended, then lifted Dominique to the ground. He took Gabrielle's arm to help her, and his hand lingered on her waist, guiding her toward the building's arched portals. It was a casual, polite gesture, nothing more, yet she was uncomfortably aware of the feel of his palm resting on the small of her back, the brush of his leg against her skirt, the nearness of his face. Though the sun beat down bright and hot on the stone steps, she shivered.

The Jardin des Plantes was the center of scientific French studies. Founded over a hundred and fifty years before, it housed laboratories and lecture halls, rooms full of rare collections and greenhouses overgrown with exotic plants. Its botanical groves and gardens stretched for acres down to the Seine.

As they entered a giant hall, Dominique clapped his hands with delight. Odd-looking anatomical specimens in jars lined the walls. Tables were loaded with sextants and quadrants, crucibles and alembics. A giant armillary sphere dominated the center of the room. Sunlight streamed in from a row of tall arched windows to light even the far back corner, where a skeleton dangled from a rope fastened to a hook in the wall.

"Look, Maman!" Dominique exclaimed, heading unerringly for the skeleton. "That man has lost all his skin!"

"Dominique," Gabrielle called out in vain as he raced down the length of the room. "Don't touch anything."

"I see the boy has gone to make the acquaintance of Old Bones," Max said on a note of amusement that burst into full laughter at Gabrielle's shudder of revulsion.

The hall was full of men, many of whom greeted Max by name. Several eyed Gabrielle with unabashed curiosity. One man, braver than the others, limped over with the help of a cane, an infectious smile creasing his round, apple-cheeked face.

"Saint-Just, you devil, so this is what's been keeping you so occupied lately. I might have known!" His chocolate-brown eyes moved appreciatively over Gabrielle, then he bowed with an exaggerated flourish. "Your very devoted servant, mademoiselle."

Max introduced her as Madame Gabrielle Prion. "Gabrielle, may I present Percival Bonville, a not-so-famous American patriot and the man who proved that lightning is actually electricity . . . and *only* a mere two months after Benjamin Franklin did it.''

The man laughed heartily. ''Unfair, unfair, Saint-Just. I would have beaten old Uncle Ben to it if I hadn't been so preoccupied with, er, other matters.''

He took Gabrielle's hand and placed it on the crook of his arm. ''He's brought you here to show off his aerostat, I'll wager. Come, come, Madame Prion, we might as well feed his conceit by going out there to gape at it with looks of rapturous wonder on our faces.''

Laughing, Gabrielle glanced back over her shoulder at Max as she was pulled toward a pair of doors that opened onto the gardens. ''Max, would you—''

He waved them on. ''Go ahead. I'll fetch the boy.''

The gardens were a painter's palette of colors. Beds of flowers and rows of blooming bushes stretched before her like a scrap quilt—too abundant and too vibrant for the eyes to absorb fully. She paused to admire a vivid green bush resplendent with huge white blossoms and a heavy floral aroma.

She cast a questioning look at Percival Bonville, who brought a handkerchief to his nose. ''Don't ask me what species it is,'' he said, his voice muffled by the cloth. ''I know nothing about plants except that the prettier they are the more the blasted things seem to reek like the inside of a bordello.''

Gabrielle laughed gaily, charmed by Max's friend. Though he was not especially good-looking, there was something attractive about the way he spoke, with his drawling American accent.

She took his arm again and they turned, walking toward the river. The sun blazed down relentlessly; Gabrielle began to wish she hadn't rushed from the shop without bringing her fan.

''Have you been in France long, Monsieur Bonville?'' she asked.

''Call me Percy. Actually, you know of Benjamin Franklin, no doubt? He's an uncle of mine. I joined up with him here after the war.'' He tapped his foot with the end of his cane. "That's where I picked up this bum leg. Fighting the blasted English."

"I've heard of your Monsieur Franklin, of course, though I've never met him," she lied, for the man had once been a frequent habitué at her mother's salon. The niece of a simple pawnshop owner would, on the other hand, have had little opportunity to meet the illustrious Monsieur Franklin.

The American patriot had come to France several years before to seek French aid for their revolution. He became a popular figure both at Paris and at the court of Versailles and stayed, even after the American war ended. She remembered that the old man had been a bit of a roué and a great admirer of the ladies.

As if guessing her thoughts, the American smiled slyly and leaned intimately toward her. "Every word you've heard about my uncle is unabashedly true, Madame Prion. Every word. And what's more, it runs in the family."

They passed through an orchard of citrus trees and into a broad meadow.

"Oh!" Gabrielle exclaimed, sucking in a sharp breath of wonder. Holding on to her hat, she tilted her head back to look up.

Strung between two masts by a cable that ran through a ring at its top bobbed a great blue and gold silken balloon. Although only partially inflated, the envelope was already as tall as a five-story building. At its base was a row of casks interconnected with pipes made of tin. A pair of men worked busily around the casks, from which there came a strange bubbling noise.

Percy chuckled softly. "Magnificent, isn't it? Ah, to sail such a ship through the heavens! Perhaps I can talk Saint-Just into taking me with him. He owes me a favor or two."

"Have you known Max long?" Gabrielle asked, realizing suddenly that here was someone who could shed light on the mysterious Maximilien de Saint-Just.

"Long enough to know that his is one of the greatest scientific minds your country possesses. Do you know that in just this year alone he has discovered two new satellites of

Saturn and the phenomenon of double stars?'' He waved a hand at the colorful globe that swayed lazily in the hot breeze. "Not to mention the work he is doing with hydrogen-filled balloons.''

Gabrielle shook her head, surprised and, yes, impressed. Yet she had known from the first that Maximilien de Saint-Just was not at heart the aristocratic dilettante he pretended to be.

"He could accomplish so much,'' Percy was saying, "but instead he plays with science and wastes his talents. Not to mention the way he risks his very life by indulging in those dangerous and nefarious games of his. He's like a great galleon being tossed about on a storm-whipped sea.'' Percy paused and turned to face her. "He needs a safe harbor.''

Gabrielle's chest felt tight, and she couldn't meet the American's eyes. She looked at the balloon instead, wondering what sort of dangerous and nefarious games Maximilien de Saint-Just played at. "I'm not sure I understand.''

Percy shrugged a pair of elegantly clad shoulders. "I'm not sure I do, either. But I do know this. There have been many women in Max's life, but you're the first one he's ever bothered to bring here—''

"Maman!''

Max emerged from the orchard with Dominique riding on his shoulders. Her son's fists were wrapped in the man's dark hair; his face was flushed with laughter. He reared back his head and took in the sight of the balloon with eyes as round as carriage wheels.

"It's big,'' he stated matter-of-factly, which caused them all to laugh.

Max set Dominique on the ground and, taking his hand, led him closer to the giant balloon. It seemed to be groaning as it pulled upward against the cables that kept it tethered.

Gabrielle followed behind a little nervously. "It isn't dangerous, is it?''

"Nonsense!'' Percy admonished.

Max gave her that beguiling, damn-the-world grin, and Gabrielle felt something tug at her heart.

"Gabrielle happened to witness one of my rare failures," he said, "and now she won't let me forget it."

He hunkered down beside Dominique and began to explain how the sealed casks around the base of the balloon were filled with sulfuric acid to which the workers added iron filings to produce the gas that was inflating the envelope. Gabrielle knew Dominique could understand little of what Max said, but his eyes bounced back and forth between Max and the balloon, a look of rapt attention on his face, his pudgy fist clinging securely to the sleeve of Max's coat.

He needs a father, she thought, and then instantly regretted the foolish, useless yearning.

She looked up to find Percy Bonville's eyes on hers and was afraid for a moment that she had spoken the thought aloud, for he smiled and nodded knowingly.

Then he turned abruptly aside and tapped Max's thigh with his cane. "When do you take her aloft, Saint-Just?"

"She should be fully inflated in another couple of days." Max straightened, brushing dirt off his knees. "It takes at least a week to create enough hydrogen gas by this process," he explained to Gabrielle. "Someday I hope to invent a faster way."

Dominique grasped Max's hand, swinging himself off the ground. "Take me with you, M'sieur Max. Take me up in that 'stat with you."

"Not this time. Someday, perhaps. When you're older."

"Promise?"

"It's hard to promise things too far ahead." Max searched Gabrielle's face, his own expression unreadable. "It all depends on your maman."

What was he really saying to her? Unsure, she mumbled, "We'll see."

Max, his mouth set into a hard line, turned away from her.

They looked at the balloon in silence—except for Dominique, who raced in a giant circle around it. Then Max suggested they walk back by way of the menagerie so that Dominique could see the animals. "I've arranged for some refreshment under the shade of the peach orchard. You're welcome to join us, Percy.''

"Thank you, but no. Though it hurts my pride to admit it, I think that in this rare instance I would be *de trop*." Grinning broadly, he presented them both with another flourishing bow. "*Au revoir,* madame . . . May the wind be at your back, Saint-Just." He winked conspiratorially at Gabrielle. "And all your harbors be safe."

Max stared after the American as he limped away. "What was that all about?"

Gabrielle pretended not to hear. She snatched her son's arm as he raced by. "Really, Dominique!" she scolded. "It's too hot to be dashing about like that."

Gabrielle brought the strawberry, dripping with clotted cream, to her mouth. She tilted her head back, sticking out a pink tongue to lick the cream. Then her lips enveloped the plump fruit, sucking it off the stem.

Max looked quickly away, bringing his knee up to hide the sudden, uncomfortable swelling in his breeches. He pressed hard against the scratchy bark of the peach tree at his back and reached with a trembling hand for the glass of champagne on the ground beside him. He tossed it back in two swallows, and the golden effervescent liquid burned down his throat.

"What's the matter?"

Max looked into a pair of eyes that were as purple as a field of heather. "Nothing," he said, knowing he sounded like a sulky little boy.

A smile played about her lips, stained red from the berries, and looking just as luscious. He knew how those lips would taste, sweet and full as they moved beneath his. He knew, God, how he knew—

"You were scowling," she said.

"I was just . . . thinking."

"What about?"

"You. Who are you, Gabrielle?"

Her eyes flickered away; faint color stained her cheeks.

She sat cross-legged on the blanket next to him. Bracing himself on one arm, he leaned forward. He cupped her chin in his hand and turned her head, tilting up her face. Sunlight filtered through the leafy bower overhead, dappling shadows on her skin. She was so fair he could see the blue veins pulsing in her forehead, and her hair was a flame, beckoning him. He wanted her, wanted her . . .

He lowered his head. She exhaled sharply, and he felt her breath, sweet and fruity, against his lips.

"Gabrielle . . ."

She turned away from him. "Not here."

"Come to my rooms tonight."

"No!" She jumped up and began to shove the picnic things into the wicker basket. "We should be going back now. It's getting late."

Max clenched his jaw to keep from cursing out loud. Had the woman been sent by the gods for the sole purpose of making him pay for his many sins? Never had he wanted anything the way he wanted Gabrielle Prion—or whoever in hell she really was. She was like one of those swamp fevers he'd come across in Le Mississippi, infecting the blood and driving the poor afflicted completely insane. He couldn't seem to stay away from her, yet to be near her was to put himself in a state of tormented agony. The only antidote for the fever was to get her into his bed, except that a part of him already knew that with this particular woman once was not going to be enough. He doubted there were enough hours left in all eternity for him to slake the hunger he felt for Gabrielle . . . Gabrielle . . . Gabrielle . . .

Damn you to hell and back, Gabrielle.

Max stood up, glancing toward a nearby hillock where Dominique played at an imaginary game of knights slaying dragons, and felt the bite of a bitter envy. Not of the boy, but of the man who had fathered him. Until now, it had never mattered to Max whether the women he took had lovers before him. Yet he couldn't bear the thought that Gabrielle, *his* Gabrielle, had known pleasure in another man's arms.

Especially when she had yet to know pleasure in his.

He bent over and with a savage gesture snatched the blanket off the ground.

Dominique came trotting up, breathing heavily, his face flushed. His pockets bulged, dragging his pantaloons down around his hips.

Gabrielle sighed at the sight of her impossible offspring. "Oh, Dominique . . . what have you got in your pockets now?"

"More rocks," he said. "For my collection. And this." He put something long and smooth into her hand.

She stared at it, perplexed. It appeared to be three thin pieces of white ivory strung together with a piece of wire—

Gabrielle shrieked and flung it away from her. "Jesu and all his saints!"

Max was instantly at her side. "What's the matter?"

She pointed at the repulsive object where it lay in the grass. "It's a . . . a *finger*."

Max stooped over and picked it up. He looked at Dominique, who gazed back up at him with round, innocent eyes. "Have you been plucking bits and pieces off Old Bones?" he said, trying to sound stern and failing.

Gabrielle heard the repressed laughter in Max's voice. "It isn't funny!"

Max raised his brows at Dominique. The boy giggled and then Max started to laugh.

Gabrielle looked from one to the other. "Why, you . . . you *men*. You're all alike!" She whipped around on her heel and stalked up the lawns toward the academy buildings.

Max and the boy looked at each other and shrugged.

"Maman is very angry with us," Dominique said.

"I fear so."

"Do you think she'll whip us when we get home?"

Max's lips twitched. "No. But it couldn't hurt to make some sort of reparation."

"What's a reprashun?"

"That's when you have to buy something pretty and expensive to get back into a woman's good graces."

Dominique frowned. "But I haven't any money."

"No? Well, then we shall have to improvise."

Max took the boy's hand and led him to a well-tended bed of daffodils and snapdragons. While Max kept an eye out for the groundskeeper, Dominique picked a peace offering.

"I don't understand why she got so angry," the boy said. "It was only a few old bones."

Max shared a sigh with Gabrielle's son as they pondered the mystery that was woman.

A woman was also the topic under discussion in the cramped and stuffy office of the minister of police deep within the cavernous Palais de Justice.

Abel Hachette sat on a creaking chair, pretending indifference to the sweat that trickled down his pale cheeks. The minister of the Paris police was not bothering to pretend. He sat behind his desk across from Hachette, mopping his brow with a sopping, ragged handkerchief.

"*Merde*, but it's hot today," the minister said.

Hachette acknowledged that it was, indeed, rather warm. It was the third time the minister had mentioned the weather. They had been carefully skirting the real reason for Hachette's visit for a half hour now, like a pair of wolves around a staked-out hen, hungry but still too cautious to plunge in for the attack and risk springing the trap.

The minister cleared his throat. "You say this friend of yours—"

"I wouldn't precisely call him a friend. More of a business acquaintance. But he's an Englishman, a visitor to our country. I thought it would hardly do for—"

"Quite, quite. I see your point. It is *fort mauvais* to have visitors, particularly Englishmen, fleeced by our local harlots, eh?" The minister smiled and winked.

When Hachette neither smiled nor winked back, the minister sobered and straightened behind his desk, drawing a piece of paper toward him. He reached for his pen.

The paper stuck to his sweaty palm and he growled an oath under his breath. "You say this Englishman met, uh, the young mademoiselle in a café on the Rue de Rivoli and took her back to his lodgings where he, uh, consummated the arranged transaction. Afterward, he claims, the mademoiselle went through his pockets while he, uh, rested.''

Hachette nodded. "Yes. Stole all his money and a valuable gold watch and fob.''

"Cleaned him out in more ways than one, eh?'' The minister started to guffaw, but stopped at the look on Hachette's face. "Yes, well . . . There are a lot of whores in Paris, monsieur.''

"But not so many who are beautiful, with red-gold hair and violet eyes.''

The minister nibbled on the end of his pen. "Red-gold hair . . . Still, Paris is a big city. Is there anything else you can tell me about the wench? Her, uh, name perhaps?'' His eyes, unable to meet Hachette's, flickered to the window, streaked with grime and partially hidden behind a splintering crate crammed with records.

Hachette watched the minister's face. "It probably means nothing, but she asked him to call her Gabrielle.''

There was a reaction there, Hachette was sure of it: a slight tightening of the man's full mouth, a quick blink of his orange-pip eyes. Hachette decided that for the moment he had gone far enough. The minister was alerted. Now he would watch to see whom the minister informed in turn. Hachette already had a man in place within the Palais de Justice to do the watching.

The minister shrugged with apparent nonchalance. "Just that? Gabrielle?''

Hachette nodded, equally nonchalant.

The minister made a careful notation on the by now damp piece of paper. "As you say, it probably means nothing.'' He laid the pen down and slowly stood up. "Well, monsieur, unless you can think of anything else? No?'' He began ushering Hachette quickly from the room. "Then be assured I shall have my men question all the pimps in their precincts. We'll keep a lookout for this redheaded whore. And, please, tell your—this Englishman—that Paris very much regrets the incident.''

Hachette had barely completed his departing bow before the door was shut smartly in his face.

He placed his tricorne on his bewigged head and turned, a slight smile on his face—

"I beg your pardon, monsieur!"

The man who had bumped into him stepped to the side, motioning for Hachette to pass. Hachette glanced up briefly into dark, protruding eyes that bulged behind a pair of thick spectacles. He noted, before looking politely away, that a nasty scar puckered one of the man's thin, pale cheeks.

Louvois watched the elegant stranger walk down the hall and turn the corner, then he entered the minister's office without knocking.

"There's a shipment due in this evening at sunset," he announced to the minister without further preliminaries.

He went to stand before a map of Paris pasted to the plaster that showed all the main thoroughfares and the surrounding city wall broken by the customs posts, called *barrières*. "Through the south. The Dijon gate." He tapped the appropriate spot on the map. "Be sure your men are briefed this time. I've already alerted the Department of Customs."

The minister fluttered nervously around Louvois. "But, of course, of course. Please be assured—"

Louvois whipped around, pinning the minister with his bulging eyes. "We don't want any more 'mistaken arrests' like we had last month, do we, my friend?"

The minister wrung his hands. "No, no, monsieur. I will tell my lieutenants. We have received a very important tip about a group of smugglers coming in from the north tonight, eh? All patrols will be diverted there." He forced out a laugh.

"By the way," said Louvois, his voice sounding so casual that even the minister was fooled, "who was your illustrious visitor?"

"My illustrious . . . ? Oh, my *visitor*." The minister's sweating face creased into a wide smile. "This you will like, monsieur. This you will like very much indeed. He is Monsieur Abel Hachette, the man who—"

"I know, you fool, who Abel Hachette is. That is, I have heard of him, of course. Who in Paris hasn't?"

"Yes, yes, monsieur." The minister nodded effusively. "But this I'll wager you don't know. Abel Hachette is the man"—he paused dramatically—"the man who can lead us to a fair and elusive whore by the name of Gabrielle."

"Gabrielle!"

A shudder of excitement ripped through Louvois's small frame, causing him to tremble visibly. For a moment the minister feared the man had been stricken ill, and he stepped forward—

Only to back away suddenly at the look of madness blazing from Louvois's bulging eyes.

Chapter 6

The farmer snuck up behind the milkmaid, pinching her on the bottom. The maid shrieked and swung around, clobbering the farmer on the side of the head with her milk bucket. The farmer stood perfectly still for a moment, then crumpled to the ground in a heap.

The audience laughed and cheered as the curtain descended over the tiny stage. It rose again immediately, and the puppets took their bows.

Dominique tugged on Gabrielle's skirts. "Maman, I'm thirsty."

"I know you are, *mon chou*," she said, putting a sou into a bucket passed by a girl dressed in a scantier version of the puppet milkmaid's costume. "Simon and Monsieur Max have gone to fetch us all something cool to drink."

Gabrielle watched the broad back of Maximilien de Saint-Just, and the smaller one that was Simon's, as they pushed their way through the crowd in front of a stall dispensing cider and ale. Whatever Max said to Simon caused the older man to laugh uproariously, so that heads turned in their direction.

Gabrielle frowned, not sure what to make of this sudden liking the very bourgeois Simon Prion had formed for the very aristocratic Maximilien de Saint-Just. And then there was Agnes, who couldn't stop talking about him. And Dominique, who gazed up at him with worship in his four-year-old's eyes. The man, she decided irritably, was much too charming to be trusted.

She looked around for Agnes and saw the girl had staked out a patch of shade beneath one of the few trees that dotted this broad, dusty field known as the Champ de Mars, where the city fairs were traditionally held. Spying Gabrielle and the boy, Agnes cupped her mouth and hallooed, waving them over.

Gabrielle deposited a string bag heavy with apples, bread, and cheese on the ground next to Agnes. As Dominique squatted beside it, she noticed a suspicious bulge in his pantaloons.

"Dominique, what do you have in your pockets this time?" she asked, dreading the answer.

Dominique showed her—three of the small wax statues that were being sold from stands all over the fair. One each of the king and queen, and one of a bespectacled old man who might have been Benjamin Franklin. She heaved a huge sigh, wondering at her son's latest propensity to pick up anything that struck his fancy. "And just where did you acquire these?"

"Monsieur Max bought them for him," Agnes said.

"Oh . . ." Smiling with relief, Gabrielle took off her straw hat and fanned her face with it. The noise and smells of the fair assaulted her—screams from a steer-and-dog fight, the cloying odor of carameled peaches and pungent scents of roasted chestnuts and sour wine, and the shriek of fifes, the wail of trumpets, the shrill voice of a boy hawking tickets to the national lottery.

Agnes motioned with her chin to where Max's dark head stood above the crowd around the ale barrels. "His eyes burn for you today, Gabrielle."

"Oh, Agnes, for heaven's sake—"

"And your eyes burn for him."

"They do not!" Gabrielle exclaimed indignantly. Collecting her blue calico skirts beneath her, she sat down on a patch of scraggly grass beside Agnes. She dug a couple of apples

from the bag, tossing one to Dominique and another into the
girl's lap, but she could not stop the telltale blush that colored
her cheeks. *Dieu,* if even Agnes noticed, then surely he . . .

Agnes's teeth crunched loudly into the apple. "I ask myself, Gabrielle, if it's a game you play with me, or with
yourself, or if you really are so blind to what is happening.
You met this man five days ago and he's been hanging around
the pawnshop like an abandoned puppy ever since. The man
is so besotted with you he can't bear to let you out of his
sight."

Gabrielle choked back a laugh at the comparison of the
arrogant Maximilien de Saint-Just to an abandoned puppy.
She watched his tall figure stride toward them, dripping tan-
kards of ale balanced precariously in his hands. She thought
perhaps Agnes was a little enamored of the man herself. Or
perhaps she was simply intrigued with the hints she had been
given of Max's shady past.

It had happened earlier that afternoon, as they had all set
out together for the fair. Simon brought up the rear with
Dominique, who not only walked at a tortoise's pace but had
a maddening tendency to want to stop and pick up anything
lying in the street that caught his fancy. Gabrielle and Agnes
walked ahead with Max sandwiched between them. Soon Max
and Agnes were bantering in an easy, friendly way, and Gabrielle began to feel strangely grouchy and out-of-sorts. Perhaps it's my monthly curse, she thought. But if so, it was a
week early. As they crossed the Pont des Invalides she managed to insinuate herself between Max and the girl, and she
immediately began to feel better.

"You should be thanking me for bringing the lovely Gabrielle into your life," she heard Agnes say to Max.

Gabrielle gaped at her, too astonished to be embarrassed.
"What, pray tell, did you have to do with it?"

"I saved your miserable life, that's what I had to do with
it. You wouldn't be here in the Palais Royal with Monsieur
Simon if it hadn't been for me, and you know it."

Gabrielle snorted. "What a fabrication!"

"I'll tell you the story," Agnes said to Max, who had

fallen judiciously silent. "It was a cold, rainy winter's day, and I was in the Place Maubert. I was making my living as a street sweeper at the time—"

"Street*walker,* you mean," Max stated, taking the words out of Gabrielle's mouth.

Now it was Agnes's mouth that popped open in astonishment. "But I didn't sleep with you, did I? I'm sure I would have remembered. Of course, I had a lot of customers, but there are some men a girl doesn't . . ." She cast an appalled look at Gabrielle. "Oh, *mon Dieu . . .*"

Max laughed and, reaching across Gabrielle's back, rubbed his hand over the short, wispy spikes of Agnes's hair. "I was never one of your customers, but if you're trying to keep your past a secret, you should wear something over that hair of yours."

On rare occasions, when public outrage began to get out of hand, the Paris police would round up the multitude of the city's prostitutes (those whose pimps couldn't or wouldn't pay the bribe), shave their heads, and make them sweep the streets for a fortnight. It would be another year at least before Agnes's hair grew out enough not to be noticeable.

"I bought her a mobcap," Gabrielle said. "She refuses to wear it."

Agnes stuck her tongue out at the older woman. "It makes my head look like a fat brioche. As I was saying, I was whoring at the time, though in truth I was sweeping the streets, too, because Paul, that whoreson turd of a diseased goat, may a million devils boil him like a black pudding, forgot to pay the bribe. I was sweeping out the gutters in the Place Maubert—and filthy gutters they have there, too—when I saw this poor wretch of a girl with a babe in her arms and her purse poking out her pocket as if she were begging for it to be lifted."

"I was tired," Gabrielle said, though more to herself. Tired and cold and wet and hungry. And frantic with fear because Dominique had been running a burning fever. He had just turned three then, but she had been carrying him because he was too sick to walk. He had weighed hardly anything, she remembered, and his breaths in her ear had been hot and shallow. They had spent the whole day out in the cold and wet in the Cemetery des Innocents because she had to work in order to buy food, and she had to bring the boy with her, because she didn't dare leave him alone. He had been so very sick and she had been so terribly afraid he was going to die.

". . . and by the most incredible coincidence Monsieur Simon was in the Place Maubert at the same time," Agnes was saying. "Well, perhaps it wasn't so much of a coincidence since it's where he goes to buy chickens for supper. Anyway, it was my bad luck he spotted Gabrielle—he knew her from before, you see, when she came into his shop to pawn her ring. Well, he saw Gabrielle and he shouted, and I—"

"He shouted because he saw you stealing my purse," Gabrielle said.

"I proclaimed my innocence."

"You ran off like the thief you were. And with my purse!"

"But Monsieur Simon caught me," Agnes went on as if she hadn't been interrupted. "And he began to beat me with his cane. Then Gabrielle came running up—she looked beautiful, too, like an avenging angel, though an angry one—and she snatched the cane away from Monsieur Simon and broke it over his head."

By now Max was laughing so hard heads turned toward them as they walked by. "P-poor Monsieur Simon," he sputtered when he could catch his breath.

"But he shouldn't have been beating her," Gabrielle protested. "She was hardly more than a child."

"The police agreed with you, Monsieur Max," Agnes said smugly. "They were going to arrest her for making Monsieur Simon's head bleed."

Max cocked a brow at Gabrielle, his eyes sparkling with laughter. "Let me guess," he said. "Simon felt sorry for both of you poor waifs and brought you back to his shop—all three of you, I should say, since presumably the babe in arms was Dominique."

"He really only wanted Gabrielle and Dominique," Agnes admitted ruefully, "but she made him bring me, too."

"Then it seems to me it was Gabrielle who saved your hide, not the other way about," Max told Agnes.

Agnes sniffed. "A lot you know then. Would Simon have even noticed Gabrielle if I hadn't tried to pick her pocket, eh? I ask you."

Max opened his mouth to point out the fallacies of this argument, then slowly shut it. Gabrielle knew he was remembering the tale she had told him about Simon being her dead husband's uncle. But though he regarded her with a hard, assessing look, he said nothing.

Agnes heaved a nostalgic sigh. "It's all well and good being virtuous now, but I miss the old life sometimes."

Gabrielle blew a lock of hair from her eyes and sighed with exasperation. "You don't know when you're well off, girl. Most likely you'd be sweeping out the dungeons of the Salpêtrière by now if you'd continued down that particular road."

"She's right, you know," Max said, using his drawling aristocratic voice. "I don't know what sort of whore you were, but when it comes to picking pockets you're a bloody amateur."

Agnes harrumphed. "I picked yours, didn't I?"

"Only because I let you," Max said. "You were as slow and clumsy as a two-toed sloth."

"And what would you know about—" Agnes's eyes opened wide at the sight of the purse that Max dangled before her eyes. "Hell and damnation! Do you see that, Gabrielle? He picked my purse right out of my bloody pocket and I didn't feel a thing!"

"I see it. And that's still no reason to curse like a stevedore from the Port-au-Blé."

"Jesu . . ." Agnes shivered and flexed her fingers before her eyes, no doubt thinking of the whipping post at the Place de la Grève. "I knew I was getting rusty."

"Well, don't rush out tomorrow and start practicing on all

the pockets in the Palais Royal and, no, I won't give you lessons,'' Max said, having gotten the measure of Agnes.

Gabrielle had slanted a covert look at Max then, wondering at this new and strange facet to his character. That was no parlor trick he had just shown them. He must have clever and well-trained, *well-practiced,* fingers to have so impressed Agnes. But though that endearing, devilish smile flirted around his wide mouth, she could read nothing in his hooded eyes. She thought about the mercury seal molds she had seen in his drawer, and the pistol. About the way he could move so swiftly and silently. And about Percival Bonville's drawling voice, saying: *He plays at dangerous and nefarious games* . . .

"Here you are, Dominique. A cup of good French ale to quench your thirst.'' Simon handed the boy a pint-sized wooden mug of thin ale which the boy immediately began to gulp down greedily.

Feeling Agnes's eyes on her, Gabrielle tried to appear indifferent to Max when he put a tankard of ale into her hand. But as he stretched out beside her on the grass, the sleeve of his silk shirt—he was coatless today because of the heat— brushed against her bare arm. She repressed a shiver, telling herself it was merely a chill from the cold tin of the tankard that sweated against her palm.

Agnes gave Gabrielle a knowing grin as she began to take the food from the string bag.

"By the headless body of Sir Thomas More,'' she exclaimed, "we've forgotten a knife to cut the cheese.''

Max bent his leg up and pulled a slender, Italian-style stiletto from his tall black boot. He handed it to an astounded Agnes, hilt first. "Th-thank you,'' she stammered.

Gabrielle, too, was so surprised that for once she forgot to admonish Agnes about her cursing. Simon, however, appeared to think there was nothing extraordinary about a man who walked around Paris with a murderous-looking dagger in his boot. Even Dominique was unimpressed.

Gabrielle met Agnes's eyes and shrugged, wondering if she would ever understand men.

Agnes handed Simon a hunk of bread and cheese, then leaned over to pluck a handbill from the pocket of his vividly striped waistcoat. "What do you have here, Monsieur Simon? More dirty pictures?"

"It's a pamphlet on the latest scandalous conduct of that Austrian woman," Simon said, softening the usual epithet for the sake of the company. Simon's staunch political sentiments were of a definite republican bent, and any stories that blackened Queen Marie Antoinette's name merely fueled Simon's distaste for the monarchy.

"It seems she sleeps on black satin sheets and has a room at the Petit Trianon tapestried with diamonds. Diamonds! When there are children starving in the streets of Paris and freezing in peasant huts throughout the land," he added, unmindful that at the moment the country was experiencing an unrelenting heat wave.

Since Agnes couldn't read, she had given the pamphlet to Max.

Gabrielle leaned over his shoulder to look at it. It was crudely printed, set in five different fonts of type. "It says she lights her bedroom with two thousand candles every day."

"I should think the whole bloody place would catch on fire," Max said, and Gabrielle laughed softly, her breath caressing his ear.

Max stiffened and pulled slightly away from her.

She studied his dark profile. A muscle twitched in his jaw and sweat trickled from his hairline, but his heavy lids obscured the expression in his eyes. Feeling suddenly bold, she leaned closer, clasping his waist to maintain her balance. She felt the hard muscle that encased his rib cage shiver slightly.

"What else does it say?" asked Agnes eagerly.

Gabrielle tried to read the crude pamphlet, but though the air was still, the paper seemed to flutter so much that she couldn't make out the words. She put her hand beneath Max's to steady it, and a lock of her hair brushed against his cheek. She heard a muffled groan.

"It says . . . *mon Dieu,*" Gabrielle exclaimed softly as she took in the meaning of the printed words. The queen, the pamphlet claimed, had taken the beautiful comtesse de Polignac for her lesbian lover.

"Do you think that's true?" she asked Max, wondering if, as the son of the comte de Saint-Just, he had ever attended court and met the queen. But as she turned to ask the question, her breast pressed intimately into his shoulder, and for a fraction of a second they both went perfectly still.

Max let out a strangled oath and set her bodily away from him. "I doubt it's true," he said in a voice that shook, brushing the sweat from his face with the ruffles on his cuff. "Marie Antoinette might be shallow and frivolous, and probably very lonely, but I don't think she's perverted."

Agnes was practically squirming with curiosity. "Is what true? Jesu, what does it say? What wicked thing has she done now?"

"I'll tell you later," Simon said, glancing significantly at Dominique. For although the boy seemed engrossed in playing with his wax statues, they all knew from experience he was aware of everything that was said or done around him.

Gabrielle had gone suddenly silent. Her breast felt on fire where it had touched Max's shoulder. She didn't need to look down to know her nipples stood out like round, smooth stones beneath the thin calico of her bodice. She raised her eyes to Max's face, and the quicksilver gleam of his eyes flared back at her. Then against her will her gaze was pulled downward, over the broad planes of his chest that quivered now with his ragged breathing, to the tense muscles of his flat stomach, to the bulging manhood in his tight breeches that swelled even more beneath her eyes—

She tore her gaze away from him, feeling a shocking moistness between her own legs.

Agnes, her skirts kilted high above her ankles, walked with Dominique down to the riverbank, where a place had been fenced in for bathing. Simon had left soon after eating, saying he had a chess match set up at his favorite café.

And so Gabrielle and Max were at last left together.

They had taken care not to touch again, even accidentally, but always throughout the long afternoon, she had been aware of him so that by now her nerves were stretched taut as the skin of a kettledrum.

She sat, her back pressed against the tree, her knees drawn up under her chin, looking across the field to the riverbank. Max was lying on the ground, braced on one forearm. There was a quality about the silence between them, an intimacy that became so tangible Gabrielle felt compelled to break it.

"Where did you learn to pick a pocket so skillfully?"

He sat up, bringing himself closer to her. She wondered if it was deliberate, if he was going to try to kiss her, if she would let him this time.

"The same place Agnes did," he said. "In the streets. The streets of the Faubourg Saint-Antoine to be exact," he added, naming a hard working-class district of crowded tenements and smoke-belching foundries.

Gabrielle thought of a period in her life when she would have, if she'd had the skill, picked pockets in order to survive. But there had been other times in her life not so desperate, times that weren't in a way much different than the life of any other daughter or son of a noble family. And in such a life one did not acquire the talents of a pickpocket.

"You've had a strange upbringing for the son of a comte, a famous *maréchal* of France," she probed.

"And what of your upbringing, Gabrielle?" He slipped his curled finger under her chin, turning her head so that she was forced to look at him. "I think you're not the common shopgirl you pretend to be. I think there must have once been a time when you wore silk and jewels and danced the minuet beneath gilded chandeliers. Who are you, Gabrielle?"

She would have been honest with him then if she'd been able to speak. But her eyes, lingering on his lips, saw them part slightly as he sucked in a sudden, sharp breath. Reaching up, she traced the length of them with the tips of her fingers.

Whatever she had been about to say was forgotten.

He pulled her against him and his mouth covered hers,

fierce and gentle, urgent and lingering. He branded her with those lips, marking her as his possession. And the burning fire spread throughout all of her, consuming her, so that she melted into him. Her arms wrapped around him, one hand massaging the bunched muscles in his back while the other stroked his neck beneath his hair. She rubbed her breasts against his chest, feeling her nipples harden instantly. She forgot to breathe so that the world spun dizzily and she clung to him even tighter—

He dug his fingers into her shoulders and pried her away from him. "Christ . . ." he exhaled on a ragged gasp.

And then he was up and striding away from her, toward Agnes and the boy wading along the river's edge.

Thunderclouds formed in the west, and it began to grow dark early.

Strings of paper lanterns hanging from poles circled and looped, like a necklace of diamonds, around the fairgrounds. As the twilight deepened, the lanterns grew brighter, and the sound of laughter and music carried further on the air.

They left the Champ de Mars, walking east along the river. Max strode ahead with Dominique balanced on his shoulders, and Gabrielle heard her son's piping voice firing an endless stream of questions which Max, with unfailing patience, tried to answer. Lightning flashed, but weakly, and there was a long pause before thunder rumbled in the distance. The storm was still far away.

Agnes slipped an arm through hers. "If you leave us, Gabrielle, don't go too far. Simon and I, we need you."

It was a strange thing to say. An unlucky thing, for Gabrielle was happy in the pawnshop in the Palais Royal, and life had taught her that happiness was ephemeral. But then so, please God, was sorrow.

"Why, wherever would I go?" she answered, trying with a carefree lilt in her voice to banish these morbid thoughts.

Agnes looked at Max, who walked ahead of them, a shadowy figure now for it was rapidly growing dark. The boy on his shoulders made him appear monstrously tall and mis-shapen. ''To him,'' she said.

Gabrielle said nothing. I *will* go to him, she thought, when he asks. And it seemed then that she had suddenly stumbled across a clue to a long, involved riddle. Now that she had it, the answer appeared so obvious, so perfect, she wondered why she had not thought of it before. How simple, she thought. How very, very simple. I love him and so, when he asks, I will go to him. And I will stay.

A camp fire flickered brightly from a nearby gypsies' camp. A soft breeze, a precursor of the coming storm, blew off the river, bringing with it the garlicky smell of sausages roasting over the flames and the mournful wail of a violin.

A pair of gypsies danced around the fire. Agnes and Ga-brielle paused to watch.

The woman had long dark hair that fell in thick ropes al-most to her ankles. She arched her back, curling her arms in the air and stamping her feet in time with the throbbing, sensuous beat of the music. There was an expression of pain on her face, almost of agony, a look of lost love and broken hearts. A young man danced with her, winding his slender, sinewy body around hers. The look on his face was one of hunger and desire. The heartbreaker.

A demijohn of wine passed from hand to hand. Someone threw a piece of wood on the fire and the flames flared up, casting light in a wider circle around the camp. Gabrielle saw Max on the other side of the dancing figures, speaking with one of the gypsies, their leader obviously from the richness of his clothes—a man with a flashing smile and a gold hoop dangling from one ear. She didn't see Dominique.

She pushed her way through the circle of people, not quite running, only a little afraid. Max would not lose her son.

When she arrived at the spot where she had seen him, Max was gone.

She whirled, searching through the faces around the fire, faces with dark hair and skin. The tempo of the music picked up; the dancers moved faster. The woman threw back her head and began to sing. There was loneliness in the song. A sudden crack of thunder ripped across the black sky.

Gabrielle left the fire, searching through the gypsy caravan. Stuck through brackets fastened to the corners of the wagons, torches flickered, casting strange shadows that seemed to perform a dance of their own. Here, the laughter and music were muted. The breeze died suddenly, leaving the air hot and still, and the sound of her own ragged breathing filled Gabrielle's ears.

Lightning flashed, illuminating for an instant the entire caravan. There was no one about; they were all around the fire, watching the dancers.

"Dominique!" she called.

"Maman?"

For a moment she couldn't tell where the voice came from. Then the wind kicked up again and one of the torches flared, picking out a flash of gold beneath one of the wagons. Dominique's hair.

She bent over and hauled him out by the scruff of his neck. Her fear had been such that the relief she felt in finding him was immediately replaced by anger.

She gave him a rough shake. "How dare you sneak off like that!"

"I didn't—"

"Where's Monsieur Max?"

Dominique wriggled free. "Don't know," he said sulkily, kicking at the dusty ground with his foot.

A little girl crawled out from beneath the wagon. She looked solemnly up at Gabrielle, her topaz eyes huge in her beautiful, dark-skinned face. She was dressed in clothes made of expensive satin, embroidered with bright gold thread. She had four heavy gold bangles shoved halfway up her thin brown arm and the wax statue of Marie Antoinette clutched tightly in her hand.

"This is my new friend, Maman," Dominique said. "Her name is Lia. I gave her a present, and she gave me this." He held up his arm, from which dangled a thick gold bracelet.

Gabrielle looked at it in consternation. The bracelet was worth far more than the little wax statue, but the girl was still too young to have any conception of the monetary value of things. Nevertheless, Gabrielle could hardly allow Dominique to accept the gift. She had heard that a gypsy girl's dowry was her jewelry, and though this girl looked hardly older than five or six, it wouldn't be too many years before she would be of marriageable age, for gypsy children wedded young.

Gabrielle knelt beside Dominique and turned him to face her. "Dominique, *mon petit,* it was very nice of your new friend to give you a present, but—"

"I'm not giving it back," Dominique stated, holding the arm with the bracelet tightly to his chest. "Lia wouldn't want me to."

Sighing, Gabrielle pulled her son into her arms. She put her palm against the back of his hair and felt, instead of the silky strands she was used to, a sticky grittiness. She rubbed her fingers briskly across his scalp. "Heavens, child, what have you been into?"

She sniffed her fingers, then licked them, tasting . . . salt.

She stood up to look more closely at the wagon. Though it was very dark now, with the stormclouds obscuring the moon, there was still a small pool of light cast by the torch. She could make out a thin dusting of something white on the darker earth beneath the vehicle's deep bed.

"Is this your wagon?" she asked the little girl. "Is this where you live?"

"No, madame," Lia answered solemnly. "The pigs live in that wagon." The wagon did, indeed, smell like a barnyard.

It was made entirely of wood, like a small cottage on wheels. There was a door in back, secured by a latch. Gabrielle started to reach for it, then turned to the girl.

"May I see the pigs, Lia?"

The girl's face brightened. "But yes, madame! It is a mother pig and three babies. We used to have another, but we ate him.'' Eager to be helpful, she opened the wagon door for Gabrielle.

The sow lay on her side in the straw, the piglets suckling at her tits. Although the wagon was quite large, except for the pigs it was empty. A thick layer of straw covered the bed, which appeared from the inside to be much too shallow for the wagon's size.

Gabrielle pushed aside a handful of the straw. More of the gritty white powder dusted the warped, wooden floorboards.

Salt smugglers.

The gypsies were salt smugglers.

Each family in France was required to purchase a certain amount of salt a year at state-controlled prices. It was known as the *gabelle*—the salt tax—and was the most hated tax in the land. To use smuggled salt and cheat the king of the *gabelle* had become a matter of pride to all Parisians, and so salt smuggling had become a profitable and noble profession. An army of customs men and police had been called up to try to suppress the salt smugglers, and instant hanging was the punishment if you were caught at the crime.

Was Max, Gabrielle wondered, a member of this salt smuggling gang? His image came to her as she had last seen him, deep in conversation with the gypsy leader. *Games,* she thought, *dangerous and nefarious games—*

''Have you seen enough, Gabrielle?''

She turned slowly. Max appeared within the circle of torchlight, the gypsy with the gold earring a step behind him. Max stopped when he was two yards away from her; he stood with his feet slightly apart, his fingers curled around the pockets in his breeches. The gypsy cradled a musket in his arms.

''Papa!'' the little girl sang out happily, and started toward the gypsy, but when she noticed the angry look on his face she stopped, sticking a finger in her mouth.

Dominique's eyes went from his mother to the tall man with the hard face and the soft voice, and for once he was silent.

"I asked you, Gabrielle," Max said, his voice silky, dangerous, "if you have seen enough."

Gabrielle flung up her head and stared defiantly back at him.

The gypsy took a step toward her. "She's seen too much."

Max put out a hand, stopping him. "It's all right, *mon frère*. I can ensure her silence." There was a movement in the shadows behind him, and Agnes appeared at his side. "Take Dominique down to the river and wait there," he said to the girl.

"Monsieur Max, you won't—"

Max said something to her, too low for Gabrielle to hear, but whatever it was it satisfied Agnes, for she gathered Dominique in her arms. "You come, too," she said, holding her hand out to Lia.

"We'll finish our business later, Prado," Max told the gypsy, and the dark-faced man flashed Gabrielle a final, baleful glare before he, too, disappeared into the night.

Gabrielle wondered why she didn't do something. Why she just stood there waiting for Max to come to her, waited with her feet fastened to the ground as if they had grown roots. She thought of the stiletto in his boot; she remembered the strength in his hands. How was he going to guarantee her silence? Would he slit her throat or strangle her?

He took a step toward her—

Gabrielle took a step backward. "Why should it matter if I know about the smuggling?" she said, her voice breaking shamefully. "Do you think I care if you've found a way to cheat the *gabelle?* It was only curiosity—"

"You have a lot of *curiosity,* don't you, Gabrielle?"

He reached her in two strides, but she was too quick for him. She whirled, dashing around the wagon and running for the Champ de Mars, back toward lights and people and safety.

She tripped over a tree root in the dark and went sprawling. Gasping for breath, she pushed herself to her feet. But Max was on her. He grabbed her by the shoulders and swung her around, pushing her up against the tree trunk. His hands went around her throat . . .

* * *

Max had never intended to hurt her; he only wanted some answers. He hadn't expected her to run from him, and when she did, it set off his hot temper like a match to gunpowder. He was tired of her teasing games. She would tell him who she was and why she was spying on him or, by God, he would—

She fell and he hauled her to her feet, furious enough now to shake the truth out of her if necessary. But the moon picked that moment to burst free of the clouds that covered it, and there before him was the haunting white beauty of her face, the depthless purple pools of her eyes, and her lips, those lips, whose softness was a memory and a promise . . .

Suddenly it seemed he wanted only one thing from those lips, and it had nothing to do with truth. He lowered his head and wrapped his hands around her neck to bring her mouth within reach of his.

She punched him in the face with her balled-up fist, striking his cheekbone and sending a shock of pain from the top of his head. She hit him again, the blow landing on his throat this time, and he choked. She seemed to have as many arms as a giant squid; no sooner would he capture one than the other would land a blow somewhere. She could hit damned hard for a girl.

"Dammit, Gabrielle, I'm not going to—Jesus!" he swore as she kicked him.

He managed at last to get both arms pinned between her back and the tree. He held her slender wrists easily in one hand and pressed his pelvis and thighs against her body so she couldn't do any more damage with her feet.

"Why did you run? I wasn't going to hurt you."

"Liar!" she spat at him.

Her fichu had pulled loose, and the short sleeves of her dress had slipped off her shoulders. She was panting heavily and the soft swell of her breasts rose and fell, rose and fell, straining against the thin calico of her bodice.

There was an achingly hard bulge in his breeches. She had to feel it, to feel him, and she did, for he saw the answering passion flare within her as her eyes darkened. She opened her mouth . . . and he covered it with his own.

He let go of her wrists to grip the sides of her head. Her hair was a golden-red halo set ablaze by the pale moonlight, a waterfall of liquid fire. He tangled his hands in it, bending her head back so he could probe her mouth with his tongue, and she sucked on his lips, tasting him, drinking him.

Desire was in the tight, exquisite feeling in his chest; the hard, urgent need in his loins. Passion was in the trembling of her woman's body in his arms, the low moans in her throat, her roaming hands that were touching him, burning him, claiming him . . .

His lips left her mouth to kiss her neck. He found a spot she particularly liked, on the side, below the gentle curve of her jaw, and he lingered there, feeling the swift pulse of the blood beneath her skin, feeling her hot, harsh breathing against his ear. There was a tangy scent to her—of salt and apples—and underlying it the faint and evocative scent of sexual arousal.

He pulled the sleeves of her dress further down her arms, yanking at the tight bodice a bit too roughly so that it tore, freeing her breasts. They were small but firm and round, just filling his hands, and he teased the hardened nipples with the backs of his fingers, then lowered his head to take one in his mouth. He heard her sigh his name as she shuddered in his arms.

He pulled up her skirts, reaching under her chemise until he found the bare flesh above the tops of her stockings. Soft. She was so incredibly soft. He stroked the length of her thigh and up, trailing his fingers along the rounded curve of her buttocks, drifting across her hipbone to penetrate the nest of curly hair between her legs . . . slipping inside her. She gasped, arching against him. He probed deeper, stroking the slick inner heat of her, and his other hand, which still cupped one breast, tightened. She writhed against him, planting kisses on his face, his neck, and he searched out her mouth again with his.

He captured one of her roaming hands and pressed it against

the hard ridge of his arousal. "Feel that, Gabrielle. Feel how much I want you," he said through clenched teeth as his control began to slip. "Gabrielle, Gabrielle . . . oh, God, Gabrielle . . ."

He was fumbling with the buttons on the panel to his breeches, so he didn't feel her hands come up to push against his chest until she had shoved him away from her. He stumbled a half step backward, letting go of her.

She slapped him hard across the face. "Damn you, Max. If you're going to make love to me you'll do it properly. Not standing up against a tree like some cheap . . . cheap *putain!*"

Dazed and breathing heavily, Max stared at her for a long moment in astonishment. His cheek stung where she had hit him. *If you're going to make love to me you'll do it properly . . .*

He laughed aloud, shaking his head to clear it of the roaring blood still pumping hard through his veins. What an incredible woman she was. He doubted there was another like her in the world.

"Gabrielle . . ." He reached for her.

She pushed his hand away. "No, Max. I've had enough of this. Of you." She was having trouble speaking around her panting breaths, her bared breasts heaving as she fought for air. "First you try to strangle me—"

"I didn't try to strangle you—though there have been times, like now, by God, when I've been tempted! I was only—"

"And you've done nothing since we first met but try to seduce me."

"If I have, it's all your fault." The pounding in his head was receding, and his chest was no longer pumping like a blacksmith's bellows, but he still wanted her with a hunger that was a heavy, hollow feeling in his gut. "You're just too damned desirable. You don't know what you do to me."

She was trying to straighten her clothing, but her hands, he noticed, were shaking. He saw her mouth tighten as she fought to hold back some emotion, but whether it was a frown or a smile, he couldn't tell.

"I'm sorry," he thought to say, trying out his best little-boy grin and wondering why it wasn't earning instant forgiveness. He was suddenly afraid there would be no forgiveness, ever. The thought appalled him, and it wasn't because of the unrelenting, unrelieved ache between his legs. Or not only that. If physical hunger was all it was, then he could walk away from her now and find release in the arms of another woman. He had left before and always there had been another woman, in the next room, the next city, the next bed. But not this time. He couldn't leave this time because he realized in one sudden, painful instant that there was, and would always be, only one Gabrielle.

Desperate circumstances require desperate measures, he thought—and he threw himself on his knees at her feet.

"Madonna, madonna, forgive me," he crooned, clasping his hands over his heart.

He was rewarded with her laughter. It came bubbling from her throat, soft and curled around the edges like rose petals. Then she covered her mouth with her hands and looked around self-consciously.

Her gaze came back to him, gentle and brimming with amusement, glowing golden in the moonlight. "Get up, you . . . you . . . Oh, Max, what if someone sees you? You're making an utter fool of yourself."

He stood up and held out his hand to her.

She didn't take it, not at first.

Not until he promised that her hand was all he would touch of her for the rest of the night.

But as for tomorrow . . . He made no promises about tomorrow.

Chapter 7

"**S**o now you see, monsieur, why we must lose no time in finding this whore with golden-red hair who calls herself Gabrielle. For if she is the same girl and she has a living child . . ."

The man's voice trailed off and he leaned forward in the gilt and velvet chair, his hands flat on the knees of his coarse black breeches. The flickering light from the many candles in the library's crystal chandeliers shimmered off his spectacles and glazed his sweat-sheened face, making the purple scar on his cheek look like a raw wound.

"In all confidence, monsieur," the man continued, "Monseigneur le Duc has not been at all well. And he is desperate to be united with his only grandchild, and heir. Are you quite sure—"

"Quite sure. I certainly have no idea where the girl can be found," Abel Hachette lied smoothly.

Hachette sat behind his rosewood desk, resplendent in a satin suit of a vivid blue color known as the king's eye. He toyed with his quizzing glass while he studied the lawyer Louvois from beneath lowered lids, which concealed his eyes and his thoughts. It was a trick he'd learned from his Black Angel, who had certainly used it to great effect often enough on him.

Hachette wanted to hide his surprise that his inquiries to

the minister of police had produced a visit by this man Louvois—who claimed to be procurator to a man of such significant stature as the duc de Nevers.

But in spite of the high connections the lawyer claimed, he was obviously of humble birth and, to Hachette's considerable disgust, he seemed to be doing little to hide it. Instead of a powdered wig, he wore his coarse black hair long and loose. His suit was plain, of rough black wool, and his shoes were scuffed and worn down at the heels. Hachette, who wore chicken-skin gloves to bed every night to keep his hands white and soft, was horrified to see that Louvois's nails were bitten down to the quick, and as for the disfigurement on the man's face, Hachette was barely able to repress a shudder of revulsion.

Louvois cleared his throat impatiently. "Perhaps if I could speak to this Englishman—"

"Quite impossible. The man has since returned to England," Hachette said, embellishing his lie. When and *if* he delivered the girl to this lawyer Louvois, he wanted to be sure he had first considered all the consequences. A greedy seductress, a rebellious son, a lost heir—the lawyer's tale was almost too preposterous to be believed. And there was something else here . . . something that flickered deep within the man's strange bulging eyes. Louvois, Hachette suspected, wanted to find this girl and her child for reasons that went far beyond pleasing his master the duc.

Reaching a decision, Hachette stood abruptly, signaling an end to the interview. "You may tell Nevers that I've initiated inquiries. If in fact the girl exists, I shall find her for him. The child as well, of course," he added with a smile.

Louvois scooted his thin buttocks forward in the chair. "If you are able to restore his grandson to him, I am sure you'll discover Monseigneur le Duc to be quite overcome with, shall we say . . ." He raised his head, fixing the older man with his protruding stare. "Shall we say *gratitude*, Monsieur Hachette?"

Shall we indeed, Hachette thought, allowing his smile to linger, although he said nothing. The duc de Nevers was one of the most powerful men in the kingdom, and it certainly couldn't hurt to have such a man in his debt. On the other hand, it could hurt a considerable amount to have such a man as an enemy. A man who possessed blank *lettres de cachet* signed by the king—arrest warrants with only the name of the victim left blank. With one stroke of a pen the duc de Nevers could have him, Abel Hachette, consigned without trial, without hope, to the deepest, darkest dungeon in the Bastille, and all the money in the world couldn't buy his way out again.

The lawyer Louvois had started for the door, but he paused, turning. "We have a lot in common, you and I, Monsieur Hachette."

Hachette's lips puckered into an involuntary frown. "Do we?"

Louvois smiled knowingly. "Oh, but we do. We do, indeed. I, too, come from peasant stock, Monsieur Hachette. And though we were born on a land rich and fertile, still my sisters and I starved because our crops were ruined by the seigneur's pigeons, pigeons we didn't dare to shoot. And till the day he died, broken and old at thirty-three, my father bore a scar on his face from the lash of a riding crop because he failed to doff his hat to a visiting lord. Yes, we have a lot in common, you and I."

For a moment Hachette was back in the sod hut in Brittany where a cold wind blew through the cracks in the eaves and he slept among the chickens and the goats on the floor because his bedding had gone to pay the tax, and he felt a pang in his belly that was like hunger although he had eaten a full meal only an hour ago. "But that is the way of it," he said. "It's always been so—"

"Oh, yes, they think they rule the world and they do, these fine aristocrats, with their thin blood and their haughty ways." Louvois's protruding eyes blazed with fervor behind his spectacles. "But their time is soon finished and ours is yet to come. Someday the streets of Paris will flow with their noble blood and they will pay for their false pride. They will pay."

"The girl Gabrielle . . ." Hachette said.

Louvois blinked. He touched the scar on his cheek. "Yes, her. Her, first of all." He blinked again and turned abruptly, seeming suddenly to realize he had perhaps said too much. "You will inform me directly should you find her."

"By all means," Hachette said.

He rang for a servant to escort the lawyer to the door, then settled back behind his rosewood desk. He was tired and his bones ached, and Louvois's last words had stirred up old and bitter memories he would sooner forget. He yawned, remembering just in time not to rub his eyes. Such a thing, he had been told, caused wrinkles. He shuddered at the thought, then shuddered again at the memory of Louvois's scarred cheek. How could the man, a mere lawyer, have come by such a wound? Hachette wondered. Had he, like his father, failed to accord proper respect to some irritable aristocrat?

Hachette looked up, studying the many reflections of his own face in the mirror-paneled walls. There was a sallow cast to his skin tonight. He would have to remember before retiring later to smear it with the special balm mixed with wine that bleached the skin, giving one the "convent complexion" so indicative of the wellborn. Abel Hachette might be the grandson of a serf, but no one, he vowed silently, was ever going to know it by looking at him.

Sighing, he fought off another yawn. He couldn't go to bed just yet. He had a lot of things to consider. What, for instance, did this girl Gabrielle have to do with his Black Angel? She had powerful enemies. She could mean trouble, not only to Max, but to the cabal and their cause.

Lettres de cachet or not, Hachette thought, he might just dare to doublecross the duc de Nevers. He had, after all, risked and gotten away with far more before this. But dare he play such games with his Black Angel?

Dark and dangerous . . .

He thought of the first time he had encountered Maximilien de Saint-Just. It was over eleven years ago now. He had been traveling in his coach at night on the road between Calais and Paris. He had wakened from a doze to find the nasty end of a pistol pointed at his face through the window of his carriage, and to hear a drawling voice, muffled by a black silk mask, telling him to deliver up his valuables.

Hachette was rich even then, but he couldn't bear the thought of giving so much as a single sou to a scruffy band of thieves. "Go to hell," he had snarled, sounding braver than he felt.

"I intend to," the drawling voice replied with a laugh. "But unless you cooperate nicely, you'll be preceding me there. And I, at least, will have the joy of spending all your money before I follow."

Hachette tried to peer out the window. The *flambeaux* fastened to the roof of the carriage cast only a small pool of light that couldn't pierce the dark shadows of the brush that lined the road. Strangely, there was no sign of his coachman and postilions and, what's more, Hachette *felt* alone.

The brigand, too, appeared to be solitary. He sat easily astride a dark horse, the pistol balanced against the wrist of the hand that rested on the saddle pommel. It seemed absurd to Hachette that one man could have dispatched five others, who had been armed against just such a possibility.

"Where are my men?" he demanded.

"With mine," the voice said, then laughed again. "I have more men than you do, and they're nastier than yours. They wait for me down the road." The pistol moved closer to Hachette's face, pointing between his eyes. "I would like your money and your other fine things, Monsieur Hachette. If you please."

Hachette started. "How do you know who I am, and who the devil are you?"

The pistol clicked as it was cocked. "Your money, Monsieur Hachette . . ."

Hachette made a pile of his valuables beside him on the leather seat—a purse bulging with gold and silver louis, his diamond cravat pin, several rings, a snuffbox, and a quizzing glass. Then to the pile, and with visible reluctance, he added an intricately carved, and very valuable, silver pounce box. "Please don't take this. It belonged to my father," he lied.

The pistol disappeared out of the window, but the carriage

door was pulled open and the masked stranger was suddenly inside. He seemed to fill the interior of the coach, and Hachette pressed back into his seat.

"I have a business proposition, Monsieur Hachette," the silken voice said.

Hachette laughed shakily. "You must be mad. Or you must think I am. I don't do business with brigands wearing masks."

"Come now, Monsieur Hachette, don't turn squeamish on me. You're as much a thief as I. Only I do it openly."

Intrigued in spite of himself, Hachette leaned forward. "What is your proposition? Brigand."

Six months before, the disembodied voice explained, the English colonies in America had revolted against the crown, and now the rebel American army was desperate for weapons and ammunition, desperate enough to pay almost any price. If Hachette would finance the initial purchase of the guns and a ship, the masked youth promised he could get them to America, where a guaranteed profit could be made.

"Damn my eyes, you must be a bloody madman!" Hachette exclaimed, reverting in his astonishment to a peasant's rough speech. "Do you think I'd trust a brigand with the ready to purchase a cache of arms and then watch him sail off in a bloody ship that *I* had paid for, by Christ?"

"I won't cheat you."

"Bloody hell you won't. Why should I trust you?"

The brigand reached up and pulled the black kerchief down around his neck. From the light of the *flambeaux* flickering through the open carriage door, Hachette could make out the face of a young man with sharp cheekbones, hooded eyes, and a hard mouth.

The youth met his eyes and flashed a smile full of mockery. "I can swear on the honor of my name."

"And what name is that, brigand?"

"Saint-Just. Maximilien de Saint-Just."

"You lie. I know a comte de Saint-Just, but it is an old, proud name and both his sons are officers in his majesty's army."

"This son isn't."

"This one is a thief."

The boy said nothing, merely met Hachette's scrutiny with a steady gaze.

"Very well," Hachette finally said, astonished that he was really doing this. "I'll think over your proposition. Come to my house on the Rue Royal this Friday at noon. I'll give you my decision then."

The boy said nothing more. One moment it seemed he was in the coach, the next moment Hachette was alone in the night with only the *chirr* of the insects for company. His purse, jewelry, snuffbox—everything was gone. Even the silver pounce box.

Abel Hachette began to laugh out loud. He hoped the boy would be fool enough to show up at his house on the Rue Royal that Friday, for Hachette would arrange to have the *gendarmes* there to greet him. Still, there was something oddly appealing about this Maximilien de Saint-Just. He had a certain *élan,* a flamboyant bravado . . .

Qualities the boy would need, Hachette had thought then with another laugh, when the day came for him to mount the scaffold steps.

Hachette thought at first it was the chime of the clock that brought him back to the present.

He sat up with an abrupt snort and glanced at the clock, to see it read straight up at midnight. The newspaper he had been reading before Louvois's visit slid off the polished desk top and onto the parquet floor. He bent over to pick it up, and that was when he saw the man standing by his library door.

The scream stopped halfway from his mouth and turned into a curse instead. "The devil take you, you scoundrel. Can't you have yourself announced like everyone else?"

"It's late. I didn't want to wake your servants."

Maximilien de Saint-Just sauntered into the room, and against his will Hachette's scowl softened into a fond smile.

"I'm sorry, but you startled me," he said. "I didn't hear you come in."

"Obviously not . . . That's a sign of insanity, you know."

"Huh?"

"Bedlam is full of people who sit alone, chuckling inanely to themselves."

Hachette felt hot with embarrassment, realizing he must have been laughing out loud in his reverie. For a moment he wished he *had* arranged to have the police there waiting for the young brigand that day eleven years ago. It would have served the arrogant bastard right.

"I didn't expect you tonight, Max. I thought you were going aloft tomorrow morning in that fool balloon. Or have you come to your senses?"

"No . . ." Distracted, Max pushed a hand through his thick hair. "No, I still intend to take her up tomorrow."

Hachette watched as Max paced the length of the room, to the windows and back again. The flickering light from the chandeliers fell obliquely on the young man's face, giving a feral gleam to his dark gray eyes. There was a wildness about his Black Angel tonight, Hachette thought. And an answering quiver of excitement rippled through Hachette, banishing his earlier embarrassment, even making him forget for a moment Louvois and the girl and the duc de Nevers.

"What is it, Max? What's happened?"

Max hooked his hip onto the edge of Hachette's rosewood desk. He toyed with the items on top—an enameled snuffbox, the quizzing glass, a horn-handled penknife—and Hachette noticed with shock that the young man's hands were shaking.

"Do you believe in hell?" Max asked abruptly.

Hachette was not sure he believed in God, let alone such a thing as divine retribution, but he nodded automatically. "Of course."

A mocking smile twisted Max's lips. "So do I." He flung the penknife at the painted wall, piercing the eye of a cherub playing a harp. "Hell, my dear Abel, is a woman with hair the color of a sunset and purple eyes that see right through to your wicked, lustful soul."

The drawling words, so full of self-mockery, made little sense to Hachette. He was more concerned about the damage just done to his wall. He gave the younger man what he hoped was a censorious glare and, rising, went to pry the knife out of the cherub's eye. "I hope you haven't come here merely to debate theology, Max, because it's late and I'm rather tired—"

Max stood up. He plucked the knife from Hachette's hand and tossed it back on the desk. "I'm here because there's another load of salt being smuggled into the city the night after tomorrow." Excitement animated Hachette's face, and Max laughed softly. "I thought that might stir that reptilian blood of yours. By this time tomorrow I'll have the names of the leaders. If you're interested."

"You've penetrated the salt ring?" Hachette exclaimed, rubbing his hands together. "Splendid, my boy! Splendid. This particular mission is coming along better than I had hoped."

Max's lids lowered until his eyes were almost shut, and his mouth stretched into a lazy smile. His voice when he spoke was soft, and deadly. "You betray my . . . associates to the police, my dear Abel, and you betray me as well."

"No, no, of course I wouldn't do such a thing," Hachette protested, shaking his head so vigorously that his wig slipped. "The cabal doesn't want to stop the salt smuggling, Max. You know that. Why should we want to stop something that can only hurt the king and the fools who control his finances? No, no, we merely want to find out who's running the smuggling so that we may run *them*. And you will get your usual twenty—"

"No!" Max said quickly. "Not this time. This is the last mission I do for you, and I do it for nothing. Call it a parting gift."

"But—"

"Good night, Abel," Max said. And then he was gone, as swiftly and silently as he had arrived, leaving Hachette standing half out of his chair with a frozen smile on his face.

Parting gift?

Hachette sat down slowly, so stunned that for a moment he forgot to breathe. His Black Angel, his Black Angel was leaving—

It's the girl, he thought suddenly. The fool boy has gone and fallen in love with this mysterious highborn whore, this Gabrielle. *Hair the color of a sunset* . . . Hachette snorted. He should have recognized the signs sooner. And all that crazy talk tonight about hell being a woman. What else but love could have put such a haunted look on that arrogant face? The cocky young rake has fallen in love, and suddenly he's not good enough for his beloved and so must reform his whole life. The next thing we know, Hachette thought with a sharp laugh, the young fool will be joining the priesthood to atone for his sins.

Well, not if I can help it, Hachette promised himself. For the lawyer Louvois was right; the time was soon coming when the king and his noble lackeys would be overthrown, and there was not only liberty but a fortune to be made in the resulting chaos. Now, more than ever, Hachette and the cabal were going to need the services of someone to help them sail around the tricky shoals such an upheaval was bound to uncover. Someone dark and dangerous . . . Someone like his Black Angel.

"You belong to France, Maximilien de Saint-Just," Abel Hachette said aloud to the empty room. "To France and to history." And no mere *woman* was going to be allowed to alter the course of history.

The great silken globe wafted in the breeze, its blue and gold stripes shining incandescent in the morning sunlight. Fully inflated now, it strained against its mooring ropes as if alive, like a huge beast struggling to burst free.

A wicker car, decorated with bright turquoise bunting, hung suspended from a cord net that covered the upper half of the balloon. Hatless and in shirtsleeves rolled up to his elbows, Maximilien de Saint-Just stood beside the car, checking the tautness of a cable that ran up the middle of the vessel's vast, gas-filled core.

"I say, Saint-Just," Percival Bonville drawled, limping up to him. Wearing yards of lace at his throat and a short coat decorated with frog buttons, Percy looked more like one of the young nobles who haunted the halls at Versailles than a rough-hewn American patriot. He waved his tasseled ebony cane at the wicker basket. "Are you sure you've no room in there for an extra passenger?"

Max looked up, giving him a slanted smile. "Sorry, Percy. The position's already been filled."

Pretending to be hurt by this rebuff, Percy turned his back on Max to survey the growing group of curious onlookers. Unlike Max's first experiment three years before (when he had helped finance the exorbitant cost of the balloon by charging the *ton* a louis apiece for the privilege of a close-up view of its ascent) there had been little advertisement for this one. Yet it could hardly have been kept a secret, and even Parisians weren't so jaded that such an event would fail to draw a crowd. There was always the exciting possibility that the balloon would explode, or fall out of the sky, and some good red blood would be spilled.

Then, too, a Parisian knew that a crowd meant there was money to be made. Percy spotted a man selling wine from a barrel on a cart, though it was barely two hours past sunrise. By his side was a woman selling waffles—half burned, by the smell of them.

Then Percy's eyes lit on the fetching sight of dazzling red-gold hair beneath a plumed bonnet. "Good God!" he exclaimed aloud as a thought struck him. He stared at Max. "You aren't seriously considering . . . ?"

Max's eyes glinted with devilment.

"Good God," Percy said again. "How on earth did you get her to agree to it?"

"I haven't actually asked her yet."

Percy's brows soared upward.

"But she will," Max said.

He hadn't actually looked at her yet, either, but he knew she was there. He had known from the moment she stepped out of the orchard onto the field. Just as he had known she would come, although last night, before they had parted, she had sworn to him that she would not.

Liar, he scolded himself with an inward laugh. You didn't *know* she was going to do any such thing. You only hoped. He figured he had as much chance of guessing what Gabrielle would do next as he did of winning the national lottery.

He couldn't understand why he was finding it so damned difficult to get this particular woman into his bed. She wasn't an innocent. She'd been married; she even had a child, for Christ's sake. Besides, he'd sported at the game of love with enough women over the years to know when a flirtation was ready to become something more. Hell, what was between him and Gabrielle had been ready to become something more the minute they first laid eyes on each other. It had never been a flirtation, even at the beginning, but an attraction of cosmic proportions. He wanted her desperately. And she wanted him, just as desperately. So what in bloody hell was stopping them?

As he bent over to heave a bag of sand into the balloon's wicker car, a sudden thought struck him with such force he groaned aloud.

Maybe she was holding out for marriage!

He groaned again, and Percy leaned over him solicitously. "I say, Saint-Just, did you strain something?"

Max straightened slowly, shaking his head. "No, I, uh, no, I'm fine." He took out his handkerchief and wiped his sweating brow. *Marriage.* He gritted his teeth. The devil will get frostbite in hell, Max swore violently to himself, before I take a woman to wife.

Marriage only ruined one of the greatest pleasures in life by wrapping it up with respectability and obligations. A man took a wife for three reasons—money, land, or lust. At least if you married for the first two, you got something tangible for your pains. Only a fool married for lust, which was short-lived and easily satisfied. As for love, which only women and poets believed really existed—

Max felt a hand on his arm. "Saint-Just, are you sure you're all right?"

Max looked into Percy's concerned face. "What?"

"You were shivering and gnashing your teeth. Maybe you hadn't better—"

"No, I'm fine. Uh, Percy? If I ever show the slightest inclination to go near a church, will you promise to stop me?"

Confusion wrinkled Percy's brow. "Church? Why ever would you—" His eyes widened and he threw a quick look at Gabrielle over Max's shoulder. Max still hadn't turned to look at her.

The American chuckled. "Sorry, Saint-Just, but you got yourself into this and you'll have to get yourself out. Personally, old friend, if I were you—though, praise God, I'm not—I'd grab her by the hand and drag her to the nearest priest as quickly as I could. Before I lost her to someone else."

Heavy lids fell over Max's eyes and his voice dropped into a silken purr. "Gabrielle is *mine.*"

An answering anger blazed from the American's dark eyes. "Spare me your jealous ravings, Saint-Just. I've never fancied redheads. They've too much spirit for my tastes."

For a moment the two men glared at each other. Then Max sighed ruefully, running a hand through his hair. "Hell, Percy, I'm sorry. You see what she's doing to me? I'm about to go out of my mind."

Percy shook his head in sympathy. "Women. They've been nothing but trouble since Eve took off her fig leaf in the garden of Eden."

With Percy offering him a running commentary of unsolicited advice on how to handle women, Max checked everything one last time. He was giving some final instructions to his assistants when he heard his name called. He turned and saw Dominique and Simon walking toward him hand in hand.

"M'sieur Max!" Dominique cried again and, pulling his hand free of Simon's, came running up to meet him.

Max swung the boy in the air in a wide arc. "Go tell Monsieur Bonville I said you could climb into the car for a look around before I take her up."

Dominique grabbed Max's neck in a tight grip, and his blue eyes opened wide. "Can I really?"

"Didn't I just say so?"

"Don't tell Maman," Dominique whispered, his lips close to Max's ear.

"Why not?"

" 'Cause she might say I can't. Agnes says she's been as cranky as a wall bug all morning."

Laughing, Max swung the boy down onto his feet. "Off with you then. While she isn't looking."

With a squeal of delight, Dominique took off running toward the balloon. Simon followed behind him more slowly. Gabrielle had stayed where she was, beneath the shade of an orange tree on the fringe of the crowd.

As Simon passed, he nodded once at Max, and then his round face broke into a slow smile and he winked. "I thought you might want to know, Dominique and I have plans to go fishing this afternoon, and I've made Agnes stay home and mind the shop," Simon said, seemingly apropos of nothing. But it made Max laugh out loud. He continued to smile to himself as he rolled down his sleeves and put on his hat and coat. Then he turned and for the first time looked at Gabrielle.

She smiled shyly as he came up to her. She was so beautiful she brought a tightness to his throat that wouldn't let him breathe, let alone speak.

She wore a green taffeta gown adorned with beige muslin ruches arranged in flounces. The dress was obviously new and probably more expensive than she could afford. He wondered if she had bought it to impress him and was secretly pleased at the thought. Her bodice had a low, square décolletage, and she had for once left it uncovered by a fichu. He wanted to plant his lips between the shadowy hollow of her exposed breasts.

He kissed her hand instead. "Thank you for coming after all."

She flushed slightly. "I . . . I decided I was being foolish."

"You were."

Her dark brows flared upward. "You needn't be so ungallant as to agree with me."

He laughed. "You really are as cranky as a wall bug this morning."

She tried to scowl at him, but her eyes betrayed her, crinkling with silent laughter at the corners. When her lower lip began to quiver, it was all he could do not to kiss it.

"I thought that by agreeing with you I would avoid an argument for a change," he said. "Are you always so hard to please? Or is it just me?" He had yet to let go of her hand. She tried to pull it free, but he held it fast. It trembled a moment, then was still. "Are you feeling adventuresome this morning?"

She looked at him, suspicion plain on her face. "Why do you ask?"

"Come with me, Gabrielle."

She looked confused for a moment. Then her eyes jerked over to the balloon and back to him. "Come with you! You must be—"

"—mad," he finished for her. "Come with me, Gabrielle. If I haven't raped you yet, I'm not likely to do so two thousand feet in the air."

"That isn't what I—two thousand feet!"

"It isn't dangerous. At least no more dangerous than crossing the Champs Élysées on a Sunday afternoon. Simon will look after Dominique, and I promise to have you home by sunset." That last part was a lie, but he was counting on the fact that by sunset they would be sharing a bed in some village inn, and she would have other things on her mind besides hearth and home.

She was weakening. He could see it in her face. She was sucking on her lower lip in the delightful way she had that made him want to ravish her on the spot.

He brought his hand to her shoulder, trailing his fingers along the edge of it to the back of her neck. She wouldn't look at him, but he saw her swallow hard. He brought his face close to hers, his lips just brushing her cheek. "Gabrielle . . . Gabrielle. Come float across the sky with me."

She pulled away from him, and he thought he had failed, but she walked toward the balloon, her shoulders squared resolutely, and then she turned, flinging her head up in a challenge. "Are you coming, monsieur? Or are you afraid?"

Percy Bonville couldn't hide his amusement as Max led Gabrielle past the ropes and *gendarmes* that separated the balloon from the crowd.

"Good morning, Madame Prion," Percy said, bowing with his usual flourish. He started to bring her hand to his lips until he caught sight of the murderous scowl on Max's face. He bowed his head over it instead. "Has Saint-Just somehow managed to convince you to join him on this wild escapade?"

She smiled nervously. "He assures me it isn't dangerous."

Percy laughed. "Oh, the aerostat isn't dangerous. Not at all." He laughed again and winked at Max. "As long as you take care to steer clear of all churches."

Max took Gabrielle's arm and pulled her toward the balloon's wicker car. "Don't pay any attention to him. He's only jealous because he wants to come, too."

Simon had just convinced Dominique it was time to get out of the basket, and there was a bit of difficulty when the boy realized his maman was going to get to ride in the balloon without him. He insisted, in a very vocal way, on coming along as well, until Simon had to bribe him with an offer of gingerbread and a promise to go fishing not only that day but all the next afternoon, too.

With her full-panniered skirts and many petticoats, Gabrielle had considerable trouble—to Max's delight—climbing into the wicker car. It gave him a chance "accidentally" to brush his arm along her breasts as he helped her inside, and he got a tantalizing glimpse of a white silk stocking stretching thinly over an ankle so small he could easily span it with two fingers. A buzz of excitement rippled through the crowd when they realized a woman was about to join this crazy scientist Saint-Just in his mad experiment.

Once inside the car, Gabrielle looked around her, and he

saw her eyes narrow suspiciously at the sight of the blankets and the basket of food and champagne.

She raised her brows at him. "You seem to have been expecting a passenger, monsieur."

"A good scientist provides for all contingencies," he countered, flashing his mocking smile.

She tilted her head back to gaze nervously at the yawning cavity of the colorful silken sphere. With an easy nonchalance, Max slipped an arm around her waist, then grinned to himself when she left it there.

"The theory," he said, "is that an envelope containing a substance lighter than air will rise until its weight matches that of the atmosphere around it."

A sudden gust rocked the great balloon, making it pull against its moorings. She looked at him with huge violet eyes, swallowing convulsively. Although they were still firmly anchored to the ground, she clutched the rim of the basket with rigid hands.

He smiled at her. "Don't be frightened."

She gave a shaky laugh. "I'm not frightened. I'm terrified. How . . . how do you make it work?"

"It's quite simple really. To go up we eliminate some of the ballast—that's weight." He kicked at a pile of sandbags that lay in a corner in the bottom of the car. "To descend, I pull on this cord here, which opens a valve at the top of the envelope, letting some of the gas escape. We're propelled through the air by the wind currents."

"Oh," she said on an expulsion of breath, and her voice quivered a little. "Where are we going?"

"You'll see."

He didn't dare tell her he had yet to discover a way to control their direction. He could get them up and he could get them down, but what happened in between was pretty much up to the wind gods.

The wicker car swayed gently again, and Gabrielle let out a tiny squeak.

"It won't tip over," Max said, although he used the excuse of her fear to hold her tighter against him. He brought his lips close to her ear. "You're perfectly safe with me. I promise."

Her mouth curled softly. "Oh, Max, you are such a shameless liar."

The wind tugged loose a tendril of her hair. It brushed back and forth across his cheek until she tucked it behind her ear. Turning slightly, she looked up at him through the veil of her lashes, though one hand still clung tightly to the rim of the car. He covered that hand and it fluttered once, like a trapped bird, then was still.

"Trust me," he said.

She sucked in a sharp breath. "I dare not."

"You've no other choice. You've come too far to turn back now."

She was silent for so long that he had opened his mouth to speak again when she turned full around to face him. She let go of the basket, and slipping her hand into his the way a child would, she forced a brave smile that tugged at his heart.

He squeezed her hand. "Are you ready, *ma mie?*"

"Yes," she said, and laughed suddenly. "But remember your promise to behave yourself."

"I don't remember making such a promise." He grinned at her. "Besides, you know what a shameless liar I am."

One of his assistants launched a small emerald-colored balloon to test the wind, and then Max gave the signal to release the mooring ropes.

Simon held Dominique above the heads of the surging crowd, and Gabrielle waved, calling out his name. He waved back so vigorously he knocked Simon's hat off. Max jettisoned the anchoring ballast and, with cheers from the crowd wafting over them, the balloon rose above the grounds and academy buildings of the Jardin des Plantes and floated out over the river Seine.

He tossed a few more sandbags into the water below, and they rose higher still as the rooftops of Paris sailed past beneath them.

Max came to stand close beside Gabrielle, and she turned to him, a look of rapturous wonder on her face.

"Oh, Max, it's so beautiful. You can see the whole world from up here!" she cried.

"And you . . ." He brushed her face with his knuckles, following the curve of a cheekbone into her hair. "You are more beautiful than the world. Gabrielle—"

She turned away from him. "Max, please . . . You're making me feel silly." Though the air was balmy, she shivered slightly and chafed her arms. "Look," she said, pointing below where a bevy of ducks took off from the river, skimming over the water. "From here they look no bigger than skitter bugs."

Max smiled to himself as he moved away from her again to vent the hydrogen, slowing the balloon's ascent. They floated over the city wall where carts and wagons lined up to pass through the *barrières* and then, within minutes it seemed, they were out in the country, and the black and gray of the teeming streets and tenements of Paris became rolling green fields dotted with clumps of trees and brush. Here and there a road sliced across the earth like a thin scar, connecting the clay and wattle farms. He saw a windmill, and he had the incredible feeling he could reach down and set it to spinning with a godlike flick of his finger.

And then, in the great, enveloping silence, Max heard the sound of laughter, and he turned to see that it came from Gabrielle.

She removed her plumed bonnet and, leaning back, threw back her head as if in supplication to the wide blue sky above them. The sun set her hair ablaze like a candle flaring suddenly in a dark room, and her lips parted in a soft sigh.

Then she straightened and looked at him with those dark violet eyes, and he saw a yearning in them, a yearning that both terrified and drew him. She was all he had ever wanted, all he needed. She was Gabrielle, his Gabrielle.

And he was a fool, the worst kind of fool—one who lied to himself. For he realized with a sudden, sharp pain that was like a jabbing blow to his gut . . .

He loved her.

Chapter 8

I love you.

The words seared across her mind like a brand as she gazed into his smoldering eyes, eyes that were the dark gray of a thunderstorm.

A violent, dangerous thunderstorm.

I don't care, I don't care. I love you.

Abruptly she turned away from him, trying to lose herself in the wonder that she was floating suspended in air like a cloud, so high that the sheep and cows in the pastures below resembled the ceramic barn animals that were part of the crèche she had played with as a child. Fields of wheat and mustard spread over the countryside in haphazard, colorful patches, like a ragpicker's clothes. They drifted toward a village in the hazy distance, the gilded cross of its church steeple flashing in the sun. A silver river slashed like a wound across the fields—

He touched her.

"Gabrielle."

He touched her, laying his fingers on her bare arm, and it was like holding a torch to wax, as if her flesh would melt beneath the heat of his hand.

I can't bear this, she thought.

His fingers moved up her arm, encircled her elbow, drew

her around. *Stop,* she pleaded silently. *Stop . . . Don't stop, don't—*

He kissed her. A full, strong kiss that plumbed her depths and took of her all she had to give, and more. Draining her until she could not stand up, so that she leaned back against the side of the car and clung to the ruffled lawn of his shirt. She felt his flesh through the thin material begin to shudder in ripples like waves curling along a beach.

When, too soon, he released her mouth, she was afraid of what he would see in her face, and so she turned her head aside. Her chest ached and she felt dizzy, and then she remembered to start breathing again. The darkness around the edges of her vision faded and she could see.

She saw the swaying treetops of a stand of pines below and the thatched roofs of the village, the church steeple with its shiny gold cross . . . Was it just her imagination, or was the steeple getting taller? And the ducks, those ducks that had seemed as tiny as skitter bugs before were definitely as big as field mice now. Could it be possible they were—

"Max!" She pulled away from him and lunged for the edge of the car. "Max, we're *sinking!*"

Max looked down. "Dear me," he said.

Dear me?

They were plunging to their deaths and all the madman could say was *Dear me!* Gabrielle wanted to hit him. Except she would have to let go of the curved edge of the wicker passenger gallery to do it, and nothing on earth was going to pry her hands loose of their fierce grip.

She squeezed her eyes shut instead. She felt the car sway as Max moved about, hurling the remaining bags of sand overboard. It slowed their descent, but not by much.

Gabrielle risked a peek. She saw wreathing pine branches beckoning to her like witches' claws. She tried to make her voice sound calm. "Max, we're still going down rather too fast, don't you think?"

He was staring up within the cavity of the balloon, frowning. "There's a leak in one of the seams on the envelope."

"I'm delighted to hear you know what's causing it," Gabrielle said through gritted teeth. "Now will you be so good as to fix it, please."

"I can't."

She sucked in a deep breath, determined not to disgrace herself by losing control and shouting at him. "Well, why don't we turn around then and sail back toward Paris?" she said, her voice falsely bright. "There are trees here, Max. And a steeple."

His eyes flickered away from her. "I can't do that either."

"Mon Dieu . . . If we're killed, Maximilien de Saint-Just, I'll never have anything more to do with you. You and these aerostats of yours that either blow up or start leaking at the most inconvenient moments—"

"We won't be killed." He heaved the food basket, champagne bottles, and blankets all overboard. Gabrielle watched them fall into a turnip field below. At least they were beyond most of the trees now, but the village still loomed ahead. As if it possessed a mischievous will of its own, the wind was sending them directly toward the church with its tall steeple. She could read the face of the clock—both hands pointed straight up at twelve. And as if on cue a bell began to peal the hour.

"There may be a bit of a jolt when we hit the ground," Max was saying in a maddeningly cheerful voice, and he even had the audacity to give her an encouraging smile.

Gabrielle glared back at him.

"We'll have to lighten our load as much as possible," Max said, pulling off his coat and cocked hat and sending them over the side as well.

He stepped up to Gabrielle. His arms reached out, and she thought he was going to embrace her. Still clinging to the rim of the car, she sidestepped around him like a matador taunting a bull. "Max! How could you even think of doing *that* at a time like this?"

He lunged for her, grabbing her waist with one hand while the other reached up under her skirts and began to tug at the strings that attached her petticoats to her corset. "Will you, for Christ's sake, Gabrielle, quit squirming,'' he growled at her.

Gabrielle was so astonished she went completely still. Obviously his mind had come unhinged with lust—their aerostat was falling like a stone out of the sky and instead of trying to stop it he was attempting to rip her clothes right off her body!

She pounded her fists against his chest. ''Let go of me this instant. I refuse to let you make love to me when we're about to be killed!''

The madman was actually laughing. He had also somehow inserted his fingers between her chemise and her bare flesh, and in spite of impending death, Gabrielle felt her stomach muscles start to quiver.

''Ahhh!'' She groaned aloud and swayed into him, shutting her eyes.

''Gabrielle, *ma mie,* you are absolutely irresistible when you do that,'' Max said between gasping breaths. ''But now isn't the time. Help me take off your pannier and your petticoats. We'll need to throw them overboard. All of them.''

Since she would have to relinquish her grip on the basket to stop him, Gabrielle let Max rip all her underthings from beneath her skirts. The three petticoats and the split hip hoops made of osier reeds were quite heavy, and their absence did noticeably slow the balloon's descent.

But not enough. ''Shoes, too,'' he said, plucking them off her feet, and then her stockings for good measure. Then, leaning against the wall of the car, he managed with a lot of grunting and grimacing to yank off his tight black leather boots. His boots and stockings followed hers overboard.

He sighed as he watched them fall. ''The devil. I paid over a hundred livres for those boots.''

Gabrielle swallowed a sob at the thought of all the money she had spent on her gown and its accoutrements, bought solely to dazzle and tantalize a certain mad, impossible scientist. She had imagined him taking off those three frothy, and expensive, petticoats one by one—

''Gabrielle . . .''

Tearing her fascinated attention away from the rapidly approaching church steeple, she turned her head to find Max regarding her speculatively.

"What—?" she began, and then her eyes widened with horror as she guessed his intent. She whirled around, actually letting go of the basket to fling her arms protectively across her breasts. "You wouldn't dare!"

"But that dress of yours must weigh at least—"

She pointed a shaking finger at his middle. "I'll see you naked long before me, Maximilien de Saint-Just. Off with those breeches."

He gave her a smoldering look that promised if she didn't cooperate she would be the next thing tossed overboard. "Gabrielle, dammit, be reasonable—"

"Reasonable!" Why you—" The steeple reared up before her eyes, so close she could count the individual red slates in its roof. "Oh, *mon Dieu,*" she cried softly and made the sign of the cross.

The basket swung about, grazing the slates, lurching and tipping onto its end. Gabrielle screamed as she was hurled across the bottom of the car to slam against the hard wicker side.

Her skirts were flung over her head, and for a moment her world was a dark and silent shroud. Fighting off waves of panic, she clawed the stiff material away and looked up into the sad face of a huge gold Christ, and she thought she must have died already and gone to heaven. Then she noticed that the gilt on the figure's halo was flecked and streaked with pigeon droppings and one of his feet was missing.

With a sudden, violent jerk the car pulled free of the steeple and flipped upright again. Gabrielle slid back along the bottom of the basket and into Max's arms.

"I knew I should have stayed away from churches," he said, and she thought then that he really was well and truly mad.

"Marry me, Gabrielle."

* * *

Gabrielle opened her eyes to a turquoise sky laced with wisps of clouds. Above her, tangled among thick piny branches, was the wicker car, its bunting ripped and flapping in the wind, the cord netting dripping down like fingers of moss.

For a moment she had no idea where she was or what had happened. She had this strange memory of being in Max's arms, of hearing his voice, low and silky in her ear, talking about churches and asking her to—

No, she couldn't possibly have heard him right. She was, after all, expecting to die at any moment. Perhaps, in her terror, she had hallucinated the words out of his mouth.

She sat up. The world tilted for a moment, then was still. She looked around her. She was on the edge of a fallow field. In the middle of the field was the balloon, which had pulled free of the car. It lay heaving on the wet, dark earth as the hydrogen escaped through the rents in its fabric, making it look alive. A plowman, who had been working the nearby acres, came trotting up to stare openmouthed at the writhing monster, then took off running for the village.

There was no sign of Max.

"Max!" she cried, stumbling to her feet. "Max, don't frighten me like this. Where are you?"

She took a step forward, toward the balloon, thinking perhaps he was somehow wrapped up in the silken envelope. The car, she remembered now, had struck the tops of the trees, flipping upside down again, flinging her out of Max's arms and hurling her into space. But perhaps Max had gotten tangled up in the balloon instead.

Her foot caught in one of the freshly turned furrows, pitching her forward. She flung out her hands to break her fall, and a flash of white in a nearby gulley caught her eye—the ruffle on the cuff of a man's shirtsleeve.

She ran to him, stumbling over the clods of earth and falling to her knees beside him. He lay on his back, his arms flung out at his sides. His face was still, his eyes shut, but his chest rose and fell steadily with his breathing. She almost sobbed aloud with relief.

"Max . . . wake up." She cradled his head, and it lolled against her breast. "Oh, Max, my love. Wake up, please."

He didn't stir, and suddenly she was afraid again. She had heard once of a man—a comte who was an intimate of the king—who fell off his horse while hunting and went to sleep never to wake up. He lay for years in his bed, growing steadily thinner as his flesh wasted away and his skin toughened like leather—

She shook him, a bit roughly. "Max, damn you. Wake up or I'll . . . I'll . . . ." She tried to remember what one was supposed to do to revive the victim of a dead faint. "Or I'll throw a pitcher of vinegar into your face," she threatened, oblivious to the fact that there wasn't even a thimbleful of the stuff to be had for miles.

She heard in the distance the peal of a bell, the tocsin sounding the alarm to the villagers. Max's eyelids flickered.

She shook him again, more gently this time. "Max, if you don't wake up this instant, I really will marry you even if I did dream the whole thing. It would serve you right."

A slight flaring of his nostrils betrayed that he had heard her, although his eyes remained closed.

Gabrielle shook him again, as hard as she could. She was furious with him for almost killing her and then almost dying himself, and for making her love him.

"I'll saddle you with a dozen babies to support," she vowed, coming up with the worst threat she could think of. "And I'll nag you worse than a Les Halles fishwife. I'll make you sleep on the floor at night and—omph!" He pulled her down on top of him, smothering her words with his mouth.

He forced her lips apart, pushing his tongue past her teeth, thrusting it deep into her mouth, and a hot, surging passion flared immediately within her. It was not enough for her to touch him. She wanted to crawl inside his skin, to fuse their bones and meld their hearts. There was nothing soft about her need of him; it was all hard, pulsating hunger. She wanted to devour him.

His mouth was a wet, hot hole to be filled. Her fingers grabbed his hair, pulling him closer so she could probe it

more deeply with her tongue. He stroked her back, pressing
the ridge of his palm against the rise of her buttocks, molding
her to him so that she could feel his desire harden and grow.
She rubbed her stomach against it in bold, sensuous circles
and her hunger grew and grew with him, swelling with him,
until she thought she would surely die of it.

He broke the kiss with such violence she thought he was
angry.

"Ah, God in heaven, Gabrielle . . ." He groaned against
her mouth, though she could barely hear him for the throbbing of the blood in her ears. She pressed her face against
his neck, unable to look at him. Only a whore, she thought,
would have behaved in such a way. What must he think of
her?

"Gabrielle?"

Reluctantly she raised her head to look deep into his eyes.
She could see shadows of his thoughts reflected in their dark,
sooty grayness. Yet they remained as obscure and unreveal-
ing as a tarnished mirror.

After a long moment—when Gabrielle was sure the entire
world waited breathless to see what he would say—he sat up,
pulling her with him. "You can do all those things," he said,
his voice shaking. "As long as you never leave me."

Gabrielle, who was still finding it difficult to breathe let
alone think, wondered what particular things he was talking
about. Yet somewhere, like a song in her blood, she caught
the echo of his voice saying *Marry me, Gabrielle.*

"Max, I . . . If it's only because you want me to sleep
with you—"

He pressed his hand against her mouth. "Christ, yes, I
want to sleep with you—so badly I ache. But I also want you
there beside me in the morning when I wake up. Every morning. I want you to saddle me with children to support, the
more the better, and starting with your own adorable son. I
want someone to laugh with during the good times, and
someone to cling to during the bad times. I want *you*, Gabrielle. As my wife."

Behind them the hot wind rushed through the trees, making

a sound like waves crashing against a rock. She could smell the peaty dampness of the freshly turned earth. She could feel the sharp, sticky pine needles under her legs. She thought he was probably the most beautiful man she had ever seen.

She didn't know it was possible to be this happy.

Suddenly she felt embarrassed, unable to meet his eyes any longer. She looked down at her lap. Her dress was ripped and stained with mud. She had no shoes or hat, and the wind blew her hair in wild tangles around her face. She tried to gather it back with her hands, then, giving up, rubbed at a smear of dirt on her skirt.

He captured her hands with one of his. With the other he tilted her face up until she could no longer avoid his eyes. "I like you looking a bit disheveled, remember? Marry me, Gabrielle."

A smile trembled on her lips. But the smile faded as it occurred to her that he had yet to tell her he loved her. And then the smile returned as she realized that in a way—his way—he just had.

Her eyes drank in his face while he waited for her answer. She savored the strong curve of his cheekbone, the firm line of his lips, the throbbing pulse in the lean muscles of his neck.

She touched the pulse with the tip of one finger. Felt it stop, then start up again, faster. "Yes," she said, and the word, from deep in her throat, came out broken and shaky.

His eyes warmed and his lips parted, and her fingers fluttered up to capture his smile. He took one of her fingers between his lips, nibbling at it gently once, twice, sucking it deeper into his mouth, then releasing it.

"Oh, Max," she said on an exhale of breath. She cradled his face with her hands. She kissed his eyes, first one, then the other. She brought her mouth close to his, but let it hover there, allowing the anticipation to build and build until it was like a high-pitched note whining through her blood.

Even then she didn't kiss him, merely slid her tongue lightly across his lips. His shirt, which had pulled loose at the neck, was twisted half off his shoulder. And she turned to put her lips to the curve of his bare flesh, licking the smooth muscle, tasting him. Her breasts, pressed flat against his chest, felt the echo of the drumbeat of his heart. Her hands roamed over his body, exploring him inch by slow and careful inch.

"Gabrielle . . ." His voice rumbled against her neck, raising goose bumps on her skin. "I think we'd better stop while we still—"

A volley of shouts, carried to them by the wind, shattered the quiet. Gabrielle raised her head from where it rested in the crook of his shoulder and looked out across the field. Her eyes opened wide, and a small laugh escaped her lips.

A group of the villagers had invaded the field, armed with pitchforks, axes, and scythes. One, who must have been the *intendant,* for he was the only one wearing breeches and a coat, approached the balloon warily. He held a long pitchfork by the end of its handle, making menacing jabs in the air.

He lunged the pitchfork like a javelin at the monster. The balloon belched, and a stream of gas jetted out with a moaning hiss. Letting out a loud shriek, the man jumped back, dropping his weapon.

"Merde!" Max exclaimed, trying to scramble to his feet, intent on rescuing the fallen beast.

But Gabrielle grabbed his waist, holding him back. "Don't be silly, Max. Do you want them to start sticking their pitchforks into you? There must be thirty of them, and besides, it's too late anyway."

Several of the men had begun to hurl stones at the fluttering, writhing envelope. It groaned and collapsed inward, shrinking. Emboldened, they approached it slowly, and when it showed no signs of counterattacking, they began to slash and hack at it with their scythes and axes.

"God, I can't watch this." Max moaned. He sat back, bracing his elbows on his bent knees, and buried his head in his arms. "They're killing her."

"Good riddance," Gabrielle said.

He flung his head up to scowl at her. "Good riddance?

Have you any idea how much in debt I put myself to build that damned aerostat?''

Gabrielle tried to decide when Max looked his most adorable—when he flashed that devilish, damn-the-world grin, or when, as now, his mouth curled into a sulky pout like a small boy's.

She kissed him. "I'll marry you anyway," she said. "Rich or poor, I love you, Maximilien de Saint-Just. I always will." And she leaned into him to kiss him again.

He drew in a ragged breath and put her firmly away from him. "If you want me to wait until we're properly married before making love to you, *ma mie*, you'd better not come any closer. Because I have only so much willpower and you are pure temptation—Jesu, what are they doing to her *now?*"

Gabrielle rose to her knees to look out across the field. The villagers, she saw, had hitched the defeated balloon to a plow horse and were about to drag it in ignominious shame off the field.

Max was up and storming after them before Gabrielle could stop him. By the time she caught up, he had already felled four men and wounded several others before being overwhelmed by sheer numbers. A short rotund man in a black cassock jumped around the pile of bodies that wrestled on the ground, waving his arms and shouting.

"Desist, I say. In the name of our savior, I command you to cease this violence at once!" He ended this tirade with a volley of violent sneezes.

The villagers desisted; Max did not. Filled with tremendous sexual energy he hadn't been able to release through normal means, Max was getting a perverse satisfaction out of pounding flesh with his fists. Two more villagers received bloody noses before he was again subdued.

He was hauled to his feet and shoved before the man in the black cassock.

"Are you responsible for the invasion of our village by this heathen beast?" the curé demanded of Max, pointing a quivering finger at the once great balloon, now withered and ripped and stained with mud.

One of Max's eyes was already beginning to swell, but he was able to look down the length of his arrogant nose at the curé. "That, you damned meddling priest, is no heathen beast. It happens to be an agnostic aerostat."

Gabrielle clapped her hand over her mouth to muffle a laugh. The curé, however, was not amused. He turned his baleful glare on her. She thought he was the ugliest man she'd ever seen. He had big, hanging jowls and a pushed-in nose deformed by taking too much snuff. He resembled one of those pugnacious dogs bred for bear-baiting.

"This man," the curé thundered, "is obviously the devil in disguise come to plague and tempt us. And this woman"— he flung a pointing finger at Gabrielle and she jumped in alarm—"is the devil's handmaiden!"

An angry rumble stirred through the villagers, and one man took a step forward, brandishing his ax.

"I will have no more viooolence!" the curé roared, punctuating it with a huge sneeze. The villager stumbled backward, flinging his arm in front of his face to shield himself from the spray.

Max had jerked free of the hands that held him, and he snatched up the priest by the front of his cassock. He gave him a rough shake, and the fat man's feet twitched above the earth as if he were a chicken that had just had its neck wrung.

"You'll keep a civil tongue in your head when you speak about my—" Max stopped in mid-word, and a strange look crossed his face. Gabrielle, worried that in his maddened state he might do murder, put a restraining hand on her man's arm.

Max relaxed his grip, letting the priest slide to the ground. He rearranged the folds of the curé's cassock, even brushing off a speck of imaginary dust. "My dear Monsieur le Curé," he said, summoning forth a truly devilish smile, "you are just the man I need."

"Need?" the curé squeaked.

"Yes." Max drew Gabrielle into his arms. "I need you to marry me to this woman."

"*Now?*" Gabrielle exclaimed.

The curé sneezed; it was an awesome sound. "I . . . marry?"

"Father?" one of the villagers interjected.

"Shut up!" the curé barked.

"Now," Max said to Gabrielle. "Before you change your mind."

The curé pushed a tremendous snort out of his deformed nose. "Impossible. Where's the contract, eh? Have the banns been posted? I'll need ten days at least to complete the necessary paperwork."

Max's eyelids slitted closed and his voice dropped to a soft, silken purr. "Perhaps, Father, I should put it in terms you can better understand. Unless I am married to this woman this afternoon, a grave sin will be committed this night."

The curé paled and licked his thick lips. "Surely you can't mean . . . sin?"

"Sin. Fornication, to be precise."

A strange sound—like the death *cheep* of a strangled bird— popped out of Gabrielle's mouth. Red with mortification, she glared at her husband-to-be, trying to tell him with her eyes just what she would do to him for this latest humiliation when next they were alone together.

But she also had to admit he spoke the truth. For, married or not, she would lie with Maximilien de Saint-Just this night.

"The consequences will be on your head," Max said to the priest. Then he flashed his sudden, mocking smile. "On the other hand, if you marry us within the hour, I'll pay you a hundred livres."

The curé flung out his arms and bellowed "Begone with you!" so loudly that a flock of pigeons in the nearby pines was scattered into flight. Gabrielle wondered if the priest truly thought she and Max were devils and was now attempting to perform an exorcism.

But he was simply shooing his own flock back to the village. "Leave the heathen beast where it is," he ordered as the field slowly emptied, although one or two of the men glared back over their shoulders.

In the ensuing silence the curé sneezed, then cleared his

throat. "A man of the cloth cannot be bribed," he admonished sternly. "However, a charitable donation to the church is always welcome." He gave his squashed nose a vigorous rub. "I am Father Étienne Benoit, curé to the village of Chênaie-sur-Seine. And you are Monsieur . . ."

"Saint-Just."

"Surely not the comte de Saint-Just? You are far too young. You are, perhaps, the comte's son?"

Max looked at Gabrielle. His face tightened, and the old bitter cynicism glinted in his eyes. "Yes, I'm the comte's son. His bastard son," he said harshly, as if daring her to love him still, now that she knew his shame.

"Ah," the curé said, imbuing an entire society's contempt for illegitimacy into that one sound.

But Gabrielle didn't care how Max came to be born. She believed he had been put on this earth for her to love, and she told him so by taking his hand and giving him the same sweet smile she gave to Dominique when he was hurt and needed comforting.

For a moment Max just stood there, as stiff and unyielding as a stone wall. Then she felt him sigh, and the smile he gave back to her reached all the way to his dark gray eyes—eyes that were for once free of all emotion but happiness.

Father Benoit had looked from Gabrielle to Max and back to Gabrielle again. "And is this marriage your wish as well, my daughter?" he asked, his voice suddenly kind.

Gabrielle opened her mouth, but her throat froze and for a moment nothing could come out. "Y-yes," she finally stuttered.

The curé sneezed. "Then it shall be done."

It was an old church.

It smelled of musty pews and mildewed missals. Streams of sunlight pushed through the narrow windows that lined the nave, showing the dust motes dancing in the air. A path was worn in the stone floor leading up to the altar, testimony to the many feet that had over the years come forward to receive the body of Christ.

Father Benoit left them before the communion railing and disappeared into the sacristy. Soon a volley of violent sneezes echoed throughout the church as he indulged his snuff habit.

Max slipped an arm around Gabrielle's waist and planted a kiss on her cheekbone. Her body responded immediately, seeming to melt into him like snow on a hot hearth.

She pushed halfheartedly against his chest. "Max, we are in a *church*."

His hand moved up her waist to cup her breast. "Uh-huh," he mumbled as his lips trailed up into her hair and he rubbed her nipple through the stiff material of her bodice. "In church. About to be married."

She groaned, turning her head so that he could lick her ear. "That's no excuse."

"I don't need an excuse."

"Ahem!"

Gabrielle jerked out of Max's arms, blushing furiously under the curé's stern eye.

Father Benoit straightened the sacramental stole around his thick neck as he waddled up to them. "I believe a session in the confessional would be in order," he said.

Gabrielle's blush deepened, and Max made a face.

"Before receiving any of the sacraments, *particularly* the sacrament of marriage," the curé intoned, wagging a fat finger under Max's nose, "your soul must be in a state of grace. Can you assure me, my son, that your soul is washed clean of all sin?"

"No," Max said with such haughtiness that Gabrielle made a surreptitious sign of the cross to ward off any stray lightning bolts.

The priest tsked and shook his head. "The worst sin of all, my son, is pride."

Max held the priest's eyes for a long moment before looking down at his bare feet. The priest looked down as well, then back up to Max, his eyebrows raised.

"It's a long story," Max said.

The curé's jowls twitched. "I imagine so. Don't bother to

relate it to me, however." He looked at Gabrielle and gestured at the confessional box. "Shall we proceed, my child?"

"That didn't take long," Max said to her when she emerged a few moments later.

"I didn't have much to say," she told him smugly. And then she blushed, for her only sins this last week had been thoughts of committing lewd and lascivious behavior with *him.*

Max was in the confessional for a long time. Gabrielle paced back and forth down the nave trying not to think, for if she pondered too much about this crazy, impulsive thing she was about to do, she would never go through with it.

She shouldn't have even gone to the Jardin de Plantes this morning. She'd only done so because Max had asked her so sweetly, and she couldn't bear the thought of disappointing him. But it had been a terrible risk to show her face at such a public event. And then she had made matters worse by drawing everyone's attention to her by climbing into the aerostat with Max. Everyone saw her, and she could have so easily been recognized—

Louvois . . . Her chest felt tight with sudden fear. Louvois himself could have been there!

Mère de Dieu, what was she thinking? She could never marry Max. If they weren't already, all of Paris would soon be talking about the mad scientist Saint-Just and his crazy experiments with balloons filled with inflammable air. And she understood Max well enough by now to know he enjoyed his notoriety. He was also the kind of man who'd want to parade around the Palais Royal with his new wife on his arm. How could she explain to him that their marriage must be kept a secret, that no one must know of her? How could she tell him that without telling him everything? And if she told him everything, what would he—

Don't think about it. Don't—

"Think about something else," she whispered aloud. Sighing, she clutched her hands together in nervousness and felt the sharp edge of the sapphire ring. For a moment the sight of it, and the memories it evoked, were almost her undoing.

Quickly she pulled the ring off her finger and put it in the pocket of her skirt.

She stared at the closed doors of the confessional box. What was taking him so long? Surely even a rake like Max couldn't have that many sins on his conscience.

A soft smile transformed her face. He might be a rake, but he was an adorable one. *I'm a bastard and I've no desire to be reformed,* he had warned her the night they went out to look at the stars. Her smile faded. Would marriage reform Max? She doubted it. He was a man who enjoyed women and the pleasure they could bring him. He might fancy himself in love with her now, but how long would it be before he came to regret this day's impulsiveness? *I'll lie to you and I'll probably use you,* he had said, *and I'll most definitely end up hurting you—*

The door to the wooden box squeaked open and Max emerged. He started to smile, and then he saw her face and his lips tightened and his heavy lids dropped to obscure his eyes.

"Are you regretting your answer already, Gabrielle? The door is right back there. You are free to use it."

She flung her head up, challenging him. "Are you, perhaps, regretting the question?"

She waited, but Max said nothing. The church was so silent she could hear the rustle of bats in the eaves. Neither of them made a move toward the door.

She wondered what he really felt for her. Surely it was love that had brought him to this church, to this moment? "What's happened to the priest?" she finally asked when she could no longer bear the silence.

He produced a smile. His mocking one.

"He insisted I enumerate all my sins and so I did. I fear he now needs a few minutes to recover from the shock."

Gabrielle laughed, remembering suddenly all the many reasons why she loved him. "Oh, Max, you are incorri—"

Just then the curé stumbled out of his side of the confessional box. His face was as white as the lawn of his stole, and he looked at Max as if he expected him to sprout horns and a pair of cloven hooves at any moment. "We will need . . ." he started to say, but his voice shook so badly he had to begin over again. "We will need two witnesses."

Max went outside and came back with two of the villagers, both with badly battered faces. They must have borne no grudge against him, however, for they grinned and slapped his back before slipping into a nearby pew.

To Gabrielle, the wedding Mass seemed interminable. She knelt beside Max before the altar, her hand in his, and let the drone of the priest's voice—interrupted by an occasional sneeze—wash over her. She slanted a look at Max. His head was bent, his eyes half shut, and she thought he was praying until she realized he was leering down the low-cut bodice of her dress. She smiled to herself as he began to caress the inside of her wrist in slow, sensuous circles. Only minutes from absolution and already he was sinning.

It all seemed so unreal, as if it were happening to someone else and she was looking down on it all from a great height the way she had looked down on the world as she floated across the sky in the balloon. She tried not to think of how selfish she was being—to wed Max when she could only bring him tragedy and pain. It would have been better to have lain with him in sin, to snatch a few glorious, love-filled nights and then disappear with Dominique into the streets of Paris the way they had disappeared before. But loving Max as she did, how could she hurt him so? No, that was not quite the truth of it, for she would end up hurting him anyway. And as for Dominique, what was she trying to save him from—a childhood of pampered luxury, a future of almost unlimited wealth and power? No, the truth was she hadn't the courage to give up either Max or her son. Not on her own, not without being forced to. Or not until they, discovering the truth, left her . . .

She realized with a start that the priest was waiting for her to repeat the vows of matrimony. It still wasn't too late.

And then it was.

When it came time to anoint the rings, Max surprised Gabrielle by removing a heavy gold signet ring from a chain around his neck. It was a man's ring, but it must have been cut down once, for it fit her finger perfectly.

Then at last it was over. The priest made the sign of the cross over their heads, blessing them and pronouncing them husband and wife.

They arose together. She looked at her husband. He seemed so serious and subdued now, almost sad. She wondered if already he was regretting this impossible marriage.

After what felt like the longest moment in Gabrielle's life, Max bent his head and gave her a controlled but gentle kiss on the mouth. Then he turned to the priest, and his lips danced into his wicked smile. "You have my gratitude, Father. And now can you tell me—where is the nearest empty bed?"

The two witnesses burst into loud guffaws.

Father Benoit's jowls turned a vivid purple. "But, but, but," he sputtered around a sneeze, "you need to sign the register. And there are forms to be filled out . . ."

"My dear Monsieur le Curé," Max drawled in his haughtiest nobleman's voice, "you see before you a man and woman—a *married* man and woman—who have been tempted to the limits of their endurance." He scooped a laughing, blushing Gabrielle up into his arms. "Dammit, man, we need a bed!"

"I see," the curé said. "That is, I don't see, being a priest, of course, but I could see if— Oh, confound it all!" He flapped his arms, and his roars sent the bats flapping in the belfry. "There's a good, clean inn on the road to Paris. Go, go, go! The register can wait."

Max carried Gabrielle down the aisle and out the church door. He paused at the top of the steps, letting his eyes adjust to the bright sunlight.

She hugged his neck and planted a hard kiss on his mouth. "Max, you're a terrible man. You positively scandalized that poor priest."

"I'll be scandalizing the entire village of Chênaie-sur-Seine soon if I don't find a bed." He looked down into her face, and she saw tenderness and desire and, yes, she saw love in his eyes.

"I want you, Gabrielle, my wife and love of my life. So damned bad I ache and, by God, I'm not waiting another minute to have you."

"And I want you, my husband."

Chapter 9

The door flew open and the innkeeper, who was bent over a cookpot at the fire, looked over his shoulder, his face screwed into a scowl.

"Here now, there's no need to barge in here like an ass with a bee up her arse!"

"I want a bed," Max said.

The innkeeper straightened to peer nearsightedly at a tall man with a battered face who appeared to have a swooning woman in his arms. "Is she dead? Is she contagious? I'll not let no room to a—"

Gabrielle burst into breathless laughter as Max set her down on her feet. She felt giddy, as if she had been sipping champagne all afternoon. "We've just been married!" she announced.

The innkeeper bowed, making a leg in the manner of the courtiers of a century ago. "My felicitations, madame . . . monsieur."

Max pulled his purse out of his waistcoat pocket and pressed a scattering of coins into the innkeeper's hands. "My good man, I want a room. With a bed. Spare no expense."

The room the innkeeper showed them to was in the back on the ground floor. He flung open the door with another old-fashioned bow. "Monsieur, madame. A room with a bed."

Gabrielle, standing behind Max's broad back, heard him

164

make a funny sputtering sound. "Praise God," he said weakly. "A bed."

He stepped through the door, and Gabrielle followed, almost falling over the end of the biggest bed she had ever seen in her life. It had clawed feet the size of an elephant's and was draped with heavy curtains of a royal purple hue. It so filled the tiny room there was barely space to walk around it.

The innkeeper, pride beaming on his face, bowed a final time and shut the door. Gabrielle, her eyes brimming with repressed laughter, looked at Max.

"You," she began, and the laughter bubbled out of her. She pointed to the enormous bed. "You've been asking for it!"

"So I have." His laughter joined with hers in husky counterpoint, dancing around the room.

Then at once they stopped laughing and looked at each other.

It was so quiet she could hear the steady thud of a hammer striking iron from the blacksmith's down the road. The sound was almost as loud as the hammering of her heart. A muted gold light filtered through the slats of the jalousie shutters. A warm breeze stirred the air, bringing with it the scent of freshly cut hay. So many times she had dreamed of, imagined, planned for this moment, and now that it was here she was frightened.

Max moved and her muscles tensed.

But the step he took was away from her. He paced the room, to the window, the door, back to the window.

He turned his back to her, stuffed a hand in his pocket, ran his fingers through his hair. "I didn't think it would be such an ordeal to take a wife. All that eternal babbling in Latin. Why couldn't the fat fool have just pronounced us married and been done with it?"

She looked up, surprised at the hard rush of words. He's nervous, too, she thought, and loved him all the more for it.

"Damn!" He spun around, took a step toward her, then stood still, his hands hanging loose at his sides, his sooty gray eyes searching her face. Outside the hammering stopped; the breeze died.

"Max, I love you."

He swallowed, sighed. "I know," he said. "I know . . . Come here."

She went.

His arms encircled her. He rested his cheek against the top of her head, and for a moment they simply held each other.

"I love you, too," he said at last.

She drew in a deep breath, filling her lungs. She felt so strange, weightless, as if, without an anchor to hold her, she would float like an aerostat up and out of the room. She reached for the bedpost. The wood was smooth and warm beneath her hand.

He ran his fingers along the edge of the blond lace that trimmed her sleeve. "Did you buy this dress for me?"

"I thought of you," she said, her throat so tight the words were but a coarse whisper. His fingers moved beneath the lace, tracing the curve of her elbow. "I imagined you taking it off me . . ."

She turned around so that he could unhook her dress. She did it thoughtlessly, without words, like a woman long married. Yet at the touch of his fingers on her neck, she shuddered and a harsh groan tore from her throat.

He gathered up her hair and brought it to his mouth in his cupped hands as if dipping into a pool of water for a drink. "Peaches," he said. "I love the smell of your hair. Like warm peaches fresh off the tree."

She shut her eyes and saw him plucking a peach off a tree, his white teeth biting into the soft flesh, his tongue coming out to lick the sticky juice off his lips.

He pulled her hair to one side, exposing the bare nape of her neck. He kissed her there. Her eyelids fluttered open, then closed again. She bowed her head, savoring the warm, moist touch of his mouth on her skin.

He released the hooks that fastened her dress. He did it slowly with single, expert twists of one finger, stopping after each one to kiss her back as it was bared to him.

When he started to uncover her corset and chemise, he worked faster, impatient. He pushed the bodice of her dress down around her waist, freeing her arms, then guided the bunched material past her hips. It slid along her legs to land in a puddle at her feet. He stroked his thumb along her shoulder blade, just above her corset, then bent his head to kiss the place where it met her spine.

"Oh . . ." She shivered, wondering how a mouth that looked so hard could kiss so gently.

"Do you like that?" he whispered, leaving a trail of more teasing kisses across her back.

He deftly undid the laces to her corset, and it split open to fall forward into her hands. She pulled it over her head and, with a sharp flick of her wrist, sent it sailing across the room.

His hands, spread wide, clasped her waist, and he spun her around so fast she almost fell. A bar of shadow fell across the lower half of his face, but his eyes glowed as he looked at her, beckoning her like the lights of a cottage window on a storm-racked night. For interminable silent seconds he stood unmoving, then his hands left her waist. He gripped the sides of her head and covered her mouth with his. She clung to his forearms, answering his kiss, meeting the thrusting invasion of his tongue. Love for him poured through her in a flood, filling her to bursting, and she gasped aloud as if in pain.

He slanted his mouth back and forth across hers, almost hurtfully, the pressure of his kiss so intense it left her lips feeling bruised. His mouth trailed down, along her jawline. He tangled his hand in her hair, pulling her head back to expose her neck, where he planted quick kisses, flicking her skin with his tongue.

Running her palms across his back, she pressed her breasts to his chest, irritated suddenly at the barrier of clothing that still remained between them. She wrenched at the buttons on his waistcoat, heard one clatter to the floor.

He stilled her hands. "Would you rip the clothes right off me, woman?"

"Yes."

He shrugged out of the waistcoat, letting it fall to the floor.

She tugged at the ruffled jabot around his neck until he choked and rolled his eyes piteously, and her laughter, low and soft, filled the room. She pulled his shirttail out of his breeches, but he did the rest, yanking it over his head and flinging it aside.

She wrapped her arms around his waist, then leaned back to admire his chest. It was just as she imagined it—brown, broad, brawny. She buried her face in it, breathing deeply and stirring the light mat of dark, silky hair into tickling her nose.

"Mmm . . . you smell sweet."

"Sweet!"

"Well, tangy sweet. Like lemon sherbet."

"Good Lord."

She licked him. "You taste good, too."

He laughed. "Stop it, you little idiot."

Then his laughter caught in his throat. His eyes roamed her face, down her neck to her breasts. With the back of two knuckles, he stroked what he could see, the soft swelling above the lacy edge of her chemise. He curled one of the ribbons around his finger.

She shook her head, covering his hand with her own. "I'll see you naked first, Maximilien de Saint-Just," she teased. And she smiled as she heard his breath catch.

She looked down. Desire that was hidden in the hammering of her heart, the hot rushing of the blood through her veins, was plainly visible on him—a hard, pulsating bulge that strained against the tight chamois. She outlined the hard ridge with the tips of her fingers, using feathery strokes that made him groan, and she saw the muscles in his stomach tighten as he forced himself to stand still.

Her strokes grew bolder, faster. Finally he could bear it no longer. He grasped her hand to stop the movement of her fingers, but held her palm hard against him. "Do you want it, Gabrielle?"

Her hand tightened around him for a moment, then she let him go. "Off with those breeches," she said huskily.

His eyes slitted half closed, his lips curled into an insolent smile. His hands rose to his waist. The breeches slid to the floor.

He took a step back, the better for her to see him. He stood before her proud in his manhood, proud in his need of her. And he let her look her fill.

In the muted light his eyes glowed silver. A muscle ticked in his clenched jaw, but she wasn't looking at his face. "Do you want it?" he demanded again, his voice rough.

Her eyelids drifted closed and she swayed slightly, as if she were about to swoon. She swallowed, nodded.

"Then say it."

"I . . . want it."

He lifted her in his arms and, swinging around, fell with her across the big tester bed.

They rolled over and over, back and forth across the broad width of it, their mouths locked together in a kiss that reverberated between them like a crack of thunder. He ended up on top, straddling her. He raised his head and looked down on her with eyes hard and hot with a hunger that seared her like a flame. She saw in his face all that he wanted to do to her, all that he would do, and her body began to tremble in an anticipation that was both joyous and fearful.

"Mine," he said. "You are mine, Gabrielle." And hooking his fingers into the top of her chemise, he ripped it off her.

Her breasts seemed to rise up to fill his hands. He kneaded them until they felt swollen, engorged. She watched his hands move over them, dark skin against white, roughness against softness. Her breaths were pushing out of her in harsh pants. And she felt his breath, fast and hot, against her neck. He lowered his head and licked the rounded curve of her breast where it rose in a swell beneath her arm. Then his mouth curled around, stroking underneath with his tongue, lips roaming up, climbing the gentle slope to capture the peak with his teeth. He drew the taut nipple into his mouth and a familiar and sweet, exquisite pain shot through her as he suckled and sucked like a babe.

"Max, oh, Max," she whispered, cradling his dark head

as he drew on her nipple, squeezing it between his lips. She felt a love for him so tender, tears filled her eyes.

He stroked her flank, following the contours of her body. In at her waist, out along the flare of hipbone and thigh. Spreading his fingers wide, he covered her stomach with his hand. He kept it there for a moment, flat against her womb, then slowly inched it lower until she began to quiver in anticipation of the moment when he would first touch her there—that tiny, throbbing knob of desire between her legs.

Even expecting it, wanting it, craving it, still she shuddered and gasped when at last, at last his fingers touched her. He rubbed and stroked her gently, slipping a finger inside her, then out, in, then out, and she writhed, arching up to press against his hand. There was a yawning emptiness inside of her that cried out for filling.

The yearning to feel him, to take him inside her, became a physical pain so that she began to whimper, "Please, please, please," and she grasped his hardness with her hands.

The breath left him in a keening moan. "Oh, dear God, Gabrielle . . ."

He pushed her legs apart roughly with his knees, and she spread them wider still, lifting her hips as he thrust into her. Her back arched rigidly as an explosion of desire tore through her, blotting out the universe, and the breath emptied from her lungs in a guttural cry.

She opened her eyes on his frightened face. "Gabrielle? Christ, did I hurt you?"

"No, no, no. Love me." She pulled him down against her, pressing on his buttocks to push him even deeper inside of her, relishing the exquisite feel of his thick, hard length filling her. "Love me."

Sealing her lips with his, he began to move inside her with hard, rhythmic thrusts, and her body joined with his, rising, falling, and rising again, each crest reaching higher and then higher than the last. The big bed began to shake, and the purple curtains quivered as the beat grew in tempo. Her fingers clutched at the velvet counterpane, twisting it into knots; her teeth clenched tightly together and her breath pushed out of her in harsh, rapid moans as she rocked with his driving thrusts. Harder, faster, higher he went, pulling her up after him, and when they reached the highest peak of all, they arrived there together.

With a muffled groan he fell across her, burying his face in her hair. She turned her head to see his profile. His eyes were still tightly clenched, his mouth partly open as his breath came out in short, harsh pants. Beneath her bare flesh she felt the velvet counterpane, sticky now with her sweat. Her heart raced and her limbs quivered with exhaustion. The weight of him pressing into her breasts made it difficult to breathe. But when he started to withdraw from her, she wrapped her legs around his hips to hold him in.

"Don't leave me," she said.

He braced himself up on his elbows to look at her. He lay his palms against her cheeks and kissed her slowly, gently. "I knew," he said, love in his voice, love in his eyes. "I knew it would be like that with you."

Gabrielle hadn't known it could be like that at all. But she couldn't find the words to tell him so.

Sighing happily, he rolled onto his back. They lay side by side, legs still entwined, for a long time in a companionable, satisfied silence, drifting in a sated state between sleep and awareness.

"Gabrielle," he murmured, nothing more. And he took her hand and placed it on his chest.

His flesh was warm, hard. It rose and fell with his breathing, and his heart beat against her palm. He seemed so strong, so alive, yet she knew how tenuous was anyone's hold on life. *Max* . . . His name filled her mind. *If I lose you, too* . . . But the thought was too terrible to finish.

She rose up to lay on her side facing him, her head braced on her fist. His male member, spent now, lay limp against his thigh. She remembered how he had felt inside her. His length, his thickness, his *difference,* had surprised her. She wanted to fondle it, to tease it back into hardness again, but shyness stopped her.

He saw what she was looking at and a smile curved his lips. "So you liked that, did you?"

She blushed and glanced away. Her hair fell forward and hit the side of his face.

He cupped her chin, forcing her head around. "Admit it, Gabrielle."

"I liked it."

"That's good, *ma mie*, because you're going to be getting a lot of it from now on."

Her blush deepened and she couldn't possibly meet his eyes. It seemed scandalous to talk about it so openly. Scandalous and exciting, and she wanted him again. Already.

"I know you want me, Gabrielle, and it isn't conceit that makes me say it. I want you just as much." He curled a hank of her hair around his fist. "I've wanted you like that, *ma mie*, from the first. I opened my door and there you were. Your hair was on fire and your eyes were snapping in anger— why were you angry?"

"You took so long to answer the door." And you were so incredibly handsome, she thought. It wasn't fair.

"Purple eyes," he said. "I'd never seen purple eyes before. I was instantly hard."

She sucked in a shocked breath. Laughing softly, he pulled her head forward until her mouth was a bare inch from his. "You came for *Fornication*, remember? You were lucky I didn't give it to you right there on the floor."

"Max!"

He pulled her down on him, rolling over at the same time and slamming his mouth down on hers in a fierce, bruising kiss. When the kiss ended every inch of her flesh felt aflame, alive with desire.

And he wanted her again. His manhood, pressing against her thigh, had begun to harden. He stroked between her legs, where she was slick and ready for him. He lowered his head to kiss her—

There was a timid knock on the door.

"Go away," Max said.

"Monsieur, madame?" came a faint, feminine voice. "My father thought you might be hungry."

Grunting, Max rolled away from her and pushed himself off the bed. She enjoyed watching the play of the muscles in his buttocks as he walked across the room—until she realized he was going to answer the door just as he was!

She sat up, snatching desperately at the counterpane in a vain attempt to at least cover herself as he pulled the door open. She heard the girl gasp and the crockery rattle.

"Thank you, mademoiselle," Max said, taking a tray of food from her hands—roasted fowl, bread, cheese, and wine. He turned away from the door, the tray balanced in one hand, and Gabrielle saw a round, pocked face crowned with braids, with two big round eyes and a huge round mouth. The eyes went from Max's partially erect manhood to Gabrielle, then back to Max.

"Oh, Jesu!" the girl cried, fleeing with a slam of the door.

"You are absolutely shameless, Maximilien de Saint-Just. And you embarrassed that poor girl—"

"She didn't see anything she hasn't seen before," he said matter-of-factly, setting the tray of food on a small stand by the bed.

Gabrielle went rigid. "Oh, really? And when, pray tell, did she see it before?"

A perplexed look crossed his face. Then a deep, delighted laugh rumbled from his chest. He knelt beside her on the bed, one knee between her legs, and leaned into her.

"You're jealous!"

She clutched the velvet material, bringing it up under her chin. "Don't be ridiculous . . . Was that girl your mistress?"

"I never saw her before in my life, you silly idiot. I only meant she couldn't have reached adulthood without seeing a naked man." He lowered his head to give her a hard, swift kiss. "How old were you when you saw your first yard, Gabrielle?"

Her eyes opened wide with shock at his frank language. "Max!"

He laughed, kissing her again. "Such outraged innocence!

Don't pretend you haven't heard that word before. That and a hundred different others. I didn't realize you Parisian shop-girls had such sheltered childhoods. I thought only a gentle-woman had to wait until her wedding night for a glimpse at a man's bayonet and balls.''

Gabrielle's cheeks burned and she was sure he could read the truth in her face. For of course he was right; she had heard all the words. What was the old saying—you can't sleep in the gutter and wake up clean? But she had been innocent once, too. And not so long ago. Even in Maman's house, with her lovers coming and going so freely at all hours, Ga-brielle had never seen a man without his clothes. Until Martin. She had been sixteen, and it had been her wedding night . . .

Tell him, she thought. Tell him now.

But Max had stood up again, turning away from her to pour wine into glasses from the jug on the tray. When he turned around to put the glass into her hand, there were still traces of laughter on his face.

He raised his glass to hers in a toast. "May this night last a hundred years and our love survive eternity," he said, his silky voice turning the words into a song of love, and she knew she couldn't tell him yet.

It was growing dark now, the shadows falling heavier in the room. She watched the movement of his throat as he drank. It gleamed with sweat for the air was still and hot. Her eyes moved over him possessively, savoring the fall of his hair against his neck as he tilted back his head, the flex of his shoulder and arm as he raised the glass to his lips, the ripple of the muscles that corded his stomach as he swal-lowed.

My husband, she thought. It filled her with a warm sense of security. It wasn't a feeling she was used to, and she was seized with a sudden and overwhelming fear of losing it. She brought the glass of wine to her lips, and her hand shook so badly the rim clattered against her teeth.

She felt his eyes on her, and when she looked up she saw that he was staring broodingly at the ring on her hand. She set her glass of wine back onto the tray and spread her fingers, really studying the ring for the first time. The band was thick, though worn, and etched into a flat oval of gold was the famous Saint-Just crest, a lion's head between two crossed swords.

The ring suddenly felt heavy on her hand, and she curled her fingers into a fist around it. "Did . . . did it belong to your father?" she asked, hoping that it did not, for she didn't want to be bound by another family heirloom.

"My father used to wear it. A long time ago." He sat down beside her on the bed, leaning back against the headboard and balancing the glass of wine against his stomach. He picked up her hand, rubbing his thumb over the etched metal of the ring. "He had it cut down to fit my mother. He gave it to her on the day they were wed."

"But I thought you said—"

"I did. The wedding was a sham, conducted by a phony priest hired by my father to play the part."

"Your father only pretended to marry your mother? But why?"

"Why do you think? She was beautiful and a virgin and he wanted her. But she wasn't of his class and he was already married anyway." His lips tightened into a bitter smile. "I suppose the randy bastard didn't want to bother with trying to seduce her honestly, so he pretended to go through with a marriage ceremony."

"What a wicked thing to do!"

"Wicked?" He laughed harshly. "He's the comte de Saint-Just and a *maréchal* of France. It made for an amusing anecdote to tell the king the next time they went hunting together." He turned his head to look at her, and through the dusky twilight she saw his face. She saw anger and shame, and the terrible hurt of a child who learned too young of evil and cruelty and sin.

"She died a whore, Gabrielle," he said, bitterness roughening his voice. "From a disease that whores get. But she never stopped loving the bastard. I can forgive her everything else, but not that."

He sat up abruptly and, bending one leg, leaned forward to pour some more wine. Tentatively she stroked his back, and when he didn't pull away from her, she pressed her face into his bare flesh. "I love you," she said. It seemed inadequate, but it was all she had to offer him.

It must have been enough, for after a moment he sighed, releasing a pent-up breath. He turned back to her, embracing her with one arm and pulling her against him. He stroked her hair, shutting his eyes. "Gabrielle," he said. It sounded like a prayer.

She held him, pressing his head against her breasts. She thought of mothers and sons. Dominique's love for her was unconditional now; she was the sun to his world. She wondered what he would hate her for when he became a man.

"What do you think Dominique will say when we tell him we are married?" she asked, voicing only one of her many fears.

Max squeezed her shoulders. "Dominique will be all right." He tossed back a swallow of wine. "He's bound to be a bit jealous at first, but he'll come around."

She raised her head from where she had tucked it into the hollow of his shoulder. "I've never spent a night away from him before."

"Simon will tell him something."

Agnes, she thought with a despairing laugh, had probably informed all of the Palais Royal that Gabrielle was spending the night with her lover. But Simon, Simon who had once named her the daughter he'd always wanted . . .

"Simon's probably frantic with worry."

The smile he gave her was suspiciously smug. "No, he isn't."

"How do you know he isn't?"

"Because he knows you're with me."

"You men think you know everything."

"We do."

"Hunh! Who says so?"

"I do."

She pretended to pout. "It seems I've wed myself to a bullying tyrant."

He slid his hand around her neck, pulling her head closer to his. His bent knee had fallen sideways against her breasts, and he moved it back and forth across her hardening nipples. "I'll bully you day and night if it makes you stick your lower lip out in that adorable fashion."

He took the lip in question between his teeth. He chewed on it lightly, then the kiss became more ardent, his tongue moving deep inside her mouth, and she tasted wine.

Something wet and cold splashed on Gabrielle's breasts. "Max! You're spilling . . ."

He pressed her back against the pillows and leaned over her. His eyes met hers, and her chest tightened at the look of desire, of raw, naked need, she saw in those sooty gray depths. She drew in a deep breath, and the pungent, rich aroma of wine filled her senses. Together they looked down, where two big red rivulets trickled through the valley between her breasts, spreading out onto her flat stomach. Slowly, while she watched, he lowered his head, and his tongue came out and licked the ruby liquid from her skin. Her eyes slid shut, and she began to drown in the rising, enveloping feel of him loving her.

His face rose above hers, and once again their eyes met.

I want you, his said.

Take me, hers answered.

He kept his eyes locked with hers as he dipped two fingers in the wine. He brought them, dripping with the sticky red juice, between her legs and pushed them deep inside her. She shuddered, her muscles jerking reflexively in surprise and pleasure. Then his head followed his fingers, licking up stray drops that had fallen on her stomach, moving lower and lower until she felt the exquisite shock of his tongue thrusting into her.

"Max!" She gasped as a jolt of white-hot sensation ripped through her like a flash of lightning.

She had seen pictures—the Palais Royal had several pornography shops that brazenly displayed their wares. Pictures of men doing this to women, and of women—

— Surely she shouldn't let him . . .

But she was letting him, for he was licking and sucking her sweet, slick cleft, and the jagged lightning bolts of pleasure came faster and hotter, until she didn't think she could bear it. She grasped his hair. "Please," she moaned, not sure if she was begging him to stop or go on.

He cupped her buttocks, lifting her. "Open to me, Gabrielle," he murmured, his breath hot, his lips moist against her. "Let me love you."

She surrendered then to the glorious, conquering assault of his mouth and lips and tongue. The canopy above her head began to whirl and licks of fire sizzled over her skin. He entered her at the peak of her climax so that it went on and on until her heart felt as if it were pressing against her chest, pushing against its fragile prison of bone and flesh, and she thought the inevitable explosion would surely kill her.

She opened her eyes to see his beloved face floating over her.

He cradled her head with gentle hands. "God, I do love you, wife."

Love for him filled her, so intense she felt smothered by it. Tears welled up in her eyes, and she squeezed her lids shut to hold them back.

But one escaped and he brushed it away with his thumb. "Gabrielle? Don't cry."

"Max, you shouldn't have done this. I shouldn't have let you."

He misunderstood. "There's nothing wrong or sinful in what we did. How could there be?"

She shook her head wildly, and the tears flowed freely now. "You shouldn't have married me. I'll only bring you trouble."

He held her tightly. "*Chérie*. There won't be any trouble. I've been a disgrace to the name of Saint-Just since my birth.

Even in my father's eyes this marriage will seem the least of my crimes.''

"No, no, you still don't understand."

"Then explain it to me."

She couldn't.

"Tell me, Gabrielle." He leaned over her. It was too dark now for her to see his face, but she didn't have to. She could feel her own fear emanating like sweat from the pores of her skin. "Tell me, Gabrielle. Tell me who you are." He said it softly, but he might as well have shouted, for the words were torn from his heart.

He was her husband and he was asking for her faith, her trust. And still she said nothing.

"Gabrielle . . . I love you. No matter what, I will always love you." It was his final plea.

Now, she thought. Tell him now.

And Max would . . . hate her.

He would hate her for not telling him sooner. He faced imprisonment and exile because of her, and he didn't even know it. She should have told him long ago, should have warned him to stay away from her. Instead she had married him, and now it was too late.

Because if he left her . . . She loved him so much, she couldn't bear—

Tell him.

—losing him. But she would survive. She had survived before, she could survive—

Tell him.

—almost anything, but not that. She couldn't survive losing Max.

Chapter 10

Gabrielle's grandfather had been a *galérien*, a galley slave.

For eight years Sébastien de Servien rowed the Mediterranean chained to an oar. Naked, his head shaven, ruled by the whip, he learned that only one thing mattered in this life—to survive.

It was a lesson he passed on to his daughter. And she in turn passed it on to Gabrielle.

Sébastien had been born a Noble of the Sword, one of his illustrious ancestors having won the title during the Crusades four centuries before. As the marquis de Servien, Sébastien could have attended the king's *coucher* had he so wished. But Sébastien disdained the frivolity, the licentiousness of court life. He had no desire to join the fawning multitudes at Versailles, begging for crumbs from the king's largess. Instead he stayed in his country château and worked his land along with his peasants and serfs. He was poor, poorer than many of his own tenants. Yet he was still their seigneur, their lord.

When he was thirty, Sébastien fell in love with a girl from a neighboring estate. The girl, Charlotte, was noble; she even had a dowry. But there was one not-so-insignificant problem—she was a Huguenot, a Protestant.

At that time the king was putting terrible pressure on the

Huguenots to give up their faith and convert to Catholicism. When the Huguenots tried to escape conversion by leaving France, the king forbade them to depart the country under pain of a life sentence to the galleys. Anyone, even aristocrats, foolish enough to aid or shelter a Huguenot was to receive the same sentence.

Sébastien didn't care about Huguenots or Catholicism or the king's laws. He wanted Charlotte in his bed and he saw that one sure way of getting her there would be to put her devoutly Huguenot father safely on board a ship bound for America. But they were caught by the king's men, and it was Sébastien who found himself on a ship—chained to an oar.

For eight years Sébastien endured the hell of the galleys. Then one day a great plague broke out in the port of Marseilles. The dead stacked up in the streets like cords of wood, for no one could be found to bury them. As the death toll mounted to one thousand a day, the provincial *intendant* became desperate. He offered the gruesome job of clearing the city of its dead to the galley slaves, who would earn their freedom if they survived the disease.

Sébastien survived.

He returned to his estate to find his fields overgrown with weeds, his manorial walls crumbling, and Charlotte waiting for him. They married and had one child—a daughter with the red-gold hair and violet eyes of her father. They named her Marie-Rose.

Her parents died together of a fever when Marie-Rose was fifteen. Alone and penniless, with nothing but her father's striking looks and his tough determination to survive, Marie-Rose left the crumbling Château de Servien and went to Paris. She took to the stage, creating such a sensation that the chef of the famous Café de Caveau named a dessert after her. Within three years she had acquired a titled husband, a daughter, and a rented *hôtel* on the Rue de Grenelle in the fashionable part of the Faubourg Saint-Germain. She had also accumulated enough debts to paper the walls of the palace at Versailles. The husband didn't last long, but the daughter and the debts remained.

Marie-Rose opened her salon to the elite of the artistic and literary world, and before long some of the most famous names of the time passed through her doors. Some found their way into her bed as well, and the gifts they gave her— the jewels and the silks and the money—all helped her and her daughter, Gabrielle, to survive. She never went to the court at Versailles; the court came to her.

Some of Gabrielle's earliest memories were of her mother's salon. The room, decorated in blue and silver, seemed to glitter with rich clothes and bright conversations. Until the early morning hours, poets recited their verses, writers read from their manuscripts. The *philosophes* argued among themselves about the power of reason, the general will, and the tyranny of kings. Everyone spoke about liberty.

But Gabrielle couldn't remember a time when she felt the carefree existence of a child. She grew up learning Latin and philosophy—and how to use a smile and a promise to get credit from a tightfisted shopkeeper. She could speak fluent Italian and do complicated sums—and she knew the location of every secondhand clothing store in Paris. She wore silk gowns in the latest fashion, while underneath, her chemise would be in tatters. She learned to pretend not to be hungry when lackeys dressed in fine livery would pass half-empty platters around her mother's table.

Gabrielle learned very young how to survive.

And then one day, the only son and heir to the duc de Nevers came to the salon on the Rue de Grenelle. There he saw Gabrielle, and there he fell in love.

I love you, Gabrielle.

The first time Martin de Nevers said those words was on a Sunday afternoon in January. They had been walking through the garden of the Tuileries, bundled up against the cold. The trees were bare, the dirt paths hard and frozen, and the fountains dry and clogged with dead leaves.

She didn't believe him. She was only sixteen, but already she knew love didn't really exist. It wasn't fashionable.

"La!" she exclaimed, laughing, teasing. She brushed her

fur muff against his pale, thin cheek. "I know how to play this game, monsieur. You protest your love and I protest my virtue. You protest your love again and I surrender my virtue."

He didn't laugh. He stood before her, with his narrow, earnest face and his wide-spaced hazel eyes looking hurt and a little sad. And she realized then that she did believe in love. She had to believe in it, for she loved him.

"I meant it, Gabrielle," he was saying, and the words condensed into vapor around his sensual lips. "If there was another way to say it, words that hadn't been used a thousand times before . . . but there isn't. All I can say is I love you." Suddenly he shocked her by kneeling at her feet. "Gabrielle . . . would you do me the honor of becoming my wife?"

"Jesu, Martin! What are you— For God's sake get up. People are starting to look at us."

He seized her hands. "Let them look. I want all of Paris to know that you are going to be my wife."

She pulled away from him, angry with him because she knew the only possible end to all of this was that she would be hurt. They lived in a society where the basest of immorality was condoned, but marrying beneath one's station was not.

"Don't be a silly fool, Martin. Monseigneur le Duc your father would never allow such a misalliance."

Martin stood, brushing bits of dirt and dead leaves off the knees of his satin breeches. "Why should he object? Your father was a Vauclair, your mother is a Servien. That's as good as a Nevers any day."

"My grandfather was a galley slave and my mother was an actress."

"And my great-grandmother was a scullery wench. Although we don't speak of it within the family." He tried to laugh, to gather her into his arms. "Gabrielle—"

"My mother takes lovers and I haven't got a dowry."

"And my father has had dozens of mistresses and he's got piles of money. Enough that he doesn't need a rich daughter-in-law. Once he sees you, once he meets you, he won't object to our marriage. I want you, Gabrielle, and my father has always given me what I want. Besides, I'm his only son. He doesn't have any choice.''

But in that Martin de Nevers was very wrong.

The duc de Nevers sent his lawyer Louvois to the house in the Rue de Grenelle. Gabrielle received him in the blue and silver salon.

She received him alone. ''If you insist on marrying this boy, *chérie,* Marie-Rose had said to her, ''then you must play the role out by yourself. If you don't mind very much, I shall only lend you my support by applauding loudly from the gallery.''

Gabrielle detested Louvois on sight.

She turned to face him as he entered, and it seemed at first that he was an insignificant man. Short and small-boned, he wore a plain coat and a short waistcoat and loose breeches. His shirt was without frills, his dark hair unpowdered and worn loose about his face. But as his protruding eyes stared unblinkingly at her from behind a pair of thick spectacles, her skin began to tingle as if a thousand ants nibbled at her flesh. She knew then that he was dangerous, and that she was afraid of him.

She lifted her chin. ''Before you speak, monsieur, I should tell you that Martin de Nevers has asked me to marry him, and I have accepted.''

''So Monseigneur le Duc has been informed. It is unacceptable.''

''To the duc perhaps, but not to me. And not to Martin. We love each other.''

Louvois inclined his head. ''Monsieur Martin needs his father's permission to marry. I am here to tell you that in your case it will not be forthcoming.'' A thin smile crossed his face. ''Go fish in other waters, Mademoiselle de Vauclair.''

Gabrielle said nothing.

Louvois sighed softly, assuming the look of a father exercising great patience with a trying offspring. ''You fail to understand. If Monsieur Martin elopes with you, he will be disinherited. His support will be cut off. The duc has promised this. It is no idle threat.''

''Then make it to Martin, not to me. I've managed to survive thus far without the goodwill of the duc de Nevers.''

''Ah . . .'' Again Louvois sighed. ''But you have yet to try surviving with his enmity.''

Gabrielle felt cold then, chilled with the premonition of the fear that was to come. She trembled slightly, and Louvois's watching eyes saw it.

''What will it take to convince you to look elsewhere for a husband?'' he asked softly.

Gabrielle smiled. ''Just what sort of incentives are you offering me?''

An expression of disappointment might have flashed across the lawyer's face as he stared at her. Then, looking away, he dipped two long, white fingers into the pocket of his waistcoat to withdraw a stiff, folded piece of paper. He handed it to Gabrielle.

It was a bank note.

Gabrielle had rarely seen one. They weren't used often, for the French had little faith in forms of currency whose worth couldn't be tested with the bite of a strong pair of teeth. The piece of paper Gabrielle held in her hands claimed to be worth one hundred livres.

''There are five hundred more bank notes where that came from,'' Louvois said. ''Fifty thousand livres. Is that sufficient incentive, mademoiselle?''

''It is indeed a lot of money,'' Gabrielle said, and Louvois smiled.

But his smile began to fade as she ripped the paper in half, then in half again. Ripped until the pieces were the size of coins and then let them slip through her fingers onto the carpet like flakes of snow.

She looked up and met the lawyer's dark, angry eyes. ''Tell your master, lackey, that I cannot be bought.''

He took a step forward until he was right in front of her. Grasping her chin between his thumb and forefinger, he lifted her face, squeezing until tears started in her eyes. But she didn't pull away or make a sound.

"You're a haughty little aristocratic bitch, aren't you?" he said with a sneer. "But everyone has a price, Gabrielle de Vauclair. Someday I will discover yours. And when I do, I will use it to destroy you."

They were married.

They took the stagecoach to a small village in the province of Lorraine, where a priest could be found who was removed enough from the Nevers's power not to be afraid of it. He married them in the church before God and before the law. *And what God has joined*, he said, *let no man put asunder*.

Until that moment Gabrielle had never believed it would really happen. She didn't think Martin had the strength of will to stand up to his father. When she saw that he had, when he placed his mother's sapphire ring on her finger as proof of it, she thought this must make her love him all the more.

That night, in a posting house, they made love for the first time.

Gabrielle sat fully clothed on the bed. Her hands were clenched into fists on her lap and she twisted the sapphire ring around and around her finger. Martin shut the door to their room and came to stand before her.

"Gabrielle . . . what is wrong? Are you sorry now—"

She laughed shakily, thrusting herself to her feet. *"Dieu,* what do you think? I'm nervous. I've never done this before." She looked up and saw her own fears reflected in his face.

Bright splashes of color appeared on his thin, pale cheeks. "I haven't done it before, either."

"You haven't?" She was surprised. He was eighteen, after all. That wasn't so young. For a man.

"I was going to before tonight," he said. "With a whore. So that I wouldn't make a complete fool of myself. But then it seemed, I don't know . . ." He shrugged. "Pointless. I don't want to make love to anyone but you."

"Well . . ." She stroked his cheek, forcing a smile. "We'll figure it out together. It surely can't be that complicated."

She turned around and lifted her hair off her back, bending her head. For a long moment he did nothing, and Gabrielle's false bravado began to crack. Deep inside herself she was worried she would be a failure at this, that she would displease him. She was married to this man now. Forever. Suddenly she was afraid she knew him not at all.

At last he pressed his lips on the protruding knob of bone at her bowed neck. But only for a moment before she heard him sigh raggedly and step away from her.

She kept her head bent, her back to him, unsure now of what to do. He's even more frightened than I am, she thought. She felt an odd sense of loss, as if she had suddenly discovered that what she thought was a diamond was really paste. She'd had to be so tough and self-reliant, so strong, all her young life. She wanted Martin to be someone she could lean on, who would be strong for her, and a part of her knew already he would never be that man.

But he was her husband, and she loved him, didn't she? I do love Martin, she told herself fiercely, trying to banish the unwelcome feelings of disappointment. I love him. I do, I do, I do . . .

"Martin . . ." she said tentatively, still unable to look at him. "I think you begin by undressing me."

She had dressed very formally for her wedding, in a gown with stays built into the bodice and a heavily embroidered stomacher fastened to the front of it. It was stiff and heavy, like an armored breastplate. He laughed nervously, saying it seemed an impossible puzzle to get her out of it as he fumbled with the hooks and laces.

But finally the gown was gone, tossed over the end of the bed. Her petticoats followed, much easier, and the wire pannier hoop that stiffened her skirts. More armor, she thought with an inward smile. She reached down herself and pulled the chemise over her head, letting it fall to the floor from the outstretched tips of her fingers. She stood before him, naked but for her shoes and stockings.

His face became transformed; a strange light flared in his eyes and his breathing quickened. The way he now looked at her made her feel suddenly shy and embarrassed. She tried to cover herself with her hands, and the sapphire stone of the ring he had given her winked like a blue flame against her skin as it caught the candlelight.

"Oh, God." His voice cracked. "You are so beautiful."

He reached out and tentatively stroked one breast. Her skin began to quiver at his touch. The muscles in her belly tightened and she felt a strange ache deep inside her. "They're too small," she said, worried about this major flaw, worried that she would displease him.

"No . . ." He rubbed his palm over her nipple and she felt it tighten, harden, and the strange ache intensified until she had to clench her teeth to keep from moaning aloud. "They're not too small," he said as he cupped both her breasts now in his palms, although now she could barely hear him, for her blood was pumping so hard, pounding in her ears. "They're just right."

Instinctively she looked down and saw that he had hardened as well, for there was a prominent ridge at his groin outlined by his clinging satin breeches. A frisson of excitement, of anticipation, rippled through her.

"Martin . . ." She swayed into him.

He gathered her into his arms, but gingerly as if he were trying to embrace a cloud, as if he were afraid suddenly of his own strength, afraid that he might hurt her. Unknowingly she rubbed her stomach against his, wanting something, needing something, but not sure what it was.

A kiss . . . She yearned for him to kiss her, and she turned her face up, putting her lips to his.

They had kissed before, but this was different. This time he ground his lips hard against hers and pushed his tongue between her teeth. Surprised, she stiffened, and he started to break the kiss and pull away. "No . . ." she protested, and pressed her palm to the back of his head, holding his mouth within reach of hers.

Tentatively she thrust her own tongue through his lips. The inside of his mouth was soft, slick. This is wonderful, she thought, as the kiss deepened and the sensations of sexual hunger and desire coursed through her. Absolutely wonderful.

Her hands moved restlessly over his arms, his shoulders, across his back, feeling, seeking. She pulled her mouth free of his. "Your coat," she whispered. "I want to touch you. Take off your coat."

He almost ripped the seams in his hurry to get it off. Laughing, pleased with herself because she was exciting him, she helped him with his shirt, easing it slowly down over his shoulders, her hands tracing the contours of the muscles in his arms. She pressed her lips on his collarbone, ran her palms across his bare chest, his breasts. His nipples, too, were hard.

Her hands drifted lower, toward the straining bulge in his tight breeches. She touched it with the tips of her fingers.

He jerked back, as if her touch was a lick of fire.

She looked up at him, a question on her face. "Martin?"

A funny, strangling sound erupted from his throat. He crushed her hard against him, knocking the breath out of her. He covered her face and throat with kisses while she pushed against him, gasping, trying to suck air into her lungs. He kneaded her breasts roughly with his fingers, hurting her now. In her struggles to get free, to get air, she rubbed her pelvis against the hard bulge between his legs.

Groaning, he fell onto the bed, bringing her down with him, rolling her over onto her back. Frightened now, she pushed against his chest. But he had her pinned down with his shoulder, pressing into her lungs. "Please, Martin," she gasped. "I can't breathe . . ."

He didn't seem to hear her. He wrenched at the buttons of his breeches, freeing himself, and heaved a shuddering sigh. She got a brief glimpse of his male member rising up out of the nest of hair between his legs. She felt a confusion of emotions. She was frightened yet drawn to what she saw, both at the same time. She wanted to touch it, to close her hand around its length and feel its hardness, but she didn't dare.

When he pressed his knees against her thighs, trying to spread her legs, she instinctively opened them for him. He jabbed at her several times with his erection, but he kept missing. So he explored her with his fingers until he found her opening. She gasped, almost screaming with the exquisite shock of his fingers pressing into her.

She shuddered and arched her back. "Oh, Martin . . ."

"Gabrielle, I want you," he panted harshly against her face. "I have to—"

He thrust into her. She cried out as she felt something tear inside her, and her legs stiffened, scissoring together. He thrust into her once more, harder, and then he went suddenly limp.

He fell in a dead weight on top of her, his breath coming in harsh gasps. Dazed, she lay inert beneath him, and after a moment he rolled off her, sitting up.

She felt a wetness on her thighs. She pushed herself up on her elbows. There was blood between her legs and on the counterpane, and there was a strange, hollow feeling inside of her. She felt an odd and terrible loneliness, and out of nowhere tears rose up to fill her eyes.

Slowly she turned her head and looked at him. She saw shock on his face, and guilt. And then, to her surprise, his shoulders shook and he began to cry.

"I'm sorry," he said, muffling the words as he buried his head in his hands. "Oh, God, Gabrielle, I've hurt you."

"It's . . . it's all right, Martin," she said. And then she actually smiled, for she knew it probably would be all right. She would make it all right.

He shook his head wildly back and forth. "No. I hurt you."

"It's all right."

He took her hand; his own was trembling. When she didn't pull away, he brought her hand to his lips. He stretched out beside her, and after a moment she turned into him so that she was encircled by his arms.

"Oh, God, Gabrielle, I've hurt you." His voice caught. "I love you so much and I've hurt you." He stroked her hair. "Don't be afraid of me. I couldn't bear it if I thought you were afraid of me."

"I'm not afraid of you," she said. Although her body felt pummeled and she ached between her legs, she wasn't afraid of him. Her maman had warned her the first time could be painful and awkward. "He's such a babe," Marie-Rose had said. "If he's had any experience at all, it's been with the wrong sort of woman. You must teach him to be gentle, *ma petite.*"

"I'll never touch you again," Martin vowed fervently, and Gabrielle knew that he honestly believed in that moment that he wouldn't. But she also knew that in time his need would overcome his guilt and he would take her again, as was his right, for he was her husband. And she remembered how wonderful it had felt at the beginning, when he had touched her breasts and kissed her.

She brought his hand to her breast. "Touch me now, Martin. Gently."

He died in the spring.

The doctor said it was a flux of the blood. The surgeon was summoned to bleed and purge him. The doctor prescribed a quinine treatment, but the treatment was expensive. Marie-Rose, looking at Gabrielle's white, pinched face, said she would take her ruby earrings to the jewelers on the Rue Vendôme to see what price she could get for them.

They had no money. No one, certainly not Martin, had fully anticipated the extent of the duc de Nevers's wrath. They lived with Marie-Rose in the *hôtel* on the Rue de Grenelle, but no one came any longer to the salon, and the dunning shopkeepers were no longer so easily put off. The bourgeois businessman who owned the house delivered an eviction notice. The furniture, the china and crystal, the paintings began to disappear, first in dribbles and then in a steady stream, to the creditors and the pawnshops.

The servants and lackeys had been the first to go. "Rats deserting a sinking ship," Marie-Rose had said with a sneer. It was the same sneer Sébastien had often given to the man who patrolled the deck with his bullwhip.

The duc de Nevers entered petitions with the church in Rome and with the courts in Paris to have the marriage dissolved. But the Vatican and the courts were slow, and Martin died first.

Gabrielle sat in the twilight shadows afterward, holding his hand long after his flesh had cooled. Her face was white, her lips bloodless, her eyes gritty and dry. She hurt too deeply to cry.

She ignored the knock on the door. The house was empty; her mother had gone to sell the last of her jewelry to buy the quinine which was no longer needed. She didn't hear the step on the stairs until the man entered the room.

It was Louvois.

He stared at the boy's body, and though he couldn't possibly have expected Martin's death, no emotion, not even surprise, showed on his face. Gabrielle stood up, instinctively putting herself between Louvois and the bed.

Louvois's protruding eyes fastened on hers. He blinked, then stepped around her.

He stared at the body for a moment. Then striking a tinderbox, he lit the single candle in a brass holder on a stand near the bed. He held the candle up to Martin's face, pried open one eyelid. He held his palm to Martin's lips, then set the candle back on the bedstand and turned to face her.

"He's dead," Louvois said.

Gabrielle flung her head up. "The duc should be pleased," she said, not bothering to hide her bitterness. "It seems a higher order than his has seen fit to end his son's marriage."

Louvois raised his brows and bowed mockingly. "Please accept my condolences over your sudden bereavement, but I've not yet told you why I've come." His eyes sparkled with malice behind the magnifying lenses. "I have distressing news for you . . . further distressing news. Your mother—"

Gabrielle wondered how she could stand it. She felt her knees begin to buckle and grasped the bedpost. Louvois didn't move, although he watched her carefully.

"Your mother," he went on, "was struck and killed by a cabriolet this afternoon while crossing the Rue Vendôme. She had just sold some jewelry, did you know?" His eyes flickered to the bed, then back to her. "Your mother's body is now in the hands of the police. There is some question as to whether the jewelry was in fact stolen goods in the first place—"

Gabrielle covered her ears with her hands. "Leave me alone. Go away," she gasped.

Louvois grasped her wrists, yanking her hands down. Then his eye caught sight of the ring on her finger and he jerked her wrist back up, pulling her hand beneath the light cast by the candle on the bedstand. "This ring belongs to the duchesse—"

Gabrielle jerked her hand free, her fist clenching tightly. "Get out of here."

"Did you know that poor Monsieur Martin wrote to his father the duc last week?" Louvois said, smiling. "A very touching letter. The boy was weakening, I think. He would not have stayed with you much longer."

Gabrielle thought she might be sick, and she was suddenly very cold. She set her teeth together to keep them from chattering.

"He wrote his father that you are with child. Is this true?"

Gabrielle swallowed. "I . . . yes."

Louvois looked back to the body of the boy on the bed, and pressed his lips tightly together. "This changes things," he said.

Gabrielle put her hands to her mouth. She thought she would probably start screaming soon and when she did she would not be able to stop.

She had them buried together.

She wanted to watch while the gravediggers filled in the

holes. The curé had thought it a macabre request, but he had allowed it. The poor child had lost a husband and a mother both on the same day. He had never seen such terrible grief before. It was all the more terrible for being so inward, so silent.

Gabrielle stood beside the open graves. The shovels scraped against the gravelly earth, and the clods of dirt made clunking noises as they landed on the wooden caskets. It was a beautiful spring day. The breeze was a warm caress on the skin, the azure sky cloudless and infinite.

A black berlin pulled up alongside the wrought-iron fence of the cemetery. The postilions and grooms wore black and gold livery. The carriage door was opened, the steps were lowered, and a small, bespectacled man got out.

She didn't acknowledge him, even when he came to stand right next to her, so close the sleeve of his coat brushed against her arm.

"He was always sickly as a child," Louvois said, looking at the graves. "Although we hoped he had outgrown it in the last few years."

"I hate you," she said.

"I know." His eyes glimmered brightly behind his spectacles, as if he enjoyed hearing her admit it. "I've come to tell you what will be."

Gabrielle turned and walked away from the graves, away from him, down a flagstone path toward the cemetery gates.

He caught up with her. "Monseigneur le Duc has dropped his petitions to end your marriage."

"How forgiving of him."

"He wants his grandchild."

"I'll see him in hell first."

Two of the postilions, she saw, had abandoned the carriage and were passing through the cemetery gate, coming slowly down the path.

She turned her back on them and went to sit on a rickety wooden bench beneath a tree. Louvois sat beside her. The lackeys stopped, hovering in the distance by the gate.

Louvois turned sideways so he could watch her face. "After the boy is born—"

"It could be a girl."

"The duc has decreed that it will be a boy." He said it wryly, smiling. Then his face abruptly hardened. Reaching into his pocket, he pulled out a thick piece of paper embossed with a seal. "Do you know what this is?"

She knew. It was a *lettre de cachet*.

"It has your name on it, Gabrielle. Signed by the king."

Her eyes flickered over to the lackeys and her lips curled into a sneer. "You require a lot of help, monsieur, to arrest one insignificant woman."

For a moment Louvois's control slipped. "You won't be arrested as long as you cooperate." Then his voice softened. "Think, Gabrielle. It is spring now, but the child is due when—in November? Would you want to whelp your bastard on a prison's stone floor in winter? Do you think either of you would survive?"

Gabrielle nudged a chipped piece of stone with her shoe. Idly she bent over and picked it up, running her fingers over its sharp edges. She thought of the lackeys lingering by the gate, but she didn't look at them again.

"What must I do?" she said, and Louvois smiled, for he heard resignation in her voice.

"You will come with me now."

"No."

"You will spend your confinement with the duchesse at the Château de Nevers," Louvois went on, relentless. "Naturally, you will never marry again. The king has forbidden it. Instead, once the child is born you will be given a dowry, a substantial dowry, and placed in a convent. It won't be so bad, not as bad as you think. Surely not as bad as the Bastille and an early death. You could be an abbess someday if you worked at it. You've got the ambition and you're tough enough to do it."

"No."

"You will have no contact with the child. When he is old

enough, he will be told you died. You will never see or even speak of him again.''

''No.''

''Gabrielle, Gabrielle,'' he said softly, like a lover. ''This is no longer a question of choice. This is what will be.''

''No!'' she screamed, slashing at his face with the jagged piece of stone, slashing until his scream joined hers, shattering the silence of the cemetery, slashing until the startled lackeys started toward her.

And then she ran.

Chapter 11

    "**G**et that bloody ass out of my yard! He's eating my roses, the bloody greedy-gut!"

Gabrielle moaned and pulled the pillow over her head.

A tormented scream filled the room—the sound of a damned soul getting its first lick of hellfire. Gabrielle sat up with a start, pushing a tangled curtain of golden-red curls out of her eyes. The scream turned into a bawl and was soon drowned out by a man's angry bellows. "Out! Get him out!"

Gabrielle started to get out of bed, then fell back against the pillows with a groan. Her body felt like a wine grape at harvest time, pummeled and trampled into liquid mush. She looked up with blurry eyes at a garish purple canopy, and for a moment had no idea where she was or what she was doing there. Then memories of the night filled her mind, overwhelming her with a tidal wave of happiness.

Max. His name was a hosanna in her heart. She ran her hands down her body, over her breasts, across her hips, but it was a stranger's skin she felt; a stranger's blood pumped through her veins. His touch had branded her flesh. She no longer belonged to herself; she was his now. She sat up and looked around her with wonder. Sunlight filled the room, brighter than sunlight had a right to be. The morning air was too soft to bear. She breathed and his love gave her life. *Max, my lover, my husband*, she thought. *My joy.*

The source of her joy, however, was not in her bed, nor even in the room. Before she could start to wonder where he was, another loud, throaty bray assaulted her eardrums. She eased her legs over the side of the bed and, getting up with a slow stretch, hobbled over to the window. She had to see what poor beast or soul was being tortured on such a bright, wonderful, beautiful morning.

She peeked out the jalousie shutters into the yard, where a youth was pulling at the head of a gray donkey while the innkeeper shouted and danced around them, swatting at the donkey's bald rump with a flat stick. The donkey seemed oblivious to the turmoil he was causing. He stood unmoving, feet spread wide, one ear up and one down, pink rose petals trickling from his grinning mouth.

Gabrielle started to giggle. Soon her rich, throaty laughter filled the room. "Max!" she sang out loud. She whirled away from the window, hugging herself, letting the happiness flood her whole being. "Max, Max, Max," she sang as she twirled, louder and faster, "Max, Max—"

She stopped, suddenly self-conscious. What if he had come in just now and caught her dancing naked around the room and shouting his name like a demented hen-hussy? He'd wonder what had ever possessed him to wed such an idiot. Where was he, anyway?

She looked around the room, searching for something of his that was proof he was coming back. There was clothing scattered all over the floor; it was all hers.

With a hand that trembled, she picked up the chemise at her feet. It had been torn in two. She remembered the look on his face in the moment before he had ripped away this last barrier that stood between him and his final possession of her body. She had seen passion and hunger blazing from his eyes, but had there been love?

She thought of the story Max had told her about his father bedding a reluctant virgin through trickery. Had that merely been a slice of his past shared with her after the intimacy of lovemaking? Or had it been some sort of a confession? Surely Max couldn't have arranged for the aerostat to start leaking right over this particular village, her heart protested. *Of course he could have*, her mind answered. But fat Father Benoit with his funny nose, surely he's a genuine priest, her heart insisted. *He could be anyone*, her mind scoffed. Max loves me, her heart proclaimed. *He wanted you*, her mind jeered, *and now he's had you, so what's to keep him around?*

"No!" she cried, burying her face in the torn chemise. It smelled of him, tangy and musky, and she was utterly convinced now that he was gone. People she loved were always leaving her.

Her head flung up at the scrape of a step in the hall. The door opened and Max entered the room. He stopped just inside, pausing to look at her before shutting the door with his heel. She drank in the sight of his beloved face, and her heart plummeted, for his eyes were flat and cold, like gunmetal, and his mouth was pulled taut into a disapproving frown.

He took a step toward her, then another, and Gabrielle backed up until she was pressed into the window. Her muscles tensed, preparing to carry her up and over the bed, when he reached out and enveloped her in his arms . . . and at his first touch she knew she had indeed been behaving like a foolish, fearful child.

"You're shivering, *ma mie*," he said gently. "What are you doing up and about and looking so gloriously naked?"

She laughed, too loudly, feeling relieved and nervous and shy. "I'm in a sad state of deshabille this morning, monsieur. It seems you spent all of yesterday ripping the clothes from my back piece by piece. I've little but rags left."

He smiled down at her. "I'll buy you an armoire full of things as soon as we get back to Paris. I'll dress you like a queen, and Marie Antoinette will turn green as a spring apple with envy."

It was his first smile of the day and its gentleness warmed her. She pressed her face against his chest and burrowed deeper into his arms. How solid he felt, how strong. "You make rash promises, my husband. There'll come a day, and soon I'll wager, when you'll be scolding me for spending all your money on feminine fripperies."

He pushed her hair off her neck and began to nibble at the tender spot below her jaw. A spasm of pure pleasure shot through her clear down to her toes.

"Now that I think on it," he said, his breath caressing her tingling skin. "I should keep you just the way you are at this moment." He ran his hands down her bare flanks to cup her buttocks, pulling her against him so that she could feel his arousal. "Gowns and corsets and other such nonsense would only get in my way—"

An agonized wail blasted through the window. Max's head jerked back and his arms tightened around her. "Good Lord, what is that awful racket? It sounds as if someone's trying to tie a cat into knots."

Laughter spilled out of Gabrielle. She bracketed his face with her palms and pulled his mouth down within reach of her lips. "It's a donkey. He's eating roses for breakfast."

"Lucky donkey," he said, a smile in his voice.

His lips molded with hers, feeling so warm and firm, so right. He fell backward onto the ravaged bed, bringing her down with him and rolling over so that she was pressed into the piles of rumpled, tangled bedclothes. He pulled back to look at her, tracing her face with his fingertips—eyes, nose, lips, down the column of her neck to her right breast. He flattened it with his hand, rubbing the nipple into an almost painful tautness.

"And lucky me," he said, before his mouth descended to claim hers once again.

They had a very late breakfast of coffee and *mignonettes* in the taproom. The innkeeper had just cleared away the plates when Father Benoit entered, sneezing and rubbing his nose, and carrying a large, moldy black book with a pen and ink pot balanced carefully on top.

He squeezed his bulk down on the bench next to Max, opposite Gabrielle. "Good morning, my children!" he exclaimed in his booming voice. "I hope you haven't forgotten about signing the register. And we must fill out the proper documents. The *intendant* for these parts is very strict. Also there are, er"—he cast an apologetic eye at Max—"certain fees to be collected." He chuckled as he dipped the tip of the quill into the ink. "God, I assure you, Monsieur de Saint-Just, is more than satisfied with your generosity, but now Caesar must be rendered his due, eh?" He opened the thick black book and, pen poised, fixed Gabrielle with a stern gaze. "Name!" he barked.

"Gabrielle Prion," Max answered for her. She could feel his eyes carefully watching her. He loved her, she knew, but after last night he trusted her not at all. And who could blame him—for she had told him nothing. She had cried and he had held her, and then they had made love. But she hadn't told him the reason for her tears, and he had not risked his pride by asking her again.

Would the marriage be valid, she now wondered, if she used a false name?

"Actually, Prion is not . . . that is to say, my given name is Gabrielle Marie Vauclair," she said to the priest, although she watched Max as carefully as he had watched her. If the name meant anything to him, he didn't show it, and she breathed an internal sigh of relief. Perhaps he hadn't even been in Paris that year she had scandalized society by eloping with the son of the duc de Nevers. But then she hadn't given the telltale "de" with her last name, which would have marked her as the daughter of a gentleman. The "de"—that coveted badge of nobility that had been throughout Gabrielle's life more of a curse than a blessing.

The priest, certainly, was satisfied with her answer. He printed it out laboriously in his black book and on various documents. She and Max both signed their names numerous times, and then Max counted out another twenty-five livres to cover the fees and bribes which would be needed to smooth over the recording of such a hasty marriage.

They left Chênaie-sur-Seine soon afterward, taking the Paris road. The sun was a hot, white ball high in the sky, and their bare feet stirred up puffs of dust behind them. Since the curé had intruded on their breakfast with his black book, Max had said not one word to her beyond the polite necessities. Now Gabrielle wondered if he intended for them to walk all the way back to Paris. Perhaps between them, the innkeeper and Father Benoit had cleaned out Max's purse, leaving him no money with which to rent a cart or carriage. She wondered, but she didn't dare ask anything of this distant stranger who now walked in silence beside her.

About two miles outside the village, Max stopped at the top of a rise. It was not too far from the field where they had been dumped from the aerostat the day before, and in fact she could see part of the vividly striped envelope through the stand of pines that had been their undoing.

Max turned off the road and went to throw himself down beneath the shade of a lone, leafy oak tree. Gabrielle stood where she was, staring after him with exasperation. They would never make it back to Paris if he stopped like this to rest every few feet.

"Max, why are you sitting under that tree?" she demanded.

"Because it's much cooler here than standing out on that hot, dusty road. Why don't you join me?"

She took several steps toward him then stopped at the edge of the shade. There was no mistaking the meaning of *that* particular gleam in his eye. "There are men over there working in the fields," she said, pointing behind him.

He gave her a slow, lazy smile. "What of it?"

"They'll be able to *see* us, Max. Making love out in the wide open like a pair of . . . of . . ." She stopped, unable to go on as the blood rushed to her already flushed cheeks.

He threw back his head in laughter. The sunlight glinted off his white teeth and burnished his dark hair to a rich walnut color, and the sight of him did something funny to her chest.

"Gabrielle, Gabrielle, for shame, you lusty wench," he taunted, his laughter winding down. "Are you asking for your love *al fresco* this time? Your daring astonishes me. Not to mention your energy."

She sucked in an indignant breath. "I wasn't asking—"

"You were hinting."

"I was not! You were the one who was leering at me with that look you get."

He screwed his face into what he evidently thought was the picture of cherubic innocence. "What look?"

She bit back a giggle. "You know the look I mean."

His features metamorphosed suddenly into those of a lunatic rapist overcome with lust, and he lunged to his feet. Gabrielle shrieked and whirled around, but not fast enough, for he was on her in two strides.

Laughing, he seized her around the waist and lifted her, whirling her around and around until tree and sky and field blended into a stream of color. When he put her down on her feet she had to clutch his arm to keep from falling while the world went on spinning dizzily.

He laced his hands in the small of her back and pressed her tightly against him. "Come sit beside me, my sweet seductress," he whispered, in that silky way of talking that turned her muscles to mush.

"*You* are the seducer," she protested, knowing he was doing it to her even now.

He brushed his lips lightly over her ear. "Only because I find you so completely irresistible. But I promise to control my lecherous inclinations, if you'll control yours. I would remind you, Gabrielle," he pointed out with affronted indignation, "that there are men working right over there in the fields."

She surrendered, laughing and leaning into him, luxuriating in the feel of his strong arms holding her. It *was* rather hot and dusty out on the road. She let him lead her beneath the tree and settled beside him within the crook of his arm.

He began to toy with her hair, brushing a curl back and forth across her cheek. It tickled a little, but pleasantly. His chest was warm and solid beneath her back, and she could feel the steady beat of his heart. She stretched her legs out straight in front of her. One of her thighs pressed against his and she felt him tense, his breathing quicken. Secretly she was pleased with this power she had to make him want her.

Smiling happily, she wriggled her toes. Already her feet

were bruised and covered with dust. "How far away are we from Paris, do you think?" she asked.

"Four, maybe five hours' ride by coach," he answered. His thumb began to stroke the cord of muscle in her neck. Slowly down to her shoulder, slowly up to her ear. Down, then up, down, up . . .

Gabrielle's stomach muscles started fluttering and her heart beat faster. "Then why . . ." She stopped, forgetting what she had been about to say. His arm had shifted. It was draped over the top of her shoulder now, his hand dangling near her breast, though not touching it. She sucked in a deep breath and her breast rose up. Her nipple, visibly hard beneath the material of her bodice, brushed against his curled knuckles.

She took another, deeper breath. And then another. "Why have we stopped so soon?" she asked. She trembled, and her hand, which had been resting in her lap, sort of accidentally drifted onto his thigh. "It'll take us weeks to walk to Paris at this rate."

The muscle of his thigh hardened and she felt his heart do a funny stutter step. "Silly goose," he said, his voice slightly rough. "I've no intention of walking to Paris."

He turned his head and began to plant gentle kisses along the side of her face. His fingers inched beneath her bodice, easily finding the bare flesh of her breast, with no corset or chemise to hinder him.

"But then how . . . Oh, Max, don't . . . I can't think when you . . ." Gabrielle's senses began to whirl, as if she were again being spun around and around—

A loud bray echoed across the fields and Gabrielle pulled away from Max with a guilty start. The mangy gray donkey with a taste for horticultural products strolled right past them on the road, driven by a youth who grinned and hooted at them, making a suggestive gesture with his fist. The donkey, Gabrielle saw, had a rosebud tucked into his halter, and the drooping petals couldn't have been any pinker than the flush of embarrassment that stained her cheeks.

She felt the rumble of Max's laughter against her back. She turned to face him, shaking a wifely finger under his nose. "Maximilien de Saint-Just, this is all your fault. You promised you would behave yourself."

"I lied."

"You are devious, shameless, truly diabolical—"

"And wicked," he added helpfully.

"Most definitely wicked." She tried to glare at him, but her mouth betrayed her, dancing up into a smile. "But you make love like an angel."

"Angels are celibate creatures, *ma mie.*"

She leaned over and gave him a sweet, chaste kiss on the lips. "Then perhaps you should pray to them for inspiration—when next you make promises you find difficult to keep."

His arms went around her, gathering her to him, and he buried his face in the curve of her neck. "I really did think I could just sit here and hold you, Gabrielle." He laughed softly. "Especially after making love with you all last night and most of the morning. But it seems that no sooner am I done having you than I want you again."

Of course she understood, for it was the same with her. "But will you want me as much a year from now?" she asked, only able to do so because his face was still buried in her neck.

He nuzzled her with his chin. "I'll want you fifty years from now."

"Hunh. I'll be an old crone then. All wrinkled and toothless."

She felt him smile. "Good. Then no other man will fancy you and I won't have to worry about keeping you all to myself."

They held each other in silence, then he grasped her shoulders and set her away from him. "Gabrielle, there are things we must discuss."

A cramp twisted her stomach. "What . . . what things?"

He gave her a hard, searching look, and she stopped breathing. Then his eyes focused on something behind her and a strange emotion crossed his face. She thought it almost might have been relief.

"Here's our transportation back to Paris," he said.

Gabrielle turned. Coming up the road from the direction of the village was a gypsy caravan, its colorful wagons corded tightly one behind the other like a beaded necklace. Max stood up and waved his arm, and a horse and rider broke away, cantering toward them.

The horse, a magnificent roan stallion, danced to a stop in front of them, rearing up on his hind legs. The rider looked down at Gabrielle, and his face registered surprise, then his attention turned to Max. His teeth flashed white in his dark face. "You didn't get far," he said. "I've been looking for you ever since Provins."

It was the man Gabrielle had last seen beside a wagon loaded with contraband salt. The man who thought she had seen too much.

"The envelope developed a leak," Max said. "We came down sooner than I'd planned. It's in a field not far from here. I'd like to salvage what's left of it if I can."

"But of course." The gypsy nodded at Gabrielle with his chin. "What's she doing here?"

"She's my wife," Max said, an edge to his voice.

The gypsy's eyes widened slightly, then a mask descended over his features. "You have my felicitations, *mon frère.*"

He turned his horse around and trotted back toward the caravan. Max started to follow, but Gabrielle grabbed his arm.

"What are they doing here—those gypsies?"

"I told you. They're our transportation back to Paris. I arranged it."

Impatient, he started to walk away again, but she held him back. "How? How could you have known we would be here?"

"I didn't know we would wind up *here* precisely. I knew generally in which direction the aerostat would sail because of the prevailing wind currents, and I asked Prado to start looking for us northwest of Provins."

As she watched him walk down the road toward the cara-van, she felt anger and confusion and an odd sense of betrayal. Why hadn't he told her about the gypsies before this? He was too good at *arranging* things. And if she still had secrets from him, who was to say he'd kept no secrets from her? She called him husband, but what did she know of Maximilien de Saint-Just? Only every inch of his body and what he had chosen to tell her about himself, which amounted to very little indeed.

About as much, her conscience nagged, as he knows about you.

Gabrielle stood where she was and watched the gypsy wagons come to her. Several men went with Max down the hill and through the pines to retrieve the collapsed envelope. They took a team and a tumbrel with them, for the huge gummed-silk envelope was heavy. The women, who were left behind in the wagons, stared at Gabrielle while pretending to ignore her. After a while Gabrielle went to sit by herself beneath the oak tree, where at least it was cool.

A small head peeked out at her from a window cut into the wooden side of one of the wagons. Gabrielle smiled and waved, for it was the girl Lia, Dominique's friend. Seconds later, the wagon's door banged open and the girl emerged.

She came slowly, shuffling her bare feet in the dirt. She stopped several feet away and glanced up at Gabrielle from beneath shyly lowered lashes that were as long and sweeping as a feather duster. "Madame, where is Dominique? Have you brought him with you?"

Gabrielle smiled, shaking her head. "He's in Paris with his . . . uncle."

Lia's face fell. "Oh. I still have the statue he gave me. I keep it in my treasure box."

"He keeps your bracelet beneath his pillow," Gabrielle said, and it was true. Along with his rock collection, and his puppet, and his top. Gabrielle had often wondered how her child was able to sleep at night with such a lumpy resting place for his head.

A huge smile had broken across the little girl's face. "Will you tell him something for me, madame? When you see him again? Tell him I had to wash my cheek, the one he kissed, though I promised I wouldn't. But Maman made me.''

Gabrielle's mouth fell open. She quickly shut it, biting her lip to keep from smiling. Her Dominique—who squirmed and made faces whenever she tried to hug and cuddle him—had willingly bestowed one of his own precious kisses on this girl child. The male species, she decided, was completely unfathomable at any age.

"Lia!"

The little girl whirled around and ran back to the caravan. The gypsy leader Prado trotted up on his roan stallion. Max rode double in back of him.

"What was Lia saying to you?'' the gypsy leader demanded as Max slid off the horse's back and started toward her.

Gabrielle glared up at the man in defiance. He was handsome, but in a flashy way, like his bright clothes and golden earring. Oddly, his eyes, although they regarded her warily, weren't cruel.

"Nothing,'' Gabrielle said. "She was only being friendly. Don't punish her for it.''

The man looked shocked. "I wouldn't!''

"Gabrielle.'' Max took her arm. There was gentleness in his touch, though none on his face. "We'll be riding in the tumbrel with the aerostat. Do you mind?''

He didn't wait for her answer but led her further up the rise to where the tumbrel waited for them with its gaudily striped load. The driver, an old man in a coat of purple velvet and a flowered waistcoat, had two gold hoops in his ear, one looped inside the other. He gave her a gap-toothed smile and tipped his tricorne.

Gabrielle eyed the conveyance suspiciously. "I suppose there's salt hidden under here somewhere.''

Prado, who had been walking beside them on his roan, shot a sharp look at Max. "You must come to an understanding with your woman, *mon frère,* else her wagging tongue could get us all branched,'' he said, referring to the custom army's method of dispatching smugglers by hanging them from the nearest tree branch.

"She'll take care. I don't think Gabrielle has any desire for a confrontation with the law. Do you, *ma mie?*"

Suspicion was plain in the mocking gray eyes that regarded her. Tears stung her eyes, and a burning pain seized her chest. She could only shake her head in denial.

"Don't worry. Gabrielle and I will be going on alone through the *barrière* and on foot, and long before you," Max said cryptically.

Prado reflected a moment, then nodded. He pulled his horse's head sharply around and cantered off, back to the rest of the caravan.

Gabrielle stared after him. "I don't like that man."

"He doesn't much like you, either," Max said, hoisting her into the tumbrel with a hand beneath her bottom. "He's convinced I married you to ensure your silence, and he wonders why I didn't kill you instead. He also loves his own wife and daughter very much and would cut off his arm before hurting them."

The tumbrel jerked into motion. Gabrielle held out her hand and Max grabbed it. With a running step, he climbed in beside her.

"Did you?" Gabrielle said.

"Did I what?"

"Marry me to ensure my silence?"

"Yes." Max lay down within the silken cocoon of the envelope, lacing his hands behind his head. "And now will you kindly provide me with a little of it, wife?" He shut his eyes. Within seconds he was asleep.

Gabrielle leaned over, bracing herself on one hand, and enjoyed the luxury of studying the face of her husband when he couldn't look back at her.

In sleep, the harsh lines around his mouth softened. His closed lids, with their incredibly long lashes, hid the mockery in his eyes. He looked gentle, trusting, innocent. In sleep, her mischievous rascal of a son looked the same—angelic.

Agnes never had that look of sweet vulnerability while she
slept; neither, Gabrielle remembered, had her maman. It must
be a talent, she decided, that belonged strictly to the male of
the species.

Smiling, she touched his cheek, and his eyes flew open,
instantly alert.

"Look," she said and, straightening, pointed ahead of
them to a horizon cluttered with buildings and blanketed by
a cloud of dung-colored smoke. A noisome smell wafted toward them on the hot breeze. "Paris."

He sat up and, putting his arm around her, drew her to
him. The smile he gave her, though not the least bit angelic,
was warm and loving. "Home," he said.

The gypsy caravan made camp outside the city wall. Max
and Gabrielle walked through the *barrière* on foot and caught
a hackney to take them to the Palais Royal.

She sat close beside Max on the cracked leather seat as the
carriage lurched fitfully through the crowded streets. Her
hands were clutched together in her lap, and Max, reaching
over, picked one up and brought it to his lips. She thought
he probably wanted to reassure her, but she felt no fear, only
joy. She was coming home, married to a man she loved with
all her heart, body, mind, and soul. And she regretted none
of it.

The hackney let them out at the garden gates just as the
sun dipped below the ducal palace walls. They walked slowly
along the arched galleries, past the shops and cafés, nodding
to the courtesans, the booksellers, the mountebanks—their
neighbors in the Palais Royal. Though they must have been
a strange sight, barefoot and travel-stained, no one stared or
looked at them amiss. Stranger sights were seen every day in
this bawdy, raucous district.

The three golden balls of the pawnbroker winked at them
through the trees. Gabrielle began to walk faster. She saw
her son; he was squatting on the stoop in front of the pawnshop, intently studying a black, box-shaped thing between
his wide-spread knees. "Dominique!" she called out, and
pulling her arm from Max's, she began to run.

Her son looked up at her and smiled. "Oh, hello, Maman," he said, pleased but not overwhelmed with excitement at seeing her. She might as well have been gone for two minutes as two days.

She bent down to see what he was playing with. It appeared to be a small wicker cage with a black cloth draped over it.

"This is my new friend, Maman. I caught him with a piece of cheese."

Smiling, Gabrielle lifted the cage, pulling aside the cloth. "And what is your new— Jesu and all his saints!" she shrieked, flinging the cage from her in horror. It split open when it hit the ground, and a huge rat the size of a puppy, with a wiry black tail and long twitching whiskers, scurried for the safety of the littered gutter.

"Maman!" Dominique wailed. "Look what you've done! You've let him escape!"

A strong hand took Gabrielle's arm, steadying her. "Dominique, you can't keep a rat for a pet," Max said. She knew he was trying to sound stern, but she could hear the repressed laughter in his voice.

"Why not?" Dominique demanded.

"Because you maman doesn't like them."

"Why not?"

"Well, because . . ."

Gabrielle shuddered. "Horrible, filthy, disgusting creatures."

"Because they're horrible, filthy, disgusting creatures," Max said. He was definitely laughing now.

Gabrielle glared at the pair of them; they had both quickly assumed the same round-eyed innocent look, but she wasn't fooled. "If you two think you can—"

The door was flung open and Agnes stood on the threshold, arms akimbo and a gloating smile on her face. "Well, what have we here?" she cooed. "May a thousand and one devils pickle me in oil. And where have you two been this last day and night, eh?"

Gabrielle looked at Agnes, unable to say a word.

"We got married," Max said.

Laughing and rolling her eyes, Agnes turned around to Simon, who was hurrying forward from the back of the shop. "Did you hear that, Monsieur Simon? They got—" She whipped back around again, her mouth a perfect O of astonishment. *"Married?* By the ever-Virgin Mary Mother of God . . ."

Gabrielle broke out of the mysterious paralysis that had suddenly seized her limbs and throat. "Agnes, don't curse," she said automatically. She took a jerky step forward, toward Simon, and her eyes went instantly to his face. "Simon, Max and I . . . we were wed yesterday. The balloon hit a church steeple. It was all Max's fault. We came down in a field and we decided to get married. There was a village nearby. Chênaie-sur-Seine? The priest's name was Father Benoit and he was nice in a funny way, although he shouted and sneezed a lot. We . . ." She stopped, bereft again of words. She felt, indeed, like a daughter who anxiously awaited her father's approval.

It came, for Simon's round face broke into a delighted smile. He wrapped his arms around her, hugging her tight. Breaking away, he turned to Max. "So you married her then?" he said, his voice gruff with emotion.

Max stared steadily back at him. "Yes."

"And you'll take care of her? You'll keep her safe?"

"Yes."

Simon nodded sharply. As he grasped Max's hand, pumping it hard, light from the candelabra glinted off the wetness in his eyes. "Come, come." He waved his arm, ushering them all toward the kitchen. "We must have wine to celebrate."

"Well!" Agnes huffed, swiping at a tear that had mysteriously appeared on her cheek. "All I can say is you look a mess, the pair of you. I certainly hope you didn't stand up in church and say your vows before God looking like a couple of Marseilles cutpurses."

Gabrielle's head tilted back, and her rich, throaty laughter filled the shop. Max felt a tingling in his gut, and a familiar tightening in his loins. She stood barefoot, her dress stained and ripped, her hair in fiery tangles around her face, and to Max's besotted eyes she was the most beautiful creature on earth.

In a voice full of happiness, Gabrielle began to recount their adventures with the aerostat as she led them all back into the kitchen. Max had started to follow when he felt something tug at the kneeband of his breeches.

He looked down at Dominique, who stared up at him with anxious eyes. His lower lip trembled slightly, but Max could see he was making a valiant effort not to cry.

"Why did you marry my maman?" he demanded in a small, choked voice. "I never said you could."

Max hunkered down beside him, grasping his small shoulders. "I love your maman," he said. "A man marries a woman when he loves her."

Dominique looked down at his feet. "Does this mean you're my papa now?"

"Yes . . . in a way."

"My other papa left. He went to heaven."

Max's chest felt tight. "Yes. I know."

Slowly Dominique lifted his head, and Max saw a terrible fear in his indigo-blue eyes. "You won't go to heaven now, too, will you?"

Max's breath left him in a shaky laugh. "I don't think that's at all likely."

"Good," Dominique said matter-of-factly. He tucked his hand into Max's larger one. "Maman was very angry at us about the rat, wasn't she?"

"It frightened her."

He heaved a loud sigh. "Will we have to pick more flowers?"

"I think you can safely leave the reparations to me this time," Max said, with just a hint of smugness in his voice.

Dominique's face brightened. *"Tiens.* Will you help me catch another rat?"

Chapter 12

The gypsy caravan entered Paris that night by the Chaillot Road. The guards at the *barrière* were surly and the gypsies were insulting, and the guards seemed to take a long time to inspect diligently every wagon in the caravan. So long a time that traffic began to back up at the gate and tempers flared. One man, a bourgeois in an elegant landau, said he would complain to the minister of police about the matter. The captain of the guard scowled and made halfhearted apologies; the gypsies' leader was seen to smile.

The caravan attracted some attention. The wooden wagons were brightly painted, and the gypsies themselves were mostly dressed in vivid silks and bedecked with golden bangles and jeweled scraves. Men, passing by on the street, made ribald comments in laughing, teasing voices, hoping to attract the attention of more than one pair of flashing dark eyes. A group of shopgirls, on their way home from dinner at a café, caught the friendly, mocking smile of one of the handsome gypsy men and, giggling, smiled back. One of the girls, sharper than the rest, noticed that the tumbrel the man drove was piled high with stiff blue and gold striped silk, and she wondered what it was. Never would she have guessed that the silk was a deflated balloon and that beneath the balloon was salt.

The gypsy caravan crossed the magnificent avenue of the

Champs-Élysées. It filed in stately procession down the Rue Saint-Honoré, where the rich bourgeoisie had built mansions as grand as any noble's. It wound through the markets of Les Halles that smelled of fish and cheese and stale beer. When it passed the hulking towers of the Bastille, the man who drove the tumbrel raised his tricorne in a cocky salute to the soldiers on duty, and the man who rode beside him, a dark-skinned gypsy with a gold earring in one ear, laughed.

They turned onto the Rue du Faubourg Saint-Antoine. They passed dyeworks, tanneries, and breweries, all shuttered and dark, for the working day had ended. An ironworks belched filthy charcoal smoke. Smaller shops, dark as well, crouched among the foundries, their trade signs suspended on gallows above the narrow street, almost touching each other in the middle and forming an arch of creaking, rusty metal overhead.

Their wagon wheels splashed through stagnant pools choked with dung and entrails, scattering a group of foraging pigs. Candlelight flickered in the grimy, paneless windows of the leaning, sagging tenements. The bells of Saint Marguerite rang out eleven o'clock, but the night air was rent with other sounds as well—babies' cries, drunken songs, screams of rage and pain. It was a hard-living, hard-drinking, hard-wenching neighborhood, this Faubourg Saint-Antoine, and it never slept easy.

The man who drove the tumbrel knew this for he had grown up on these streets. Most babes born in the Faubourg Saint-Antoine never survived their first year. The tough weeds—those that made it through infancy—were hard to kill after that. Not that death wasn't everywhere. The gallows, the pox, a knife in the gut, waited around every corner, in every dark alley. Maximilien de Saint-Just had done things on these streets that filled him now with shame. But he had learned how not to die.

It became an addiction, this cheating of death, so that after a while life was insupportably boring if he wasn't living on the edge of it—what Percy Bonville called playing at dangerous games. Max had led his employers to believe he did it for the money and as a result, to keep him doing it, they had paid him well. The truth was that, more than the money, he did it for the sheer bloody excitement of it all. But tonight his heart wasn't in it.

Tonight his heart was with Gabrielle . . . his wife.

My wife. The words filled him with an incredible joy that he had not known was possible. They also filled him with terror. For the first time in Maximilien de Saint-Just's twenty-eight years he had something more than just his life to lose.

And already things weren't going well.

It was his fault. Mostly his fault. They had spent the evening at Simon's pawnshop, drinking wine, laughing, telling stories. Max had filled many nights of his life with revelry— carousing, gambling, whoring—but never had he been happier than at that moment, sitting at the scarred kitchen table with Dominique on his knee, his arm draped around his wife's shoulders, sharing such simple joy. He thought this was what it must feel like to belong to a family, to be loved and needed.

They were a little tipsy by the time they left the pawnshop and crossed the garden to his apartment. They had left Dominique with Agnes for one more night, until a carpenter could be hired tomorrow to build him a closet bed on the wall near the fireplace in Max's apartment. Tonight Max and Gabrielle went home alone, arms wrapped around each other's waists and laughing over nothing, stopping every few feet to exchange kisses that got hotter and hotter so that by the time they had made it up the stairs to his apartment, he had Gabrielle's breasts in his hands and she had her hands down his breeches.

From the beginning her passion had surprised him. He had never known a woman who so delighted in sex and who gave so freely in bed as Gabrielle. She brought him pleasure as no other woman ever had, and it wasn't done by artifice or experience. He guessed that her first husband must have died shortly after they were married, and he didn't think there had been many others, if any, since then.

Martin, the fellow's name was. Max had wormed that much

out of Agnes—along with the comforting opinion that this Martin must have been a moonstruck youth who didn't know his yard from a dyemaster's stick. He wondered if the boy really had been a wigmaker's apprentice. The wigmakers Max knew went through life coated head to foot with flour, looking like a mackerel ready for the fry pan. He couldn't envision such a ridiculous figure appealing to his glorious Gabrielle. Still, he hated the thought of this Martin. Not so much that the boy had been in Gabrielle's bed—although to be truthful that did bother him a little. What he hated was the thought that she had loved him, loved him enough to marry him and bear his child. She was the one and only love of *his* life, and Max wanted to be the same for her.

There was something else . . . This Martin was part of the secret that she refused to share with him. The secret that kept him—no matter how deep and strong his love—from completely trusting her.

The secret that forced him to keep secrets from her.

And so, once inside the door of his apartment, he had reluctantly pulled away from her. Lighting a taper on the mantel, he had turned, and the sight of her was almost his undoing. She stood before him—her hair a flaming cloud around her face; her eyes glowing purple, warm with desire; her lips swollen and parted, ready to be kissed again—and he didn't know where he found the will not to pick her up and carry her off to his bed.

"Gabrielle . . ." He took a deep breath to steady his voice. "I have to leave for a few hours. Will you wait up for me?"

The dreamy smile slid off her face. "Leave now? But why?"

"I have some business to take care of."

She recoiled as if he'd slapped her. "What business?"

He didn't answer her. He knew that at this moment his face looked hard and cruel, about as unrelenting as granite. He couldn't help it. It was something you learned early in the Faubourg Saint-Antoine when you were a thief and your mother was a whore. Never allow your feelings to show, for feelings make you weak. Your enemies will use your feelings to destroy you. So will your friends.

Gabrielle had wrapped her arms around her chest, hugging herself. "You're going back to those gypsies, aren't you? You're going to help them smuggle the salt into the city."

"Yes."

"Oh, God . . . I didn't marry you only to become a widow again." Her fists clenched and she squeezed her eyes shut. But when she opened them a moment later, they were dry, and he admired her guts—her refusal to cry in front of him.

"Gabrielle . . ." He reached for her, but she jerked away, turning her back to him. "I swear to you it isn't dangerous. The guards at the *barrière* have been bribed. The smuggling is being run by someone high in the government. There's no chance of getting caught." He wondered if he should have trusted her enough to tell her even that much, but he couldn't bear the anguish on her face.

She had turned away from him, but now she whirled back around, and he saw she had gone from being hurt to being angry.

"Why?" she demanded. "Why must you do this?"

"It's a favor I owe."

"To Prado?"

Max said nothing. He couldn't trust her with knowledge of Abel Hachette and the cabal. Not yet, not until he found out what it was in her past that she wouldn't, or couldn't, tell him.

Her hot, angry eyes glared at him from beneath flaring brows. "Is that how you support yourself, Max—by smuggling? Is that where the money came from to buy all this?" She waved her hand around the room, encompassing his instruments and books. "Or did it come from picking pockets?"

That had hurt, but only deep inside him where she would néver see it.

He dropped his voice to a low, dead-level tone. "I'm not asking for your permission or your sanction, Gabrielle. You knew what I was when you married me because I warned you, right from the start . . ." He paused, letting the implication that she had not been so forthcoming with him hang in the air between them.

Then he felt his lips tighten into the cold smile that came when he was angry. "I'm a bastard, Gabrielle. Remember?"

She flung her head up and stared back at him steadily, and her words burned him with their bitter sarcasm. "I haven't forgotten. I just didn't think you would spend our marriage trying to prove it."

After that there had been nothing more to say. He went into his bedroom and changed into a clean pair of chamois breeches and a plain buff coat, then put on his second, older pair of boots which weren't as fine as the ones he'd lost but felt better on his feet. He thought about taking the pistol, decided against it, and took his stiletto instead. He sat on the bed to slip it into his boot.

He felt the owl watching him in silent condemnation from the perch near the window. He looked up and actually felt his cheeks flush. A man doesn't have to answer to his wife, he defended himself to those censorious, all-knowing eyes. Why should I have to change my whole life just because I'm married? I was perfectly happy with the way things were before she knocked on my door.

The big bird blinked once, and Max raised his brows. All right then, not perfectly happy. You're supposed to be so smart, what would you do?

The bird flapped his wings, and Max frowned. That's easy for you to say, my feathered friend, but I haven't got wings. And then he pressed his lips together to stop a burst of laughter. God. Gabrielle already suspected him of being half mad. What would she think if she came in here right now and caught him silently communing with an owl?

When he went back into the other room, she was still standing where he had left her, and he could see she had been crying. He started for the door, but he couldn't leave it like that. He crossed the room in three strides, crushing her against him before she could even think of getting away. She turned her head to the side, but he grasped her chin, jerking it back

around again. His mouth came down hard on her lips, and in
his kiss were mixed all the love and anger and frustration that
he felt.

She hadn't kissed him back, but then she hadn't slapped
his face, either. He took that as a positive sign.

The gypsy caravan passed the burned-out shell of an abandoned slaughterhouse. The dark-skinned man on the big roan
peeled away and the tumbrel followed him, rolling silently
on oiled wheels through a crumbling brick arch and into a
black cavern that had once been the bleeding and gutting
yard.

The place stank, although it hadn't been used in years.
Max remembered it from his childhood, and it had been a
ruin even then. But the smells of blood and rotting entrails
had seeped into the stones and packed earth long ago and
were there to stay. The fire had destroyed the roof, so that
the night sky showed dark and shadowy through the fallen
timbers overhead. A hot wind had come up and stormclouds
shrouded the moon. There was the feel of rain in the air.

Torchlight flared in back of them, casting their shadows
against the far wall. Prado dismounted; Max stayed in the
tumbrel and pulled his tricorne forward so that the brim came
to just above his eyes.

A man, flanked on each side by minions carrying torches,
came through the arch. "Couldn't you have picked a better
place for this?" he said in an aggrieved voice. "It stinks like
a butcher's midden in here."

Prado laughed and said something soothing and apologetic
while Max sat in silence and watched the man with shadowed
eyes. He was a small man, dressed all in black, with long,
shaggy dark hair that hung loosely over his shoulders. The
torchlight glazed the lenses of his thick spectacles, obscuring
the man's eyes. Max committed the face to memory; it was
easy for there was a deep, puckered scar on one cheek, like
a brand. The man had never told Prado his name, so Prado
called him the Scarred One.

The Scarred One came over to the tumbrel to look inside. "Whatever in the name of heaven is that?"

"It's an aerostat," Prado said.

"A what?"

"A balloon."

"And the salt?"

"It's there."

The man blinked. He had, Max saw, protruding eyes with thick lids, like those of a turtle, that were grotesquely magnified by the spectacles. His attention fell on Max. "Who's he? You've never brought him with you before."

Prado's teeth flashed. "My cousin Ludo. He's an ox."

Max stared down at the man, the vacuous look of the dimwitted on his face.

The man blinked again, then brought a scented handkerchief to his nose. "Have him unload the stuff then, and make him hurry. Christ, it stinks in here."

A large black berlin was driven through the arch. With the help of the two minions, Max unloaded the salt from the tumbrel into the carriage. The low voices of Prado and the Scarred One drifted over them while they worked. Max didn't bother trying to listen; Prado would recount the whole conversation to him later.

The Scarred One insisted that Prado and Max should leave first. It had started to rain, hard enough to turn the narrow street into a gulley of filthy, rushing water. Max, sitting in the tumbrel with icy water dripping down his neck, wondered why it always rained when he had to follow someone at night.

He drove the tumbrel for several blocks at a leisurely pace, with Prado walking the roan beside him and humming tunelessly under his breath. When they rounded the corner, a shadow emerged from an alley and leaped on board the tumbrel. Max slid off the other end, running on silent feet back toward the slaughterhouse. When the black berlin emerged from beneath the archway, it acquired an extra and unseen passenger.

* * *

Two hours later Max stood in the door to his bedroom, a puddle of water forming around his feet. She was there— lying on her side on the very edge of the bed, her face turned toward the window. Relief overwhelmed him, so intense that tears stung his eyes and he swayed slightly on his feet. He hadn't known how afraid he was of finding her gone.

The jalousies were open, and wind blew rain into the room, no doubt staining the floor. But the owl's perch was empty, so he didn't go to shut the window. He stood, instead, at the door and listened to her breathing. She was awake. "Gabrielle?" he said softly, and when she didn't answer he undressed in the dark, in silence.

He got into bed beside her. She didn't move. He lay on his back, looking up at the ceiling. He thought he could, with his practiced touch, make her want him in spite of her anger. But he didn't want to treat her that way—like a mere vessel to be used to slake his own hunger. He wondered if he could win her forgiveness with words, but although he tried several sentences in his mind, none sounded right. So after a moment he closed his eyes and turned onto his stomach, away from her.

The bed moved beneath him. Then her naked body rubbed against the bare flesh of his buttocks. His manhood grew thick and stiff where it was pressed between his stomach and the mattress. It was all he could do not to roll her over right then and plunge into her, deep and hard, to bury himself in her hot, wet softness. He clenched his teeth, fighting for self-control.

Her hand lightly, tentatively touched his arm. "Max . . . ? Please don't be angry with me. I can't bear it when you're angry with me."

He turned, gathering her into his arms. God, but he loved her. For a moment he couldn't breathe. "I thought you were angry with me," he said.

She had shuddered when he first touched her. Now she was pressing the whole length of her body onto his. Her tautened nipples scraped across his chest. He tightened his jaw, and sweat filmed his eyes.

"I was so furious with you, I could have branched you

myself," she said, and her voice again took on an angry edge as she remembered. "But after you left I began to grow afraid you weren't coming back."

He stroked her, his hands cupping her buttocks and pulling her pelvis up and onto him, making her feel the hard proof of his desire. He started to rub himself against the soft curly nest of hair that was the fount of all his torment and his joy. But then he had to stop because he was so desperate for her by now, he thought he might possibly burst.

"I'll always come back, *ma mie,*" he said, while he thought, Gabrielle, Gabrielle, I know it's important to talk this through, but I can't right now. I want you so badly. I need you. I have to—

She shuddered again, then a harsh, strangled sound tore from her throat. He felt the wetness of tears where her face lay buried against his neck, and his heart plunged into his gut.

"Oh, Jesus, Gabrielle, don't cry." He hugged her tight against him, hating himself. "Oh, God . . . I'm sorry, I'm so sorry—"

Her mouth smothered the rest of his words, her lips pressing down on his, grinding them against his teeth and driving his head back against the pillow. He pulled her leg over his thighs and she rose above him, swinging her hips up and around to straddle him. He could make out her shape in the darkness but not her features. Then a stray beam from one of the lamplights outside pierced the night and the rain, and came shining through the window to turn her hair into a crown of fire. Or a halo. He smiled at the thought. Gabrielle, his angel of fire and passion.

As he watched, she rose above him, high on her knees, and taking his hard length in her hand, slowly, slowly, impaled herself upon it. And slowly, slowly he shut his eyes and, though he had no wings, he felt himself fly.

Afterward, Max lay holding his wife within the crook of his arm. His muscles felt heavy with exhaustion and his thoughts were filled with her, his Gabrielle . . . Winning her had been hard enough. Keeping her, he now realized, was going to be even harder. Somehow he would have to make amends for tonight. And although he couldn't yet give her what she wanted, which was his unconditional trust, he could at least give her a slice of his pride by groveling at her feet for forgiveness.

He took a deep breath to gird himself for the coming ordeal and constricted the muscles of the arm that held her. "Gabrielle?"

Her hand lay on his heart. Sighing, she twisted and coiled her fingers through the hair on his chest. "No," she said.

"But you don't even know what I was going to say."

"I do know. If you think, Maximilien de Saint-Just, that I'll forgive you for going out smuggling on our wedding night—"

"Our wedding night was last night."

"—just because you bestow a few kisses—"

"A *few* kisses!"

"Or a lot of kisses." She pinched his nipple. "No, no, I shall exact a greater payment."

With growing trepidation Max waited to hear what she would demand of him. He couldn't possibly make love to her again tonight. At the moment he couldn't raise his little finger, let alone anything else.

"I saw the most adorable little hat in the window of Madame Bertin's," Gabrielle was saying.

"It's yours," Max said, laughing, and trying not to think about the fact that Madame Bertin made hats for the queen, and charged accordingly.

Then a sudden thought struck him that brought a strange lump to his throat. Out of love, he had been about to offer Gabrielle the gift of his pride and she, out of love, had given it back to him unopened. Out of love.

And in that moment he believed, truly believed, that what they had was special and could survive anything—anger, disappointment . . . even secrets.

And so, with his wife's hair spread across his chest and her head nestled in the crook of his arm, Maximilien de Saint-Just shut his eyes and fell asleep listening to the rain.

* * *

It was still raining the next afternoon.

Abel Hachette stood at his library window, scanning the passersby in the street below and growing more impatient by the minute. Max had promised to stop by late last night to report on the smuggling operation, but he never came. All that morning, Hachette had waited, and still no Max. It wasn't that he was worried—Max could take care of himself. No, Hachette wasn't anxious; he was excited. He had a surprise for his Black Angel and he could hardly wait to give it to him.

Hachette remembered the first time he had stood at this window waiting for Max. Until the last moment, he really had planned to have the *gendarmes* there to arrest the young brigand. He had even tried out in his mind several biting remarks he would thrust in that handsome, arrogant face as the boy was hauled off to a well-deserved scaffold.

But he had never sent for the *gendarmes* after all that day eleven years ago, and when the clock on the mantel chimed first twelve and then twelve-thirty, Hachette had felt a keen disappointment. At least there was some consolation, he had thought, in that he hadn't made an ass of himself by dragging the police out on a fool's errand. After the clock chimed one, Hachette rose from behind his rosewood desk and rang for his servant. His feet, of their own accord, carried him over to the window for one last look at the throng of pedestrians and vehicles that as usual clogged the busy Rue Royal. There was still no sign of the young aristocrat.

One half of the double doors opened behind him.

"Bring my hat and cane, if you please," Hachette said, turning around, "I'm—"

"Forgive my tardiness," came that mocking, drawling voice, this time unmuffled by any mask, and Hachette felt a chill dance down his spine. "I was unavoidably detained. I had this foolish suspicion you would summon the police."

Sweat started out on the financier's white brow. "How . . . how did you get in?"

Mocking brows arched upward over cool gray eyes. "Through the front door."

Hachette walked stiffly over to his desk. He felt for the seat of his chair with his legs and slowly sat down. He assumed a stern face. "Well, brigand—"

"My friends call me Max."

"And what do your enemies call you?"

"They don't live long enough to call me anything."

Hachette started to sneer at this bravado until he saw the glint of self-mockery in the boy's eyes. He laughed instead. "I'll have to remember what a dangerous character you are . . . Max. Since we are going into business together."

They made three shipments in all in the two years before France openly entered the war on the side of the Americans and the secret gun running became unnecessary, and therefore unprofitable. When he met with Max on a wharf at the busy port of Nantes on the morning the first shipment was to sail, Hachette was beset with fresh doubts, thinking what a fool he'd been to trust a stranger—a highwayman, no less—with a fortune in muskets and paper-wrapped cartridges.

"Once you sell the guns . . . how do I know you won't disappear into the Caribbean with my ship and the profits?" he said, trying to hide his nervousness.

Smells from the dock came through the open porthole with the breeze—cinnamon, tobacco, coffee, and over it all the stink of rotting fish. Max, who was bent over the captain's table studying a chart of the harbor, didn't even bother to look up. "You don't know, you can only hope. The same way I hoped you wouldn't deliver me to the hangman the afternoon I walked into your house unmasked and unarmed."

"Were you unarmed?"

Max smiled slowly until his eyes were nearly shut. "Hell, no."

When Max returned with the profits from the final shipment, Hachette was there to meet the ship at the dock, as he was at the end of every shipment. For always Hachette never quite believed Max would return. Yet when Max handed over the gold bullion and silver coins the Americans paid for the guns, Hachette wondered why he'd ever doubted the boy.

As Hachette counted out Max's percentage for this, their final shipment, he realized with real sorrow that his strange association with Maximilien de Saint-Just was about to end.

Curious, he asked the young man—a man he had drunk with and eaten with, a man he now trusted as a son, but whom he knew not at all—if he intended to join the cream of the French aristocracy who, following the example of the marquis de Lafayette, was volunteering in droves to fight for glory and liberty in America.

Max, who was packing the last of his belongings into a battered sea chest, shrugged indifferently. "I don't take orders very well."

"But you'd be giving orders, boy, not taking them. You're a nobleman, so you can buy yourself an officer's commission. Your father the comte is a *maréchal*, after all. Surely he—"

Max's laugh was bitter. "My father wouldn't spend a sou to buy me a seat on a coach going to hell."

"Pity then you have such a poor relationship with the comte," Hachette said, wondering aloud. "With his influence at court you could go far, even get a pension."

"I'm his bastard, Abel. My father acknowledges my existence. That's the extent of our relationship."

"I see. Still, you've made enough money in the last two years to buy yourself a dozen commissions—"

For the first time, Hachette saw Max lose his temper. The young man slammed the lid of the chest down so hard it bounced. "Dammit, Abel, what the hell business is it of yours anyway? If you must know, I see no compelling reason why I should want to fight for a country that isn't even mine and means nothing to me."

"I thought it did mean something to you." He waved his arm around the cabin. "Why do this then, these shipments of arms?"

"I did it for the money, Abel. The same as you. To fight for something means you have to be willing to die for it."

"You're willing to risk you life for money but not for liberty?"

"What is liberty? It's only a word."

Hachette stared at the youthful, handsome face, browned by the weeks at sea and flushed now with anger. "What does matter to you then?" he asked. "What do you want out of life?"

Max stared back at him for a moment longer, then his breath left him in a sigh. "To discover things. To invent the things that can't be discovered because they don't yet exist. Hell, maybe I just want to keep from being bored."

He isn't one of us after all, Hachette had thought then, hiding his disappointment, and the subject was dropped.

Hachette hadn't really expected to see the young brigand again after they had parted that day but, as was so often the case with Max, he had been wrong. For Max had shown up at his house in the Faubourg Saint-Honoré a little over a year later and he had brought with him the key to the English ciphers, the code used by the enemy in their battle communications.

Abel Hachette had sat behind his rosewood desk, holding the cipher key with hands that shook. *"Dieu,* this is incredible. Where did you—"

"From a bedroom in London."

"But how . . ."

"I stole it."

"This is incredible, Max. Do you realize what this is worth to the army, to the king?"

Max smiled. "That's why I brought it to you, my dear Abel. Because you would know how much it's worth. And you can sell it for me."

Hachette glanced sideways at the young man, who paced with restless excitement across the parquet floor. It was time, he decided, for the boy to choose just what sort of man he was to become.

"France's treasury is depleted," Hachette said. "This American war has turned out to be more expensive than anyone anticipated. Why not sell this back to the English instead?''

Max stopped, whirling to stare at Hachette in astonishment.

''England can afford to pay whatever you ask,'' Hachette said. ''I doubt our king could scrape together a hundred louis—''

''Then give it to him for nothing, for God's sake!'' Max threw himself into one of Hachette's fragile gilt chairs. He scowled at the old man, then began to laugh. ''Don't look so shocked, Abel. I do have some principles and I even try to live up to them occasionally. When living up to them doesn't interfere with my survival.''

''Then you do care what happens to France?''

For a moment Hachette thought he was going to get the flippant reply that was so typical of the boy, but Max had said, ''Hell, I'm a Frenchman. Of course I care.''

''How old are you?'' Hachette asked suddenly.

Max shrugged. ''I don't know. Around twenty, I guess.''

''Twenty! *Dieu*, that means you were only seventeen the year you captained our first shipment of muskets!''

Max flashed his cocky smile. ''I'll tell you another secret, Abel. I had never sailed before that day. I'd never even set foot on a ship before in my life. I didn't know a poop deck from a sparsail.''

Hachette burst into laughter. He laughed until tears ran down his cheeks, and he had to mop them up with his lace-edged handkerchief. Then he sobered suddenly and stared hard at the younger man.

''Max, my dear boy, I have a business proposition to put to you . . .''

And until this moment it had been a very profitable partnership, indeed. Profitable for the cabal and profitable for France and the cause of revolution. Abel Hachette thought of that now as he spotted the dark head of the man he had been waiting for coming toward him on the rain-slick Rue Royal. And he made a silent vow to that man, to Maximilien de

Saint-Just, whom he now realized was as dear to him—as *necessary* to him—as a son.

I will let nothing, or no one, come between you and your destiny.

Hachette barricaded himself behind his rosewood desk and waited with breathless impatience for the majordomo to announce his visitor. He actually had to stop himself from bolting out of his seat when the door was at last flung open and Max entered the room.

"Monsieur le Vicomte de Saint-Just," the lackey announced in stentorian tones.

Hachette couldn't help smiling as he saw Max stop as if stunned by a blow. He had never been able to disconcert that arrogant presence before.

He didn't have long to enjoy his triumph, however, for the arrogant presence was recovered in seconds. Max waited until the lackey had shut the door, then he turned slowly, eyebrows raised. "My dear Abel," he drawled, "are you in that most subtle way of yours trying to tell me something?"

"Your brother is dead," Hachette said bluntly. "A hunting accident."

Except for an almost imperceptible twitch in his cheek, Max's expression didn't alter. He sat down in the gilt and velvet chair and regarded Hachette from beneath sleepy lids. "Poor François . . . he never did learn how to sit a horse properly."

Hachette pushed his breath out his pursed lips in exasperation. *"Mon Dieu,* Max. Don't you realize what this means?"

The eldest boy of the comte de Saint-Just had died ten years before, fighting for the Americans in their revolution. Yesterday, the second son had taken a fence wrong and broken his neck. The bloodline of Saint-Just rested now with the comte's sole surviving son, a bastard, true, but one formally acknowledged years before. It would be nothing to make Max his heir, to give him the newly vacated title of the vicomte de Saint-Just. Hachette almost shivered with excitement as he thought of the heights his Black Angel could now achieve with a powerful title and his father's backing, what offices he would be offered, what knowledge would pass through his slender, aristocratic hands—

"I know what it means," Max was saying, "and you need to study your law, Abel. My half brother's death doesn't mean I get his title by default."

Hachette waved his hand. "Bastard or not, you're the only son the comte's got left. He'll give you the title now if only to keep it away from the Guillard branch of the family. I hear they all detest one another."

Max shrugged. "We'll see." It was obvious he didn't want to talk about it, and Hachette reluctantly let him change the subject. "I came here expecting to find you all agog to hear about the smuggling," Max said, pretending to be hurt. "I could have caught an ague running around in the rain last night finding out who their leader is, and now I discover you aren't even interested."

Hachette smiled, flicking open his snuffbox. "So tell me then. Who is the wicked man cheating our wicked king out of his ill-gotten *gabelle?*"

"His name's Louvois. He—"

The snuffbox bounced off Hachette's lap and clattered to the floor, scattering brown dust all over his champagne satin breeches.

"—works for the duc de Nevers," Max went on as if nothing had happened. "Which makes sense when you remember that one of the duc's lucrative pensions is the collection of the *gabelle,* and why the hell did I spend four hours last night tracking down the identity of a man you already know?"

"I don't know him!" Hachette felt sweat trickle down his chest. He forced himself to look up and meet those sharp, assessing gray eyes. "Well, I might have met him once. I'm surprised at the duc de Nevers's involvement in this smuggling," he said quickly, wanting to steer the conversation away from Louvois.

"I don't think the duc is involved," Max said in a neutral voice. "Why should he be? He skims thousands off what he collects for the king through the *gabelle.* The more salt that gets taxed, the more money Nevers makes. It's more likely Louvois figured out the smuggling on his own, as a way to do damage to his rich master and make a few livres on the side.''

Max smiled, and for the thousandth time Hachette wished he could tell what thoughts lay behind those mocking eyes.

''Then this lawyer,'' Hachette said. ''What was his name—Louvois? He would be easy for us to control. Louvois can run the smuggling and we can run Louvois, and the king and his duc can remain in blissful ignorance of what is allowed to pass through the *barrières* on certain days.''

For what seemed an eternity to Hachette, Max said nothing. Then his lips curled into a slow, lazy smile. He stood up. ''Do you want me to explain things to Louvois? Or shall you do it?''

Hachette cleared his throat. ''No . . . you do it.'' He got to his feet, surprised he was able to support himself on legs that felt like jelled consommé. Hachette stopped Max when he was halfway out the door by softly calling out his name.

Max turned, and from the look of pain on his darkly handsome face Hachette thought that the younger man must know already what he was going to say. He said it anyway.

''You said the other night that this would be the last mission you would do for us . . .''

''It is,'' Max said. ''And I'm sorry, Abel. Truly sorry.'' Then the sadness abruptly vanished from his eyes and the smile he gave Hachette was full of a strange, lilting happiness that almost had Hachette smiling with him. ''It's time I grew up and quit playing at dangerous games, Abel. I've got responsibilities now. I got married yesterday.''

Hachette felt the color drain from his face. ''How . . . how wonderful for you. And your wife . . . is she this mysterious girl with hair the color of a sunset?''

Max's face softened, and something glinted silver in his eyes. ''Gabrielle,'' he said. ''Her name is Gabrielle.'' And then the door shut behind him and he was gone.

Abel Hachette sat behind his desk in the library of his magnificent townhouse on the Rue Royal. Outside the rain had stopped and the afternoon grew warm. His servants, thinking he was working and knowing how he hated to be disturbed, left him alone. But he wasn't working, he was thinking. When the brass clock on the mantel struck six, he picked up paper and pen and began to write.

Although his fingers trembled so badly at the beginning that he had to rip the paper up twice and start afresh, by the time he finished his hand was as steady as the blade of the executioner's ax. As steady as his conviction that he had done the right thing.

For the cabal. And for France.

Chapter 13

∽◇∽

"When I get married I'm going to wear a white dress trimmed with the sheerest Lyons lace," Agnes said to Gabrielle, who leaned over the fire to stir the negus—a spiced mixture of water, wine, and lemon juice—which warmed on a trivet by the flames.

"Uh-huh," Gabrielle answered, not really listening. A fat pullet roasted over the fire, hissing and dripping grease onto the coals, and she was debating whether to take it off the spit before it overcooked. Max had disappeared hours ago, to God alone knew where; if he didn't return soon he was going to be late for supper. The first supper she had prepared for him on this, their second day of marriage.

"—with a wreath of orange blossoms in my hair," Agnes was saying. "And I'm going to be a virgin."

Gabrielle did look up then. For a change, Agnes's wispy hair was hidden beneath a mobcap, and Gabrielle had to admit the girl's head did resemble a fat brioche. "A virgin!" she scoffed. "Even a man besotted with love would never be such a lackwit as to swallow that fishmonger's tale."

Agnes's eyes crinkled at the corners with her knowing smile. "Oh, there are ways. A certain poultice of vinegar and—" She stopped in mid-word, emitting a whistlelike shriek as a flurry of flapping wings thundered from the bedroom. The shadow of a giant flying creature streaked across the wall and she shrieked again, stiffening in her chair as if getting ready to bolt for the door.

"Jesu, Gabrielle, there's a bat in here!"

"That's only Socrates," Gabrielle said. She took the negus off the trivet and began to pour it into the waiting cups. "He was out getting dinner. He likes the pigeons that roost on the roofs of the Hôtel de Ville."

Agnes cast nervous eyes into the bedroom where the flapping sound had died to a quiet rustle. "Socrates? You *name* your bats?"

Gabrielle laughed. "It's Max's owl."

"Owl? Gabrielle, I hope you will not be insulted, but I must tell you I think Monsieur Max is a little—"

"—mad," Gabrielle said. A secret smile transformed her face. "I know. It must be one of the reasons why I love him so much."

Agnes shrugged. *"Chacune a son goût."* Her stomach growled and she looked longingly at the pullet. "By the belly of Saint James, I'm starved. If you're waiting for Monsieur Max, I don't think he's coming. I just saw him, on my way back from the baker. I went to the one over by the Café Monoury this time—"

"But that's clear over in the Place de l'École."

"So? It was worth the walk. I refuse to patronize old Rosière another day, not with that witch he's married to working behind the counter. She always tries to palm off the burned loaves on us, have you noticed? Anyway, I happened to look through the windows of the Café Monoury and there he was, Monsieur Max I mean, not old Rosière. He'll be hours yet getting home. When a man gets to drinking with his cronies— even one who's a little mad—he loses all track of time, and his stomach. And while we're speaking of stomachs . . ."

Gabrielle laughed. "Really, Agnes, how can you possibly be hungry? After eating all that gingerbread barely ten minutes ago."

"Dominique ate most of it. It was a strange man, this friend of Monsieur Max's," Agnes went on without pausing for breath. "Dressed rather plainly, but he has money enough because he was wearing spectacles. He had the strangest eyes, big and round and smooth like pebbles, and a nasty scar on one ch— Gabrielle! *Mort de ma vie,* what's the matter? Do you have a pain?''

Gabrielle was half bent over, one hand clinging to the back of a chair, the other pressed against her stomach. Her eyes went immediately to Dominique, sitting on the floor beneath Max's telescope, as if to reassure herself he was still there. He was playing happily by himself with his new toy—thin, painted pieces of wood cut into odd shapes that made a picture when put together. Max had called it *un puzzle,* and he had given it to Dominique that morning.

Max. Her husband, her lover, her joy . . .

Her betrayer.

No! She couldn't believe that, not of Max. Not the man who had taught her the sweet ecstasy of love, who had said the words, those precious words, though surely they had not come easily to him. The man who had married her. My husband, she thought . . . And she felt a sick despair that almost made her gag. My husband, a man who brazenly admitted to being a thief and a liar. A man who had said to her once, *I will do anything for money.*

Agnes had started for the door, but Gabrielle seized her arm, holding her back. ''Wait!'' she hissed beneath her breath, not wanting to alarm her son.

Agnes struggled to pull free. ''Oh, *mon Dieu,* Gabrielle, you're ill. I'm going to run over to the shop and get Monsieur Simon.''

''No! There's not—'' She drew in a tight, deep breath. ''Agnes, you must do what I say without an argument.''

''But—''

''*Please.*''

Agnes gulped and nodded.

''You must take Dominique and leave here at once, but nonchalantly, as if nothing has happened.''

''Oh, Gabrielle . . . what *has* happened?''

''Later. I haven't time to explain. You'll take Dominique

to . . . to the Port Royale," she decided, naming one of the city's southern gates. "And tell no one. Not even Simon."

Tears ran down Agnes's face in two shining streams, but her head bobbed convulsively in compliance.

Gabrielle gave her a swift, hard hug, then kissed her wet cheek. "Wait for me at the gate, but if I'm not there by nightfall—" She stopped. She *would* be there. She would risk a lot for love, but she wouldn't risk losing her son. She squeezed Agnes's shoulders. "There's bound to be a café near the gate. Buy Dominique some chocolate while you wait for me. Agnes . . . you're the only one I can trust."

Agnes bit her lip to stifle a sob and produced a watery smile. "Of course you can trust me. Wasn't it me who saved your miserable life in the first place?"

Gabrielle tried to smile back, but she couldn't. She doubted she would ever be able to smile again.

Twenty minutes before, in the Café Monoury, a liveried servant had entered through the elegant, etched-glass double doors, inquiring after the lawyer Louvois. The waiter pointed him out willingly, for Louvois was a regular customer at the café, never failing to eat his supper there—a black pudding followed by a plate of sausages, followed by a beetroot salad, and accompanied by two glasses of Beaune wine—whenever he was in Paris. The waiter allowed this disturbance of his customer's meal, for the lawyer Louvois was often interrupted by minions coming and going with messages; it was understood he was a busy and important man.

The waiter, keeping a discreet eye on his customer, had watched the servant deliver his message and leave. Whatever it was, it must have been startling news, for the lawyer had almost leaped right out of his chair after reading it. Then he had tucked it into his waistcoat pocket and, shoving the half-eaten salad aside, had gulped down the last of his wine in two swallows (a sacrilege, the waiter had thought with a sniff, but understandable in a peasant). Louvois had tossed five livres on the table (two too many) to cover the bill, and the waiter, trained to anticipate a patron's desires, had already started forward to help the lawyer out of his chair when a tall, broad-shouldered man stepped between them. Louvois hissed something beneath his breath and then slowly sat back down, and the waiter discreetly retired.

Louvois's eyes had blinked with confusion as he looked up into a darkly handsome face with sooty gray eyes and a mocking smile. The face looked familiar, but he couldn't remember . . . and then he did. It was the face of the dim-witted gypsy he had last seen driving a tumbrel filled with smuggled salt.

He stood half out of his chair and his protruding eyes bulged with sudden anger. "Are you mad? What are you doing approaching me here?"

"A minute or two of your time, if I may, monsieur. To discuss a matter that concerns us both."

Louvois sank slowly into his chair, for the man had spoken with the drawling, dulcet accents of the courtier, and the granite-gray eyes that bored into him now were not those of a fool. "What matter?" he asked warily.

"Why, smuggling of course."

"Ah," Louvois said on an expulsion of breath. He thought he ought to be frightened, but the letter . . . the letter made all other things, even this, seem unimportant. He thought he could actually feel it smoldering inside the pocket of his waistcoat, like the slow match of an old-fashioned pistol.

Behind him a waiter leaned over to light the candles in the brass sconces that lined the wall, throwing light on the other man's face and making it seem less harsh. The discordant drone of other conversations passed over their heads, sounding like an orchestra tuning up before the performance. The remains of his half-eaten meal lay scattered on the table between them, and the smell of the vinegared dressing on the salad made Louvois suddenly nauseous.

Louvois always ate supper here, at the Café Monoury. Not only was it near his apartment, but he liked the ambiance of the black and white tiled floor reflected over and over in the mirrored walls. He always sat at the same table, in the corner by the circular blue and white porcelain stove. His predictability, he thought, his mind whirling in disjointed circles, had made it easy for the servant bearing the letter to find him. And easy for this man, who spoke of smuggling, and who knew . . . who had to know everything.

"You've cost your master the duc—not to mention your sovereign king—a lot of money these last few months," the stranger was saying. "I don't expect either one will be too gentle or forgiving." He was twisting the empty wineglass around and around in his long, slender fingers. As the sense of what the man was saying penetrated Louvois's befuddled brain, he felt as if the words were twisting his guts.

Louvois looked longingly toward the door, but his chair was backed up against the wall. He couldn't leave now until the stranger let him. "Have you been sent to arrest me?"

"Sent by whom, the duc?" The stranger smiled and Louvois couldn't repress a shudder. "No, no, I fear you misunderstand, monsieur. We don't want the smuggling stopped. We like the idea of someone stealing from our poor king's already bankrupted treasury. It further weakens an already weak and corrupt government."

And who is "we"? Louvois wondered. The gypsies? Surely not. "You are revolutionaries?" he asked, not really expecting an answer.

The stranger smiled again. "I have a business proposition to put to you, monsieur. One that will allow the smuggling to go on, with only . . . minor adjustments."

Louvois began to breathe easier. Blackmail, of course. Well, he could handle that. He would let the fellow spew his empty threats, and then he would fob him off with a purse full of louis and a threat or two of his own. No matter his own republican sympathies, Louvois certainly wouldn't allow a band of fanatical rebels to horn in on a profitable smuggling operation.

His mind wandered back to the letter. He wanted to take it out and study the words again, although they had been seared onto his brain with only one reading. *The woman you seek has been seen entering and leaving an apartment above the Café de Foy in the Palais Royal.* Nothing else, no signature, not even an initial. But he had no doubt of the message's origin.

The woman you seek . . . The Palais Royal.

Gabrielle, he thought. Gabrielle. I have you at last.

Her breath burning raw in her throat, Gabrielle peered through the tall arched window of the Café Monoury. At first she saw only the reflection of her own tortured face. Then slowly her eyes focused on the interior of the brightly lit room.

The tables were packed with patrons, a few having supper but most enjoying a game of chess or arguing politics while lingering over a carafe of wine. Even the tiled bench that circled the café's porcelain stove was jammed with the cotton-covered posteriors of a group of students who were having some sort of drinking contest.

And there, at a table pushed against the far wall, was a small, black-garbed man wearing spectacles. He was nodding his head, and one slender, pale hand drifted up to touch the puckered scar on his cheek.

Louvois.

The muscles in Gabrielle's legs began to twitch like those of a rabbit that has just gotten scent of the fox. Every nerve screamed at her to run, but her heart held her fast. A waiter stood before the table, a tray of brandy snifters balanced on the outstretched fingers of one hand, and the waiter's fat back blocked Gabrielle's view of the other man who sat across from Louvois. She had to know . . .

And then she did, for the waiter stepped back and turned aside, and Gabrielle saw who the other man was.

Perhaps he sensed her eyes on him, for he lifted his head sharply around, the way a stag, feeding in a glen, will suddenly glance up at the snap of a twig. For an eternity she stared at the profile of his beloved face, the high cheekbone, the haughty nose, the hard lips that had not been hard at all but soft and tender beneath her kisses. She swayed forward, making a throaty, moaning sound like a woman in the throes of passion, and her hand came up as if beseeching mercy, or forgiveness.

He turned his head around again and said something to Louvois, and though she couldn't see his face, she knew he smiled. Her hand fell to her side and she started to stumble away, and then, like Lot's wife, she turned back again for one last look at the destruction of her world.

She saw Louvois smile and shrug and reach into his coat pocket. He brought out a heavy purse—she knew it was heavy for he hefted it in his hand, showing off its weight. He held it out, balanced on his palm, across the table the way a servant would present a missive on a gilt tray.

And Max—her lover, her husband, her joy—stretched his hand across the table and took it.

"No." She stumbled backward, shaking her head wildly. "No."

Darkness, thick and black, fell like a blanket over her eyes, blinding her. She whirled around, slamming into a lamppost, and fell to her knees. Wrenching spasms racked her stomach and she doubled over, vomiting into the street.

A pair of carriage wheels clicked dizzily past her face, splattering mud into her eyes, but she didn't notice. There was a strange moaning sound in her ears, like the distant wail of a thousand mourners, and through the moans she heard voices speaking above her head, and someone leaned over and touched her arm.

"She's drunk."

"No, she's ill. Help her."

It was her instinct for survival—as much a part of her as her golden-red hair and violet eyes—that propelled Gabrielle to her feet. She pulled away from the solicitous hands that helped her and took several tottering, blind steps, swaying out into the street. An enormous gray dog snarled and snapped at her, straining at a leash held by a man in silver and blue livery.

The man knocked her roughly aside. "Out of the way, you fool. Do you want to get run over? Make way for Monsieur le Comte."

An emblazoned barouche, its path cleared by the runners and dogs, careened around the corner, clattering over the cobblestones at breakneck speed. The whirling spokes of its high-set wheels missed clipping Gabrielle by inches. Reflexively she jerked aside, and in that moment the darkness around her eyes receded and the moaning wail in her ears died, and only then did she fully understand what Max had done to her. And why.

She ran, weaving blindly through the streets, driven by panic and heartbreak, until her heaving lungs and trembling legs could carry her no further. She stopped in the middle of the Pont Neuf and, leaning over the balustrade, looked down on the oily flat surface of the river while tears streamed down her face to fall into the water below.

Max, Max, Max. His name was a dirge in her heart. She loved him, loved him, loved him. And he . . . he had said he loved her, he had made love to her body, he had married her and then he had destroyed it all for a few dirty coins. He had *sold* her. And Dominique, her son, who had already come to love and trust his new papa . . .

"Max!" she screamed, her voice echoing over the river. "How could you do this to us!"

People stopped to stare; she didn't see them. She saw only the dark depths of the water so far below, the beckoning, peaceful water where there was no love and no betrayal and no pain, and she almost jumped.

But she had the blood of Sébastien de Servien in her veins, and the house of Servien always survived. Galley masters, dunning shopkeepers, even lovers who betrayed—all those and more could be endured. Only death defeated a Servien, and Gabrielle was not ready to die.

Instead she did what she had done before—she ran.

Max strode across the gardens of the Palais Royal with the quick, lilting step of a man madly and passionately in love and on his way to his beloved.

Gabrielle . . . her name was a song in his blood. He wanted

to throw back his head and shout it to the world. He had found the fountain of eternal joy, and she was his.

Not that things were perfect. There would, for instance, be a little storm to weather tonight—he had forgotten to tell her he would be late for supper. He wasn't used to considering someone else in his comings and goings, and so it had completely slipped his mind. Obviously, being married was going to require some adjustments on his part. He didn't mind; he would do whatever was necessary to make her happy.

She didn't know it yet, but already he had taken the first step by quitting the cabal. And that was the other small blight on his otherwise rosy world. His last mission for the cabal was completed, but it had left him feeling vaguely uneasy. Louvois had acted strange, distracted, almost as if he didn't understand what was happening, or didn't care. Except for a single, token effort at a bribe, the lawyer had agreed to all of Max's demands without an argument—almost, Max thought, as if he were in a hurry to be done with it and on to the more important thing that was occupying his mind. The whole thing smelled to Max like a three-day-old herring, but it wasn't his worry any longer.

Max supposed one of the other ''angels'' would direct the smuggling now in his place. He had told Abel Hachette this would be his last mission, and he had meant it. He'd half expected Abel to make one last attempt to talk him out of it this evening when he had gone to the house on the Rue Royal to make his final report. But like Louvois, Abel, too, seemed to have other things on his mind.

The owners of the Café de Foy had recently strung paper lanterns through the chestnut trees. Tonight, they swayed and bobbed in the moist summer air, almost as if they were dancing to Max's internal song of joy. The café was busy, and laughter spilled from its open doors, drawing him on.

As he turned his head briefly away from the dazzling lights of the café, Max thought he saw a glimmer of spectacles and a white, scarred face. His step veered off the path, but a second later, Louvois—if it was Louvois and not a figure of his imagination—had disappeared. Now he saw only a pair of whores lingering in the shadows of the peristyle.

He considered investigating further, then changed his mind. Gabrielle was waiting. If the lawyer Louvois had taken the trouble to follow him home, Max would be generous and let the man have his fun. It would do him little good.

Max slowed his steps as he approached his apartment. He looked up and saw the welcoming flicker of candlelight in the window and felt a warm glow in his heart. He had lived in many rooms in his life, from garrets to palaces, but this was the first time he had ever had a place to come home to.

He lingered a moment, hoping to see her silhouette pass by the yellow square of light, but it remained empty. He shook his head, smiling at his own besotted foolishness, and strode through the entrance into the stairwell—

"Bastard!" A slight figure hurled itself out of the shadows, flailing at his chest. "You bastard!"

"Agnes! What—"

She raked his face with her nails, drawing blood. He seized one wrist, then the other, pulling her hands around to the small of her back. He forced her up against his chest and turned her around so that he could see her face in the light spilling in the door from the paper lanterns. It was blotched, swollen with crying and rage. Her chest heaved with her sobbing.

Max felt a coldness wrap slowly around him like a shroud. He heard his own voice speak, hard and controlled, from a long way away. "Gabrielle. What's happened to Gabrielle?"

Agnes jerked against his arms. "You promised to keep her safe, you bastard. And instead you drove her away!"

"Where is she?"

"Bastard."

He shook her, so hard her head snapped back and her teeth rattled. "Goddamn you, where is she!"

"She's left you! She and Dominique. They've gone where you'll never find them."

He squeezed her wrists until she screamed from the pain of it and shoved his face up against hers. His own harsh pants mixed with the girl's whimpers. "Where. Is. She."

She burst into hysterical laughter. ''Do you think she would tell me where she was going? She's too smart for that. She knew you would try to throttle it out of me.''

Max thought that this was what it must feel like to drown. To know you are dying, to open your mouth to scream, and have the water, the killing water, come pouring in.

''Why?'' he whispered, and the question was torn from his gut. ''Tell me why.''

She spat in his face. ''You know. Bastard.''

He let her go. She backed away from him, rubbing her wrists. The look she gave him was full of hate and contempt, and something else—confusion. She doesn't know, Max thought. She knows how, she might even know where, but she doesn't know why.

It didn't matter, he knew why. She had given him the answer anyway, with the first word out of her mouth.

Bastard.

He'd spent his life earning the epithet his father had branded him with at birth. What had made him think he could change overnight—could make himself into someone good enough for her? He had no one but himself to blame if Gabrielle had come to see him clearly just for what he was. A bastard in both meanings of the word.

''If I were a man, I'd kill you,'' Agnes said.

If I were a man, he thought, I'd probably kill myself.

He climbed the stairs to his apartment because there was nowhere else to go. Just as he knew without looking the moment she entered a room, so he now knew that she was truly, irrevocably gone.

He went into the bedroom anyway. She hadn't had time to bring many of her belongings over from the pawnshop. What few she had were now gone. But she had found, after all, a way to tell him goodbye. It lay beside the candelabra, on the marble surface of his commode table—the gold signet ring he had placed on her finger just two days before.

His fist closed around it, and he pulled his arm up and back, wanting to fling it away from him, wanting to throw it and all that he was feeling halfway across the world. Instead his arm fell to his side and his hand opened. The ring bounced once as it struck the floor and rolled away from him. He didn't look down. He stared unseeing at the wall. Something had torn loose inside of him. He could feel it bleeding, leaking his life's blood into his chest.

His fists clenched and his head fell back, the tendons of his neck standing out like ropes. "Gabrielle!" he shouted, and her name reverberated in the still night air.

"Gabrielle! *Gabrielle!*"

Part Two

1788-1789

Chapter 14

The three vagabonds—a man, an old woman, and a youth—were huddled close around the fire, for a bitter wind blew that November night and clouds, soggy with rain, draped the moon.

Their camp was in a small copse just off the Lyons road. All three were strangers to each other, but they had come together and camped within sight of the road because it made them feel safer from the bands of brigands that roved the countryside. Not that they possessed much to steal but a few turnips. Still, others had died for far less.

They didn't speak much, but waited patiently for the half dozen turnips that roasted over the flames to be done. The youth, a scrawny lad of about seventeen, had said he was so hungry he could feel his belly button rubbing against his spine, but it was an old joke and the other two didn't laugh.

Which was why he waited a long time before calling their attention to the apparition on the side of the road. Eventually fear overcame his pride. "Look," he said, pointing. "Do you think they're ghosts?"

The old hag and the man turned to follow the direction of his finger. They saw the silhouette of a woman standing, feet braced apart, a small child clinging to one hand. The wind whipped the edges of her ragged cloak, making it flap like bats' wings against her legs.

"They look solid enough to me," the man said. He was an odd sort, almost dainty in his mannerisms and with an educated way of speaking. His breeches were so caked with dirt they had crackled when he first squatted before the fire, but anyone could see they had been satin once. He said he was called Louis-Prosper, which was a toff-sounding name.

"What do you think they want from us?" the youth—whose name was a very ordinary Gaston—wondered aloud.

"The fire, *mon petit gars*," the old hag said. "And some company. Same as us." She sucked on her toothless gums and poked a stick at the smoking roots. "They mean no harm."

Gaston sighed. "They'll want some of our turnips."

The woman and the child had started to approach the camp fire, but warily, like pigeons sensing a trap. They stopped while they were several feet away.

"Good evening, messieurs . . . madame," the woman said in a low, rasping voice, and Gaston thought she sounded young and perhaps beautiful, but he couldn't see her face for it was shadowed by the hood of her cloak. The child who clung tightly to her hand was a boy of about five with flax-colored hair and a pair of blue eyes that filled the whole of his thin, white face. His feet were wrapped in rags, but where the flesh showed through it was blue with cold.

While Gaston was trying to decide what to say, Louis-Prosper pushed to his feet. He dusted off the seat of his filthy satin breeches and made a courtly bow. *"Enchanté* . . . Please enter, pull up a chair. I'll ring for some tea," he said, and the old hag burst into cackling laughter that turned into a fit of coughing.

Stepping forward, the woman pushed back the hood of her cloak, and Gaston sucked in a sharp breath, for her hair was as bright as the flames of their camp fire. She held out her arm, and two plump rabbits dangled from the end of it. "I have meat to share," she said, this time with a dazzling smile, and Gaston's breath expelled from his pursed lips in a low whistle. "If you'll allow me the use of your fire, and one or two of your turnips."

The vagabonds would have traded a field of turnips for one of the rabbits. And Gaston would have traded the rabbit for a chance at a tumble with the woman, for never in his life had he seen anything so fine.

He changed his mind a moment later when, sitting down, she pulled a wicked-looking knife from a makeshift sheath around her waist and began to skin and gut the rabbits. Looking up, he met Louis-Prosper's laughing eyes. The man leaned close to him and whispered loudly. "Best keep your yard in your breeches where it belongs, my randy young friend. She could slit a hole in your belly and weave your guts into a basket with the likes of that."

Gaston's cheeks blazed with embarrassment, but if the woman had heard she gave no sign of it.

The old hag had scooted over for a closer look at the rabbits. She poked one with her stick. "These are plump little darlings, they are."

"Maman stole them," said a clear, piping voice.

They all looked at the boy where he squatted beside the woman, clutching her knee with his fist.

"Hush, Dominique," the woman scolded. A faint blush colored her cheeks, but the fingers that were wrapped around the hilt of her knife tightened their grip. She stared back at the vagabonds, forcing them one by one to drop their gazes to the fire.

After a long silence Louis-Prosper slapped his hands together and massaged his knuckles. "Stolen, are they? And why not, eh? They taste better when they haven't been paid for."

While the meat cooked, the vagabonds fell to discussing politics, for winter was coming and already there was famine and no work. The queen was to blame, they all agreed. Marie Antoinette, who cared more about being queen of fashion than being queen of France. Who bankrupted the treasury by draping herself with clothes and jewels and gambling a year's wages against the faro bank on the turn of a card. They were calling her Madame Déficit in the newspapers now. Nor was the king entirely guiltless, foolish and beguiled though he might be by his frivolous and greedy wife. It was said he spent his days hunting and his nights gorging on the one hundred and eighty dishes prepared for his table. And this while his people starved!

As they argued over what was to be done about it, the woman pulled the boy within the warmth of her thin, ragged cloak, wrapping it tight around their bent legs. She took no part in the conversation, and the others began to suspect she thought herself too grand for the likes of them, although it was kind of her to share her rabbits.

She stirred when a goatskin was passed around the fire. "It's only water, more's the pity," Louis-Prosper said, holding it out to her across the flames.

Her hand shook as she reached for it, and Gaston saw that her face was blotchy and covered with a light film of sweat. "I say, you don't have the pox, do you?" he asked.

Her eyes stared at him, wide-open and unblinking. He had thought them blue, but they were too dark to be blue. Purple, he thought. They're purple. He'd never seen purple eyes before.

She gave some water to the boy first, then drank thirstily herself, tilting back her head. Her hair rippled like a sheet of copper down her back, and Gaston sighed.

But when she went to pass the goatskin on to him, she swayed dizzily and would have fallen into the fire if he hadn't grabbed her arm. Her flesh, he noticed, was as icy as the wind.

"Where are we?" she said to him suddenly.

Gaston's mouth fell open. "Huh?"

The old hag snorted. "The road to Lyons, *fille,* where did you think?"

"Where do you want to be?" Louis-Prosper asked in a strangely gentle voice.

"The Château de Nevers," she said, her voice thick and wandering with the fever. The boy had fallen asleep with his head in her lap. She stroked his fine blond hair. "I must take him there, you see? To the Château de Nevers. I thought to give him a mother's love, but I've brought him only misery. I must take him there or he will die.''

Gaston had seen many deaths in his seventeen years. The towheaded boy looked cold and half starved, but he wasn't close to dying yet. The woman, he thought, making the sign of the cross, already had one slender foot in the grave.

The *diligence* that had taken them away from Paris that day fifteen months before had been crowded with passengers so that Dominique had to sit on Gabrielle's lap. They were wedged between a plasterer coated with white dust and smelling of pickled herring and a laundress smelling more pleasantly of soap.

Dominique asked a million questions: Where were they going? What were they going to do once they got there? How was that man able to make his eye float in his head?

The man, who sat across from them, did have something wrong with his right eye. The pupil, which couldn't seem to stay focused on any one object, drifted up and down and from side to side like a pearl onion in a bowl of broth. Gabrielle flushed and apologized to the man for her son's rudeness.

''Don't be distressed. The child means no harm,'' he said. ''It's refreshing to find curiosity in one so young.''

He couldn't help overhearing, he said, that they were going to Dijon. To visit family perhaps? Himself, he was going a little further, to Beaune, where he resided with his wife (alas, they were childless) and where he ran a business. He was a vintner; he bottled and shipped wine. His name was Baptiste Balue—had madame perhaps heard of the Balue label? He didn't mean to brag, but his circumstances were comfortable, very comfortable indeed, though he worked hard for what he got. Did madame know how many vines it took to produce a single bottle of good burgundy?

He talked on. Gabrielle was grateful for the distraction. Her throat ached and her eyes burned from the effort it was taking to hold back her tears. She still wanted to crawl into a hole somewhere and die, or to drown in one of Monsieur Balue's vats of wine. It seemed a monumental effort just to breathe. *Max, Max, Max.* The pain wouldn't go away. It wasn't ever going to go away.

It took the stagecoach an hour to cover five leagues, and that wasn't counting the stops to pay tolls or change horses or clear the fallen logs and boulders from the road. They were a very long time getting to Dijon.

Baptiste Balue was a big man, with thick bullocklike shoulders and a round, jutting head, and with his strange eye he would have seemed menacing if not for his gentle smile and childlike, easy laughter. He was also an astute man. By the time they arrived in Dijon he had guessed that the lovely Madame Prion and her son were running away from something. A cruel father, an abusive husband, a jealous lover, perhaps? He didn't care. He could see that madame wasn't one of the *canaille*—the rabble. She was educated, polished; she had style. Would she be interested, perhaps, in journeying on to Beaune to become a companion to his invalid wife, who was lonely and needed someone of a genteel disposition with which to pass the time?

To Gabrielle, Monsieur Baptiste Balue seemed a nice enough man—when one got used to his floating eye. He was offering her a living, a roof and food for her son. She told herself if she didn't like it she could always leave. She didn't care where she lived or what she did; she didn't care about anything anymore. Besides, Dominique seemed to like the man.

Although the town of Beaune was not large, it was the center of the great wine-producing district known as the Côte de Beaune. The *hôtel* of Baptiste Balue was the finest in the region—finer even, Balue told her with pride, than the local seigneur's. It had a staff of twenty-three, including two maids whose sole job it was to clean up after the other servants. Gabrielle and Dominique were given a room all to themselves, on the fourth floor with the rest of the live-in staff.

Dominique liked the room because it was high above the other roofs of the town and he could pretend he was floating in a 'stat with M'sieur Max. Every day he asked Gabrielle where were his new papa and Agnes and Simon and when were they coming, and every day she told him they were all still in Paris and couldn't come.

One day a sudden thought struck him and he went running to Maman to share it with her. "I know what we can do!" he said, so excited he was hopping from foot to foot. "If they can't come to us, *we* can go back to Paris!"

She knelt down so they were face to face. "But we can't, *chéri*. We must stay here and take care of Madame Balue, who is very ill and needs our help."

"I don't like Madame Balue. She stinks. And she cries a lot—worse than a baby."

"She only cries when she's in pain."

"*I* never cry."

She hugged him until he began to squirm and make a face. "That's because you're my little man," she said.

Dominique's chest puffed with pride and he forgot for a time about going back to Paris.

Eventually Dominique decided that Monsieur Max must have gone to heaven like his other papa, because every night, when she thought he was asleep, he could hear Maman crying Monsieur Max's name and begging him not to do something. And then one Sunday Maman took him to Mass and he heard the priest say they should all pray to heaven, to ask and you shall receive, and so Dominique began to pray to Monsieur Max, asking him to leave heaven and come to Beaune, which was nice but not as nice as Paris. It was true that Maman took him fishing here, although it was only a tiny little creek, not big like the river Seine. The cook made him gingerbread sometimes, but it was not as good as what Agnes used to buy. He liked Monsieur Balue, who laughed a lot, but he never put him up on his shoulders the way Monsieur Max used to do.

And Maman was sad all the time. She had never been sad before, especially when Monsieur Max was around.

Gabrielle was able to spend a lot of time with her son, for her duties to Madame Balue were not exacting ones. The nature of the woman's illness was never precisely explained, except that she had to be bled three or four times a week.

The poor woman's arms and legs were covered with thick ridges of scars made by the barber's knife and she was left so weak she couldn't rise up from her bed. In between bleedings she would recline on the settee while Gabrielle read aloud to her, always books with a strong religious theme. She liked to talk about her childhood in Provence and how she had wanted to become a nun, but her father, who knew, of course, what was best, had said she must marry instead.

Instead of eating in the servants' hall, as part of her duties Gabrielle ate upstairs with monsieur and madame. And when madame took one of her bad turns, Gabrielle dined alone with monsieur—chaperoned by a butler and two servants and separated by fifteen feet of polished mahogany and a ton of silver plate. Balue's cheerful voice, punctuated by his hearty laugh, would rattle on about wine and politics and the weather, while Gabrielle ate and smiled politely and even listened a little because it meant she didn't have to think. Or remember.

Except at meals, she rarely saw Balue. Occasionally he would listen for a time while she read to his wife. Once or twice she had been in a room alone and looked up to find him watching her, his strange eye floating eerily in its socket. He would stay and chat politely for a few minutes, and then leave. He was gone from the house for many hours at a time, for his business kept him busy.

And so the hours passed and became days and the days slipped into months, until a year had come and gone. And there was not a minute of the hours, days, and months that Gabrielle did not think of Max and mourn. Not for what she had lost, but for what had never been.

She had been in Beaune for over a year when Baptiste Balue invited her and Dominique to come with him to watch the grape harvest.

It was a beautiful October day. The air was dry and mild, the sky a vivid turquoise-blue, dotted with small clouds as thin and lacy as dandelion puffs. They made a picnic of it, supping under the shade of a group of cottonwoods that grew beside the vineyard. They watched the pickers walk up and down the rows, baskets swinging down their backs, hanging by straps across their foreheads. As the baskets filled with grapes, they were emptied into a cart and brought to the vats to be crushed.

Gabrielle, with Dominique's enthusiastic help, filled a couple of baskets herself, while Balue walked beside her and explained in laborious detail the process of making wine. Gabrielle let his voice drone on above her head and luxuriated in the feel of her muscles stretching and bending after so many cramped and tedious hours spent indoors.

That evening they all joined in a celebration to mark the beginning of the harvest. With the other village girls, Gabrielle kilted her skirts above her knees and climbed into the vat to crush the grapes.

Someone began to play a guitar and they all stamped their feet in time to the music in a strange, clumsy dance. The sticky juice oozed between her toes and slapped up to coat her calves. It felt wonderful—cool and sensual. The smell of the must rose up to fill her head, making her feel a bit drunk.

Gabrielle threw back her head, and her golden-red hair hung down her back to catch the rays of the dying sun. She laughed out loud and the sound of her joy bounded across the fields. It was the first time Balue had heard her laugh, and he stood looking up at her, transfixed.

That night he tried to rape her.

She always locked her door, but he must have kept a key, for suddenly he was there with no warning except the crash of the door against the wall, crushing her down on the mattress with his big bulk, smothering her screams with one hand while he tore at her nightdress to paw at her breasts with the other, whispering harshly about her beauty and how she was driving him mad and how he could see she wanted this, was begging for this . . . His hands left clammy trails of sweat on her skin and his breath smelled of sour wine and garlic, and though she fought him she knew she couldn't stop him. He was so heavy, so strong . . .

She heard someone crying. Dominique, she thought as she scratched and clawed and kicked with her legs, feeling the obscenity of Balue's hard shaft jabbing at her thighs. Dominique is watching this, Dominique is going to see—

Suddenly Balue screamed, a high-pitched woman's shriek, and arched up, his face twisted into a rictus of agony. He rolled off her, clutching his thigh, swearing and sobbing. And Dominique, her five-year-old child, stood beside the bed with a knife in his hand.

"Maman, I gutted him!" Dominique cried, his voice shaky, almost hysterical. "I gutted him like the fishes!"

"You damned brat! I'll kill you for this!" Balue roared. He clawed at the bedclothes, trying to pull himself up. Even in the dim light cast by the moon coming in the narrow window, Gabrielle could see the shining wetness of the blood on his thigh.

Gabrielle leaped off the bed and, snatching up her son, began to back into the hall. Balue tried to lunge to his feet after her, but his leg collapsed beneath him and he fell to the floor, swearing and sobbing. Gabrielle heard a door open somewhere downstairs and a man call out. Balue was screaming loud enough for all of Beaune to hear.

"And you, you bitch! I'll see you branded and whipped through the streets! I'll make you wish you—"

Gabrielle whirled and fled from the horror in the room.

The other servants were all too intent on discovering the source of the terrible shouts to try to stop her. She burst into the night, Dominique in her arms, and ran for the open country where there would be ditches and ravines and places to hide. She didn't know for how long she ran or where she was when she stopped. There were trees all around, and she could hear somewhere nearby the trickle of water flowing over rocks, but it was nothing compared to the roar of her own harsh breathing. She leaned her back against a large boulder and slowly sank to the ground with Dominique in her lap.

She looked down and saw that her son still had the knife clutched tightly in his hand. It was of a set that came from the kitchen. She wondered how he had come by it, but then he had always been attracted to things that were shiny and sharp. *Oh, Dominique, Dominique* . . . There was blood on the sleeve of his nightshirt.

"Dominique," she said softly, not wanting to frighten him. He wasn't crying, but she could feel tremors shaking his small body. "Give me the knife, *chéri.*"

He gave it to her. "He was a bad man, Maman."

"Yes, he was. A very bad man."

"I gutted him."

"Oh, *chéri* . . ." Silent tears streamed down Gabrielle's face. Oh my son, my son, she thought. What have I done to you?

It was said that November of 1788 was the coldest anyone could remember. Rivers and streams froze solid. Hailstorms ravaged the countryside, ruining the crops. It was so cold that wine bottles burst in the cellars and windmill sails had to be doused with warm water to melt the ice.

Gabrielle and Dominique had fled Beaune with nothing but a knife and their nightclothes. Before dawn, at the first village they came to, she broke through the window of a laundry and stole enough things to make them decent and keep them warm. She stole more clothes later, and food, too, enough to live on. She begged some days, but times were hard, and she and Dominique were strangers, vagabonds, and the country folk were more used to taking care of their own. She was too afraid to stop in any one place long enough to find work. Balue's threat was not an idle one—he could have her whipped and branded for what had been done to him.

Once a cobbler, seeing them barefoot, took pity and gave them each a pair of sabots. She thought their luck was really turning when the next day a farmer gave them a ride in his cart all the way to the next village. But then, after the cart disappeared over the crest of the hill, it began to rain and Gabrielle looked down, thinking to grab Dominique's hand so that they could run for the dubious shelter of the ditch along the road. And then she saw her son's bare feet.

She seized his shoulders, giving him a rough shake. "What

have you done with your sabots?'' she shouted at him, her voice cracking.

He stared up at her, looking small and wan and rebellious while the rain fell in icy, nugget-sized drops.

"Don't know. I left them in the cart, I guess."

"You guess! Oh, Dominique, what were you thinking? You can't walk across France in the middle of winter in your bare feet!'' Her voice caught on a sob as the terrible uselessness of it all struck her then. They were running away, but they had nowhere to go and there was nothing for them once they got there.

She knelt beside her son and pulled him into her arms. She could feel through the rags of his clothes the sharp bones of his ribs. His nose was running and his lips were blue and she was killing him through her selfishness.

Her throat felt raw, as if it had been grated with sand, and she knew she was burning with a fever. She was getting sick. What if she became too ill to care for him? What had she brought him to anyway—to starve or freeze or to die racked with fever, pummeled by icy rain in a ditch?

She would give him up, taking him to the Nevers family. They were of his blood. They would care for him, love him probably. *Dieu,* but didn't they want him enough to hound her for years, trying to take him from her? After all she had done, they would probably think a cell in a convent too good for her now, but it wouldn't matter what happened to her, as long as Dominique was safe and loved.

She held him at arm's length and forced a bright note into her voice. "Dominique? Would you like to go see your *grand-mère?* She is a grand duchesse and she lives in a big château not far from here, I think. Would you like that?"

Dominique nodded, wiping his nose with the end of his sleeve. "I suppose so. But will M'sieur Max be able to find us there? He's coming from heaven and he might not know where to look for us."

A sob tore from Gabrielle's pain-ravaged throat and she crushed Dominique against her breast. *Oh, Max,* her heart cried out to him. Max, her husband, not in heaven but safe in Paris. Was he laughing at the thought of her and Dominique running like flushed pheasants across France, with nothing, not even a pair of sabots? Did he hate them that much? Why? Why had he done this to them?

Oh, God, Max. I loved you. I thought you loved me, you said you did, you married me. I love you, love you, love you . . .

But though her heart called out to him, she heard only the moaning of the cold November wind, and as the rain beat down hard on her bent head, she felt for the first time in her life defeated.

Chapter 15

The grand ballroom in the palace of the duc d'Orleans sparkled with colored silks and satins and shimmered with gilt and brocaded velvets. Chandeliers, dripping with candles, dangled from the domed, frescoed ceiling. An orchestra played a minuet, but no one was dancing.

Across the crowded room a woman caught the attention of a pair of sooty gray eyes and tilted her chin toward a curtained alcove. Then she turned back to her companion, who just happened to be the comte d'Artois and brother to the king. She laughed at something he said and rapped him lightly on the cheek with her fan—but not too hard for it was, after all, a royal cheek. From time to time her eyes would stray back across the room.

The object of her attention leaned against a wall to wait, content for the moment just to watch her. In her silver gown garlanded with lamé roses and white feathers curling from her silver-blond hair, she shone like a diamond among paste jewels. Shone brighter, in fact, than the very real circlet of diamonds that graced her slender neck.

The comte d'Artois bowed and turned from the woman, and she started to make her way across the room, angling slowly toward the alcove. She had stopped looking at him by now, but the bright spots of color on her cheeks were not entirely due to her rouge. When he saw her pull the curtains aside and disappear, he followed.

He had expected only a bay of windows on the other side of the curtains, but instead he found a door. It opened easily beneath his hand.

A heavy floral perfume enveloped him, and then soft arms wrapped around his neck. Lips, cool and moist, fastened onto his.

"You swore you weren't coming," she said a moment later.

He pushed the sleeve of her gown down her arm to trail his fingers lightly across her collarbone, and only when he heard her moan did he move lower to caress her bared breast. "I changed my mind."

"My husband is here." The sentence ended with a gasp as he pulled on her tautened nipple.

"So?"

"He took me tonight, on the way here. In the carriage." She undid his breeches and stroked him with both hands, and he set his jaw to steady his breathing. "Are you jealous?" she asked, unable to hide the catch in her voice as he pressed his knee between her legs and began to rub her there, hard and fast.

"No," he said. "Perhaps next time he takes you I can watch."

"You are cruel."

"You like it cruel. What you need, Madame la Marquise, is a master."

Her laugh held both fear and excitement. "And do you, Monsieur le Vicomte, fancy yourself my master?"

For an answer he put his hands on her shoulders and pushed her onto her knees before him. "Oh, Max," he heard her sigh as she took him in her mouth.

He shut his eyes, giving himself over to the pleasure that would, as always, be all too brief and leave him feeling empty.

* * *

When the Vicomte Maximilien de Saint-Just emerged from the alcove later, the ballroom was less crowded, and the powder on the faces of those who were left was melting with the heat of the hall. The orchestra, which was now playing Mozart, was being drowned out by a cacophony of loud moans mixed with cheers and laughter drifting from a pair of double doors that opened onto a smaller room. The faro bank had been reopened.

"Back the pharoah and the king of hearts!" he heard someone shout. He had started toward the card game when he felt a hand on his arm and looked down into the boyish face of Percival Bonville. For once it wasn't smiling.

"I didn't expect to see you here tonight," Percy said.

Max sighed. "Why do people insist on believing everything I say?" He felt a dull pain begin to throb behind his eyes. It meant he was getting sober again, and he plucked a glass of champagne off the tray of a passing servant to avert such a catastrophe. "Excuse me, Percy, but I believe I hear a king of hearts calling my name."

The young American continued to hold his arm, and though Max gave him a baleful look he didn't release his grip. "Why aren't you on your way to the Château de Morvan?" Percy said. "I thought your father had taken ill and was asking for you."

"What have you been doing, *mon ami?* Steaming open my correspondence?"

Percy didn't smile. "That's more your line of work. If your father's dying—"

"To hell with the son of a bitch," Max said with a crudity that matched his mood. His eyes went to the double doors from which came another burst of groans and laughter. "I'd rather play at faro than the prodigal son."

"Really? I should think you'd want to make sure of your inheritance. How much have you lost already tonight?"

"It so happens I've won thirty thousand livres. You know I never lose at anything." Max gave a sharp, bitter laugh. "Except, of course, for that one memorable and soon to be forgotten occasion." His eyes went to a woman whose silver gown matched her hair. She was speaking to a plump matron in puce silk, but she watched Max from behind her fan. He smiled at her and lifted his empty champagne glass in a mocking toast. "I'm working hard at forgetting it."

"Forgetting *her*, you mean," Percy said, and he wasn't looking at the woman in silver.

Still smiling, Max returned his attention to the American, although he failed to hide the pain that flared for a brief moment in his eyes. "Yes, her. Gabrielle. My wife."

But you don't forget a woman like Gabrielle, my poor friend. You go on loving her until it kills you, Percy thought, wishing he dared to say it aloud.

Percy turned to look at Max's new mistress, and his chocolate-brown eyes darkened with scorn. "Thirty thousand should just about pay for the likes of that high-class *grande coquette*."

Max laughed again. "She's married to the marquis de Tessé. *He* pays for her."

"And he'll kill you when he finds out you're bedding his wife."

"If he can. If he knows. And if he cares."

"He knows and he cares and he's in the billiard room," Percy said, then cursed himself when he realized too late his mistake.

Max headed unerringly for the billiard room and trouble, with Percy following, leaning on his cane and wondering if he could knock his friend down or get him passing-out drunk before any one of the million and one disasters that could happen happened.

But later, as he watched Max send one of the ivory balls at a corner pocket and miss, Percy began to think he had been wrong to worry. If Max lost this game, he would have to pay his opponent, the husband of his blond-haired mistress, an incredible fifty thousand livres. The wager had been all Max's idea and Percy hoped he would lose. Then perhaps the marquis de Tessé would feel that his honor had been satisfied without resorting to pistols or swords.

"Alas, you fail again, monsieur," the marquis de Tessé was saying, his black eyes flashing with taunting laughter as he picked up his cue stick to take his turn. "I hope you don't make love with the same lack of skill you exhibit at billiards."

Max said nothing, but his mouth stretched into a cold, lazy smile and his heavy lids drooped over his eyes until they were half shut. Percy, who knew just what that look portended, swallowed a sigh. Perhaps honor wouldn't be satisfied so easily after all.

Of course the real cause of all this, Percy knew, was not that silver-haired marquise in the ballroom. The real cause was a woman named Gabrielle, who had been more beautiful than the marquise ever hoped to be, and who had been loving and laughing and giving. Who had, damn her to hell, done more than break his friend's heart. She had broken his soul.

Percy had thought Gabrielle would be Max's salvation, and he couldn't understand what could have happened to drive her away. One night, shortly after she had first left him, Max had gotten drunk enough to try to explain. "I tried to warn her about me, but she wouldn't listen," Max had said, the words so slurred Percy could barely hear them. "I guess when she discovered the truth, she couldn't stomach it."

None of it had made any sense to Percy.

Nor did any of Max's actions in the subsequent months. For over a year, Max, who had been one of the worst rakes in Paris, avoided women the way the devil would cringe and cower at the sight of a crucifix. Then just when Percy had adjusted to this strange, morose celibacy on the part of his friend, Max resumed his old carousing ways by entering into a blatant and torrid affair with the wife of the marquis de Tessé, a man known for his hot temper and his love of dueling . . .

Maximilien de Saint-Just, Percy thought with a sigh, no longer played at dangerous games; he embraced them.

As the billiard game dragged on, the animosity between the two men became a tangible thing in the air, like mist. Word of the contest began to spread, and a crowd gathered in the room. Everyone knew that the Vicomte Maximilien de Saint-Just, bastard son of the famous *maréchal* and now his acknowledged heir, was bedding the marquis de Tessé's wife. Now the two men had brought their rivalry to a game of billiards. It was just the sort of scandal and reckless wager the raffish, dissipated aristocrats of the Palais Royal set loved. A set where it was *bon ton* to take lovers and gamble away a fortune. And where duels, although outlawed, were fought with the smallest provocation.

To the delight of the crowd, the two opponents began to exchange thinly veiled insults faster than they could trade shots.

When the marquis de Tessé made a particularly difficult carom, the crowd sighed in admiration, and Tessé smiled triumphantly at Max. "I do hope you can afford this little exercise in humility, *mon petit salaud.*"

Percy winced at the insult, but Max didn't even blink. He was probably used to being called a bastard, Percy thought. Then he heard Max say, "How odd that your wife isn't here to watch your triumph . . . but then perhaps she doesn't care," and Percy bit back a groan.

The marquis, whose hands were braced on the green woolen cloth of the table as he bent to study his next shot, slowly straightened. Two white ridges of anger bracketed his mouth. "At least my wife is with me tonight," he said. "Where is yours?"

All the blood drained from Max's face, and the knuckles of the hand that gripped his cue stick whitened. "I'm not married."

"Aren't you? I heard you were. To some little shopgirl, wasn't it, who shared your bed less than a week and then fled from you in horror—"

Max lashed the cue stick—a thin, flexible shaft with an ivory tip—through the air and struck Tessé's cheek. Tessé screamed and reeled backward, his hand flying to his face. Blood spurted between his fingers.

Percy grabbed Max's arm and wrenched the stick from his hand, but there was really no need. The damage had already been done.

"Name your weapons," the marquis said in a pain-clipped

voice as blood leaked from the hand that cupped his face to drop onto the floor in bright red splashes.

"Pistols."

"Max, for God's sake—" Percy began.

"Tomorrow at dawn," Max said. "In the Bois de Boulogne."

"Agreed."

The marquis de Tessé allowed someone to lead him from the room. There was no sign of the marquis's silver-haired wife. Soon the crowd dispersed until only Max and Percy were left standing side by side next to the billiard table.

Percy stared at the hard face of his friend, feeling anger and a terrible sadness. "If he kills you, it will serve you right. You marked him for life."

Max said nothing. He went instead to a sideboard, where brandy and glasses were set out, and poured himself a drink. Max had started to raise the glass to his lips when Percy knocked it from his hand with his cane. Seizing his arms in a grip that would leave bruises, Percy turned Max to face a huge, gilt-framed mirror that hung on the wall.

"Look at yourself!" He gave Max a rough shake. They both stared at the reflection of the dark, patrician face that was still handsome in spite of the puffy flesh around the bloodshot eyes and the slack, drunken mouth. "What are you trying to do? Prove to the world that Gabrielle was right to leave you?"

Max jerked out of Percy's hands so violently that Percy stumbled backward. His cane clattered to the floor, and he had to grasp a chair to keep from falling. Although Percy was half a head shorter, he stood up to Max, toe to toe.

"What are you going to do now, Saint-Just? Cut my face, too? Pity I don't have a wife you can bed."

Max was breathing heavily and the muscles in his neck and jaw were drawn taut. "I want you to keep your nose out of my life."

"Well, I won't." He flung his arm toward the ballroom. "That particular tart isn't worth killing for, and she certainly isn't worth dying for. She might have a title and dress in satin and jewels, but she's still a whore.''

''And I took her like a whore.''

''So what does that make you?''

Max's lips curled into a tight smile. ''A man who sleeps with whores.''

Percy sucked in a sharp breath. ''You are a bastard.''

''I know. Will you be my second?''

''No. Yes. Damn you.''

The old to-hell-with-it-all smile flashed across Max's face. ''Quit worrying. If I was going to kill myself, I'd have done it by now. Tessé's a master with a sword, but he can't crease the back end of a cow with a pistol. Whereas I, as you know, can shoot the pip out of a card at fifty paces. And I wouldn't have hit the fool so hard if he hadn't made me lose my temper.''

Percy smiled back shakily. ''Christ . . . what in hell are you talking about?''

Max laughed. ''I hit him first so he would challenge me, which made the choice of weapon mine. I won't kill him. I'll only wing him so that everyone's honor will be satisfied. I'll even give him his wife back. Now are you happy?''

''No,'' Percy said.

Mist, as thick as milk, dripped off the skeletal branches overhead. Gauzy like a shroud, the gray dawn light filtered through the trees. There was an empty feeling to the air. Even the squirrels and blackbirds seemed to have fled from the Bois de Boulogne that cold November morning.

His back to his opponent, Max marched off the fifteen paces, only half listening to the echoing voice of the man doing the counting. The pistol dangling from his fingers felt heavy; his boots sank deep into the wet earth, mulchy with fallen leaves. The dull throb behind his eyes was now a full-fledged headache. He had tried to sober up just enough so he wouldn't get himself killed. Now all he wanted was a glass of brandy and some sleep.

Suddenly he felt adrift, unable to remember why he was

here, why he was dueling with this man over a woman he didn't love and wouldn't even want to see again after this day. This is pointless, he thought in the split second before he heard the call to fire.

He had always been able to move fast, and with an easy, athletic grace—even when not completely sober. He did so now, spinning around, raising the pistol, and pulling the trigger in one fluid motion.

The marquis de Tessé didn't have time to turn all the way around let alone raise his weapon and get off a shot. As a result Max miscalculated his aim, and instead of hitting the man in the shoulder, the ball pierced him high on the chest, knocking him off his feet. His white shirt turned instantly crimson.

Someone shouted and a pair of men brushed against Max, running toward the man lying still and bloody on the ground. Max stood where he was, unable to move.

The marquis's hand twitched once and was still. At last, Max started forward, but Percy got up from where he knelt beside the body and came limping back to stop him.

Anger mottled the American's face. "I hope you're satisfied, you damned fool. You'll go to prison for this."

A cold wind fluttered Max's shirt against his chest, and he shivered. "Is he dead, then?"

"Not yet. But the doctor says the ball's come perilously close to a lung, so he will be soon. Unless you're luckier than you deserve to be."

Lucky? Max fought off an urge to laugh. On its heels came a fierce, desperate need to be held and comforted. Simply that—to have someone put her arms around him and hold him tight. He hadn't felt that need since he'd been a small boy and listened with his ear pressed against the door to the creaking of the bed and the sound of his mother's moans. When had she stopped holding him? He thought it must have been the year he learned that her moans were not those of pain.

"You'd better leave Paris immediately," Percy said. "Go make peace with your father. Then when—*if*—Tessé dies, your father can intercede with the king on your behalf."

"Yes. All right," Max answered, not really listening.

Gabrielle, I need you, he thought with a yearning so physical he almost groaned out loud. *Why, Gabrielle? Why did you leave me when you know I need you so much?*

Chapter 16

Max drove the cabriolet at a fast, reckless speed. Too fast for the twisting, rutted road and the black night. A heavy snow was falling. It pelted against his face, so cold it burned. He was wrapped in a thick woolen greatcoat, but his hands and feet, in spite of his gloves and boots, had long ago grown numb. The coldness of the night matched what he felt. He was numb inside as well.

If he hadn't already been so close to his father's château, he would have stopped at some roadside inn. Only a madman would be out on such a night, he thought, and then laughed out loud. Hadn't *she* accused him of being mad often enough? Perhaps that was why she had left him. Perhaps she had feared he would go berserk and strangle her some night while she slept. Perhaps—

"What in fiend's name!" he exclaimed aloud.

As the cabriolet whipped around a sharp turn, a wraith rose out of the ground at the horse's head. The horse whinnied in fright, rearing up in its traces and sending the cabriolet skidding across the slick, muddy road. The carriage tilted precariously, and Max felt the right wheel skim along the edge of the deep ditch that lined the road. He hauled back on the reins, trying with brute force to turn the horse's head.

The wheel dug through the slush, biting into the firmer ground underneath, and the carriage righted. Max cursed and wrestled the horse to a standstill, then leaped to the ground and ran back to where he had seen, or thought he had seen, in a brief second and from the corner of his eye, a body lying in the ditch.

It was a body. It was curled into a tight ball and covered with a black cloak. Beside it, guarding it, was the wraith that had spooked his horse. The wraith seemed to be waiting for him, its form floating above the road, its face a blank white oval. It raised a beseeching hand, and Max, who was not normally a superstitious man, felt the hairs spring up on the back of his neck.

"Please, M'sieur," said the wraith, who was not a ghost after all but a small child wrapped in a ragged, pale coat two sizes too big for him. "You must do something. M-my ma-man won't wake up."

Max scrambled down into the ditch and knelt beside the body. He couldn't see much of her, but he could tell she was a woman. She had evidently been trying to claw her way out of the ditch, for one hand was stretched above her head, and her fingers had dug deep into the wet earth. She had been lying there for a long time, however, for at least two inches of snow covered the top of her thin, sodden cloak.

Max picked up the wrist of her outstretched hand. It felt as frail as a sparrow's wing, as cold and stiff as a block of ice.

Max looked up at the child. He was a very young boy, Max thought, although it was too dark and snowing too hard to see the child's face. "She w-wouldn't wake up," the boy said.

"I'm going to pick her up and carry her back to my carriage," Max explained, not wanting to alarm the child. He gathered the woman in his arms and climbed with her out of the ditch. She was as light as an ell of silk.

"She'll be all right," the boy said with false brightness as he trotted beside Max's legs. "After she wakes up. She's only a little sick."

She's dead, Max thought. The poor lad.

The cabriolet, a light, fast vehicle, was not designed to

accommodate extra passengers. Max positioned the boy between his knees and propped the woman beside them on the
seat.

He whipped the horse into a trot, going as fast as he dared
with the heavier load. The woman was beyond help, but the
boy wasn't. His frail body was racked with shivers, and Max
saw he wore only rags on his feet. And it was snowing harder
now; he couldn't see much of the road beyond the horse's
ears.

Max had spent part of his adolescence at the Château de
Morvan, his father's country estate, and he knew the way
well. Although it was dark and the ground blanketed with
snow, he found the turnoff easily. He pulled up before the
great gilded iron gates.

"You there!" he shouted, and his breath billowed out
around his face in white puffs. "Open up!"

He was about to climb out of the carriage to ring the bell
when a man emerged from the front door of the gatekeeper's
lodge. He lifted a hooded lantern aloft, shining it on Max's
face.

"Monsieur le Vicomte! We weren't expecting . . . You
sent no word, otherwise I would have—"

"Quit dithering, you fool, and open the gates. I've a de—"
He stumbled over the word as he felt the boy stiffen. "A sick
woman here. And a freezing child."

The gate creaked open and Max drove through. As the
cabriolet spun briskly down the winding drive, he heard the
tocsin sounding his arrival.

The huge carved wooden doors of the château swung open
as he pulled up, and a pair of servants formally dressed in
silver and blue livery ran down the marble steps. Max handed
the boy into their arms, but he himself carried the woman
into the château's great hall.

It was so bright in the *flambeaux*-lit hall after the darkness
of the snow-shrouded night that for a moment Max saw nothing but swirls of light and black spots dancing before his
eyes. "One of you ride to Chaumard and fetch the doctor,"

he called over his shoulder as he started for the sweeping marble stairs.

"What are you going to do to my maman? Where are you taking her?" cried a small voice, and now Max felt something tug at the edge of his greatcoat.

Impatient, he paused to look down into a dirty, thin face streaked with dried tears. A lock of hair had fallen across the boy's forehead but, though it was grimy and limp, its golden color was unmistakable. As unmistakable as his vivid blue eyes.

Max felt his heart stop.

"Dominique?" he said. He didn't believe it, didn't want to believe it.

The boy stared back at him, and his blue eyes widened until they filled his face. "Papa!" His lips trembled into a smile. "You came! I *told* Maman you would come. She kept saying you were busy in Paris, but I knew you were really in heaven and that you would come when I prayed to you."

Max's arms tightened around the burden in his arms. And, slowly, for the first time, he looked down into the dead woman's face.

Gabrielle.

It was she—the same dark, flaring brows; the same wide, generous mouth; the same translucent, blue-veined skin. And her hair . . . it was still the bright color of flame, in spite of being wet and matted with dirt.

An emotion beyond defining ripped through him with such force he shut his eyes and leaned into the gilded banister. "Gabrielle . . ."

He had been living for this. It had been his sole reason for living at all. This moment, when he would once again look into those lying purple eyes and have within his hands the power to make her pay for what she had done to him. The only woman he had ever loved. Gabrielle, his wife. Gabrielle, his betrayer. She had used him, lied to him, deceived him, and left him, and now she was here, in his arms, and she was beyond hurting, beyond revenge, beyond hate. And beyond love.

"Monseigneur . . ."

Max looked up into the face of Guitton, his father's *valet de chambre*.

"The rose room is being prepared, monseigneur. Shall I take her there?"

"No . . . no, I'll take her." He looked down at Dominique, who still clung to his coattail. A line had formed between the boy's light brows, and a dark shadow flickered in his eyes. He's guessed she's dead, Max thought, but he doesn't dare ask the question out loud. "See to the boy," he told the valet. "Take him to the kitchens and get something hot inside him. I've already sent for the doctor. But don't tell him—"

"I understand, monseigneur," the well-trained Guitton put in smoothly, and within seconds the hall was cleared and the vicomte de Saint-Just was left alone to carry his wife up the stairs.

There must not be an ounce of flesh left on her bones, Max thought. Her clothes were rags, barely enough to cover her, let alone keep her warm during the worst winter in centuries. Christ, how had she come to such a state? Why had she left him in the first place? Why, why, why?

He laid her gently on the rose silk counterpane. The light from the candle on the bedstand highlighted her face. Illness and deprivation emphasized her boldly sculptured features. She was more beautiful than ever, still the most lovely thing he had ever seen.

He knelt beside the bed and brought her hand to his lips. Unexpectedly, hot tears stung his eyes, and he squeezed them shut, fighting them down. Life had taught him to smother his feelings, and he wasn't about to let himself cry over *her*. Even in death he wouldn't give her the satisfaction of knowing how badly her leaving had hurt him. Time had not tempered the pain, or the hate. But looking into her dead face, he could at least admit that mixed with the hate were all the love and longing and need that had drawn him to her in the first place. Losing her again, this second time, seemed almost unbearable.

Leaning over, he started to press his mouth to her lips for a brief and final kiss when something broke inside him. He smothered his face in her neck, and his shoulders hunched over as a silent sob shuddered through him, and then another. And then they were no longer silent—but the harsh, tearing sobs of a man who never wept.

"Why, Gabrielle?" he cried. "Oh, my God, Gabrielle, Gabrielle . . . I loved you!"

Loved her and believed in her. Believed in *himself* for the first time in his life. She had given him the world and then walked away, leaving the world shattered at his feet. And he would go through it all again, all the pain, the suffering, even go through *this,* for those few glorious hours they had shared together.

He brushed her cold, still lips with his. "I love you, Gabrielle," he said softly. Then he laid his head on her breast . . . and heard her heart beat.

He sprang up so fast he knocked over the bedstand, almost causing a fire. He stamped out the flames with his boot, then slowly backed up until he was standing flat against the far wall. He stared at her in stunned disbelief, his chest heaving, his breath sounding harsh in his ears.

Then he lunged for the bell rope.

The doctor pulled the thick woolen blanket over Gabrielle's chest, tucking it under her chin. "The humors have retired to the center of her body."

Max wiped the sweat that dripped down his face with his sleeve. A huge fire blazed in the hearth, and the room was stifling hot. "Humors? What the hell does that mean?"

The doctor glanced up at him. There was a supercilious smile on his face, and Max, who was feeling helpless and hating it, clenched his fists to keep from punching that smile out the back of the man's head.

"It means, monsieur, that she has a fever. She must be given an infusion of centaury and purged with a Seidlitz powder. Naturally, she must be bled."

"Bled! Christ, she hasn't blood to spare!"

"Monsieur le Vicomte, I trained for three years at Paris University. Are you presuming to tell me I don't know what I'm doing?"

Max's lids slid shut and a cold smile thinned his lips. "If she dies, I will bury you with her."

Disconcerted, the doctor stared at Max. Then, shrugging, he said, "You are distraught," and beckoned to the surgeon who stood waiting discreetly just inside the door. It would be the surgeon who would perform the vulgar labor of handling the lancet for bleeding.

The surgeon removed Gabrielle's arm from beneath the covers. It looked so thin and white, Max couldn't imagine how it was going to produce any blood. The surgeon placed a shallow brass bowl beneath the bend in her elbow and, taking a small, pointed knife, slit through skin and flesh and into the vein. Within seconds, blood welled out of the cut and began to drip into the bowl.

And Max—who had thought he had seen enough of life's horrors to inure him to anything—had to flee the room.

The valet Guitton found him pacing the hall a few minutes later. "Monseigneur, I've taken the liberty of having a light repast prepared. It awaits you in your antechamber."

Max pushed a trembling hand through his hair. "Thank you, Guitton, but I'd choke if I tried to eat anything. Where's my father? I would have thought all this commotion would have wakened him long ago."

"But, monseigneur, I thought you knew. The *maréchal* has gone to Rambouillet for the month. To hunt with the king."

Max gave a sharp laugh. "The old bastard! I thought he was dying. What revived him? I bet it was a wench."

Guitton didn't even blink. But then it was impossible, Max had learned after fruitless years of trying, to shock or disconcert his father's valet.

"Monsieur le Comte was hearty enough when he left here last week, monseigneur," Guitton said. He hesitated, clearing his throat. "Monseigneur . . . ?"

Max stopped pacing and turned to stare at the valet's thin,

sharp-featured, and politely blank face. Never before in his memory had Max seen the inimitable Guitton at a loss for words. "Yes?"

The valet took a deep breath. "The child . . . he is asking after you. He seems to be under the sad misapprehension that you are his father."

For a long time Max said nothing. Then his lips twisted into one of his bitter, mocking smiles. "I'm the boy's step-father. The woman lying in there bleeding into a cup is his mother. My wife."

He headed for the kitchens, leaving Guitton standing at the top of the stairs. If he had looked back, Max would have had the satisfaction of seeing a look of pure astonishment on the va-let's face.

"*Sacre bleu!*" Guitton exclaimed beneath his breath. "A wife! The comte will burst his spleen when he hears of this." Then he smiled as he thought of what the others belowstairs would say when he told them of the irrepressible Monsieur Max's latest escapade.

Max found Dominique sitting on a tall stool before the kitchen table. A chocolate mustache coated his upper lip and he clutched the half-empty cup tight between his hands. A plate wiped clean even of crumbs sat before him. A serving girl, looking sleepy-eyed and disheveled and annoyed at having been roused from her bed, hovered by the fire. Max dismissed her and pulled up a chair beside the boy.

Dominique stared back at Max with solemn, frightened eyes. He swallowed hard. "W-where is Maman?"

"The doctor's with her. She's sleeping."

"But will she wake up?"

"Yes," Max said, hoping God wouldn't make him out to be a liar.

The relief on the face of Gabrielle's son was patently visible. He pumped his legs against the stool and squirmed a bit. "What was heaven like?"

"I wasn't—" Max stopped himself. He forced out a smile. "It was boring. Too many angels and not enough devils . . .

Dominique? What were you and your maman doing out on that road at night and in the middle of a snow storm?''

"We were going to *grand-mère's*. She's a duchesse and she lives in a grand château. Like this one, I 'spect. But we got lost."

"Your grandmother is a duchesse?" asked Max, thinking the boy was confused, or perhaps indulging in a bit of make-believe. "What's her name?"

Dominique took a long swallow from his cup, then wiped his wet mouth with the back of his hand, smearing the chocolate across his cheek. "Don't know."

Max decided to try a different tack. "Do you remember the day you left Paris?"

Dominique screwed up his face. "I guess."

"Why did you leave? Was it to go visit your *grand-mère?*"

Dominique shook his head vigorously. "We had to go to Beaune to take care of Madame Balue. I didn't like her. She smelled bad. And she cried a lot. I don't cry because I'm Maman's little man."

Beaune, Max thought. It was miles from here. And leagues away from Paris. "Did Madame Balue die? Is that why you left Beaune?"

A haunted look darkened the boy's eyes. "No, we had to run away. Because of the bad man. Can I have some more chocolate?"

Beating down his impatience, Max got up and went to the fire where the pot of cocoa and milk sat on a trivet.

He refilled Dominique's cup. "What bad man?" he asked carefully, feeling like a toothdrawer yanking on a stubborn molar.

"He tried to hurt Maman. But I gutted him."

"God in heaven . . ." Max slowly sat down, the pot of chocolate forgotten in his hand. He remembered the rusty kitchen knife he had seen strapped to Gabrielle's waist when he had stripped her and bathed her with hot water and wrapped her in blankets warmed before the fire, trying to bring life back into those stiff, frozen limbs, wondering how she had survived those hours in that snow-filled ditch, wondering how she had come to be there in the first place, wondering so many things . . .

The cup clattered onto the table and rolled against Max's hand. Startled, he looked up. Gabrielle's son had fallen asleep, his head pillowed on his folded arms. His blond hair lay in the spilled chocolate, getting sticky.

The faces haunted her dreams.

Once Agnes came, her hair covered by a huge mobcap and her mouth scowling in anger. "You promised you wouldn't go too far," Agnes said. "Instead, you went all the way to Beaune."

"But it was Louvois," Gabrielle tried to explain. "I had to go where Louvois couldn't find me."

Agnes didn't want to listen. She went away and Simon came. "What happened to the ring? How could you let someone steal it when you know how much it means to me?"

Tears filled Gabrielle's eyes. "That was all a mistake. He didn't steal it; Dominique had it in his pocket. And then I left it in Beaune. I had to leave everything in Beaune."

But she wasn't talking to Simon after all; it was Madame Balue, who looked at her with bruised eyes and held out her arms. "See the scars. I wanted to be a nun, but instead I bleed, I bleed for Jesus Christ." And then Madame Balue was taken away by the surgeon, who lifted his lancet and slashed and Gabrielle screamed because she felt the pain as if it were her own. Somewhere far away she heard a voice shouting in anger. "That's enough! Christ, do you want to kill her?" And the dreams faded into a heavy, still blackness.

She liked the blackness. It was peaceful, not angry like the faces. But Dominique wouldn't let her stay in the warm, gentle blackness. He kept calling to her and so she had to leave because he was sick and cold and needed her to take him to the duchesse de Nevers, who would love him and dress him in satin.

But the faces waited for her on the road.

Baptiste Balue, whose eye rolled demonically in his head,

smiled and said, "You asked for it, my dear. I wouldn't have tried to give it to you, if you hadn't asked for it."

And Louvois, who smiled, too, so that the scar, raw and bleeding, puckered his face. "I will use him," Louvois said. "I will use your love for him to destroy you."

And then *he* was there, leaning over her, his eyes narrowed in anger, his mouth drawn taut, not smiling at all.

"No!" she cried, turning her head away. "Oh, Max, Max. Why did you do it?"

His fingers dug into her shoulders, hurting her and pulling her up, out of the dream. "Damn you, Gabrielle! Why did you leave me?"

"I love you!" she cried. She wanted to take his face between her hands and kiss away his anger. But when she reached for him, he faded away and the blackness returned. The blessed, welcoming blackness.

She opened her eyes to a strange and luxurious room. Its walls were all gold and white, with hangings of turquiose- and rose-colored silk. She lay in a bed of white cotton softness, and beneath her hands was a bedspread of pink watered silk. On her body was the finest nightgown she had ever seen.

She turned her head. A strange girl in a starched, lace-trimmed mobcap leaned over her. She had a pert, turned-up nose, and there was a bright smile on her heart-shaped lips.

"Where am I?" Gabrielle said. Or thought she said, for what came out of her mouth was barely a croak.

"Oh, madame! Are you awake at last?"

Gabrielle swallowed. Her throat was sore and she was very thirsty. It took her several tries to get the words out of her mouth, and even then her voice squeaked like a rusty hinge. "Is this . . . is this the Château de Nevers?"

The girl covered her mouth with her hand to smother a laugh. "Oh, heavens no, madame. Nevers is way over in the next province. I must go tell Monsieur le Vicomte that you've awakened. He's been half mad with worry. I fear he'd begun to despair you would ever recover from your fever." She giggled. "He kicked Monsieur le Docteur down the steps!"

Gabrielle tried to focus on what the girl was saying, but it was too difficult and her head hurt too much. "Thirsty . . ." she whispered.

A strong hand cradled her neck, lifting her head. "Here, madame, drink this. It's an egg beaten in boiling water with cinnamon and sugar. It will soothe your throat and keep the cough down."

Gabrielle painfully swallowed the draft. Her eyes drifted closed. The light was too bright; it made her head pound. What had happened to the gentle blackness? She felt the girl move away from her.

Her eyes flew open. "No!" she cried out hoarsely, and thought to hold the girl back, shocked to discover she was too weak even to lift her arm. "Dominique! Where's my son?"

The girl had paused at the door. She laughed. *"Tiens!* Don't worry your head over that one. The *petit coquin* is riding old Marthe round and round the paddock. Monsieur le Vicomte put him up on that old nag's back two weeks ago and I swear he's not been off since!"

Two weeks? No, that wasn't possible. She needed to see to Dominique. It had been over a day since they'd eaten. And it had started to snow. They were still a long distance from the Château de Nevers. They still had to walk all the way to the next province, and he would die if she didn't get him out of the ditch.

Tears spilled unheeded from Gabrielle's eyes. "Please . . ." she begged the girl. "You must bring him to me."

"But of course, madame," the girl said, misunderstanding. "I am to fetch Monsieur Max the moment you awaken."

Gabrielle thought she must somehow have slipped back into one of her dreams. Exhaustion washed over her and she closed her eyes. It felt as if the bed were tied onto the tail of a kite, being whipped and flung around the room by the wind. "No . . ." She turned her head from side to side. "Not Max . . ."

She heard the girl's voice echoing to her as if from a deep well. "Oh, please forgive my impertinence, Madame la Vicomtesse. I was so used to thinking of monsieur your husband as Monsieur Max, I forget sometimes that he is now the vicomte. I will bring him to you now, if you please, madame . . .''

''No . . .'' Gabrielle felt herself slipping into sleep again and she tried to fight it, but she was so tired . . . so tired . . .

When next she opened her eyes, it was to the sound of footsteps approaching the bed and, though she faced away from the door toward the wall, she felt her heartbeat stop and then start up again. She knew, oh, God, she knew it was he, for hadn't she always been able to tell when he entered a room, even without looking? The world glowed when he was near, and her heart took wings. It did so now, still, even after everything he had done and she had done and all that had somehow been done to them.

She sucked in a deep, painful breath and slowly turned her head . . . to look up into a pair of sooty gray eyes.

''So you've decided to live after all,'' he said in that silky voice of his that could weave songs around her heart.

It had been a year, over a year, and nothing had changed. She loved him still. She battled back tears and wanted to look away, but she couldn't. Her eyes and heart drank in the sight of his beloved face after so many days and months apart.

He looked stunningly handsome in an English hunting coat with a high collar and tight leather breeches tucked neatly into tall riding boots. The plain white linen neckcloth knotted at his throat set off his dark skin and hair. She wasn't surprised to find him here at what had almost been her deathbed, for wasn't he part of her destiny? Hadn't he been put on earth for her to love?

And to hate. ''What have you done with my son?'' she demanded in her pain-roughened voice.

The closed expression on his face didn't alter except for a slight flaring of his nostrils. ''Your son, madame? I've clothed him and fed him and taught him how to sit a horse—the same as any other *father* would do.''

She shut her eyes, summoning her strength. She tried to

push up on her elbows, but she was too weak. She fell back, her head bouncing against the pillow. "I don't believe you."

He went to the door and flung it open.

"Maman!" Dominique came hurtling into the room, although he slowed as he approached the bed, remembering just in time that his maman had been very, very sick and needed lots of rest and quiet. "Guess what?" he said, trying hard to whisper and not succeeding very well. "Papa is teaching me how to ride a horse! And soon I can go hunting with him—he said so! We'll shoot some rabbits and then you won't have to steal them anymore."

A huge smile lit her child's face. It was still thin, but his cheeks bore the bloom of health. His blond hair had been brushed until it shone and tied back with a riband, and he looked the picture of a little gentleman in navy-blue velvet breeches and a matching coat with silver buttons. There were even silver buckles on his shoes. Tears flooded Gabrielle's eyes and overflowed to run down her face, dampening the pillow.

Dominique's smile slid off his face, and a worried frown creased his brow. "Don't cry, Maman. Monsieur le Docteur won't hurt you anymore. Papa punched him in the nose and kicked him down the stairs."

Laughter bubbled from Gabrielle's raw throat. She felt weightless with a strange happiness. But when she unconsciously turned to share the happiness with Max, she found that he had gone.

Chapter 17

"**D**rink it."

"Ugh!" Gabrielle wrinkled her nose and twisted her head to the side. "It smells like cow's piss."

"Drink it or I'll force it down your throat."

"You wouldn't dare!"

Max grabbed Gabrielle by the jaws, pulling her mouth apart. He held the steaming cup to her lips. "Now. Are you going to drink?"

She blinked and tried to nod her head. Max tilted the cup and the liquid, which also tasted like cow's piss, poured down her throat. She swallowed reflexively and tried not to gag.

Only when the cup was completely drained did Max let her go. Her face tingled where his fingers had pressed into her skin, and she felt something quiver in her chest. Damn the man. He was a liar, a deceiver, the worst sort of villain imaginable—and all he had to do was touch her, even in anger, and she lost control of her senses.

He straightened and moved away from the bed, but he didn't leave the room as she half expected him to. It was the first time he had been to see her since she had awakened from her fever two days ago. She should have known he would return only to torment her.

She wiped her mouth with the back of her hand. He watched her with that maddeningly arrogant smile of his that made her long for the day when she would once again have the strength to slap it off his face. "I hate you," she said. "What was that vile stuff?"

The smiled deepened, putting a dimple in one cheek and making him look boyish, making her want to kiss it.

"You don't want to know," he said. Then his face smoothed and tightened and the heavy lids fell over his eyes. "You should see your face, you little fool. You're still burning up with fever. Do you *want* to die? Think about Dominique if you refuse to care about yourself!"

She flung her head up defiantly, which wasn't easy since it was buttressed on all sides by mounds of pillows. "I should think my death would please you well, Monsieur le Vicomte. Then you would be free to sell my son all over again. Or do you no longer need the money now that you've come into your inheritance?"

He had turned to look out the rain-washed window, but he whipped around again, and she almost cringed at the harsh anger on his face.

"*Sell* him! What the hell are you talking about?"

"You know."

He crossed the room in two bounds. His powerful hands grasped her arms, half lifting her from the bed. "Oh, no, Gabrielle, I'm not playing any more guessing games with you. A year ago last August you stood up in church and took me as your husband. Two days later you disappeared. Now I'm going to hear the reason why if I have to turn you upside down and shake it out of you."

Angry tears threatened to choke her so that she had to swallow several times before she could hurl the words right back at him. "Two days later I saw you in the Café Monoury selling us to Louvois!"

"*Louvois!*"

He let go of her and she landed back on the bed so hard that she bounced. His face was the epitome of bewildered shock, and if she hadn't seen the proof of his deception with her own eyes she would almost have believed him innocent.

"Don't pretend you don't know him," she said.

"I do know him. He heads the smuggling ring. Or did."
Smuggling . . . ?

No, she thought, I don't believe this, I can't believe this. He's lying. He has to be lying.

He had returned to the window. He had his back to the light, facing her, which left his eyes in shadow. His mouth was a tight, straight line. She wished she could see his eyes.

"You're lying," she said.

He shrugged. "Why not ask him yourself, since you seem to be on such intimate terms? What precisely is the nature of your acquaintance with him? Or is that one of the many secrets you refuse to tell me, my lady wife?"

Gabrielle's chest felt tight. She heard her own voice say from a long way away, "You know. You must know. He had to have told you."

"I beg to differ, but your name never came up in the conversation."

She shook her head wildly back and forth. "You're *lying.*"

He made a movement as if collecting himself to walk away.

Gabrielle struggled to sit up. "No, wait . . . please . . ." She squeezed her eyes shut, summoning all her courage. "He—he works for the duc de Nevers."

"I know that." Max's voice was flat, detached. "It's how he was able to run the smuggling. I still don't see what that has to do with you."

"The . . . the duc de Nevers was my husband's—my first husband's—father."

He said nothing for the longest time. Then he made a small sound that was part exclamation of surprise and part laughter. It was the spontaneity of that sound, more than anything else, that convinced her of his innocence.

"My God . . . This Martin fellow of yours was the duc de Nevers's *son?*" He left the window and came to stand beside the bed. She turned her face away, for now that she could see his eyes, she couldn't bear what they told her.

His hand cupped her cheek and forced her head back

around. "Just who in the name of all that's holy *are* you, Gabrielle?"

She told him then. She told him everything. By the time she finished it was the hour of the evening when the lamps were lit, although he had dismissed the servants, allowing the room to grow dark. Her voice spoke to him from the bed, sounding disembodied, while he listened from as far away as he could go and still be in the same room, leaning against a mantel on the opposite wall. She thought he probably felt it, too—that impossible, uncontrollable attraction that had always been between them. And she decided he probably mistrusted it now as much as she did.

"Why didn't you tell me?" he said when she had at last finished.

"It's not the sort of thing you blurt out to someone you hardly know."

"Hardly know! You were my *wife.*"

"It wasn't exactly a long betrothal. We met and married within a week. I *wanted* to tell you. I tried to tell you on our wed—" She choked over the word. "Our wedding night."

"That would have been a good time, Gabrielle. It was, I believe, the night I told you I loved you."

She flinched as if his words were a whip, flaying her. She tried not to cry, but the tears were choking her throat. "I was being *hunted.* By marrying you I made you hunted as well. I was afraid you would hate me for it. That you'd leave me."

He gave a sharp, bitter laugh. "So you left me instead."

The tears were pouring from her eyes, harder than the rain that beat against the window. She thought they would flood the room until she drowned in them. "But I s-saw you with Louvois. He-he gave you money. You s-said you would do anything for m-money."

Again he laughed bitterly. "Did I say that? One of these days I'm going to learn that not everyone shares my sense of humor."

He was silent for a long time. Then he sighed. "You saw me with Louvois. And he gave me money, although if you'd waited another second or two you would have seen me give it back to him. I'm not the kind of man to condemn a woman, any woman, to the fate Louvois had planned for you . . . If you had trusted me, believed in me, loved me, you would have known that."

"Oh, God, Max, *please* . . . I do love you. I never once stopped loving you."

He shook his head. "If you loved me you would never have left me. No matter what you saw, or thought you saw—"

She held up her hand in an unconscious supplication. "They were trying to take away my *son.*"

He pushed away from the mantel and started for the door. "Max!"

He paused with his hand on the latch and turned to look back at her. In the dusk his eyes shone like polished glass. "I loved you, Gabrielle. I thought I would love you forever."

Two weeks later, Gabrielle—still feeling a bit wobbly— leaned against the paddock fence and looked up at her son with anxious eyes. Dominique sat astride an enormous cinnamon-colored horse, his stubby legs barely able to straddle the animal's withers.

The horse tossed its head and snorted, baring a pair of huge yellow teeth. "Jesu!" Gabrielle exclaimed. "Does he bite?"

Dominique giggled. "She's a lady horse, Maman. She's very nice. Her name is Marthe."

Gabrielle thought perhaps she should give Marthe a pat, as a token of friendship. Keeping a careful distance, she leaned far over at the waist and stretched out her hand to rub the horse's gray muzzle. The wind gusted, kicking up the velvet skirts of her new green riding habit and fluttering the tall heron feather in her hat. The feather was dyed bright orange.

Marthe's cavernous jaws stretched open and she lunged her neck, snapping at the feather.

Gabrielle shrieked and leaped backward. "Jesu and all his saints! He's eating my hat!"

Dominique cackled with laughter. "She thinks it's a carrot."

Gabrielle looked around her quickly to be sure no one, in particular a certain *someone,* had seen her making a fool of herself. She smoothed her skirts, trying to recover her dignity. "Very well, Dominique. You may show me what you've learned now."

Dominique nudged the horse into the center of the ring. "Are you watching, Maman?" he called out.

"I'm watching, *mon petit,*" Gabrielle answered faintly, thinking that her life would have been much quieter all the way around if she had given birth to a girl.

Suddenly the horse broke into a fast trot and Gabrielle dug her nails into her palms to steady her nerves. Dominique and the horse seemed a blur as they sped past her, breaking into a canter around the ring, and Dominique waved. She forced out an encouraging smile and waved back. "Use both hands, *chéri.*"

She sucked in a lungful of the crisp winter air. It was a clear day, the sky a chilly, pristine blue, the sun a hazy yellow orb hovering low on the horizon. A snappy wind blew, stripping the trees of the last of their leaves and flattening the surrounding fields of rye. It brought with it the smell of burning wood. They were making charcoal in the nearby forest, burying stacks of wood, setting them alight and covering them with layers of turf.

During the last two weeks, Gabrielle had felt as if she, too, had been smoldering, just like the charcoal, as she fought with a desperate will to recover from her illness and regain her strength. She forced down tisanes that smelled vile and tasted worse; she drank countless bowls of turnip bouillon and endured mustard baths that left her skin feeling pickled. She made herself walk—from the bed to the water closet and back again.

The water closet had amazed her. It was all white marble and porcelain and luxurious beyond imagining. But then, so was the whole château. The floors were made of precious, fragrant wood and covered with priceless Aubusson carpets.

The walls were lined with silk and decorated with Gobelins tapestries and paintings by the grand masters—Titian, Rubens, Raphael. Luxury was evident everywhere, even in the small things such as the use of white wax candles instead of tallow, and whitewash on all the outbuildings. Everything proclaimed nobility and tax-exempt privilege—even down to the gold-plated weathercock on the stable roof.

The chambermaid, whose name was Louise, told her that all this belonged to the comte de Saint-Just, Monsieur Max's father. Now that Monsieur Max was the comte's only surviving son they had managed to set aside their differences. Well, not completely set them aside, mind you, for they still butted heads like a pair of old bulls whenever their paths crossed. Gabrielle had the impression the servants were waiting with bated breath to see what would happen when the comte returned from his hunting trip to discover his rake of a son ensconced in his château, and with a suddenly acquired wife and son. Knowing Max's sarcastic tongue, Gabrielle could almost sympathize with the poor old comte.

Since that first evening of accusation and revelation, Max had not been back to see her. Sitting in a gilded armchair by the window, wrapped in satin quilts, she had watched him cavort with her son around the château grounds, teaching him to ride, chasing him across the sweeping green lawns. Even with the window closed against the winter air she could hear their laughter, and she felt a longing that was an actual ache in her chest to be a part of it. She envied her own son, that he was to be given Max's love so unconditionally. But then, he had done nothing to forfeit it.

Gabrielle knew it was going to be difficult to win back her husband's love. He was not the sort of man to give his heart lightly or easily, yet he had allowed his careful guard to relax long enough to fall in love with her, only to be terribly wounded as a result.

To Max, who had never loved before, love was a gift to be given without reservation. He couldn't believe it had been possible for her to mistrust him, to leave him, while still loving him. In his mind she hadn't loved him *enough*, not if she could suspect him capable of betraying her to Louvois. And he would be damned before he would ever trust her with his heart again. He might as well have been clanking around the château in an old-fashioned suit of armor, so fortified was he now against letting her near him.

The only ammunition she had on her side, she knew, was the chance that she might be able to make him want her physically again. Unfortunately the fever had melted what little flesh she had left off her bones, so that her figure resembled a witch's broomstick. Her complexion was so ruined she looked like a blanched and wrinkled prune. Worse, she literally hadn't a single thing to wear.

The first day she felt well enough to get up and sit in the chair by the fire, she asked Louise what had happened to her clothes. With a sniff, Louise said if she was talking about those old rags, they had been burned days ago. An hour later, the girl returned with a beautiful blue quilted-silk dressing gown folded in her arms. And the next day a *modiste* arrived at the château bearing ells of silk, satins, and gossamer muslins.

Since this generosity could only have come from Max, Gabrielle had spent the next two days humming and smiling to herself. When the first of the new clothes arrived—a dress of soft peach silk with coffee-colored flounces—she waited impatiently for him to come see how it looked on her. She waited in vain . . .

"Look, Maman!"

Dominique thundered past her on the huge cinnamon-colored horse. Gabrielle had just opened her mouth to shout at him that he was going too fast when, to her utter horror, he put the reins between his teeth and stretched his arms straight out in the air like angels' wings. His feet flapped against the horse's sides and his hair billowed like a flag around his head, and he was going to fall off and break his neck.

Gabrielle waited until he had slowed the horse and trotted back to her. Only the ominous tapping of her foot on the ground was there to warn Dominique of the coming explosion, but he didn't notice it.

"Did you see me, Maman? Did you see?" he exclaimed proudly.

"I saw you, young man, and if you ever do such a reckless, harebrained, addlepated thing again I'm going to give you the whipping of your young life!"

Since she had never even raised a hand to him before, Dominique was not particularly impressed by this threat. "But it wasn't dangerous, Maman. Papa says I have good balance."

Gabrielle clenched her teeth and vowed to have a word or two with the Vicomte Maximilien de Saint-Just. "Get down," she told Dominique in a tone of voice that brooked no argument.

Dominique nudged Marthe over to the fence and used the rails to climb down. He grinned up at her. "Do you want to go for a ride now, Maman?"

Gabrielle opened her mouth, then shut it. She looked at the big cinnamon-colored mare, standing docilely beside them, munching on a tuft of grass. Surely it was ridiculous that she'd passed the age of twenty-two and had never once sat on a horse. How difficult could it possibly be if a five-year-old child could master it?

She looked around to be sure there were no snickering eyes watching her. "Well . . . perhaps a gallop or two around the ring."

With lots of unsolicited advice from her son, Gabrielle managed to get herself onto the mare's broad back. It had not been at all as easy as it looked, and for several terrifying seconds she found herself lying stomach down and crossways on Marthe's broad withers, with the beast making terrible snorting sounds and whipping her tail ominously back and forth. Finally Gabrielle was upright—and a long, long way off the ground.

Marthe had gone back to munching the grass. "She doesn't seem to want to move," Gabrielle said nervously.

"Kick her in the side with your heel, Maman."

Gabrielle gave her the merest nudge.

Marthe stamped her foot.

Gabrielle shut her eyes. *"Mon Dieu . . ."*

"Give her a good thump, Maman."

Gabrielle gave her a good thump.

Marthe bolted across the paddock, snorting and kicking up her hooves. Gabrielle did a somersault over the mare's hindquarters and landed on her tailbone with such force that she grunted.

Familiar laughter, rich and husky, joined with Dominique's high-pitched whoops to fill the air. Gabrielle's cheeks burned. She might have known he would arrive just in time to witness her humiliation.

She pulled aside the heron feather, which was drooping over one eye, to glare toward where her husband and son stood outside the paddock, laughing at her expense. Immediately they tried to assume their wide-eyed, innocent looks.

"Is something amusing you, Monsieur le Vicomte?" she asked icily, lifting up one hip to rub her sore bottom.

He bowed. "I beg your pardon, madame." He had managed to assume a somber expression, but a tic at the corner of his mouth gave him away.

Gabrielle scrambled awkwardly to her feet. She marched toward them, and they started to back away from her. She pointed a shaking finger at Marthe, who had once again gone back to her grazing. "That . . . that wild beast is dangerous!"

Max made a noise that sounded like one of Marthe's snorts. "That wild beast was born the same year I was. She wouldn't hurt a honey bee."

"Ha! She tried to eat my hat!"

"Maybe she thought it was a carrot."

Gabrielle stopped before him, her hands on her hips. The heron feather fell over her eye again, and she pushed it away impatiently.

Their eyes met and Gabrielle stopped breathing.

The smile that brightened his face slowly faded. His eyes darkened until they were almost as black as the charcoal that burned in the forest. His mouth looked hard, inflexible, and she wanted to press her lips to it, to feel it soften, melt, succumb to her. Love for him overwhelmed her, making her chest ache.

She leaned into him, touching his hand. "Max . . ."

He recoiled as if her fingers were a burning brand and, indeed, their skin had seemed to sizzle at the contact.

He backed up a couple feet, but he didn't leave. He looked out across the fields. She looked with him. They stared together at a man in the distance who turned over the dark earth with a large-wheeled plow. Nearby was a mill, and the water tumbling over the wheel caught the sun's rays and shimmered like shards of glass. She felt his body beside her, coiled as tightly as the spring in a mousetrap.

"If you're well enough to be out cavorting around the countryside, then you can join me for supper this evening," he said, although he made it sound like a command.

She gave him her sweetest smile. It had some effect, for she saw a vein begin to throb in his temple. "If you wish," she said. She smiled again. "I haven't had a chance to thank you for all the lovely gowns and things."

"There's no need. I'm your husband and it's my duty to provide for you. If you *are* going to go cavorting around the countryside, I won't have you doing so dressed as a beggar—" He cut himself off, but it was too late. The were both remembering the condition he had found her in, and how she had come to be that way.

He turned away from her. "I'll tell Guitton to have us served informally in the small dining room. We'll begin with a glass of brandy in the library."

At the sound of a door opening and closing upstairs, Max quickly knocked back his fourth glass of brandy. There was a pleasant hum in his head and his fingertips were starting to feel numb. It was just the state he wanted to be in—drunk enough to be as cruel as it would take to survive the coming battle.

That it was going to be a battle he had no doubt. The only

question was the nature of the enemy. The worst enemy, he had decided, was his own treacherous body. How had he allowed himself to get to such an impossible state where only one woman on earth was capable of satisfying him? And what fiendish god had decreed that the woman would be Gabrielle?

Gabrielle.

Lying, deceiving, falsehearted Gabrielle. He refused to believe he still loved her. He refused to *let* himself love her. The minute he did she would hurt him again. Leave him, probably, or take a lover. Only a man who enjoyed suffering would deliberately let himself in for that kind of pain.

A part of him wanted to flee to the other side of the world, where he would be sure of being out of reach of that damned spell she could cast with just one of those sweet smiles. On the other hand, she was his wife, which meant he could avail himself of her body, that glorious, sensual body, whenever he felt in the mood. And tonight he was definitely in the mood.

The door opened.

She stood with the oil lamps in the hall backlighting her hair, so that it blazed like the sun. Her gown was of flesh-colored vaporous silk and in the flickering light he thought he could almost see right through it to her naked body. She had laced her bodice so tightly that, as she breathed, her breasts rose and quivered, threatening to spill over the top of the deep décolleté, and the lace that trimmed the edge of it was so sheer he had a hard time telling where it left off and her bare skin began.

Max set his teeth to bite back a groan. How was he ever going to win this war when the enemy possessed such formidable weapons?

He splashed more brandy into the glass, spilling a good portion onto the ruby and blue Aubusson carpet. He lifted the glass to her in a mock toast and fought back with the only weapon he had—words.

"You shouldn't wear that gown in public, *ma mie*. You're liable to start a revolution."

A blush spread slowly across her cheeks, then she raised

her head to stare proudly at him. "I had hoped you would be pleased with the dress, Monsieur le Vicomte. Since it is you, after all, who has paid for it."

"Actually, I charged everything to my father's accounts. I hope it was outrageously expensive."

"Oh, but it was!" Her eyes crinkled at the corners and she laughed softly. Max emptied half the brandy snifter down his throat.

He went over to the sideboard to refill his glass and pour one for her. She glided into the room as if on a bubble of air. She paused to look around her, taking in the lustrous mahogany and gilt furniture, the shelves of books bound in gold-embossed leather, the wainscoted walls broken up by double French doors that led to the gardens. Max glanced at her.

She walked over to the fireplace, gazing up at a portrait over the mantel of a stern-looking man in a uniform dripping with gold braid. "Your father," she stated. "I can tell. You have the same arrogant nose."

"Do we?" Carrying both brandies, he came to stand close enough to her that the sleeve of his shirt brushed her bare arm. The fine hairs rose on the back of her neck and he smiled to himself. She might have the ability to drive him half mad with desire, but at least he'd always had the same effect on her.

He pressed one of the brandy glasses into her hands, allowing his fingers to linger in hers, smiling again as he heard her breath catch. She smelled wonderful—of spring flowers and sun-drenched meadows.

He looked down. She was breathing rapidly and he could see her nipples pressing against the lace of her bodice, like two dark red rosebuds . . . Jesus, he wondered. Had she rouged them?

He jerked away from her. He stumbled stiff-legged over to a chair by the window and flung himself down on it. Draping one leg over the chair arm, he cradled his brandy glass in his lap to hide the hard bulge in his breeches. His hands were trembling.

She had noticed the other portrait opposite the one above the mantel and she went now to study it. This one was of a woman with rich chestnut hair and glowing hazel eyes, and a melancholy smile on her full lips that left just the hint of a dimple in one cheek.

"My mother, the whore," Max said.

Gabrielle looked at him in surprise.

"The comtesse, the real comtesse, has been banished to the attics." He got up and went to stand before the portrait. The bulge in his breeches was still there; he decided not to care if she noticed it. "The real comtesse died, you see, and my father thought to go looking for his other wife. He found her in the Faubourg Saint-Antoine, walking the streets, and me"—his lips curled into a bitter smile—"doing things you don't want to know about. I was twelve. He brought us back here and she died six months later." He waved his glass at the portrait, and brandy slopped over the rim. "Since then the old bastard's convinced himself she was the one true love of his life."

"Perhaps she was." Gabrielle had spoken in such a strained voice that he barely heard her.

"He had a strange way of showing it then, didn't he? Abandoning her to a life of prostitution. But maybe I'm a sentimental fool when it comes to marriage and love."

The color drained from her face and he felt a spasm of self-disgust. To quench it, he finished off what was left of the brandy in his glass.

She tilted her head back to look again at the portrait. "I was wondering where I had seen her before . . . You have a miniature of her in the apartment back in Paris."

"Ah, yes, I'd forgotten about that day you stole into my apartment and rummaged through my drawers. I never did discover what you were really looking for. But never mind telling me now, Gabrielle. Anything you said would probably be a lie and, besides, I find the air of mystery that always surrounds you to be something of an aphrodisiac. It seems I'm never making love to the same woman twice."

As she turned to face him, he saw tears glinting in her

eyes. Even as he watched, one spilled over and rolled down her cheek.

"Damnation!" he exclaimed, hurling his empty brandy glass across the room.

She brushed the tear impatiently away. "If you're trying to make me pay for what I did, Max, then you are succeeding. What will it take for you to forgive me?" To his horror she fell to her knees before him. "I beg—"

He seized her arms, hauling her to her feet. "Don't do that, for Christ's sake!" He shook her and her eyes fluttered shut and her mouth fell open. He started to lower his head, stopping himself in the second before his lips touched hers.

He flung her away from him and, whirling, fled from the room and the sight of that white, hurt face, and the knowledge that he had loved her then, loved her now, would always love her, no matter what.

No matter what.

Two days later, Gabrielle stood before the full-length mirror that hung on the armoire in the rose bedroom, not knowing whether to laugh or to swear. She hadn't dared to light a candle, and in the dawn light of a cloudy day, she could barely make out her reflection. What she did see looked ridiculous. When she had imagined fleeing the château in a male disguise she had pictured herself looking like a dashing cavalier, not a court jester.

The clothes—Max's clothes—were much too big for her. Why hadn't she anticipated that? His breeches spilled out the tops of his floppy boots, and she had to hold them up by looping a tasseled cord from one of the window curtains around her waist. His tricorn hat fell down to the bridge of her brows, and she kept having to push it back, only to have it fall forward again. It seemed that two of her could have fit into his coat.

Well, it would just have to do, she thought; she had come too far to turn back now.

So far, except for this slight miscalculation with the clothes, her plan had fallen out just as she imagined it. Dominique stood beside her now, muffled in a thick coat, a sack of food clasped tightly in one fist. Beside her was a cloak bag stuffed with several changes of clothes for both of them. In the pocket of her coat was a purse full of coins, and a pistol. The world was full of men like Balue, and she was determined this time to be prepared for them. Of course, she had never fired a pistol before, but what could be so hard about it?

She had stolen all these things yesterday afternoon from Max's room while he was out in the paddock with Dominique, playing the part of a father by teaching him how to ride that nasty cinnamon-colored horse with the gray muzzle. In a moment she would steal that horse and one for herself. True, her one experience at riding a horse had been something of a disaster, but she refused to believe she couldn't master a thing the rest of the world seemed able to do almost by second nature.

She had no qualms about stealing these things from Max— well, not *too* many qualms. She reminded herself that it was either do this or stay here and live with a man who didn't love her. A man who'd made it obvious he would never care for her again except, perhaps, as a means of slaking his lust. In all those years alone, struggling to support herself and her son, she had never resorted to selling her body. Now she would be damned before she would allow Max to make her his whore.

They crept down the stairs and out the French doors that led into the gardens from the library. It had started to rain, a steady, icy drizzle that made Gabrielle glad that she had Max's big, thick coat.

Dominique had told her that the cinnamon-colored horse was a "lady horse," but Gabrielle didn't believe it, for surely only a male of the species would be so contrary. The stupid beast refused to stand still long enough for Gabrielle to get the saddle on her back. She bared a pair of wicked-looking teeth and made so much racket banging her hooves against the stall that Gabrielle expected the stables to become full of curious grooms at any minute.

Finally Gabrielle was forced to give up on the saddle. She

also decided against taking two horses. One was obviously going to be almost more than she could handle.

It was Dominique's idea to coax Marthe out of the stables by offering her one of their precious apples from their food sack. The mare was obviously a treacherous beast, just like her master, because once through the stable door she got a whiff of freedom and jerked away from Gabrielle, almost tearing her arm out of its socket and knocking off her hat.

Gabrielle watched with dismay as the mare cantered away, tossing her head and flicking her tail. The sound of her hooves clattering on the pebbled drive drowned out the noise of the horse and rider that emerged from behind the stables.

Until she heard a familiar voice, drawling with suppressed amusement, say "Are you going somewhere, Gabrielle?" and she turned to look up into a pair of mocking gray eyes.

"You look ravishing this morning, *ma mie*. Although it's a trifle early in the day, isn't it, to be going to an opera ball?"

Gabrielle whipped back around to glare at her son. "You told him!"

"I didn't!"

"He didn't," Max said. He sat at ease on an enormous black horse, his wrists crossed over the saddle pommel. "Did you think, my devious little wife, that I would fail to see that someone had rifled through my drawers again, stealing my pistol? Speaking of which, I'll have it back now if you don't mind. It's loaded and you're liable to shoot your foot off."

Gabrielle took the gun from her pocket, but she didn't hand it to him. Instead she pointed it at his chest. "Let us go."

His face tightened and his hands jerked involuntarily on the reins, causing the horse to back up a step. "Oh, no, Gabrielle, you're not running away again. You're my wife, and my wife you will stay. Willingly or unwillingly."

"Let us go, or I'll shoot you."

He threw back his head and laughed.

She shot him.

Chapter 18

The horse reared up and came down again with a clash of hooves. The sound of the shot bounded across the fields, muffled by the misty air. A bright red stain appeared on the sleeve of his buff-colored coat.

"Maman, you shot Papa!" Dominique exclaimed.

She hadn't meant to shoot him. The heavy pistol just seemed to go off of its own accord. It startled her so much that she flung it away from her with a scream, as if the ball had hit her, not Max.

He touched his arm, then stared in astonishment at the hand that came away bloody. He raised his brows at her. "I didn't know you were such a good shot."

"I missed. I was aiming for your treacherous heart," she lied.

He laughed and the horse danced sideways, its ears back and its eyes showing white. He kicked out of the stirrups, slipping off its back to slap it on the rump, sending it toward the stable, where a half dozen goggled-eyed grooms were already spilling from the doors. One look told them that the vicomtesse had shot the vicomte, and they decided that what happened next would be something they would be better off not witnessing.

Dominique stared from one to the other of his parents, his eyes as round as carriage wheels. "Papa, Maman shot you."

"Dominique, go inside."

"But, Papa—"

"Now."

Gabrielle had never seen her son obey with such alacrity. He abandoned her to be murdered by his precious papa without even a backward look.

Max took a step toward her.

She backed up. "W-what are you going to do?"

He kept coming. "It's time you were taught how a wife is supposed to behave, Gabrielle. For instance, a wife is not allowed to leave her husband. Nor is she allowed to shoot him—"

"You laughed in my face!"

"—no matter what the provocation."

She stopped backing up and stood her ground, lifting a quivering chin into the air. "You don't *own* me, Maximilien de Saint-Just."

He thrust his face so close to hers that she could see the fine lines around his eyes and the stubble of the beard he had yet to shave off that morning. He peeled his lips back in a nasty smile and she backed up two more steps.

"Oh, but I do own you," he said, his voice silky, dangerous. "The law is most specific on that point. My authority over your property and your person is absolute."

"And who were those laws written by? Men! Men, who—"

"Be quiet. I haven't finished dealing with this matter. In fact, I have only just begun. As your husband and master—"

"Master!"

"Master, dear wife. It is my moral duty to instruct you in all the wifely virtues of obedience, submissiveness, and humility, and I intend to do so. Come here."

She shook her head no, but her treacherous legs obeyed him of their own accord. When she got within striking distance, he seized her around the waist and hefted her upside down over his shoulder like a sack of grain. The laughter of the men in the stables followed them as he carried her up the sweeping steps of the château.

She kicked her feet; he pulled off the big boots easily, flinging them aside. She pummeled his back with her fists; he smacked her backside. She was so angry she was crying. "How dare you! Put me down this instant—*ow!*" she cried as he smacked her again.

"That didn't hurt. Yet. But if you don't quit fighting me, it will be many a week before you're able to sit in any comfort."

Gabrielle went rigid. He wouldn't dare! Would he? According to the law he could, as her husband, beat her as much and as often as he liked, as long as he didn't endanger her life. And what would the law say to the fact that she had shot him? Oh, *mon Dieu* . . .

He carried her all the way upstairs and into the bedroom, his bedroom. He flung her down on the big tester bed. She started to sit up and then she saw his face and she lay back down again. She bit her lower lip to stop its trembling. She noticed the muscle begin to throb in his jaw, and she hoped he was trying to master his temper.

He kept his eyes on her as he removed his coat, grimacing a little as he pulled on his wounded arm. There was a lot of blood on his shirt, and Gabrielle felt sick with guilt and shame. She deserved everything that he was going to do to her.

"Max? About the pistol . . . It was something of an accident. I didn't mean—"

"Take off those ridiculous clothes."

She flinched as if she'd already been dealt the first blow. Then she sat up and with trembling fingers worked at the buttons on the coat. She took it off and handed it to him. He dropped it on the floor. The shirt came next. She had to stand up to pull down the breeches.

She stood before him stripped to her own sheer cambric chemise.

"That, too," he said, his voice a rough burr.

He stood tall, looking down at her from beneath heavy

eyelids, and she knew in that moment it was not a beating he was going to give her.

She yearned for him to take her—with every breath, every thump of her heart. But pride kept her stiff before him and pulled the words from her mouth. "I'll not be a wife to a man who doesn't love me. I'll not let you—"

"Shut up." He yanked impatiently at the jabot around his neck, and his shirt fell open, baring half his chest. "You'll be what I say, and you'll do as I say."

She lowered her head. His manhood, hard and swollen, pressed against his breeches. There was a slight tremor in his rigid thighs, and his shirt fluttered with his breathing. Whatever he said, he could not control what he felt.

Slowly her hands went to the ribbons of her chemise.

His eyes watched her. His harsh breaths thundered in the room. Through the veil of her lashes she thought she could see his heart beating against the brown skin of his chest.

He made a sound, almost like the hiss of a cat and, shoving her hands roughly aside, he grasped the delicate material of the chemise and ripped it down the middle. "You were taking too damned long," he said, and she shuddered violently as if it was her flesh he had rent.

His arms went around her waist as he fell onto the bed, bringing her with him. He lowered his head to her breast, opening his lips wide around the nipple, sucking it hard into his mouth, and so he missed the look of triumph that flared in her purple eyes.

He pinned her to the bed with his weight. *Mine,* he thought. *Goddamn you, you are mine.*

He felt like a starving man suddenly confronted with a banquet of food. His mouth went from her breast to her lips to the pulse in her neck and back to her mouth again. His hands were everywhere, stroking her soft slopes and firm curves. He was gorging himself on her, trying to possess all of her at once.

His hand went around her back, crushing her tighter against him as if he could merge their flesh, and pain lanced through his arm. Perversely he welcomed it, as if he should suffer, deserved to suffer, for this weakness of the flesh, for needing her so desperately.

He reminded himself that he could possess her body without surrendering his soul, and forgot it instantly when she fastened her mouth onto his to kiss him hard and hungrily. He entangled his fingers in her hair and pulled her head back so that he could probe deep into her mouth with his tongue. Her hand pressed against his stomach, pulling at the waistband of his breeches, and his muscles clenched as tight as a fist.

He rolled off her and sat up.

He had trouble getting his boots off—they were wet and slippery with mud, and he was in a hurry. He felt her move against his back and her leg swung around—

"Stay," he said. He hadn't meant for it to sound so much like a command, but she took it as one, straightening her legs and lying back down.

At last his boots and stockings were off. Standing up, he kept his back to her as he peeled down his breeches. The muscles in his buttocks tightened, for he could feel her eyes on him.

He kept forgetting to breathe, until his lungs began to burn for air, and his jaw throbbed from the pressure of keeping his teeth clamped so tightly shut. Never had he felt so big, so hard. He felt enormous. He was near to exploding, and if she so much as touched him he would spill his seed.

He turned and looked at her.

She lay flat on the bed, her arms at her sides, her legs spread slightly apart. The sacrificial virgin, he thought; it didn't make him smile. Her hair was spread over the pillow, a pool of fire. He had seen skies at night over the ocean that were the purple of her eyes. I would die for you, he thought. I would grovel at your feet. How could he worry about the loss of his pride when with her he'd never had any pride to lose?

Her eyes glowed; her voice was a tiger's purr. "Come here," she said.

He knelt between her legs. He kept his eyes riveted onto

her face as he lifted her thighs, bringing them up over his shoulders, raising her pelvis off the bed. He hung poised above her for the space of a heartbeat, and then he drove into her.

A harsh moan burst from her throat, and her legs tightened around him. He pushed in deeper and her slick inner muscles enveloped him. He pulled out again, almost immediately, until only the tip of him was still inside her. He watched her face, and she watched him, as he plunged his length in again, then out, again and again, until he saw her eyes flare wide and her mouth go slack, and she arched her back as the tremors shook her.

He throbbed inside her, letting the passion course through him, draining him, emptying him, consuming him. *Mine*, he thought in triumph. And through his clenched teeth the words were torn from him in a harsh cry.

"Christ, Gabrielle . . . I love—!"

He lay facedown, one leg flung across her thighs. She relished its heavy weight, the warmth of his skin, slightly damp with sweat. Her heart thundered in her ears, keeping tempo with the beat of the rain against the window. The skin of her face and breasts tingled where it had been rubbed by his whiskers.

His leg moved off her. Unconsciously she held her breath, waiting to see what he would do, what he would say. Would he admit to the words that had spilled from him during the peak of his passion?

He leaned over her. She opened her mouth to breathe and he slid his tongue over her lips. He pulled back and surveyed the length of her body.

"*Merde.* There's blood everywhere."

Tension made her laugh too loudly. "Look at us. We're painted with red stripes like one of those savages from America."

He sat up and peeled off the blood-soaked shirt. He examined the wound. The flesh was red and pulpy, gaping open like a slice of raw meat, and she felt the gorge rise in her throat.

"Oh, Max . . . I'm so sorry."

"Hell, I deserved it." He looked up, giving her one of those adorable damn-it-all smiles. "No one likes being laughed at."

"Perhaps we should summon the doctor."

"So that I can be drained of even more blood? No, thank you. It's only a flesh wound. There's some brandy on that chest over there. Will you get it for me, please?"

She scrambled off the bed and ran to fetch it. She had started to pour some into a glass when she heard him laugh.

"Silly idiot. I'm not going to drink it."

"Oh." She hurried back to the bed with the decanter.

The ball had left a deep crease in the fleshy part of his muscle. He pulled the cut as far apart as he could stand it. "Pour it in there."

The room began to darken and spin before Gabrielle's eyes. She sucked in a deep breath and tipped the mouth of the decanter, pouring the brown liquid into the wound.

His arm jerked spasmodically. "Jesus God Almighty!" he roared, falling back against the headboard. Sweat filmed his face, his breath coming in hash pants. After a moment he opened his eyes. "That's good, *ma mie*. Now do it again."

"Oh, no, I couldn't . . ."

"Just do it. Before I lose my nerve."

He didn't curse again, but his lips turned white. After she had finished, he took the decanter from her trembling hands and poured a hefty measure of what was left down his throat. He looked at her and smiled, reaching up to wipe the tears from her cheeks. "What are *you* crying for?"

She gulped back a sob. "I—I can't bear to see you suffer."

He stiffened and his eyes flared with sudden anger. The words hung in the air between them, like raindrops caught fast in a web.

Then he turned aside and pulled a linen slip off one of the pillows, ripping it in two. He tried binding his wound one-handed and using his teeth until she took the makeshift bandage away from him and did it for him.

"Max . . ."

"Leave it, Gabrielle."

"I can't. I can't bear loving you and having this . . . this great wall between us."

"What do you want from me? I can't make things the way they were before."

He flung himself off the bed. He paced the room, magnificent in his nakedness. A strong, lusty male animal—and she felt a primitive stirring in her loins.

"You could try to forgive me."

"It's not that simple." He gave a hollow laugh. "Do you know, in those hot, miserable nights after you first left me, I would lie in bed and dream of you crawling back to me, begging to be forgiven. Even the *thought* of revenge tasted sweet."

"I've begged, Max. I'll beg some more if that's what it takes to tear down the wall." She got up and went to him. His back was to her, and she pressed her face against it. "If it's revenge you want, my love, then take it."

He pulled away from her. For an eternity he said nothing, then he turned, and her heart broke at the anguish on his face.

"I no longer want revenge. But the hurt is still there, Gabrielle. It's like a canker. It aches and festers, and the only time I can forget it is when my yard is buried deep inside you."

She would settle for that. For now. There was some hope that if she loved him hard enough, long enough, he would love her once again.

"You're my husband," she said. "And I love you."

A muscle ticked in his jaw, and a corner of his mouth turned down. She thought he was going to say something, but he was interrupted by shouts and the jangle of harness coming from below.

He went to the bedroom window. "It's Percy!"

Grabbing his breeches off the floor, he struggled into them. "Better put some clothes on, *ma mie*. If Percy saw you in that utterly delightful state of nakedness he'd do something foolish and I'd have to fight another duel.''

Before she could ask him what he meant by that remark about a duel, he had bounded from the room. She heard his feet thundering down the stairs, the bang of the front door, and his voice bellowing, "Percy, you whoreson! What the hell are you doing here? Was Paris too boring for you without me around to lead you down the pathways of sin?''

Shielding herself behind curtains of embroidered muslin, Gabrielle peered out the window to see Percy Bonville in a coat of purple velvet and a flowered waistcoat descending from a traveling chaise pulled by mud-splattered horses with dripping trace chains. The two men embraced and thumped each other on the back, then Max led Percy up the château's steps and into the great hall.

"Paris is boring and Versailles is even worse. The peasants are starving and surly and about ready to revolt, and the marquise de Tessé pines for you. Are you going to give me something to drink or do I have to sing for it?''

Percy stood in the middle of the library, leaning on his cane to look around the room. Only the French, he thought, could take opulence to the point of decadence and get away with it.

Max pressed a snifter of brandy into his hand.

Percy gestured at the bandage around Max's arm. A spot of fresh blood was already seeping through the thin linen. "Did you fight another duel and lose this time?''

"Gabrielle shot me.''

"Gabrielle!"

Percy studied his friend's face. He saw the clear eyes, the smiling mouth. He laughed. "If she shot you then, by God, you probably deserved it. Where is she?''

"Here. Upstairs.''

Percy laughed again. Then he suddenly noticed that Max was standing before him in nothing but a pair of breeches. "Did I, er, interrupt the reunion?''

Max's mouth tilted up in a crooked smile. "No. We'd finished. For now."

"Finished! And it's only the middle of the morning. You must be wearing down in your old age." Percy chuckled and took a sip of the brandy. "That's wonderful about Gabrielle being back. Is she going to stay this time?"

The gray eyes clouded and the dark, handsome face stiffened, and Percy cursed his careless tongue. "I don't know," Max said.

Percy limped over to the fireplace where a thick, gnarled log burned invitingly. He set the glass of brandy on the mantel and held his hands before the flames. He looked up at the portrait above his head.

"I ran into your father the other day. I can see where you acquired that cutting tongue of yours." He turned to grin at Max. "I offered him a friendly hello and tried to strike up a harmless conversation about the weather, and he told me that if it was French I was trying to speak, I needed to be given lessons. I get the feeling he doesn't like Americans."

"He doesn't like people who like me. Why are you here? Has Tessé died?

"No. He's going to live. That's why I rode all the way out here in that miserable chaise, freezing my ass off. I've come to tell you you can come back to Paris if you like—we all miss you." The smile left Percy's face and he gave Max a hard, assessing look. "I can't pretend to have ever liked Tessé, but he's pretty much the invalid now, can't leave his bed for more than an hour at a time. And you've scarred him for life."

Max gave Percy his cold, lazy smile. "My heart bleeds . . . He pimps for the marquise his wife, did you know? He encourages her to take lovers and he makes her tell him all about it in great detail. Then when he tires of the game he kills the man in a duel. The bastard deserved everything he got."

Percy stared at Max in astonishment. Then he laughed. "By God, you do have a knack for knavery if nothing else. You made Tessé pay dearly for the privilege of watching you make love to his . . . wife.'' Percy's voice trailed off as he caught sight of the woman standing in the doorway.

She was wonderfully deshabille in a quilted dressing gown of blue silk, her hair hanging loose around her shoulders in fiery disarray. She looked stunning. And furious.

''Oh shit,'' Percy said.

Max found her standing with her back to the door before the big tester bed. It was in a shambles, the counterpane stained with his blood and their lovemaking, pillows and clothing strewn around the floor.

''Gabrielle—''

''No! I will not listen to your lies!'' She flung her head around. Two bright spots of color stained her cheekbones. Her eyes were hot with fury. He had never seen her angry like this before.

A lock of her hair had fallen across her face. She brushed it back with a shaking hand. ''How *could* you have made love to another woman?''

''I wouldn't call what Claire and I did making love.''

She sucked in a sharp breath. ''She has a name!''

He almost laughed—except that it wasn't at all funny. ''Of course she has a name.''

She cradled her elbows with her hands and turned away from him again, but she couldn't hide the pain in her voice. ''Do you love her?''

''No.''

He thought of himself as he had been then—drunk half the time and hurting so bad he wanted to die. How could he ever explain the complicated feelings of pain, loneliness, and anger that had driven him into the all-too-willing arms of the marquise de Tessé? The final irony was that he'd had to close his eyes and imagine it was Gabrielle's lips, Gabrielle's hands, Gabrielle's body opening to him before he could even come.

He stared at her rigid back and felt his own anger building as he remembered all over again the misery she had put him through. ''You left me, Gabrielle, remember? As far as I knew, you were never coming back. It's a little hard being faithful to a memory.'' There came to him suddenly the thought, Had she been faithful to him?

Her shoulders shook, and he thought she was crying. Then she whipped around to face him, and he saw she wasn't crying at all.

''That night you found me in the ditch,'' she said, ''you were on your way here straight from that woman's bed.''

''Yes.'' He gave her a tight, angry smile. ''After a little detour to the Bois de Boulogne, where I shot her husband.''

''She was your mistress.''

''Yes. For a while.''

''Then what you have done was utterly despicable. You let me humiliate myself, begging to be forgiven for making you suffer when you never suffered at all, did you? You had this *Claire* to comfort you. Were there others? Was there any night during the past year that you spent alone?''

''She was the only one,'' he said. He could feel his face hardening into the mask of indifference he always wore when he was hurting. ''Although if you're going to damn me for it, then I'm sorry there weren't a dozen others. Sophie Restonne offered me a different girl for every night of the week. I should have taken her up on it.''

Gabrielle sucked in a ragged breath and at last the tears came, falling in gentle drops, like dew, onto her cheeks. ''Oh, God . . . I'll never forgive you for this.''

He bowed mockingly. ''Then it seems, madame, that we are now even.''

Chapter 19

The hunt thundered across the road, the baying of the hounds and the mournful wail of horns rending the air. Percy Bonville leaned out the window of his traveling chaise to watch it pass.

The dogs, following the deer scent, led the purebred horses with their purebred riders through a small group of clay-and-wattle farms. The horses' sharp hooves slashed through the moist earth, ruining the newly plowed fields. One nobleman, for sport, fired his musket at a cow, and the beast fell dead facefirst into the turf. The peasants cowered within the doorways of their cottages, a mixture of terror and anger on their faces.

One man, braver than the rest, stood beside a tottering hen roost and raised his fist in the air, shaking it. A horse and rider veered toward him. The rider swung out one brightly polished boot and kicked the man in the chest, driving him to his knees, and the horse's powerful shoulders knocked against the hen roost, toppling it. There was a flurry of squawking chickens, and feathers filled the air.

Shaking his head, Percy pulled back inside the body of the chaise. "You French aristocrats are an arrogant lot. It costs more to buy a loaf of bread than a man can earn in a day, the people are simmering on the edge of revolt, the *philosophes* are crying for liberty—and you all behave as if things will continue as they have for the next thousand years. Can't you see what's happening beneath your own haughty noses?''

''No doubt,'' Max said, obviously not listening. Gabrielle, sitting as far from Max as she could get, didn't bother to respond at all. The boy Dominique was asleep between them, his head leaning against his mother's arm. The tension between husband and wife was stretched so tightly it could almost have been plucked, like the strings of a violin. Percy reflected that for all the company he was getting he might as well have been traveling back to Paris alone, and he smothered a yawn in his scented handkerchief.

With the hunt having cleared the road, the chaise resumed its journey. As they passed the group of farms, Percy again looked out the window. He started to raise his hand to wave, then let it fall. Mistaking his carriage for that of a nobleman's, the peasants stared at it with hatred plain on their thin faces. Once, they would have cheered and doffed their caps. Now they stood insolently straight, their hands stuffed deep into their pockets.

''The trouble with France today,'' Percy said aloud, amusing himself, ''is that ninety percent of the population is dying of hunger and the other ten of indigestion.''

No one laughed at his joke. He doubted they had even heard him. He saw Gabrielle steal a look at Max, who was staring out the window with such a forbidding expression on his face it could have been chiseled from granite. There was a look of such love and anguish on Gabrielle's features that Percy wondered how Max could resist it. What's more, she looked positively scrumptious in a gown of pink tiffany with blond lace scallops topped by a short, fur-trimmed pelisse and matching hat. Percy had to sternly remind himself she was the wife of his best friend, and that he didn't like temperamental redheads.

Resigning himself to many more hours of this uncomfortable, taut silence, Percy leaned his head against the leather seat cushion and shut his eyes. They popped open immediately at the sound of Gabrielle's voice, sweet and clear, filling the chaise.

"Monsieur le Vicomte?"

Monsieur le Vicomte turned to regard his wife with upraised brows.

"I have been thinking," Gabrielle said.

"It's about time," Max retorted, and Percy stopped himself from snickering just in time.

"I have decided that you may have all the mistresses you like—"

"Thank you, but—"

"—and I shall take lovers."

Percy's eyes opened wide at this remark. "By Christ, I'll see you dead first!" Max snarled, predictably.

"We shall have an accommodating marriage."

"I'll accommodate you black and blue if I so much as catch you looking at another man."

She lifted a haughty chin into the air, and Percy grinned. "Hunh!" She sniffed. "Your threats don't frighten me."

Max gave her a wolfish smile. "I'll thank you to remember that you are mine. I'll keep you chained to my bed if I find it necessary, but you will be a lover to *me*, Gabrielle, and no other."

Percy broke into a sudden fit of coughing. He smothered his entire face with his handkerchief, while dark gray and violet eyes sent sparks flying at each other across the confining carriage.

It was obvious to any fool that those two were madly in love with each other, but Percy wisely kept such an opinion to himself. After dinner yesterday at the Château de Morvan, he had tried to get Gabrielle alone long enough to undo some of the damage caused by his earlier tactless remark. He thought to convey some of the torment his friend Saint-Just had gone through during her absence, but she had seemed unmoved. Then he had made the supreme error of mentioning that a man like Maximilien de Saint-Just had certain physical needs that could be suppressed for only so long.

"And, pray tell," she had said, opening wide those great purple eyes, "what needs are those?"

Percy could feel his face burning hotly. "Well, uh, that is

. . . a man who's never had trouble finding a woman whenever he gets the urge becomes used to the, er, regular physical release.''

''Ah. So that then is the reason why Max took a wife. So he could have the convenience of regular physical release without taking the trouble, however small, to look for it.''

Percy had once fought a skirmish against the redcoats in a swamp in North Carolina, but this ground he now tread felt far more dangerous. Sweat trickled down his cheeks, and he struggled hard to come up with just the right words that wouldn't further damn his friend.

''A man can take a woman without feeling any affection whatsoever, and think nothing of it,'' he finally said, ''but I would stake my life that Saint-Just not only loves you very much, but that you are the only woman he has ever loved.''

Gabrielle lifted her head, and he could see plainly how hurt had marked her face. ''I would die before I let another man touch me. If Max loved me at all he wouldn't have been capable of making love to another woman.''

Percy had no answer for that. Women, he decided, were made differently than men in more ways than the obvious. It was why life with the opposite sex could be so delightful, and so maddening.

He had tried to explain this theory to Max later that night as they got drunk together over port and brandy in the library.

''Women,'' Max had responded, sounding as surly as he looked, ''are good for only one thing. And the man who forgets that is a fool.''

Percy sighed. ''It's only because Gabrielle loves you so much that she can't forgive you for—''

''Love!'' Max sent his glass crashing into the flames, and the spilled brandy caught fire in a *whoosh* of blue light. ''How can she claim to love me and have thought me capable of such despicable acts? If she loved me, she would never have been able to leave me—no matter what she saw or thought she saw.''

Percy, who had earlier been told the full story of the reason for Gabrielle's flight, tried to think it through from her point of view. "She was frightened—"

"If she was frightened, why didn't she come to me for help? Why keep it all hidden from me?" Max pounded his fist so hard on the delicate arm of the chair that it cracked. "As my wife she had an *obligation* to tell me."

"I don't know why she didn't tell you, although I can guess. That perpetual sneer you wear on that handsome face of yours doesn't do a lot to encourage confidences. What I fail to understand is why the pair of you are now putting yourselves through all this added misery." Percy waved a hand in the air. "It's obvious you're still in love with her—"

"I'm not."

"Horse manure. And she still loves you. You should both swallow your damnable pride and go to each other, admit your mistakes, and build a life on the love you share, rather than tormenting each other by denying your feelings."

Max thrust out a square and stubborn chin. "I'll admit Claire de Tessé was a mistake—when Gabrielle admits she drove me to do it in the first place!"

Thinking back now on this conversation, Percy leaned against the leather seat of his chaise and used his handkerchief to smother a sigh. He was glad he had thus far escaped the misfortune of falling in love. It turned even the most reasonable of men and women into utter idiots, and wreaked more havoc than a plague of locusts.

The chaise bullied its way slowly down a Quai des Tuileries that was congested with traffic. They had left Percy at his lodgings in Versailles and continued on by themselves to Paris, borrowing the chaise. Max, Gabrielle had just learned, no longer leased the apartment in the Palais Royal, but lived instead in a grand *hôtel* on the Rue de Lille that he had inherited with his title.

Dominique sat on Gabrielle's lap and leaned out the window, offering a running commentary on everything he saw. "Look, Maman!" he exclaimed loud enough for all on the quay to hear. "All those ladies have big, fluffy white feathers in their hats."

Gabrielle looked. Indeed, it seemed every hat she saw sported an ostrich feather—obviously the *dernier cri* in millinery fashion this winter season—and she made a mental note of it.

Dominique screeched in her ear and pointed at a fat woman who sat wedged tightly into a sedan chair that had been dumped into a pile of kitchen rubbish while her bearer indulged in fisticuffs with a clumsy carter. "Maman, that lady curses even worse than Agnes!"

Beside her she heard Max swallow a laugh. Unconsciously she turned to him, and they both shared a smile until they each remembered their anger and looked away. But the smile eased some of the tension between them, enough so that she could say, "Paris seems different somehow."

"Percy would say it is the sedition you smell in the air," he drawled, and his smile caused her heart to give a little leap.

It was a dark, drizzly day, and the city seemed as gray as the weather. Piles of frozen garbage lined the streets, and surely there were more beggars than usual sheltering beneath the stone parapets that lined the river Seine. Many of the shops along the quay had their green wooden shutters pulled down tight, although it was only midday. There were long lines outside the bakeries, and in the gutter beside a butcher's shop Gabrielle spotted a skeletal old woman stuffing a handful of raw animal innards into her mouth.

But as the chaise crossed the Pont Solferino and entered the fashionable Faubourg Saint-Germain, the look of the city changed. Here the tree-lined streets were quiet and swept free of refuse. Looking at the stately carriage entrances to the great stone houses, it was easy to believe, as Percy had said, that things would continue as they had for a thousand more years.

The chaise rolled up before a *porte cochère* with the shield of the house of Saint-Just carved into the stone arch over the gates. They were pulled open by a pair of lackeys in silver and blue livery, and the chaise continued forward along a short white-pebbled drive.

A valet ran up to open the door of the carriage and let down the step, and more servants were there to hold open the front door of an enormous mansion that seemed to be all windows and marble facing. Max stepped into the hall, letting fall his greatcoat and hat into the hands of a porter without even bothering to look around to ensure the man was there to catch them. If Paris was, indeed, seething with sedition, Gabrielle thought, then the disease had yet to infect the household of Saint-Just.

The huge entrance hall was the most magnificent Gabrielle had ever seen, with so much gilt scrollwork it made her feel slightly dizzy. The majordomo magically appeared to lead them up the sweeping marble stairs—first to the nursery, where a sleepy-eyed Dominique was put down for a nap, and then to what was termed "madame's room," where unseen minions had already deposited the many trunks filled with all the clothes and accoutrements Max had bought for her.

"Madame's room" was decorated in soothing green and mauve colors, and separated from "monsieur's room" by a connecting door. She could hear Max's voice speaking on the other side of it, and she stood in the middle of the splendid room wondering whether she should go to him, wishing he would come to her, and regretting the need to think about it at all.

Instead she went to look out one of the room's three velvet-draped windows.

The Hôtel de Saint-Just backed up to the Quai d'Orsay. She could see the river from here. For the first time in her memory it had frozen over solid enough for skaters to cross back and forth on their swift, sharp blades. Chunks of ice had caught against the pilings of the bridges. Cookfires burned orange on the ships that were locked into their moorings, and the cries of the peddlers on the quay carried far on the cold air.

The view blurred as shameful tears filled her eyes. Five days and nights had passed since Percy Bonville had come to the Château de Morvan, and Max had not touched her once since then.

Gabrielle tried to convince herself she didn't care, that—husband or not—she would never let him take her as he would a whore, without love. She felt so betrayed by him. In some ways it was worse than when she thought he had sold her to Louvois. Every time she closed her eyes she saw Max with a faceless woman, their limbs entwined in passion, and she felt a bitter and angry hurt that throbbed in her breast like a raw wound.

Yet still . . . still . . . One look at his dark, sensual face, at his hard, demanding body, and she knew she would accept him back into her bed on any terms. When it came to Maximilien de Saint-Just she had no pride, no shame, no sense.

She heard a knock and whipped around, her heart in her throat, but it was the wrong door that opened.

A serving girl entered bearing a large brass can filled with water. "Monsieur le Vicomte said the vicomtesse would wish to wash off the grime from the journey." She set the can and a pair of thick white cotton towels on top of an ornate dresser with a marble top and gilt bronze mounts. She poured some of the water into a large Sèvres porcelain bowl and turned to smile at Gabrielle. She had a friendly face with round, plum-like cheeks and slightly crooked teeth that gave her a gamin look.

Gabrielle tried to produce an answering smile. "Thank you, mademoiselle . . ."

The girl curtsied. "I am Henriette, Madame la Vicomtesse . . . Madame, do you desire that I unpack for you now?"

"No, thank you. Later, if you please, Henriette. There's a green silk dressing gown in that cloak bag just there beside the door. If you could lay it out on the bed for me . . ."

"But of course, madame."

"I prefer to undress myself."

The girl curtsied again. "As you wish, madame."

Left alone, Gabrielle rapidly stripped off her clothes. She pulled the pins from her coiffure, shaking her head until her hair tumbled like a mantle over her shoulders. She stood naked in the middle of the room, shivering, for the place was large and a bit drafty in spite of the thick rugs that covered the floor and the fire that blazed in the grate.

Lavender-scented steam rose from the water in the bowl. Gabrielle spread one of the towels on the floor and, taking a sponge, began to dribble water over her body, luxuriating in the sensuous, oily feel of it coursing softly over her skin. Her eyes drifted closed and she imagined it was Max's hands caressing her flesh, Max's hands setting her blood afire. She rubbed the perfumed water between her thighs, trailing her fingers through the curly, silken nest of hair. She trembled and her mouth parted on a soft sigh—

There was a small sound behind her. She whipped around, the blood leaving and then rushing back to her face in a wave of furious color. Max stood just inside the room, within the shadows of the muted winter afternoon light.

She reached frantically behind her for her dressing gown, her eyes unable to leave the dark oval that was his face. She belted the gown tight around her waist. "You—you could at least have had the courtesy to knock," she stuttered, feeling hot with guilt, shame—and something else. Excitement.

He came into the room. Now the firelight fell on his face. It was very pale, and a muscle twitched in his cheek. For a moment his eyes rested on her breasts, where the silk clung to her wet skin, outlining her tautened nipples, and she saw hunger flare hot and bright within the sooty gray depths.

He averted his head, showing her his sharp-boned profile. He had removed his coat, and she saw the thin cambric of his shirt flutter against his chest as he breathed.

"I thought I should tell you," he said, a rough edge to his voice, "so that if you should happen to see us together you won't take it into your head to run away again . . ." He jerked back around and looked hard into her eyes. "Tomorrow afternoon I intend to pay a visit to the duc de Nevers."

Gabrielle felt the color drain from her face, and she saw Max's reaction to it in the way his mouth twisted down at one corner into a sneer. Even now, even in the midst of this renewed worry over her son, she wanted to kiss that sneer away, to make him smile at her again, to make him love her.

He lifted his head and stared down at her from beneath half-closed lids. "What's the matter, Gabrielle? Don't you trust me?"

She clenched her fists to control her trembling. "But if you tell him about us, he'll take my son! I'll be arrested. The duc has a signed *lettre de cachet* with my name on it. And you could be arrested as well. I was forbidden by the king ever to marry again."

He waved his hand impatiently and took a step to bring himself closer to her. She could read nothing in his hard mask of a face, but she felt the heat of his nearness as if his body were a flaming torch.

"What did you plan to do, Gabrielle?" he said. "Skulk inside the house here until Nevers dies, or until Dominique becomes a man? This matter with the duc must be resolved so that we can all live a normal life." Again his lips twisted downward. "Or at least as normal a life as is possible given the circumstances of our marriage."

This was important; her son's future was at stake. She had to consider all the consequences and all she could think was that Max was here in her room, they were alone together for the first time in days, and she wanted him with a raw, primitive hunger that was an ache in her belly.

Sucking unconsciously on her lower lip, she looked down at the floor and missed seeing the telltale muscle in his jaw clench and unclench. "But what . . . what will you say to him?" she said. "How can it possibly be resolved?"

Max lifted his hand, hesitated a moment, then lightly stroked her cheek. The harshness on his face eased somewhat. It was all she could do not to melt against him, not to go into his arms seeking comfort.

"You are the wife of the vicomte de Saint-Just. It's a name that counts for something in this country." A small dimple appeared and disappeared in his taut cheek. "Thanks to my great and noble parent."

"But the duc—"

"Hush and listen." His voice took on that silky resonance that never failed to send chills up and down her spine. "I know certain things about the duc de Nevers that he probably wouldn't like whispered into the ear of the king. I think we can reach a fair exchange. He gives up his persecution of you; in return he can visit his grandson occasionally. Dominique is the old man's heir, after all, and he should come to know his—"

Gabrielle jerked away from him. "Never! I will not let that monster near my son! He would carry him off and I would never see him again."

He clasped her upper arms and turned her around to face him. She shuddered at the frisson of feeling that ripped through her at his touch. But Max, evidently thinking she feared or was repulsed by him, released her so abruptly that she almost stumbled.

He backed up a step and his eyes, under their drooping lids, looked mockingly down on her. "Come, come, Gabrielle, the mighty Saint-Just pride is at stake here. Do you think I'd allow anything to happen to Dominique? He's my son now and I'll protect him." His eyes darkened to charcoal-black with some emotion she couldn't begin to fathom. "I would never let harm come to the boy. Can't you find it in you to have a little faith in me, Gabrielle?"

Her throat closed up and she almost couldn't get the words out. "Oh, Max . . . of course, I have faith in you."

He gave a bitter laugh and started to turn away from her, but she grabbed his arm to stop him. Whipping around, he seized her by the neck and slammed his mouth over hers.

Their teeth grated together, and then his tongue, rigid and thrusting, was in her mouth while his hands loosened the belt around her waist and the damp material of her robe fell aside to expose her breasts. He cupped them in his hands, his fingers twisting her nipples to the ecstasy side of pain, and she arched her back, pulling their mouths apart.

His lips swooped down to her breast. His hands cupped the underside of her buttocks, pulling her hips up onto the column of his body, while his tongue and teeth toyed with her nipples. She rubbed her mound against the marble-hard muscles of his abdomen and felt his thick male ridge, tightly encased in his satin breeches, pressing up between her thighs. She lifted her knee and rubbed it against him and she could feel him pulsate and throb beneath the thin slick cloth.

He shuddered and his hands slipped, and she slid down the length of him. Her fingers tore open his breeches and suddenly his thickness was filling her hands. He spanned her waist, lifting her, sliding his shaft smoothly deep inside her until he was buried to the hilt and she wrapped her legs around his waist and drew him in tighter, deeper.

He tried to carry her like that to the bed, but they fell onto the floor, panting with laughter and passion. He rolled onto his back and she was on top of him. She pulled open his shirt, exposing the bare flesh of his chest in a deep V. Falling forward, she rubbed her breasts across the light mat of hair, feeling it tickle and tingle her sensitive flesh. She sealed his mouth with hers, diving into him with her tongue. Then she reared back and began to move up and down on him, and he lifted her breasts like a feast before his eyes as she rocked and plunged wildly in the saddle of his hips.

This, she thought—although it was not a thought at all, more a sudden, primitive awareness—this is what it feels like to ride across broad, windswept plains with a powerful stallion galloping hard between your legs, with the wind in your face and the blood pumping hot and fast in your veins.

She threw back her head and let loose a guttural cry. As the tremors of passion wrung her empty, he filled her up again.

She slumped forward onto his chest, her face nestled into the crook of his shoulder. Their lungs rose and fell together, rapidly at first, then slower and slower, as they began to wind down. Where her skin met his it was moist with sweat. One of his hands was spread over one cheek of her bottom, and he began to knead it gently. He was still inside her, although he had begun to shrink and soften. It always made her a little sad when he withdrew from her. It left her feeling empty, or as if something vital to her life had been pulled out of her.

Perhaps to lessen the sadness this time, she pulled away from him first, rolling up onto her side to look down into his face. She thought his eyes were closed, but as she opened her mouth to speak, he covered it with his palm.

"No. Don't say anything."

The words piled up in her mouth, pressing against his hand, straining to come out. *Do you love me? Was it me you wanted just now, or would any woman have served?*

In silence he lifted her into his arms and carried her to the bed. In silence he settled her beneath silken sheets. Then to her pleased surprise he undressed and joined her. He fell asleep with one heavy arm draped across her breasts, and when he awoke a couple of hours later he took her again, in silence still, slowly this time, and with exquisite tenderness.

But he didn't speak of love. And neither did she.

Chapter 20

❧❧

G abrielle had her son's hand tucked tightly into hers. They stood beneath the bare and withered branches of a thick-trunked chestnut tree and looked around them at the Palais Royal. The libertines and streetwalkers were as numerous as ever, but now the gardens appeared to be a hotbed of political activity, as well as sin.

The bookstalls were overloaded with pamphlets and tracts, so fresh off the presses that the heavy, acrid odor of printer's ink filled the air. A man standing on a garden bench and reading aloud from one of the pamphlets about the rights of man was gathering quite a crowd. A huge throng of people stood in front of the Café de Foy listening to an orator shout about a plot on the part of the king to starve Paris.

"Maman!" Dominique pulled hard on Gabrielle's hand. "I thought you said we were going to visit Agnes and Simon."

"We are, *mon petit*. In a minute."

Gabrielle looked up at the sign of the pawnbroker. The three golden balls needed painting again, and she wondered why Simon had not seen to it. A spasm of fear tightened her chest. Was he ill? Had business been bad?

Through the front window she could see the flickering of the candelabra on the desk. She remembered the first time she had stood in this place, trying to summon up the courage to enter Simon's shop. How strange sometimes were the vagaries of fate, for how different her life would have been if she had chosen somewhere else to pawn Martin's ring.

The bell above the lintel rang as she pushed open the door. Simon sat on the stool behind the counter, covering a piece of paper with a loose, bold scrawl. It was a moment before he looked up—not until Dominique pulled out of her hand and began to run toward the back of the shop, shouting, "M'sieur Simon! M'sieur Simon!"

His head flung up and he blinked several times, then Dominique hurled himself onto Simon's knees, burying his head in Simon's plump lap.

Simon's outstretched hand hovered over the top of the boy's blond head, then it fell and a funny twisted look came over his face. "My dear God have mercy . . . Gabrielle. Is it really you?"

Simon's round face blurred and wavered as tears filled Gabrielle's eyes. She stumbled toward him and he stood up, bringing Dominique with him. Wordlessly he wrapped his free arm around her and pulled her tightly against him. She pressed her face into his chest. He smelled of the same old Simon—rosewater and beneath it the musty smell of old coats.

"Gabrielle, Gabrielle," he began to croon, swaying back and forth as he held them both.

A loud shriek made them pull apart. Agnes stood in the doorway to the kitchen, her hands covering her mouth, her face mottled with color beneath a monstrous mobcap. "Is it you? May the devil peel me like a raw onion. Gabrielle!"

Dominique crawled down Simon's leg and ran to Agnes, wrapping his arms around her knees. "Agnes, guess what! I can ride a horse! Her name is Marthe."

"Can you, my precious one?" Tears began to spill from Agnes's eyes and she brought a shaking hand over her mouth again. "Oh, Jesu . . . I can't believe you're really here."

Gabrielle felt strangely shy. There was so much to tell and explain and she didn't know where to begin. Instead all she could manage was to mumble, "I'm here."

Agnes picked Dominique up and gave him a smacking kiss

on his cheek. Setting him on his feet, she stepped back and put her fists on her hips. "Let me look at you, child. My, but I swear you've doubled in size, just like a boiled *beignet.*" Then she surveyed Gabrielle up and down. "By God's spleen, girl, you're as skinny as a splinter."

"Don't curse, wife," Simon said.

Gabrielle had been about to laugh, and her mouth stayed open as she whirled to gape at Simon. *"Wife?"*

Agnes chuckled, but her magnificent bosom swelled with pride. "Can you believe it, Gabrielle? Simon's gone and made himself my husband, the old fool." She cuffed Simon on the arm. "And now he thinks he's God himself."

Simon sniffed. "Whoever said that if it's trouble a man wants, then he should take himself a wife, knew well what he was talking about." But Simon's eyes glowed with happiness as he regarded Agnes.

Gabrielle looked from one round, smiling face to the other. "I don't know what to say . . . except to wish you well." She flung her arms around Agnes.

"Agnes!" Dominique cried, pushing between them. "Do you have any gingerbread?"

"I've been praying for the day you'd come home to us," Simon said. He sat in his chair before the hearth while Gabrielle perched next to him on an oaken settle, cradling a cup of tea in her hands. Dominique and Agnes were at the kitchen table, making a feast out of gingerbread, biscuits, and a type of jam called *raisiné*, which was made from pears, sugar, and grape juice.

"But I can see by those fancy clothes you and the boy are sporting that it's *him* you've returned to." Simon's lip curled. "The vicomte de Saint-Just, or so he styles himself now."

Gabrielle met his angry eyes. "Maximilien de Saint-Just is my husband."

Simon thrust out a stubborn lower lip. "That's as may be, but if you had reason to flee from him once, who's to say he won't give you reason again. I don't know what it was he did, but I'm never going to forgive him for it. I told him so to his face when he came poking around here, trying to find out where you'd gone.''

"Told him!" Agnes exclaimed around a mouthful of gingerbread. "You attacked him with a broom. Poor Monsieur Max. He just stood there and let you hit him.''

Tears filled Gabrielle's eyes, but she was laughing as well. "Oh, Simon . . .''

Simon shook his fist in the air. "I'll go after him again if he ever sets his foot across my threshold!''

"Simon, it wasn't Max's fault,'' Gabrielle said.

He shook his head stubbornly. "He promised to keep you safe. Instead he drove you away.''

"By Saint Christopher's whiskers!" Agnes snorted, spewing out a mouthful of gingerbread crumbs. "If you'd shut up, husband, long enough for her to get a word in, maybe Gabrielle can explain—''

Simon scowled at his wife. "You forget yourself, woman!''

Agnes sniffed. "I remember well what I'm about. It's the whereabouts of your head lately that has me worried." She grinned at Gabrielle and pointed at Simon. "He's joined that silly club—those Freemasons. Now he does nothing but write pamphlets and spout politics all day. And nights, too, when I don't keep him otherwise occupied.''

Simon blushed furiously, and Gabrielle took a sip of tea to hide her smile. Simon and Agnes married! Who would have ever thought it?

Agnes harrumphed. "He sees a plot of some sort or other in every bowl of soup.''

Simon pushed his bulk out of the chair, flinging his arms out at his sides. "And should I stand idly by and watch my country be destroyed by the Austrian bitch and that outdated monarch, her husband?'' He reached into the rubbish bin and pulled out a dark and crumbly loaf of bread that had a sour odor to it. He waved it beneath his wife's nose. "Do you see this? This is what the people of Paris are forced to live on while Madame Déficit drapes herself in diamonds!''

"You're scattering crumbs about, you fool. Do you want

us to get mice?" Agnes rolled her eyes at Gabrielle. "Three hours I wasted standing in line for that. But you don't see me wasting another two writing a tract about it."

"The warehouses are stuffed with rotting grain while the speculators wait for prices to rise." Simon appealed to Gabrielle, ignoring Agnes. "Yet a thousand sacks of flour are used each day to powder the heads of the aristocrats." He looked at Gabrielle's hair, which was styled simply to hang loose down her back, unpowdered. "At least you haven't forgotten who—"

He stopped and she could almost see the question forming in his mind. *And just who are you really, Gabrielle?*

But she could tell him nothing yet. At this very moment Max was meeting with the duc de Nevers, using a combination of blackmail, political influence, and his incredible charm to win freedom for herself and her son. He had asked for her faith and she knew if her marriage had any hope of surviving she must give it to him unconditionally.

Her eyes strayed to where Dominique now sat beside the coal scuttle, his mouth ringed with the *raisiné* jam, building a castle out of the briquettes and getting his blue satin suit filthy in the process. In trying to win back Max's love she risked the loss of her son, and her stomach roiled with fear at the thought.

A heavy silence had descended on the kitchen. She could feel Agnes's and Simon's eyes on her, waiting for her to tell them where she had been this past year and why she had run away in the first place. Someday, when she was sure she and Dominique were free of the duc, she would tell them both everything. But until then she didn't want to risk involving them too deeply in her affairs with her dangerous enemies. She repressed a smile. She could just imagine Simon going after the duc de Nevers with a broom!

Instead she said, "Simon, those pamphlets you write . . . Do you remember how I used to draw those caricatures of the queen—"

"But of course!" Simon exclaimed, slapping his hands together. "What a splendid idea! I'll speak to my printer about how it can be done. My tracts will have a much greater impact with your drawings to accompany them.''

Agnes heaved a huge sigh. ''Jesu, Gabrielle, I was hoping you would put an end to this foolishness of his, not encourage him.''

Gabrielle thought of the duc de Nevers and his lackey Louvois, and the terror and misery they had brought her during the last five years. Her face hardened and a fiery light burned in her eyes. ''No one, by the simple virtue of his birth, should have absolute power over another human being. If that is the meaning of liberty, then I will fight for it.''

Simon beamed. ''There you see, Agnes. I couldn't have put it better myself.''

Later, as they were leaving, Agnes walked with them into the gardens of the Palais Royal. Dusk had started to fall and the place had a festive air, with its strings of Chinese lanterns and the bustling and colorful crowd. At the palace, the decadent duc d'Orleans was giving yet another rout, and streams of carriages lined up to disgorge the satined and bejeweled revelers.

''Stay within sight of me, *petit,*'' Gabrielle called out to her son, who had darted ahead, chasing a squirrel.

Agnes entwined her arm with Gabrielle's. ''I know what you're going to say. You think Simon is much too old for me.''

''Simon is a good man.''

Agnes heaved a huge, nostalgic sigh, straining the bodice of her dress. ''I know you'll think I'm lying like a mountebank, but I fell in love with Simon that very first day.'' She giggled. ''When he tried to beat me with his cane for picking your pocket. Of course he never saw me as anything more than a nuisance he had to put up with for your sake.''

''Don't be silly.''

She squeezed Gabrielle's arm. ''No, it's true. But after you and Dominique left, we both felt so lonely. And then one day we realized, I guess, that we didn't have to be lonely. We had each other.''

Her irrepressible smile dimpled Agnes's cheeks. ''We

were married at Saint Roch's and I wore a white lace gown.
It was just as I'd always dreamed it would be." She giggled
again. "Of course, I couldn't pretend to be a virgin with
Simon—"

"I should hope not."

"But in a way it was like a first time because always before
when I lay with a man, it was just work. I didn't like it or
dislike it, as long as the man wasn't cruel, but with Simon
it's so different. He makes me feel special. He touches me
so gently. It's as if he fears I'll break."

In the soft light of the lanterns, Agnes's face glowed with
happiness and she looked almost beautiful. For a moment
Gabrielle envied her. Not for having Simon, for Gabrielle
could never think of him in any terms other than as the father
she had never had. What she envied was the security Agnes
felt—of knowing she was loved and cherished.

Agnes stopped and turned her around so that they were
face to face. "Gabrielle . . . are things all right now between
you and Monsieur Max?"

"Yes . . . of course," she lied.

Agnes sighed, mistaking the reason for the look of sadness
in Gabrielle's eyes. "Simon is the most stubborn man alive.
Once an idea gets into his head it takes root there and a team
of oxen couldn't drag it out. He was very fond of Monsieur
Max once, so perhaps he will come around. Then it could be
the way it was before—all of us friends again."

"Maman, look what I found!"

Gabrielle's eyes opened wide with dread at the excited note
in her child's voice, and she turned slowly, expecting Dominique to have in tow anything from a mouse to the king of
France.

Her impossible son came tottering toward her, clutching
an enormous orange and white striped cat to his chest. The
cat was so long its tail dragged along the ground between
Dominique's legs and its ears pointed straight up on either
side of his nose. A paste-jeweled collar twinkled around the
cat's fat neck.

"Oh, Dominique . . ." Gabrielle bit her cheek to keep

from laughing. Beside her, a whooping Agnes wasn't even bothering to try.

Dominique looked up at her with wide blue innocent eyes. "She's trying to follow us home, Maman. Can we keep her?"

Gabrielle, dragging a sulking Dominique behind her, approached the gates to the Hôtel de Saint-Just slowly, keeping a wary eye out for a heavy black berlin with postilions dressed in black and gold.

There was, in fact, a carriage parked in the white pebbled drive, but it was a splendid white landau, not a berlin, and the lackeys wore blue and silver. Even the horses had silver and blue cockades and matching ribbons pleated into their manes. And painted on the door of the coach was a lion's head between two crossed swords.

The *hôtel's* majordomo, a thin, creaky man with a mournful face, approached on silent feet as soon as they entered the vast Italianate marbled hall. Two other servants hovered nearby to remove their hats and cloaks.

"I'm not speaking to Maman," Dominique announced so loudly that his voice bounced off the tall, domed ceiling. "She wouldn't let me keep my cat."

The majordomo looked down his nose at Gabrielle's son, who was covered with soot, gingerbread crumbs, and bright orange cat hairs. The man's long nose twitched like a rabbit's. "Indeed, Monsieur Dominique?"

Gabrielle smiled apologetically to the steward. Even as a child she had always felt ill at ease around her mother's servants and Max's majordomo, Aumont, seemed especially intimidating. "We just went out . . . for a walk," she mumbled, though she knew as the vicomtesse she needn't explain her actions to anyone.

Aumont bowed. "Madame la Vicomtesse." His face was completely blank, but Gabrielle thought she saw something, amusement perhaps, flicker in his pebble-black eyes. "Monsieur le Comte awaits your presence in the grand salon."

It took Gabrielle a moment to absorb what he had said.

Then she paled and exclaimed without thinking, "Max's father is here to see *me?*"

"Madame. If you please, I shall conduct you there." He left no doubt that the great *maréchal* had issued a command that was expected to be obeyed instantly.

"I'm going, too," Dominique stated. He was now clinging to Gabrielle's skirts, and his mouth had changed from pouting to stubborn.

The steward looked down at the boy, and Gabrielle was surprised to see his thin, angular face soften. "I believe I heard Monsieur le Vicomte mention something about a surprise in the nursery," he said. He snapped his fingers and a servant appeared, but Dominique had already started running for the stairs, exclaiming something about a red 'stat his papa had promised to make for him.

Gabrielle expected Aumont to lead her toward the grand salon, but he hesitated a moment longer. "Madame . . . I wasn't sure you would approve." His face left no doubt that he didn't approve at all. "It is a . . . *creature* Monsieur le Vicomte has installed in the nursery."

Gabrielle paled. "A creature?"

Aumont's nose twitched. "An owl, madame."

"Oh . . ." She swallowed a smile. "Well, I shall have a word with monsieur."

He bowed. "Thank you, madame."

As Gabrielle followed the majordomo's spare frame toward a pair of double gilt-paneled doors, she caught a glimpse of her reflection in a mirror and almost sighed aloud. Her undressed hair had been whipped about by the damp winter wind and now frizzed and swirled around her head like a lion's mane. She had deliberately chosen the plainest of her new gowns to visit Simon and Agnes—a soft gray wool with just a hint of lace at the bodice and sleeves—not wanting to seem as if she were flaunting her new status as the wife of a vicomte. She had thought the dress elegant when she put it on earlier; now she decided she lacked only a mobcap on her head to keep from looking like a charlady.

Aumont swung open the doors and stepped aside. "Madame la Vicomtesse," he announced.

Gabrielle squared her shoulders and flung up her chin to march into the room. As she swept past the majordomo she had the oddest impression that he winked at her.

The *maréchal* stood at the far end of the room, his arms folded across his chest, his back to the fire. He was tall—taller even than Max—with a thick, round chest, shaped and corded like a wine barrel, and thighs that resembled tree trunks. He was in court dress, wearing a coat of yellow velvet heavily laced with gold and white satin breeches. His fashionable clump-heeled, square-toed shoes were adorned with diamond buckles and an elaborate, powdered wig curled down around his shoulders.

He would have looked foppish but for his massive size and the harsh lines on either side of his haughty, thin-lipped mouth. Instead, he looked like what he was—a man whose mere word could command armies.

He raised a quizzing glass to one eye and surveyed her through it, and his lips curled into a sneer that so resembled one of Max's that it was all Gabrielle could do not to smile in spite of her nervousness.

"For over the past year I've been hearing a ridiculous rumor that my son had taken a shopgirl to wife," he drawled, speaking in the heavy, pompous *style noble*. "But although Maximilien has always delighted in dreaming up schemes to besmirch the noble name I gave him, I had thought such a thing beyond even him." He sighed and dropped the quizzing glass, looping its string around his finger. "Alas, I see I am mistaken. Not only is he capable, he seems to have done it."

"Monsieur le Comte." Gabrielle performed a deep and respectful curtsy as befitted a dutiful daughter-in-law, but when she straightened she proudly met the comte's hard gray eyes, and said nothing. She refused to defend her lineage or her past to this arrogant man.

"I understand there is a child. A boy," the comte said. "Is it my wastrel son's?"

"No, monsieur."

He raised a pair of thin, dark brows. "Indeed?" He shrugged his broad, elegantly clad shoulders. "Then I shall not ask who the father is." Again he surveyed her with the quizzing glass. "I can understand what caught Maximilien's eye. You're rather beautiful in a windblown way. But I would have thought you too small through the hips to produce a boy. Are you breeding now?"

Angry color stained Gabrielle's cheeks. "That is none of your affair, monsieur."

"On the contrary, it is very much my affair. For if you aren't yet breeding, then perhaps it isn't too late for me to have this preposterous union annulled."

Gabrielle almost burst into wild laughter. She couldn't believe this was happening to her again. She wouldn't have been surprised if the comte next produced a *lettre de cachet* and waved it beneath her nose, threatening her with the Bastille.

Suddenly she was consumed with an indignant anger. She was tired of having these *men* wreak havoc with her life merely because they were obsessed with bloodlines and titles and who would be occupying a moldy old château five hundred years in the future. Why was it only women understood that what mattered in this life was not tomorrow, but now—having a mate you loved and who loved you to share your bed and your table; having happy, healthy children to nurture and watch grow. Why should it matter to this pompous, arrogant man what woman his son chose to marry, as long as Max found happiness and love?

She flung her head up and glared at the comte with violet-eyed fury. "If you intend to offer me threats or money with your next breath, monsieur, then I suggest you save it. For I was married to your son before God and married I shall stay until God chooses to sever the union, preposterous though it may be."

"Better take warning, my dear father," said a silky, sardonic voice, "my lady wife is frighteningly proficient with a pistol. If you insult her further she may challenge you to a duel."

Maximilien de Saint-Just leaned with negligent ease against the door frame, his long legs crossed at the ankles, his hands tucked into the pockets of his breeches. As usual the sight of him brought an automatic smile to Gabrielle's lips and a funny, shivery feeling to her chest.

On the other hand, the sight of his son brought a scowl to the *maréchal*'s face. "Speaking of duels, I hear you've killed the marquis de Tessé. He happened to have been a friend of mine."

"As far as I know he still is." Max sauntered into the room. Though she wasted not an ounce of pity on the comte de Saint-Just, Gabrielle couldn't help thinking the mocking smile on Max's face would have tried the patience of even the most sweet-natured parent.

"Why not rush over to Tessé's sickbed right now?" Max drawled lazily. "I'm sure he'd be delighted to see you."

The comte waved an imperious hand. "Never mind about that. It's this marriage of yours that I've come about—"

"You've come to congratulate me. I knew you would be thrilled."

"You have a year to rid yourself of her," the comte said, speaking of Gabrielle as if she were no longer in the room. "I've already arranged it with the marquis de Sévigné. You're to marry his daughter next Epiphany."

Max threw back his head and laughed. "Good God! The girl can't be more than fourteen!"

"And her husband will inherit half of Brittany."

"Then you marry her." Max slipped his arm around Gabrielle's waist and drew her to him. "If you enjoy your marriage bed as much as I do mine, you'll soon have a whole new crop of sons to replace me with."

Gabrielle blushed at Max's frank language, but the comte wasn't looking at her. His eyes, dark with anger, were boring into his son's face, and his hands clenched into tight fists.

"By God, I might have named you as my heir before the court and the king, but that doesn't mean I still can't rectify the error!"

Max shrugged. "Then do it."

The comte turned on his heel and marched to the door. But he paused at the threshold to look back at his son, who still stood in the middle of the room with his arm around Gabrielle's waist. "I often wonder what devil possessed me the night I sired you."

Max's arm squeezed Gabrielle so tightly the breath was pushed from her lungs, but his voice as he spoke was light and mocking. "Yes. Well, a lot of people have suffered over the years for that one mistake of yours."

The comte's face turned puce and he looked for a moment as if he would choke on his fury. Then the doors closed behind his broad back with a resounding and childish slam.

Gabrielle sagged against Max's shoulder. He smelled of tobacco and brandy and she wanted to kiss him, but something about the reserved way he held himself prevented her.

She sighed and he misunderstood the reason for it. "Don't pay any attention to my father. He's always been more bluster than bite—which maybe explains why France can never seem to win a war." He cupped her chin and lifted her face. "Would you mind if I were suddenly poor and titleless again?"

"Don't be an idiot." She shivered. "But he's a terrible, nasty man."

"Forget about him. I have something for you." Max released her to take a piece of paper from his coat pocket. It was a *lettre de cachet*. The one with her name on it, signed by the king.

She took it with a hand that trembled and looked up at him with shining eyes. "Oh, Max . . . How?"

"I traded for it with a vow of silence. There are certain tidbits of information the duc de Nevers would just as soon never reach the ear of the king." He smiled wickedly. "Actually it's the queen he fears even more, for he was once responsible for the disgrace of a particular favorite of hers. If she ever discovered it was Nevers in back of the plot, she'd have his balls fried in oil and brought to her on a silver platter—"

"Max!"

He laughed. "Sorry, *ma mie*. I forget sometimes you're such an innocent." He leaned into her and she thought he was going to take her into his arms, but at the last moment he pulled back and she tried to keep her disappointment from showing on her face.

"The duc has begged to see his grandson," he said, in a voice that was clipped and dry. "I told him the decision's yours, and he has agreed that's how it is to be."

She stiffened. "I'll think about it." She looked down at the *lettre de cachet* that she still clutched tightly in her fist. There were so many things she wanted to ask him. How had he come to possess the kind of knowledge that so frightened a powerful man like the duc de Nevers? Did all this mean that Max had decided to forgive her for running away? Did there remain within his heart even the tiniest spark of love for her?

He was staring at her, and his face looked hard, indifferent, almost cruel. It was how he always looked at her now, except when in the throes of passion. But passion wasn't love. Or was it?

"Max. I . . . I don't know how I can ever repay—"

"A husband has certain obligations to protect and care for his wife," he said stiffly.

Shameful tears welled up in Gabrielle's eyes and she turned away so he wouldn't see them. "Nevertheless, I'll always be grateful."

He took a step backward and bowed formally. "As you wish. I bid you good evening, madame."

He was almost out the door before she stopped him.

"Max, will . . . will you be home later tonight?" She clenched her hands behind her back to control their trembling. "Dominique was asking," she lied shamelessly.

"I have an engagement."

"Oh," she said, feeling sick.

His lips twisted at the corners into a knowing smile. "Does Dominique want to know where the engagement is, and whom it's with?"

Gabrielle sucked in a sharp breath. "Why you . . . you

rake! If you're going to see your mistress, I'd just as soon not hear about it!''

He laughed. ''Then I'll take care not to tell you. *Au revoir, ma mie.* ''

Late that night, the black berlin pulled up before the duc de Nevers's townhouse in Versailles. At the top of the steps, as he waited for the door to open, the lawyer Louvois looked across to the palace next door—where Louis XVI rested his royal, and probably drunken, head.

Louvois smiled to himself. At this very moment throughout the land, elections were being held to select representatives to a meeting of the Estates-General. It was the first time this parliamentary body would meet in a hundred and seventy-five years, and they were not going to be in a congenial mood. The king hoped to bail France out of bankruptcy by getting permission to tax the privileged orders, the clergy and the nobility. The privileged orders had other things on their minds—notably to wrest as much power as they could from the king. The bourgeoisie, the great and heavily taxed middle class that had wealth but no privileges, wanted to be given what the nobility already had.

And the people? Louvois laughed out loud. The people wanted bread for three sous a loaf.

Soon, my fat old King Louis, he thought, there will be no more highborn lackeys willing or able to hand you your nightshirt and empty the royal chamber pot.

The door opened behind him, and Louvois turned to follow a lowborn lackey up the stairs and into the bedchamber of the duc de Nevers. The duc was lying in bed staring at the portrait of his son. Louvois repressed a sigh and unconsciously touched the scar on his cheek. Must we, he thought, go through all this once again?

Louvois had never quite recovered from the crushing disappointment of last year—when he thought he'd had *her,* Gabrielle, that haughty little aristocratic bitch, at the very tips of his outstretched fingers only to find she had somehow slipped from his grasp. He had railed at that fool Abel Hachette for giving her a chance to escape, only to have the financier shrug and reply in icy tones that he had provided Louvois with all the information he had. If Louvois could do nothing with it then he, Hachette, could hardly be blamed.

To this day, Louvois still haunted the entrance to the apartments above the Café de Foy. He'd had it watched every minute when he couldn't be there. But if she had ever been there in the first place, she certainly never came back.

". . . and if the vicomtesse agrees, then I shall be able to see my grandson soon," the duc was saying.

"*What did you say?*" Louvois exclaimed, realizing too late by the shocked expression on the duc's face that he had shouted the question. He lowered his voice and tried to remain calm. "Did . . . did you say you've found your grandson?"

"My dear Louvois, that's what I've been telling you. It seems the bi— my son's wife has remarried. To the vicomte de Saint-Just, son of the great *maréchal.*"

Darkness clouded the edges of Louvois's vision, and he had to blink several times. "Are you telling me that Gabrielle has *married* the vicomte de Saint-Just? That you know where she *is?*"

The duc gazed dreamily up at the portrait. "Gabrielle . . . Yes, I remember now. That was her name. Gabrielle. Monsieur le Vicomte says the child is called Dominique. He has blond hair and blue eyes." He frowned. "Is the girl a blond? I don't remember."

"She has golden-red hair," Louvois snapped. "And violet eyes. Haven't you sent anyone yet to arrest her, you—" He stopped himself just in time from calling the duc an old fool. "She's slippery and dangerous as a viper. *Dieu,* she could be anywhere by now. And could have taken the boy with her," he added, thinking that at least would break through the duc's nostalgic reverie.

The duc did whip his head around to rivet the lawyer with agate-hard eyes. "The woman is to be left alone. Do you understand me, Louvois? Monsieur le Vicomte de Saint-Just has made that very clear. If I have any hope at all of ever seeing my grandson, the boy's mother is to be left in peace.''

Louvois saw a shadow of fear flicker across the duc's face. ''I understand,'' he said, and he did.

But he didn't care. It was Gabrielle he wanted, not the boy. The duc's wants didn't interest him in the slightest.

Still, Louvois thought, almost trembling in his excitement, he could afford to be patient now. She wouldn't be running away this time. This time she thought herself safe. He could afford to leave her where she was, thinking herself protected by her powerful, titled husband.

Louvois repressed a shiver at the memory of his one brief encounter with the dangerous man who had turned out to be the vicomte de Saint-Just. No, he would need to play very, very carefully if he was going to safely wrest the bitch from beneath that haughty nose. But he could do it, oh yes, and he knew just exactly *how* he was going to do it.

Again excitement gripped him, and he had to hold his breath to keep from laughing out loud. He thought of a certain jewel box, locked within a chest in his apartment. It contained no diamonds or rubies, but something far more precious—his own signed, blank *lettre de cachet* that he had appropriated years ago against just such an eventuality, that he would have an enemy who needed to be disposed of, quietly, and without a trace.

Chapter 21

 — decorative flourish

His dark, sardonic face, half obscured by the black moiré domino, leaned close until their lips almost, but not quite, touched. He ran his finger along the edge of her bodice where the stiff silver lace just covered her nipples. Gabrielle shivered, and her mouth parted as she sucked in her breath.

Max's lips twisted into a satisfied smirk as he pulled away from her to settle back against the leather seat. He turned his head to look out the carriage window. Carnival revelers, roaming the streets of Versailles on foot, pressed against the coach's sides. Some, dressed in grotesque costumes, looked like demons from a particularly colorful hell. Others were nymphs, dressed in gauzy costumes that revealed too much.

"We'll be another five minutes at least, just reaching the palace gates," Max said.

Although she had a perfectly good window on her side of the black japanned coach, Gabrielle leaned across Max's lap to look out his side. As she pressed her palm on his satin-covered thigh to brace her weight, she felt the hard muscle tremble, and she laughed low and soft in the back of her throat. Max was usually the one to start this teasing game of seduction, but she always won it.

Ahead of them, to the gilded gates of the royal residence of Versailles, streamed a glittering cortege of coaches—carved, painted, and pulled by shining, caparisoned horses.

The road was lined with dozens of Swiss Guards bearing torches, and the palace rose up against the purple night sky, looking as if it were on fire with its hundreds of high windows filled with blazing light.

Gabrielle felt the heat of Max's eyes on her, and she turned her shoulders slightly so he could get an even better view of her shockingly deep décolletage. His breath caressed her neck, causing her diamond chandelier earrings to sway and tickle her skin. The coach lurched, and she pretended to lose her balance, grasping him between the legs—

He groaned aloud and, grabbing her wrist, lifted her off his lap and pushed her back against the seat next to him. He held her in place with his arm pressed across the rising mounds of her breasts and brought his face so close to hers she could have licked the corner of his mouth with her tongue. She wet her own lips instead.

A muscle twitched once in his cheek. His eyes devoured the sight of her in a gown of vaporous silk garlanded with hundreds of tiny pink silk roses, each with a sapphire chip in its center so that she twinkled like a sky full of stars. "I don't think I dare present you to the king wearing that dress, *ma mie*. It's too seductive by far."

She lowered her lashes demurely. "You needn't worry, Max. The king has always been faithful to *his* wife."

Behind the black mask, Max's eyes glittered with dangerous lights. "That may be true, but then the queen has never once left *her* husband's side."

He removed his arm and turned away from her as the coach entered the palace gates into the Cour Royale. The three-sided courtyard shimmered like a bowl of molten gold from the lights that shone from every window and the great *flambeaux* that lined the palace walls.

Max descended first to give her his arm. Gabrielle put her loo mask—shaped like the head of a bird and covered with white silk feathers and tiny glass beads—in front of her face and stepped down from the coach. She looked up through wide-open doors to a great marble staircase heavily encrusted with gold and filled with people.

"Oh, Max." She sighed softly. "It's so . . ." But there were no words to describe what she saw.

"Welcome," he drawled mockingly in her ear, "to the mournful splendor of Versailles."

The ball was being held in the Galerie des Glaces. One wall of the great long hall was entirely covered with mirrors, and opposite were as many windows that opened onto the sweeping lawns and canals and fountains of the palace grounds. Chinese lanterns cast mysterious shadows into the Grand Canal and caused mist from the fountains to twinkle like thousands of fireflies. Inside the hundreds of candles in the crystal chandeliers were reflected in the mirrors and windowpanes again and again, on into eternity. Shells, garlands, palm fronds, and cupids were gilded, carved, and painted onto every available space that wasn't already glass.

There was no place to sit down. But then, only those with the rank of duchesse or above were allowed to sit in the presence of the queen. And then only on a *tabouret*—a three-legged stool. It was the princesses of the royal blood who got the chairs with arms.

The gallery was so crowded that Gabrielle could only stand in one place anyway and turn in a circle. The skirts on the gowns of the women were so widely panniered that they tipped and rang against each other like bells. Their frizzed and powdered hair was elaborately dressed and topped with plumes, and they looked in danger of catching on fire from the dripping chandeliers. One woman sailed past Gabrielle's nose wearing a headdress comprised of a wooden ship, including sails and a flag on top of the mainmast.

It was supposed to be a fancy dress ball in celebration of the carnival—a final day of revelry before Ash Wednesday and the beginning of the dull season of Lent. Some of the revelers wore only dominos and loo masks, but others were dressed in complete costume. The queen's coterie, which were huddled jealously around the royal couple at one end of the hall by the fire, were dressed alike as fantasy milkmaids and shepherdesses. They had daringly hitched their skirts high above their silk-clad ankles and pulled their satin overskirts up into poufs on their hips.

Max took Gabrielle's arm and began to lead her down the length of the hall. She tried to drag her pearl-embroidered slippers across the glossy, parqueted floor to slow him down.

Max stopped and lowered his head to speak softly into her ear. "I thought you wanted to be presented to the king."

"I've changed my mind."

She had turned her head to look at him. The candlelight overhead was reflected in the glass beads and feathers of her mask, and her face shimmered as if it had been gilded with gold dust. She had left her glorious golden-red hair unpowdered, and it blazed like the copper headdress of some ancient goddess. Beside her, Max thought, every other woman in the gallery paled into insignificance.

He didn't know it but the smile he gave her was full of an aching, tender love. She didn't see it because his domino cast a dark shadow across the lower half of his face.

He ran his palm up her arm, stroking her as he would calm an excited horse. "Don't be nervous, *ma mie*. You are by far the most beautiful woman in the entire palace."

"Thank you for the compliment, monsieur, but what does that have to do with anything?"

He laughed. "Why, Gabrielle, surely you've learned by now. Even a king will forgive a beautiful woman anything . . ." His voice trailed off. It seemed that every conversation they started tonight was destined to remind them both of all the hurt and anger that still lay between them.

Gabrielle gazed up into her husband's face. The lower curve of his mask emphasized his perfect, taut cheekbones. He looked magnificent in a suit of silver cloth embroidered with gold metal thread. Ruffles of the finest lace fell over his hands, and a diamond sparkled in the thick lace that cascaded from his throat.

"Tell me again what I'm supposed to do," she said, wanting to get back onto a neutral subject, wanting more than anything to savor the simple pleasure of just looking at him, of being the woman at his side.

He shrugged. "Just be yourself," he said unhelpfully.

She knew what to do anyway. Marie-Rose had once paid fifty livres she could ill afford to have a dancing master teach Gabrielle all the various bows and curtsies decreed by court etiquette. There was one kind of curtsy for the king and queen, another for princes and princesses of the blood, one for ducs and duchesses, and still another for lesser mortals. As Max once again began to lead her down the hall toward the king, Gabrielle frantically went over all the procedures in her mind.

Graceful and at ease in any situation as usual, Max made his obeisance and spoke for a moment to the king, then stepped back and drew Gabrielle forward by the hand. "Your royal highness, may I present my wife, the Vicomtesse Gabrielle de Vauclair de Nevers de Saint-Just."

Keeping her eyes respectfully downcast, Gabrielle lowered her loo mask and sank into so deep a curtsy that her knees cracked like a cannon shot. She was sure the sound had been heard throughout the entire hall, and the flush on her cheeks deepened. Then to her horror she noticed that the king of France was wearing one blue shoe on his very big right foot and a clashing turquoise shoe on his left, and she was possessed of a wild desire to laugh. She held her breath, bit her cheek, and ground her palms into the sapphires on her dress.

Her eyes began to tear and her ears roared from the lack of air, but she thought she heard from a long way away a voice saying, "My dear vicomtesse, please rise so that we may look at you."

Slowly she straightened, praying that her legs wouldn't collapse beneath her. By now she was so starved for air she had to draw in such a heaving breath her bosom quivered. Her eyes were moist and her lips were parted as she raised her head to look at her king, and the fawning courtiers who surrounded him sighed collectively. "How enchanting!" she heard one exclaim.

Throughout her life she had seen the fat, hook-nosed face of Louis XVI embossed on silver coins. In person he appeared much less imposing. Indirectly this man had caused

her much misery, but she realized now he had no idea who
she was. He, too, was merely a marionette of the duc de
Nevers, jerked around by strings much as she had been.

He smiled at her with kindly blue eyes that had just a touch
of sadness in their depths. "Madame la Vicomtesse, we are
pleased to be able to have this word with you," he said in a
thin, reedy voice that rose in an undignified squeak at the
end. "We wish to have your esteemed husband as our royal
astronomer. We beg of you to release him from your side for
just the few hours a week that he will need to perform for
his king and country this small service."

The king's announcement created a stir among the surrounding courtiers. The nobles of France depended on lucrative pensions such as this to maintain their expensive
positions, and the office of royal astronomer was quite a plum.
Gabrielle cast a frantic look at Max. Did he want this post
or not? It was impossible to tell by the expression on his face.

"We are overwhelmed with the honor your royal highness
has chosen to bestow upon us," she equivocated, curtsying
again, and she thought she caught a flash of a smile in Max's
eyes.

"Splendid!" the king exclaimed, his voice squeaking
loudly. "You must tell me of your experiments with balloons, Monsieur le Vicomte. And you must allow me to show
you my laboratory sometime."

"I would be honored, sire," Max replied, flashing his
charming smile. The king was also known to enjoy the ple-
beian hobbies of making locks and blacksmithing, much to
the annoyance of his wife.

Until now Queen Marie Antoinette had chosen to ignore
Gabrielle's presence, but at Louis's mention of his laboratory, she turned her head sharply. Her eyes rested for a moment on Gabrielle, who got a glimpse of ash-blond hair and
a long face with a high brow and a pendulous lower lip.

The look Marie Antoinette gave her husband was openly
contemptuous. "My lord, now is not the time to speak of
such things." She slipped her arm through the king's and
began to turn him away. "Look, here is the comtesse de

Polignac. She's pining because you've chosen to ignore her all night.''

With obvious reluctance the king obediently turned to greet the honey-blond–haired woman. Thus summarily dismissed, Gabrielle kicked back her train and made a perfect backward curtsy without cracking a single joint.

As she glided down the gallery on Max's arm, he reached over and squeezed her hand. "You did splendidly, *ma mie,*" he said, giving her a devilish smile. "Next time, however, we'll have to remember to oil your knees."

She tilted back her head to laugh, so relieved the ordeal was over she felt almost giddy. "It seems you're now the court astronomer, Monsieur le Vicomte. You must discover a new star and name it after the king."

"That particular pension pays fifty thousand livres a year," Max said dryly. He flicked one of her diamond chandelier earrings with his finger. "I'll need the money if I'm to keep you decked out in baubles such as these."

She tried to scowl at him, but her lower lip gave her away by trembling. Glancing up, she caught a look of such naked hunger in his eyes that her knees felt weak. With his black mask he resembled more than ever a devil on the prowl.

She turned her head sharply away. "Oh, Max, look," she said, her voice shaking slightly. "There's someone with a glass of burgundy and a plate of cakes. Where do you think he got them? I'm starving."

But Max's eyes were still fastened on his wife's flushed face. "Let's go home," he said gruffly.

"Home! But we only just got here."

He slipped his arm around her waist and lowered his head so that he could project his silken voice to her, and her alone. "Since I first saw you in that dress, Gabrielle, I've thought of nothing else but taking it off you. Very, very slowly. I'm going to take my time with you tonight, *ma mie.* I'm going to make love to you again and again until you beg for—"

"Why, if it isn't *le beau* Max," said a voice dripping with honey. "I thought you had gone to your château in Morvan."

Gabrielle felt Max stiffen, and she raised her loo mask to

shield her eyes, turning to look into the beautiful face of a
woman with silver-blond hair and icy blue eyes. The woman
clung to the arm of a dashing, mustachioed officer of the
Garde de Corps, but the look she gave Max was one of in-
vitation and promise. And yearning.

The woman's eyes flickered to Gabrielle and she bared her
teeth in a smile. "You must be Max's little shopgirl of a
wife."

Behind her mask, Gabrielle raised a pair of flaring dark
brows. "And you must be Max's little whore."

Beside her Max made a funny sound, halfway between a
groan and a laugh. The officer looked shocked. The woman's
face had paled beneath its thick coating of rice powder, and
her mouth opened and closed like that of a goldfish feeding
on crumbs. Before she could say anything, Gabrielle swept
her skirts aside and, holding her head high, walked away
from them and down the crowded gallery toward the doors.

She had gone about ten feet when a strong hand fell on her
arm, pulling her around.

"Gabrielle—"

She tried to jerk out of Max's grasp. He tightened his grip.

"Let go of me!"

"Not until you listen."

She swung her loo mask at his face. He ducked and,
snatching it from her, tossed it over his shoulder.

She glared at him. "People are starting to look at us."

"Then quit making a scene."

"I'll show you a scene, you bastard. If you don't let go of
me this instant, I'm gong to throw back my head and scream
at the top of my lungs."

Max didn't take any changes. He clamped his free hand
across her mouth and marched her through the press of bodies
to where he had spotted a small door camouflaged by a painted
panel between two pilasters. He yanked it open and flung her
roughly inside. He had to duck his head to follow after her.

He slammed the door shut behind him with his heel and
locked it. They were in a small receiving room, furnished
with only a small tapestried chair and a bureau, gilded and

intricately decorated with marquetry. The room was lit by a pair of candles set in brass sconces on the wall.

Gabrielle stood before him, her eyes flashing, her hair tumbling loose and looking like a waterfall of fire. She was breathing hard, and her breasts heaved, threatening to tumble right out of the low-cut bodice. She looked magnificent, and desire burst upon him—full-blown, hard, and demanding.

"I hate you, Maximilien de Saint-Just," she said, rubbing her mouth with the back of her hand and sounding so much like a little girl indulging in a temper tantrum that he almost laughed. "I don't know why I bother with this marriage. I should let you go to *her*, your mistress. It's where you want to be anyway."

"The devil take you, Gabrielle, I am where I want to be and she isn't my mistress." He advanced on her and she backed up, until she was pressed against the edge of the bureau. All the old anger and pain came rushing back to him. He wanted to strangle the life out of her. He wanted to crush her against him and kiss her until she admitted she loved him still, had always loved him, no matter what, no matter what . . .

He lowered his face until it was but inches from hers. He saw her eyes widen, and he thought it was from fear. "I haven't touched Claire de Tessé since the night before I found you freezing to death in a ditch." His hands seized her shoulders, and he shook her roughly. "And I wouldn't have gone near the bitch in the first place, damn you, if you hadn't *left* me!"

Suddenly her face crumbled. Hurt filled her eyes, turning them from vivid violet to almost black, and Max felt a funny, tight ache in his chest.

"How could you have done it, Max?" she said, so softly he barely heard her. "How could you have made love to that woman?"

He shook her again. "I didn't make love to her. I fucked her. There's a difference, and it's time someone showed you what it is." He gripped the sides of her head, crushing his mouth down hard over hers.

He kissed her cruelly, without feeling, and she held herself stiff, keeping her teeth clamped tightly together. But when he eased the pressure of his lips, she slipped away from him, lunging for the door.

She scrambled frantically, feeling for the latch. He seized her from behind, wrapping one powerful arm around her and flinging her around, slamming his mouth back down onto hers, impaling her against the wall with his hard, bulging loins and his invading tongue.

This time she fought him, going for his face with her nails, and he encircled her wrists in a crushing grip, twisting her arms behind her back. Still she heaved and thrashed about so violently that he had to press his entire weight against her body, pinning her to the wall. He hadn't realized she was so strong, and her fury made her stronger. Suddenly he felt trapped, frightened of hurting her yet more terrified that if he let go of her now she would run away from him again, and this time she would be lost to him forever.

He released her mouth. "Don't fight me, Gabrielle."

"Damn you, Max, I'm not your whore!"

"You're my *wife*. Can't you understand what that means to me, what it did to me when you left? Can't you see how much I—*omph!*"

She had jabbed an elbow into his chest, taking him by surprise. But she got no more than a step away from him and he was on her again, catching her by one of the ruches on her dress. It ripped partway, then held fast, and he enveloped her in a bear hug with both arms, lifting her. His foot caught one of the legs of the chair and they went stumbling and sliding, locked together, across the slippery polished parquet floor. He struck the bureau so hard with his hip that he swore, and it, too, went skidding across the floor and banged against the wall.

They wound up with her back arched over the rounded top of the bureau and him covering her with the hard length of his body. He was panting so loudly it sounded like a summer windstorm had invaded the tiny room.

"Goddamn you, Gabrielle. You are mine!"

"Never!" she managed to spit back in his face before his mouth crushed down on hers again, forcing her lips apart.

He had snarled the words at her, but his kiss this time, though hard and desperate, was no longer cruel. Love, in all its anguish and all its ecstasy, came pouring out of him. His lips softened, gentled, moved over hers rhythmically, possessively, tenderly. He didn't know it, but with his kiss he was crying out to her, proclaiming his love, and something deep within her heard it and instinctively reached out to answer him.

All he knew was that he felt the anger leave her and desire slowly suffuse her, taking its place. Tentatively he released her wrists, and her arms came up and curled around his neck while her mouth slanted hungrily across his.

He pushed the narrow sleeves of her dress down to her elbows and yanked at the bodice, freeing her breasts from their loose restraint. Her nipples were turgid with arousal. He pulled at them gently and then rubbed them between his fingers. Their kiss deepened, their tongues possessing each other, and he thought then that he had won. Or perhaps it was she who had won. He no longer gave a damn.

He lowered his lips to follow the sweet curve of her jaw, then down along the taut column of her neck, pausing to lick and nibble at the pulse point until she began to writhe and make cooing sounds in the back of her throat. Then lower, down to her breasts. He lifted them in his palms, squeezing them together, and delved his tongue between the deep, moist cleavage. Her face fell forward onto the top of his head and she pressed her mouth in his hair, then rubbed her cheeks in it, back and forth, like a cat. She made a purring sound, too, like a cat showing contentment.

His thick manhood strained against its tight satin sheathing and he moved it in slow and sensuous circles against her pelvis. The rough sapphires on her dress scratched maddeningly through the thin material of his breeches, and he clenched his teeth on a deep, chest-shattering groan.

His strong hands spanned her waist, lifting her until her hips were braced on the rounded front of the bureau. Her knees fell wide apart and he came between them. He bunched up her skirts and underthings around her waist and his hand moved up the long, firm muscles of her thigh. He found the soft nest of hair and he burrowed inside it, sliding his fingers deep into the warm, pulsating core of her. She was wet, quivering, ready for him. Her hands clutched his shoulders, digging in, and she arched her spine and her head fell back, her mouth open.

He pulled his fingers from her to stroke along her slick nether lips, back and forth, faster and faster, while he kneaded the nub of her womanhood with his thumb. With his other hand he fumbled for the opening to his breeches, then at last, at last, he was free. He cradled himself with his hand, and then her hand took the place of his and she guided him into her, wrapping her legs around his hips.

She was so hot, so tight, so incredibly fine. It was as if God had made her just for him. He knew it was irrational, but it seemed that no other woman had ever *fit* him the way Gabrielle did. It was as if he were the sword and she the sheath, made by a master craftsman, one for the other.

"Gabrielle, Gabrielle, Gabrielle . . ."

He crooned her name, over and over, as he plunged into her, again and again, and the bureau knocked against he wall, thudding like a big bass drum, and the candles started to teeter in their sconces. He felt her inner muscles contract around him, and giving one last mighty thrust with his hips, he smothered her scream with his mouth and exploded deep inside her.

He lay hunched over her, his forehead pressed against her breasts. Her lungs pumped hard, and her heart skipped wildly, and her legs were still wrapped around his waist, her skirts bunched up in a crushed wad between them. He would have felt smug at what he had reduced her to, except that he had been left in the same state. *This*, he thought. As long as we have this together, then I have some hope of keeping her.

Gingerly he pushed himself upright, tucking his shirt back in place and fastening his breeches. He drew her to her feet, helping her straighten her own clothing. The rouge she had put on her cheeks and lips was now smeared across her face; her hair was a mess, half still pinned to her head, the rest cascading in fiery tangles over her shoulders. She tried to pull her bodice, with its built-in corset, up over her breasts, but it had been ripped partway down the middle and she had to hold it together with her fist to keep it up.

Her lower lip fell open and started to tremble, but Max, who had seen her do that before, knew it was from repressed laughter. "Look at me," she said. "I look like . . ." She couldn't finish as amusement overwhelmed her.

His arms went around her and he laced his hands in the small of her back. He dipped his head to rub his tongue along that adorable lower lip. "What you look like, *ma mie*, is as if you've been well and thoroughly—" He stopped himself, remembering just in time what he had said that had started all this.

She stiffened in his arms, as he knew she would, and he repressed a sigh. She lifted her chin and the candlelight fell full on her face, and he felt a cold dread steal over him for he could read nothing in her face, not even anger.

"That was some lesson you taught me, monsieur. Is that what you did with the marquise de Tessé?"

He opened his mouth to say something cruel and cutting that would pay her back for this time and all the other times. But something—perhaps just plain damned weariness— stopped him, so that what came out of his mouth was, for the first time since she had returned, the uncensored truth.

"No, *ma mie*. It has never been so wonderful, so passionate, so perfect, with any other woman. Only with you."

She lowered her lashes to obscure her eyes, but he saw her mouth soften into a tiny smile.

Chapter 22

❦❦

"Where are you going?"

Gabrielle dropped the latch to the front door and whipped around, a guilty flush suffusing her face. Unconsciously she clutched the roll of drawings tighter to her chest. She had deliberately chosen this early hour to slip out of the house so that Max wouldn't question her about where she was headed. She didn't think he would approve of her caricatures lampooning his noble class—especially now that he was the king's astronomer.

Max finished coming down the stairs, pulling on a pair of gloves. He was wearing his tall leather riding boots and English hunting jacket. He raised his brows at her. "You've neglected to answer my question, Gabrielle."

"Out. I'm going out."

A look of supreme impatience crossed his face. "And alone, I see. There are times, *ma mie,* when I would dearly love to wring your neck. Haven't you heard there was another bread riot in the Place Maubert yesterday morning?"

"I'm not going to the Place Maubert."

He laughed suddenly. "Of course you aren't, my little revolutionary of a wife." He plucked the caricatures from her hands before she could stop him. "You're taking these seditious drawings to your erstwhile Uncle Simon, who will have them printed up in hopes the mob will be incited to further rioting and the monarchy will fall.''

She thrust out her chin. "And what is wrong with that? We're working for liberty.''

He didn't comment, but flipped through the caricatures, amused cynicism on his face. To her surprise he handed them back to her.

She frowned. "I suppose now you're going to forbid me to go.''

"Would it do any good if I did?''

"No.''

"Then I won't bother.'' He tipped his tricorne at her. "Good morning, Madame la Vicomtesse.''

He brushed past her and pulled open the door. But he whipped around suddenly and seized her by the waist to plant a swift, crushing kiss on her mouth.

"Max!'' she called after him when she had recovered her breath. "Where are *you* going?''

He was already halfway down the front steps, but he turned to give her a wicked grin. "Out,'' he said.

Gabrielle stewed about Max's irrational behavior all during the hackney ride to the Palais Royal. It was April now; they had been reunited for over four months, living as husband and wife, sharing the same bed—she smiled to herself—as well as the floor, the sofa, and any other surface that happened to be handy whenever passion struck them. Once they had made love in the carriage on the way home from a day at the Vincennes race track, and another time they had done it in their private box at the opera during the second act of Mozart's *Don Giovanni*. Although they followed fashion by keeping separate bedrooms, he never slept in his.

She sighed. That part of their life was perfect. It was the only part that was.

For in many ways, they all seemed to lead separate lives. Even Dominique was busy in his own world now. He had a tutor and a riding and a fencing master, and he seemed to think his mother, a mere *woman*, wasn't capable of discussing even the rudiments of these manly pursuits. As the vicomtesse she had a horde of servants to supervise. In her spare time she was supposed to write letters and do embroidery. Instead she drew biting caricatures of the king and queen and their coterie and helped Simon write tracts calling for a republican form of government. As for Max, he had his new duties at court and his scientific experiments with balloons in his laboratory at the Jardin des Plantes. He never discussed any of it with her. He certainly never told her what he thought of the wave of political unrest that was sweeping the country.

That was the trouble, for they never spoke to each other, at least not about anything serious. They played teasing games of seduction that eventually erupted into draining bouts of passion, but they never sat down and simply *talked*. Every time one or the other of them would drift to a subject that was the least bit personal it would dredge up all the old feelings of hurt and anger. She had left him, and he had taken another woman while she was gone. *If you had loved me,* one of them would begin. *If you had loved me,* the other would say. And neither of them was willing or able to forget, or to forgive.

But still, still . . . Though he refused to believe it, she had loved him then, and she loved him now. Every day she spent with him she felt her love for him spread and grow deeper, like the roots of a giant oak tree. And as the oak provides shade and holds down the earth, so had Max become essential to her life.

Perhaps, she thought for the hundredth time, I should take the first step. But what that step should be she had no idea, and still, still . . . she was certain that although she loved him, he no longer loved her, perhaps had never loved her, and so she did nothing.

Suddenly Gabrielle became aware that the hackney had stopped moving. She could hear shouts and the pounding of running feet coming from the street, and she raised the window shade and leaned out to see what was happening.

The hackney had come to a standstill in the middle of the Pont Royal. A crowd of angry, shouting people marched toward them down the middle of the bridge, quickly engulfing everything in their path the way the tide swallows shells and rocks lying on the beach. At first she couldn't make out what they were shouting and then she caught a phrase here and there.

"Hang the rich!"

"Death to all grain speculators!"

"Cheap bread! Bread for two sous!"

It wasn't only men in the mob—there were women and children as well. The men were armed with pikes, pitchforks, and iron bars. The women had clubs made from the staves of dismantled fences and had loaded their pockets and aprons with rocks and bits of cobblestone. Two or three of the rioters even brandished muskets which they fired into the air. But although their slogans were full of hate, a holiday atmosphere prevailed. Gabrielle even spotted a vendor pushing wine from a cart and another selling paper twists of chestnuts and strings of tobacco.

The traffic on the bridge had been completely enveloped by the mob. There was a fancy calash—a light, low-wheeled carriage with a folding top—directly ahead of her hackney, and the rioters suddenly swarmed around it. It rocked and swayed precariously for a moment and then tipped over onto its side. Its occupant, a man in a satin suit with curled and powdered hair, was dragged out to be swallowed up by the hostile crowd. And Gabrielle felt the faint stirrings of fear.

The roar of the mob sounded like the rumbling of a giant waterwheel. She heard a horse whinny in terror and her driver shouting to make way. An almost irresistible compulsion to get out of the hackney and try to run for safety overcame her. Isolated in the carriage this way, she felt as conspicuous and vulnerable as a parrot tied to a pole and, indeed, at that moment she heard a thud as something, a stone perhaps, struck the side of the carriage.

Gabrielle pushed open the door.

It was a mistake. Rough hands clutched at her arms, dragging her out. Without the steps being let down, it was a long drop to the ground, and she landed with a jarring fall on her hands and knees. Someone wearing a hard sabot kicked her in the side, and then the crowd started to move again. She flung up her arm, just managing to curl her fingers around the handle of the carriage door, and tried to pull herself upright before she was trampled beneath hundreds of feet. Faces swirled around her, mouths agape, eyes bulging white with anger and frenzy. She was kicked again, so hard this time that the breath was driven from her lungs and her vision darkened around the edges. Her grip on the door handle started to slip, and then one of the shouting, twisted faces took on a familiar shape.

"Simon!" she screamed.

A strong hand clasped her beneath the armpit and hauled her to her feet. Simon leaned her up against the wheel of the carriage and put his bulk between her and the seething mass of people that eddied around them.

"Gabrielle! What are you doing here?"

"I came . . ." She started to shake. She pressed her hands to her cheeks. "Oh, God, Simon . . . what's happening?"

"Some rich aristocrat has been caught hoarding grain," he proclaimed, with all the passion of the righteous in his voice. "We're going to force open his warehouse and distribute it to the people."

Holding her arm, he began to drag her forward, back into the flow of people moving across the bridge. Gabrielle had no choice but to follow.

Earlier that morning, Abel Hachette had stood at his library window, feeling the satisfaction of a man who believes all is right with his world.

Someone had planted red flowers in the windowboxes across the way, which gave the neighborhood a nice touch of spring. In front of the house next door a carriage was being loaded with bandboxes and trunks for Monsieur Costaine's annual trek to take the waters at Vichy. Monsieur Costaine was a silk merchant with an income of five hundred thousand livres a year, and dropsy.

Hachette heard the tinkle of a cowbell and looked up the street. There, as he did every morning, came a drover poking along with a stick his tiny herd of six mangy cows. Hachette wondered, as he did every morning, why the drover found it necessary to drive his animals down this particular street. Where did the man come from, and where was he going with his pathetic herd of—

Just then Hachette spotted a familiar figure dodging in and out among the usual crush of carriages and carts. He actually had to blink several times—the first to be sure he wasn't seeing things; the second time because he didn't want to believe what he saw. Unconsciously his hand drifted to his throat; suddenly his cravat felt tight and he had difficulty swallowing.

During the past year and a half, Hachette had spent many a sleepless night worrying over what would happen if his Black Angel ever discovered that he, Abel Hachette, had tried to betray that damnable nuisance of a woman to her enemies. It didn't matter that the fool Louvois had somehow bungled it, or that the woman and the boy had somehow escaped on their own. What mattered was *intent*. And if his Black Angel ever discovered what his intent had been that hot August day, then Hachette was doomed. For Maximilien de Saint-Just was a man who never forgot, and never forgave.

The final irony was that, in spite of the fact that the girl had mysteriously disappeared from Max's life, Max had refused to come back to the cabal. Hachette had put one of the other angels to spying on Max, and the angel had reported Max to be interested in nothing but drinking and gambling and occasionally, when he sobered up enough, those foolish experiments with inflammable air-filled balloons. Then four months ago, the girl had just as mysteriously reappeared. No more drinking or gambling, the reports had said lately. But still Max would not return.

Until today.

Why? Hachette wondered. Pulling out his perfume-scented handkerchief, he patted his sweating brow and walked stiff-legged to the fortress that was his rosewood desk. He had just managed to get himself safely barricaded behind it when the lackey swung open the double doors and the Vicomte Maximilien de Saint-Just strolled through.

Hachette quickly scanned the young man's face. He saw the drooping lids, the lazy, mocking smile. They did nothing to reassure him.

"Good morning, Max."

The smile deepened. "You've always been a master of understatement, Abel. We haven't spoken to each other in nineteen months, yet you act as if it were only yesterday."

Hachette shrugged, pretending indifference. "You said you no longer wished to work for us. I've respected your decision."

"Bloody hell you have. You've been spying on me. Not that I've minded. It's been rather flattering."

Hachette didn't need to glance at his reflection in the mirrored panels to know that disgusting color had flooded his cheeks. He started to reach for his quizzing glass, noticed his hand shaking, and pressed it flat on the desk instead. "Is that—" he began, then stopped to clear his throat. "Is that why you're here?"

Max came forward and leaned over the desk, bracing his fists on the polished surface. Hachette stopped himself from shrinking down into his chair.

"I've come for the key to your grain warehouse," Max said.

Hachette's mouth fell open. "You *what?*"

Max's voice was slow and silky and it brought the hairs up on the back of Hachette's neck. "The people are starving, Abel. They're paying ten sous a loaf for bread made from rotten grain that makes them sick, and you sit here with a full warehouse waiting for prices to rise even higher."

Hachette smiled thinly and shook his head. "You know profit isn't the real reason why I haven't released that grain, Max. We want liberty, and the only way we're going to get it is through revolution. There can be no revolution if the bellies of the people are full. It may not be an easy thing to accept, but for a just cause some sacrifices must be—"

"No!" Max slammed his fist down on the desk and Hachette jumped. "You don't want liberty. It's power you're after. You want to take the power from those who have it and keep it for yourselves—you and that damned cabal. You're only using the word 'liberty' as a cloak for your own brand of tyranny. And like a naive fool I believed in you once. Or maybe I was simply lying to myself. No, not maybe. I *was* lying to myself. I liked the excitement of the games you played, and I liked the money you paid me. But no more. I'm going to make amends, Abel, and you're going to help me do it.''

He stepped around the barrier of the rosewood desk and hauled Hachette to his feet. His voice went low and soft. "Give me the key."

"I can give it to you," Hachette squeaked, "but it won't do you any good. The overman won't open the doors unless I'm there in person. Those were my instructions.''

Max smiled. "Then get your hat, Abel, because you're coming with me.''

The crowd began to run and Gabrielle was carried with them, the way a twig is carried downstream by rushing rapids. Once, she tripped over a bundle of fagots set out at the curb for sale. She went sprawling down on her hands and knees and would have been trampled underfoot if Simon hadn't again hauled her to her feet.

The mob spilled into the Place Maubert. Normally filled with the stalls of fishmongers, greengrocers, and butchers, the square looked eerily empty this morning. The rioters spotted a bakery and began to take up the chant—"Cheap bread! Bread for two sous!''

French Guards, in their fringed cocked hats and blue coats with furled skirts, with bayonets fixed in their muskets, had ringed the shop. A group of men in the forefront of the mob, armed with pikes and shafts, surged forward, and the soldiers lowered their muskets. Everyone could see by the looks on their faces that they were more frightened of the people than the people were of them.

The baker had shoved a barricade of chairs in front of the door to his shop, and he climbed up on it to address the crowd.

"Please!" he tried to shout above the clamor for cheap

bread. "I've no bread to give you. I don't even have any flour to make it with!"

"To the warehouse!" someone shouted, and soon the shout was taken up by others. "To the warehouse!" The crowd surged forward again, pulling Gabrielle and Simon with them like so much flotsam.

The warehouse was a massive, rectangular building, three stories high, made of brick, and with a sloping slate roof and iron-grilled windows. It covered the entire south end of a tiny square that was known for its pastry shops. The square had been turned into a fortress by a troop of French Guards, a hundred strong, ordered there by the governor of Paris to maintain order and protect private property.

The captain of the French Guards, however, had no sympathy for the aristocrat who supposedly owned this warehouse and was speculating with the grain stores inside it, and he had a lot of sympathy for his hungry fellow Frenchmen. "Open the doors, monsieur," he growled to the warehouse overman.

The overman, a plump fellow with a head that bobbed up and down on his thick neck like that of a turtle, swayed back and forth on his feet, moaning and wringing his hands. "I can't, *mon capitaine*. I haven't got the key."

The captain thought he could feel the earth shuddering beneath the thin soles of his fancy officer's boots. The din of the ringing church bells seemed to be causing the very air to vibrate. There was a strange roar in the distance, like the low growl of a lion. It was the roar of the approaching mob.

"To hell with the key!" he shouted. "Break down the doors, if you must, but get the goddamned doors open before we all get ourselves goddamned killed!"

The overman didn't want to be killed. He also didn't want to account to Monsieur Hachette for a pair of damaged doors and an empty warehouse, the cost of which was sure to come out of his salary. *Dieu!* Didn't he have six children, all under the age of ten, and four of them girls too puny to work?

He gnawed on his lower lip, drawing blood. "Perhaps Monsieur Hachette should be sent for."

The captain whirled around, swearing, and kicked at the

brick wall with his boot, ruining the glossy polish. "We haven't time to send for anybody!" He pointed down the length of the square. "Listen!"

The roar had grown steadily in volume. The captain had never fought in an actual battle, but in his daydreams of glory he had imagined the thunder of artillery would sound just like this. But this wasn't a dream; it was a bloody nightmare. "I'm going to get an ax and break down the door," he said, though he stood with his feet welded to the ground and watched in horror as the first wave of the mob poured toward him.

The first of the rioters to spill into the square were momentarily diverted by the sight of the pyramids of iced cakes and rows of glistening tarts in the windows of the pastry shops. Rocks and stones sailed through the glass and soon the succulent desserts were being passed from hand to hand. But the windows were soon emptied and those in the back of the crowd became even more incensed and began to push forward, demanding their share of the loot. One man had found a barrel and was beating on it like a drum. Again the chant was taken up. "Open the warehouse! Cheap bread!"

Some of the rioters took to the surrounding roofs and lampposts to throw a hail of tiles, rocks, and cobblestones onto the captain and his troops. One of the pastry shops had caught or been set on fire and now a stinking, oily smoke filled the air, obscuring everyone's vision. The guards began nervously to finger the triggers of their muskets even though the captain had ordered them to hold their fire. In respect of the muskets and bayonets, the rioters had so far kept a careful distance from the cordoned warehouse.

A coach came rumbling through the alley in back of the warehouse and careened into the square. The overman tugged on the sleeve of the captain's blue coat and shouted above the chants and the screams and the crackle of flames. "It's him! Monsieur Hachette! With the key!" The captain lifted his eyes to heaven in thanks.

A tall, imposing young man alighted from the carriage, followed by a frail old man who looked positively terrified, and whom the captain took to be the nobleman's factor. He ignored the old man, addressing the younger. "I hope to God you've brought the key, monsieur, because—"

Max's hand fell on Abel Hachette's shoulder and he hauled the old man forward. "Open the doors, Abel. Now."

Hachette was mesmerized by the sight of the turbulent mob. In all his visions of a revolution he had never imagined it to be like this. The power of violence such as this was awesome. If only, he thought, if only it could be controlled, why a man truly could topple a throne with power such as this. Topple it, or seize it.

The sight of the carriage with its well-dressed occupants had whipped the mob into a frenzied rage. One woman, with sores on her face and black, toothless gums, began to shout, "Kill, kill, kill," and others took up the chant, stamping their feet, making a ditty out of it that ended with a final cry of "Hang the bloody aristocrats!"

Hachette jerked free of Max's grip and started toward the rippling edges of the crowd, which had so far left a space of about twenty feet between themselves and the guards with their bayoneted muskets. Max started after him, only to be restrained by the captain and two of his men.

"Forget him!" the captain bellowed in Max's face, his eyes white with fear. "Get the goddammed door open before we have a massacre!"

"Kill the aristocrats!" the mob chanted. "Hang the rich!"

"No, wait!" Hachette was shouting, his palm upraised in the universal symbol of peace. "I'm not an aristocrat. I'm one of you. I'm one of the people."

The mob didn't hear him, or didn't believe him. Or perhaps they were beyond caring. A young boy who had climbed a lamppost took aim with his slingshot and sent a rock spinning for Hachette's head. It struck him directly between the eyes, driving him stunned to his knees, blood pouring down his face. When they saw him go down, the mob fell upon him with their makeshift weapons.

Max strained against the hands that held him. "Let me go, damn you!" Then he abruptly ceased his struggle and could only watch, horrified, as a pike rose in the air, flashing in the sun, and descended in a wide, slow arc—to bury its tip in the small of Abel Hachette's back.

"Max!"

At first Max thought it had been Hachette, screaming his name in his death throes. Then he caught a flash of flaming hair and heard her scream again and, amid all that press of roiling humanity, his eyes locked onto hers.

"Gabrielle!"

She stretched out an arm to him and nothing, not even three strong men, was going to keep him from her. He literally tore himself free of the soldiers' rough embrace. He ran toward her, just as the mob—made savage by their first taste of blood—surged forward toward the warehouse. The guards, outnumbered and frightened, opened fire.

A flash of bright light blinded him, and a searing pain in his head made him gasp. Sheer, desperate will carried him two more steps toward his beloved before he fell to his knees. But he kept his head up and his last image before the world was covered with a bloodred haze was of Gabrielle, his Gabrielle, her eyes and mouth open wide in terror and the mob surging around her, engulfing her.

Maximilien de Saint-Just lay still and white in Simon's bed above the pawnshop in the Palais Royal. His head was wrapped turban-style with a bandage, hiding the deep groove in his head left by a musket ball. The doctor hadn't been at all helpful. "If he wakes up, he'll probably live," the man had said. "But first he's got to wake up."

Gabrielle sat beside the bed with her husband's hand pressed between hers, as if she could transmit her strength, her life, to him, palm to palm. From time to time, Simon or Agnes would appear in the door, but she always sent them away. Once she heard the sound of raised voices coming from downstairs, and she knew they were arguing over Simon's part in the riot. But Gabrielle thought that no matter what Agnes said, Simon wouldn't stop now. That morning, like a lot of people in Paris, Simon Prion had discovered the power of the mob.

To Gabrielle, this day had taught her the true meaning of

terror. She had seen her love, her whole reason for being, be struck by musket fire and go down. Although she had tried to bite and scratch and claw her way to his side, she had known she would be too late, was already too late, that she had lost him again . . . this time forever.

She had prayed, not coherently, but a cry of anguish sent up to heaven, offering to trade her life for his, begging for a miracle. And a miracle had occurred. For just when she thought the mob was going to tear him apart, a troop of cavalry, riding five abreast, had burst onto the square from each of the surrounding streets, swinging their sabres, and the rioters had fled, terrified.

Among the chaos of the screams and the drifting pall of smoke and the litter of pikes and staves, Gabrielle had knelt beside Max and put her hand on his heart, and she had thought that if it no longer beat, then her own heart would surely stop as well.

Now, her eyes fastened on his face, his hand clutched in hers, she willed that heart to go on beating.

He stirred and moaned and opened his eyes, and she saw a terrible fear in their dark gray depths. She squeezed his hand and leaned over him. "Hello, my beloved."

The fear left his eyes. "Gabrielle . . ." One corner of his mouth twisted upward. "My head hurts like bloody hell."

She smiled, not even realizing that tears were streaming down her face. "Hush. You're not supposed to talk."

"No . . . things I must say."

She brought his hand to her mouth, pressing her lips against his knuckles. "Later. Sleep now."

He sighed and his eyes drifted closed. He mumbled something, and she leaned closer.

". . . love you, Gabrielle."

She thought he had said it, but she could not be sure.

It was late the next afternoon before he awoke again. This time his breathing was regular and his eyes were clear. Gabrielle's own eyes were bloodshot, and her back ached from sitting up all through a night and a day in the chair. She felt a mess. Max thought she had never looked more beautiful.

She tilted his head up and held a steaming cup to his lips. He sniffed at it and wrinkled his nose. "What is it?"

"Drink it. Or do you want me to pour it down your throat?"

"You are a vengeful woman," he accused. He drank it down, but not without a lot of gagging and grimacing.

"I am very angry with you, wife," he said, trying to recover some of his manly authority. "You gave me the fright of my life when I saw you caught up in that mob. Do you realize how close you came to being killed this morning?"

"It was yesterday morning, and you are the one, Maximilien de Saint-Just, who has been lying there bleeding all over Simon's bed."

"Simon . . . is that where I am?" He looked around the room, which was filled with the clutter Simon couldn't or hadn't the heart to sell. "How did I get here?"

"Simon and some of his friends carried you." She gave him a trembling smile. "The soldiers wanted to arrest you for inciting the riot." Gabrielle had clung to him at the time, shielding him with her body, calling out that she was the vicomtesse de Saint-Just, and the soldiers, seeing her fine clothes, didn't dare not believe her.

He patted the blankets beside him. "Come lie by me."

"Only if you promise to behave yourself."

He gave her his most devilish smile and promised nothing.

She stretched out on the bed beside him. He pulled her closer until her head leaned against his shoulder. He buried his face in her hair.

"You smell all smoky," he said.

"And you're burning up with fever." She raised up on one elbow and stroked his cheek, roughened by two days' growth of beard. His skin was hot and flushed.

She started to draw away, but his arm tightened around her, surprisingly strong. "Don't leave me. I have a confession to make."

She leaned over and kissed his lips. They were dry and cracked, but they were his and they felt wonderful. "Should I summon a priest?" she teased, although a part of her cringed inside. Was he in some terrible pain he was hiding from her? Did he fear he was going to die?

In the next instant she was relieved to feel his chest rumble with laughter. "God, spare me those priests with their eternal babbling in Latin." He threaded his fingers through her hair and rubbed his thumb across her temple. "I have a confession to make to you, *ma mie.*"

He fastened his eyes on hers. They were filled with such sadness they brought sympathetic tears to her own eyes. "I should never have married you," he said, and Gabrielle's heart plummeted.

She lowered her gaze and addressed his neck. "I understand, Max. You've made it very plain these last months that you no longer love me."

His hand tightened in her hair and he pulled her head up. "But I do love you."

She shook her head. The shameful tears threatened to gush from her eyes and she squeezed them shut. Her throat felt as if a vise had been tightened around it. For a moment she couldn't breathe or swallow and words were impossible.

"Gabrielle, dammit, I said I love you."

She drew in a shuddering breath. "You-you only w-want me physically."

"Hell, yes, I want you physically. And every other damned way there is." He brought his other hand up to her face. "Gabrielle, Gabrielle . . . You'd have to be an idiot not to see how much I love you."

She was an idiot. Joy filled her. Again she couldn't breathe or swallow because of the thick lump in her throat, and her eyes started leaking tears like a rusty ladle.

"Why are you crying? Gabrielle, say something. Jesus." He spoke gruffly, but he was smiling.

She stuttered and blubbered, but she finally got the words out. "But if you love me still, then why did you say you should never have married me?"

The smile left his face. His hands drifted down her neck and settled on her shoulders. "Because you deserve better than a man like me, Gabrielle. It didn't really surprise me when I came home to find you gone that day. I knew I was never worthy of you.''

''Not worthy of me! Oh, Max, I'm the one not worthy of you. I let you marry me knowing I would only bring you trouble. I—''

''No. Let me finish. Why can't you ever be obedient and submissive like a proper wife, and allow me to have the last word?''

She thrust out her chin and her eyes flashed. ''Why, I'm so very, very sorry, my lord and master. I try to be a good wife. It's just so hard sometimes, especially when you men get to make up all the rules.''

A corner of his mouth twitched, and his eyes filmed over with a strange wetness. His hands squeezed her shoulders and he gave her a tiny shake. ''God, Gabrielle, I do love you.''

''Oh, Max—''

''Be quiet, woman. There are things I have to say, things I should have said months ago, and I'm going to say them if I have to rip the cover off this pillow and gag you with it.''

But first he made her help him sit up, supported by the pillows. Then he drew her down to sit beside him, their left hands entwined, her head within the crook of his right arm. The room grew dark while he spoke and a soft breeze came up, bringing with it the scent of printers' ink and frying crêpes from the gardens below. He told her first about his childhood in the Faubourg Saint-Antoine and the days of his youth spent as a brigand. Then he told her all about Abel Hachette and the cabal and the spying he had done for them over the years.

''I had myself half convinced I was doing it for France, but a part of me always saw through the hypocrisy of Hachette and the cabal. But at the time none of it mattered, because I was more interested in getting revenge on my father by dragging the noble name of Saint-Just through the mud.'' He sighed, shifting the arm that held her, and his fingers and thumb began to caress her ribs. ''Then you knocked on my door that day and suddenly I began to care what sort of a man I was. I couldn't bear the thought of letting you down, of failing you. And, of course, that's exactly what I did.''

Her fingers tightened around his. "But you didn't, Max. It was my own stupid fault for jumping to the wrong conclusion—"

He stopped her words with his mouth. But when she started to respond to his kiss he pulled away.

"Let me finish, *ma mie* . . . I hated you for leaving me only because I knew I deserved it. I blamed you for believing I had done the very despicable acts I knew in my heart I was capable of doing. Hell, why should you have trusted me? There was nothing I had done in my entire life up until the moment of our meeting that made me worthy of your trust. Or your love."

She put her palm against his cheek and turned his face back within reach of her lips. She kissed his eyes and rubbed her nose around his cheek, stroking his mouth lightly with her own. "You judge yourself too harshly, my darling. I'm sure a lot of what you did for the cabal, whatever their motives, was good for France. Percy told me once you've the best scientific mind this country has." She had her lips to his ear, and he could feel her smiling. "You certainly are the best lover in all of France. Probably in all the world."

His chest heaved in a soft grunt. "How would you know? You've only had me and that Martin fellow of yours, and he couldn't tell his yard from a dyemaster's stick."

She flung up her head. "Max!"

"Don't turn all wide-eyed innocent on me, Gabrielle. You know I'm right. Besides, Agnes said so."

"Agnes! What does she know?"

"A lot. She came to see me, you know."

"She didn't! When?"

"A few days ago. The day after you told her and Simon all about what had happened to drive you away—about Nevers and Louvois."

Last week Gabrielle had at last allowed the duc de Nevers a few closely supervised minutes with his grandson. That afternoon, she had told Agnes and Simon everything, and in telling them she had, in some strange way, freed herself of the past, and of the hatred she bore for Dominique's grandfather.

Max was laughing against her hair. "That little buxom

urchin accused me of being as blind as a one-eyed mole, unable to see the obvious right under my nose—which was that you loved me, and that I was breaking your heart.''

''You *were* breaking my heart, Max. I was so miserable all these weeks thinking you no longer loved me. I couldn't forgive—''

''Shh.'' He pressed his fingers against her lips to stem the flow of words.

She had been about to say that she couldn't forgive herself for hurting him. But he thought she was going to say she couldn't forgive *him* for the marquise de Tessé, and the look on his face reminded her of Dominique when he had been naughty and came to her seeking absolution and reassurance.

He picked up her hand and sandwiched it between his own. ''Of all the mistakes I've made in my life—and there have been a whole soup pot full of them—the one I most want to have back is the marquise de Tessé. I was miserable before it happened and I was miserable afterward. I was even miserable *during* the act, if such a thing is possible, and I swear to you, Gabrielle, by all that's holy, that I will never, ever, even look lustfully at another woman in my life.'' He put her hand over his heart and held it there.

She had let him make his act of contrition because it warmed some tender spot in her to hear the words. But now Gabrielle waved her hand—the one that wasn't pressed against his heart—across the air as if shooing away a mosquito. ''Oh, pooh! I no longer care about that.''

His eyes widened in astonishment. ''But—''

''Agnes said it would have served me right if you'd taken a dozen mistresses. She said I was a ninny lobcocks if I expected you to be as celibate as a monk after I had disappeared from your life. She said you couldn't be expected to know you'd ever see me again, and she thinks you're a saint for taking me back.''

''A saint!''

''Her exact words were, 'May pork and peas choke me if Monsieur Max shouldn't be canonized for putting up with your foolishness.' ''

He laughed, cuddling her against him. Then he threaded his hands through her hair and tipped her face up to meet his lips.

His kiss began gently, but the fires of passion, always so easily ignited between them, burst into flame. It was Gabrielle who finally pulled away from him. "We mustn't, *chéri*. You're feverish and weak, and if you up and die on me now I would truly never forgive you."

"My head does still hurt like bloody hell," he admitted. He brushed the hair from her temple with the tips of his fingers. "Agnes said something else. She said I already knew well how to survive, but that I would never understand a thing about *living*, or about loving, until I learned compassion. Until I learned how to forgive."

Gabrielle bit her lower lip and lights of amusement danced in her eyes. "That's odd . . . she said the very same thing to me."

Max smiled and nuzzled her with his chin. "She's a very wise woman, that Agnes." And his mouth sought hers in a tender kiss, as they told each other in this ageless fashion how they wanted, needed, loved each other.

After a moment their mouths parted long enough to let them settle themselves more comfortably among the pillows. "Do you believe now, *ma mie*, that I love you?" Max said.

"I believe," Gabrielle answered solemnly. "And do you believe—"

He stopped her with his lips. "Of course I do," he said against her mouth, giving her that smile she loved so much. "How could you not love the best lover in all of France, probably in all the world?"

"Are you the best?"

"Yes. And I can prove it to you."

And then he did.

Chapter 23

Gabrielle sat up in bed and watched her husband as he dressed by the light of a small oil lamp. In the muted glow she could barely make out the scar along his hairline left by the musket ball three months before.

The bread riots of that spring were, from the perspective of this July of 1789, being called a revolution. But, although the orators of the park benches and cafés in the Palais Royal had hailed it as the birth of a new era, the price of bread had continued to rise.

"Must you leave so soon?" Gabrielle asked, not caring a thing now about liberty or bread or what the king of France would or would not do on the morrow, for she had seen little of her husband during the last two months. "It's not yet dawn and you got so little sleep last night."

He pulled his shirt on over his head and came to sit on the bed beside her. He traced the edge of the sheet, which she had pulled up over her naked breasts. "I didn't come home to sleep. I came to make long and passionate love to my irresistible wife."

"Which you have done. Several times." She put her hand on his bare chest where his shirt gaped open at the neck. "Take me back to Versailles with you."

He brought her hand to his lips. "It's too dangerous, you know that. You wouldn't want to bring Dominique and yet

377

you'd worry about leaving him behind with just the servants. Besides, I won't be able to concentrate if I'm worrying about you." He smiled at her. "Just missing you and wanting to be with you are enough of a distraction as it is."

In May the parliamentary body, the Estates-General, had at last been summoned to meet at Versailles. Max was to have been one of the deputies representing the Second Estate, or the noble class. Gabrielle and Dominique had been at Versailles to watch the procession of the opening session. The First Estate, the clergy in their black and red robes, came in first, followed by the nobility dressed in white with gold-braided cloaks and plumed hats, and wearing swords. But, although Gabrielle had stood on tiptoe, craning to see above the heads of the crowd, there had been no sign of Max.

She had begun to grow worried by the time the Third Estate, the deputies who were to represent the people, marched in. That was when she saw him, his tall, lithe figure in white and gold satin standing out among the black suits of the bourgeois, and her heart swelled with a fierce pride. She had lifted Dominique high above her head so that he might see his father. "Look, *mon fils*," she said to him. "Look at your papa marching for liberty."

From the first day of its meeting there was within the Estates-General a tug-of-war for power. The bourgeois against the nobility and the clergy; the bourgeois and the nobility against the king. One day in June, the king had locked the deputies out of their meeting place, posting troops with bayonets at the doors, so the delegates had met in a tennis court to declare themselves to be a National Assembly and vowed not to disband until France had a constitution.

Louis XVI, his monarchy threatened, decided to fight back. His latest move had been to dismiss Necker, his finance minister, who was popular with the people because he had asked the king to tax the nobility. Earlier, Louis had called up regiments of foreign mercenaries to ring Versailles, and it was now rumored that the Bastille was being readied to accommodate mass arrests.

"Max," Gabrielle said, her fingers tightening around his, "perhaps you shouldn't go back. If it's that dangerous—"

"There are twelve hundred of us delegates. He can't arrest all of us." He flashed his cocky smile. "Besides, we voted ourselves immune to arrest."

Gabrielle sniffed. "And no doubt you think the king's musket balls will bounce right off your chests."

Laughing, he bestowed a kiss on her nose and stood up. As he sauntered over to the commode, Gabrielle watched the play of muscles in his naked thighs. Her smile turned into a sigh of desire as he leaned over to look in the mirror while he brushed his hair, and his shirttail rode up, exposing a generous section of his bare buttocks.

Gabrielle slid out of bed and slipped into her dressing gown, although she left it hanging open down the front. She came up behind him and pressed her bare chest against his back. She moved her breasts in sensuous circles, luxuriating in the feel of his shirt scratching across her tightening nipples. She rubbed her hands across the taut cheeks of his bottom, kneading them gently.

Her hands slid around to the front of him—

He grabbed her wrists, turning around. "Gabrielle, I'm trying to get dressed. Pretend that you are a properly submissive wife and pour me something to drink. Brandy. And don't lecture me about the hour," he added when her mouth opened.

She went obediently to the silver serving cart that had been pushed up beside the bed, but she poured him wine, not brandy. "Tell me what you do all day," she said, setting the glass on top of the commode and helping him tie his hair back with a narrow black riband.

"Sit and daydream about you."

"Besides that."

"Mostly we yell and argue a lot." He laughed. "A full-fledged meeting of the National Assembly is about as noisy as an open fish market. Although usually we meet in smaller groups. I'm in charge of a committee that's supposed to be drafting a Declaration of the Rights of Man. So far we've

managed to agree on one sentence—"Men are born and remain free and equal in their rights"—and why are you looking daggers at me all of a sudden?"

She faced him, her hands on her hips. "You seemed to
have forgotten, Monsieur le Député, to include in your declaration one entire half of the human race."

"Huh?"

She flung her arms up in the air. *Women,* Max. Won't
women be considered born free and equal in this new government of yours?"

"Well . . ." He wrapped an arm around her waist, drawing her tightly against him. "Have a heart, Gabrielle. I'd be
laughed out of the assembly if I suggested we add the word
'women' to the Declaration."

She pretended to pout. "It seems so unfair. We women
are never allowed a say in anything."

He nuzzled the top of her head with his chin. "There is
one place, *ma mie,* where you have absolute power over me.
You command and I tremble—quite literally, I might add—
to obey."

Her dark, flaring brows swooped upward. "Hunh. And
where, pray tell, is that?"

Lifting her in his arms, he carried her to the bed, where
he laid her down gently within the nest of silken sheets.
"Here," he said. "In my bed. Or"—and his mouth stretched
into that devilish smile—"whatever serves as my bed."

He straightened and pulled off his shirt.

Stretching like a cat warming herself in the sun, Gabrielle
actually purred. "I thought you had somewhere important to
go, Monsieur le Vicomte."

The smile Max gave her overflowed with love. "France,"
he said, "can wait."

He came into her arms. She rose up on her side and pressed
him back into the pillows. She felt bold of a sudden; master-
ful and mastering.

Her mouth fluttered over his face, her lashes caressing his
cheeks like butterfly wings, her lips dipping down to draw
nectar from his eyes, his brows, his mouth. She ran her tongue

along the curving line of his hard jaw, traced the lobe of his ear. She raised her head and looked at him.

"That's a rather self-satisfied smile you're wearing."

The smile deepened, putting a dimple in one cheek, and she kissed that, too. "Not satisfied," he murmured into her hair. "Not yet."

"Oh, so my kisses aren't enough?"

"I love your kisses."

"But you want more than kisses?"

"Well . . . I wouldn't turn down anything else you cared to offer me."

She moved a knee between his legs, gently grinding it into the short, springing curls. Her hand wrapped around his rising, swelling erection, proof of his desire, proof of her desirableness.

"This." She tightened her grip, almost but not quite to the point of pain, and he drew in a sharp breath that ended in a moan. "You want this to be satisfied."

"Only you," he said, his breath ragged, "can do it."

Still gripping him, tightly, for she knew he liked it hard and a bit rough, she brought her mouth down to the hollow in his throat. She could feel his blood pumping, hot and swift, beneath his skin and, as she sucked on his neck, she began to stroke his length, vigorously and rapidly, in time with that pulsating beat.

He moaned. "Jesus . . ."

Moving his hand over the rising curve of her hip, he slipped his fingers into the crack of her buttocks, tracing the soft flesh down and up between her legs, pressing into her from behind, and she shuddered as she always did at the first touch of his fingers there.

For a moment it seemed she hung poised in the air, connected to him, connected to reality, only by that thrusting, flicking finger. She was swirling, rising, drifting toward the edge, and she pulled herself sharply back because she wasn't ready to go over it just yet.

She shifted her position so that she straddled him now, her thighs on either side of his legs. She sat up tall and straight, looking imperiously down on him, and again she felt that heady sense of power, of possessiveness. She let her eyes roam over him, starting with his face; claiming as hers those eyes of molten silver, the hard mouth that parted with each breath he took in and pushed out, rough and ragged; moving down his chest, ridged and corded with muscles that rose and fell jerkily; and down to his vigorous maleness that sprang up thick and long between her knees.

Arching her back, she pressed her hands to his sides and pushed her bottom down his thighs, lowering her head until her lips almost touched the tip of his swollen manhood. "Mine," she breathed.

"Gabrielle . . . ?" he said tentatively, threading his fingers through her hair, for she had never done this before.

"I want to," she said. "If you do."

His fingers tightened, pressing down on her head.

"Yesss . . ." he hissed, as slowly, slowly she drew him into her mouth.

He was iron encased in velvet, rigid bone and smooth flesh. She explored him with her lips, her tongue, the inside of her mouth, discovering new sensations of pleasure in the giving of it. Pausing for a brief moment, she looked up, past the tensed, clenched muscles of his stomach and his heaving chest, to his face. His eyes were squeezed tightly shut, his mouth twisted into a blissful grimace.

When her mouth enveloped him again, he started to tremble. Suddenly he lifted her up and off him, rolling her onto her back. He loomed over her, his hands pressing deep in the mattress, bracketing her head, his face over hers, and he thrust into her so hard that she cried out—not with pain, but ecstasy.

"I," he said.

He pulled all the way out of her and drove into her again, deeper.

"Love," she said on a gasp.

He pulled out again and stopped there, the tip of him barely brushing her quivering mound, and he kept his eyes wide open and locked with hers as he drove into her a final time.

"You," they finished together as the driving tremors of passion and release coursed through them.

The next evening Gabrielle sat on a windowseat, her son kneeling beside her, and looked down on a river Seine pockmarked with rain. They were in her favorite room, a small receiving salon next to her bedchamber, enjoying a late snack of chocolate and sweet biscuits. Although it was the thirteenth day of July, they had a fire burning because the day was cool and damp.

Dominique pointed to the quay below, where small forges glowed on every corner. "Maman, why are those men making horseshoes out in the street?"

"They aren't making horseshoes, *petit*. They're hammering pikes."

During the last couple of days, since the finance minister Necker had been dismissed, the revolution had again turned ugly. Workers from the faubourgs roved in gangs armed with cudgels and pikes, chanting "Cheap bread!" and "Arms to the people!" One of the city prisons had been attacked, and several of the hated customs *barrières* had been burned. Gabrielle, remembering her terrifying experience on the day of the bread riot, stayed off the streets and kept Dominique close by her side. She missed Max terribly, but she was glad now she had not gone with him to Versailles.

Suddenly a soft knock on the door startled her, and she jumped up, her hand fluttering to her throat, her heart beating fast. The majordomo, Aumont, entered the room on silent feet, and Gabrielle sternly admonished herself for turning into a bundle of vaporish nerves.

Aumont bowed. "Madame, there is a gentleman come from Versailles asking to see you." A slight curl to his lip suggested the term "gentleman" was to be considered loosely. "He claims it is an emergency."

"*Mon Dieu* . . . bring him here immediately, Aumont. Please."

The premonition of disaster that had struck Gabrielle with the knock on the door was now intensified tenfold. Her heart drummed so loudly she couldn't hear anything else, and she had to clutch the back of a chair to hold herself upright.

Aumont returned with the visitor, a man Gabrielle had never seen before. He was dressed in black, as a bourgeois, but his suit was of expensive material and he reeked of a heavy floral perfume. He had an oily complexion ravaged by the pox and tiny, darting, rabbitlike eyes.

"Madame la Vicomtesse . . ." He bowed awkwardly, and she noticed that he wore a cockade made of green chestnut leaves, the latest symbol of the revolution. "I am Jacques Marot. I fear I bring you grave news from Versailles—"

Gabrielle gasped. "Max!"

"I regret, madame . . . the vicomte collapsed today during the assembly. Earlier he had been complaining of a terrible pain in his head. I understand an old wound . . . ?"

Gabrielle nodded automatically. Max still occasionally got headaches where the bullet had creased his skull, but lately he had assured her they were getting better.

"He's had a few lucid moments, madame," Jacques Marot was saying, "when he repeatedly asks for you and the boy."

"I must go to him at once! Aumont—"

Aumont, who was standing discreetly by the door in case Madame la Vicomtesse needed his services to chuck the visitor out, responded immediately. "I will have the carriage brought around, madame."

"If you please, madame," Marot said. "My chaise is ready and waiting directly out front. You and the boy can journey back with me." He offered a thin smile to Dominique, who stood, stretching to his full height at Gabrielle's side, with a fierce scowl on his face as if to protect her.

"Thank you, monsieur," Gabrielle said distractedly. She would need to bring a mantelet for it was raining. And Dominique would need a coat and hat. Should she bring extra clothes? No, she hadn't time for that, and besides, they could be sent for later.

Outside the damp wind carried the odor of smoke from the smoldering *barrières*. A group of men armed with sticks stood beneath the lamppost beside the *hôtel*'s gates, but a wineskin was being passed from hand to hand and the men didn't appear threatening so much as drunk.

was the chaise rolled by, one of them raised a clenched fist in the air, shouting, "Death to the rich!" Marot pulled the leather blinds partially down over the windows.

"Maman," Dominique whispered loudly, "I don't like this man."

"Hush, child. It's impolite to dislike someone you don't even know," she scolded.

A beam of lamplight momentarily illuminated the interior of the carriage, and Marot smiled, showing yellow teeth. "The lad's quite a handful, is he?"

Gabrielle said nothing, for, to tell the truth, she didn't much like Jacques Marot, either.

The chaise clattered across the Pont Solferino, but with the lowered window blinds obscuring the view, it took Gabrielle a moment to realize they had turned, not left toward the road to Versailles, but right, heading east along the Quai des Tuileries.

She started to point out that they were going the wrong direction when another flash of lamplight fell momentarily on Jacques Marot's face, and she caught the expression in his eyes.

She reached for the door handle, but Marot's hand fell over hers. And then she saw the pistol pointing at Dominique's head.

"Don't do anything foolish, madame. You wouldn't want an unfortunate accident to occur to your son."

"Maman, is that man going to shoot me?"

Gabrielle pulled Dominique against her, wrapping her arm tight around his waist. "No, *petit*. Not if you listen and do everything he says."

Marot smiled. "There you see, lad. Your maman's right. You're to do everything I say, eh?"

"I take it my husband is not ill," Gabrielle said.

Marot laughed. "Madame, I've no idea of the state of your husband's health. I've never met the man."

"Are you taking us to the duc de Nevers?"

"You'll find out soon enough."

The carriage made several turns, and Gabrielle soon lost all sense of direction. She could tell by the street noise and the smell of smoke seeping in from the window that they were still in Paris. Suddenly there was a change in the sound the wheels made, going from stone to wood and then back to stone again. The chaise rolled to a stop and the door was jerked open.

Gabrielle looked out into a vast courtyard lit by torches. She saw a pair of massive stone towers that flanked a huge clock held by granite nude male figures draped with chains. There were soldiers in the courtyard, but they all faced away from her, toward the gray stone walls. A shadow loomed up before the carriage door and she looked down . . . into dark, bulging eyes that blinked rapidly from behind thick spectacles.

"Welcome, Gabrielle," Louvois said, and his smile, the first she had ever seen from him, puckered the scar on his cheek. "Welcome to the Bastille."

Chapter 24

The darkness was absolute. The air, so fetid and damp, had a smooth feel to it, like velvet.

She had been locked in here for a long time. Long enough to know hunger and thirst and every permutation of fear. She leaned against a stone wall that seeped with moisture. Although her legs trembled and ached with exhaustion, she didn't dare sit down, for the floor of the cell was covered with unspeakable filth. She could feel it oozing up around the soles of her feet and between her toes. She smelled the rank stink of it with every breath.

"Max, please . . ." she whispered hoarsely. Oh, God, where was he, why wasn't he coming? "Max, damn you!" she screamed, her voice bouncing hollowly off the stone walls. Then she began to cry for she knew he was only a man, not a god capable of miracles, and she hated him for being only a man and not a god, and she hated herself for hating him, when she loved him so much and it was not his fault, not his fault . . .

It was cold in the cell and she was naked. The guards had stripped her of her clothes when she was first brought here. She had been afraid from the lewd looks they gave her that she would be raped, especially when they began to paw at her—twisting her nipples painfully and thrusting their fingers inside of her. Only Louvois seemed indifferent, merely watching with those protruding, unblinking eyes.

When one of the men began to unbutton his breeches, Louvois said, "There'll be time enough for that later. I want her to think about it for a while, to imagine how it will be." He lifted a long, slack hand and stroked Gabrielle's cheek with one finger. "There are thirty-two guards here at the Bastille, my dear, and every man of them will have you, and more than once, before you leave these walls. What will your haughty, titled husband think of you then, I wonder?"

Gabrielle spat in his face. Louvois stood perfectly still for a moment, letting the spittle dribble down his cheek, then he raised his arm and backhanded her with such force that he sent her reeling against the wall.

He grabbed her chin between two fingers and twisted her head around. "Gabrielle, Gabrielle . . . before I am through with you, you will be begging me for death."

Gabrielle stared back at him unflinchingly, although tears of pain from the blow filmed her eyes. "And you, Louvois, are a dead man already. The vicomte de Saint-Just will kill you merely for presuming to lay your filthy hands on me."

He blinked then and fear flickered in his eyes. Then he smiled, releasing his painful grip on her chin. "But he doesn't know I have you. No doubt he will merely assume you have disappeared again."

Black despair welled up inside Gabrielle, almost choking her. Of course Max would believe she had run away, left him again, and her heart ached for the hurt he would feel. He had allowed himself to love her again; he had trusted her with his heart. What would he think, what would he feel, when he came home from Versailles to find her and Dominique gone?

"Still, if the thought of my death gives you comfort," Louvois was saying, sounding almost cheerful, "then you're welcome to it. You will need some comfort, however meager, in the coming weeks and months and years."

Gabrielle flung up her head and hatred blazed from her face. "Where's my son, you bastard? What have you done with my son?"

Louvois's smile froze her heart. "You'll find out soon enough."

Dominique had been taken from her while they were still beside the carriage in the courtyard. She kept telling herself that no one would be so fiendish as to subject a child to a filthy, dark cell with no food or water. She screamed his name though, long after her own cell door had banged shut leaving her alone with the darkness. She screamed until she was hoarse.

She had heard only silence, and the thin echo of her own voice. Then within the last hour, she thought she heard something else—a deep rumbling sound far in the distance, like thunder.

She was so thirsty. She pressed her mouth against the wall, and the dampness helped a very little bit to relieve her parched tongue. Strange lights began to dance before her eyes and her head whirled. She dug her nails into her arms, deep enough to draw blood, hoping the pain would keep her from fainting.

The cell door banged open and she flung up her arm to shield her eyes from the sudden flare of a bright light. With the door open she could hear the thunder rumbling again, much louder now.

She blinked several times, until her eyes became adjusted to the light. Louvois stood in the middle of the cell, and four guards with him. Two of them carried torches which they stuck into brackets on the walls. Another guard carried a stool and chains, while a fourth had some sort of animal horn and two large buckets of water.

They're going to torture me, she thought. But, strangely, she felt no fear. She didn't really believe this was going to happen. Not to her.

But it was happening.

The guard set the stool and chains down in the middle of the cell, while two others grabbed her arms and dragged her roughly forward. She struggled, kicking and jabbing with her elbows, until one of them punched her hard in the stomach. She choked back sobs of pain as she was bent backward over the stool and her wrists and ankles were chained to each of

the stool's four legs. Now fear, sudden and engulfing, overwhelmed her.

Max! her mind cried out. *Save me from this. God help me.
Max, Max, Max* . . .

Louvois's face loomed over her. "Did you know, Gabri-
elle?" he said in a strangely conversational tone of voice.
"Everyone doomed to execution is tortured in this way be-
fore he goes to his appointment with death in the Place de la
Grève. This isn't designed to kill, but only to cause suffering.
To punish."

Gabrielle thought of Louvois's promise to make her beg
for death. To her bitter shame, she already wanted to plead
with him not to hurt her. But she knew by the way he looked
at her that he had no intention of sparing her what was to
come. Pride was all she had left now, and pride held her
silent.

Louvois's face disappeared. A rough hand clamped down
over her nose, and her jaws were pried open. The animal
horn was shoved into her mouth, down her throat. She
watched with terror as the bucket was tilted above her head
and the water was poured into the horn.

She couldn't swallow fast enough and she began to choke
and gag and gasp for air. Her chest burned as the water poured
into her lungs. Her stomach, stretched and distended over the
stool, began to swell. She felt engorged, bursting; the pain
was excruciating, and she was going to explode, die. She
wanted to die, to escape the terrible, terrifying pressure, the
pain, which grew and grew and grew until she was screaming
inside her head, she was drowning, suffocating, dying, and
the pain, the pain went on and on and on—

When she came to her senses she was on her hands and
knees in a puddle of water on the floor. She sucked in a
painful gasp of air, heaving, and water came gushing out of
her throat in a torrent. She choked, gagged, and vomited until
she lay exhausted on her side, clutching her stomach. Her
chest felt on fire, her throat flayed raw.

Something scraped against the stone next to her ear and
she opened her eyes to see a pair of black, scruffy shoes.

"Did that hurt, Gabrielle?"

"Please," she said and the single word felt as if needles were being driven into her throat. She would beg him now; she knew she couldn't bear that again.

"Next you will watch me do it to the boy."

"No!" she cried out hoarsely. More water erupted from her throat and she choked on it, almost strangling.

"Are you going to beg me now, Gabrielle?"

"Yes . . . I'll beg. Please . . . please, don't hurt my son." She clutched his ankles and looked up at him through the wet streams of her hair. She tried a pathetic smile. "I'll give myself to you, Monsieur Louvois. I'll go away with you, wherever you like, willingly, and Monsieur le Duc can have his grandson. Only please, please don't hurt him."

He lifted his foot and, planting it on her chest, thrust her onto her back. She lay sprawled at his feet, and he let his eyes roam contemptuously over her naked body. Her flaming hair was wet and matted with filth, her violet eyes black, bruised holes in her faces. He doubted anyone would think her beautiful now.

"All women are whores and you're no different," he said with a sneer. "I've never wanted your disgusting whore's body. It's your pride I want to own, Gabrielle. Your soul." He touched the scar on his cheek, and his bulging eyes seemed to glow unnaturally. "Your son, on the other hand, is beautiful. Very beautiful. Normally I prefer them a couple of years older, but he is tempting, yes tempting indeed."

Gabrielle's stomach heaved at the filth that was spewing from Louvois's mouth. God, God, God, she prayed. This wasn't happening. He was only trying to frighten her. He couldn't, wouldn't, no one could be that depraved. Virgin Mary, Mother of God, protect and save my son . . .

She pushed herself up on her elbows, clawing with her nails on the filthy stone floor for a purchase. She would kill Louvois. Kill him with her bare hands—

The cell door banged open and Louvois whipped around, backing out of her reach. Dizziness engulfed her, and a strange, milky fog clouded her vision.

Her muscles turned liquid and she slumped slowly to the floor, her cheek pressing against the cold, wet stone. She heard the thunder again, and voices above her head speaking plainly, but she could see nothing but the cool white mist.

"What the devil is going on?" Louvois snarled.

"The mob is storming the Bastille!"

"How the hell can they storm the Bastille? This is a bloody fortress. It's supposed to be impregnable."

"They've got cannon. I'm going to surrender."

"You can't!"

"I'm the commander here, monsieur. It's my decision."

Louvois ground out another oath. Gabrielle heard boots clumping across the floor and the creak of the cell door swinging shut.

"Dominique . . ." Gabrielle cried out weakly.

Then the darkness returned.

Early that morning of the fourteenth of July, the Vicomte Maximilien de Saint-Just had awakened bleary-eyed and groggy after a miserable night of little sleep and strange, feverish dreams.

With the twelve hundred deputies of the National Assembly meeting daily, the small city of Versailles had been hard pressed to handle the sudden influx to its population. Max, who was being hailed at the moment as one of the heroes of the revolution, had managed to appropriate a tiny flea-infested garret. At least he had it to himself, and he knew he was better off than most.

It was not the fleas, however, that had kept him awake last night. He had felt vaguely uneasy all during the evening before. The meetings had gone on until well past one o'clock, and several times he caught himself staring into space, having lost track of what was going on for long minutes at a time. Something was wrong; he just didn't know what it was.

When he finally fell into his bed that night, he was tormented over and over by the same dream. He would see Gabrielle running across a field toward the edge of a cliff. She was being pursued by something, but he could never see what it was. He would call out to her, warning her of the cliff, and then he would begin to run after her, to save her. But always he would be just a couple of steps too late. He would lunge, his hand outstretched, and catch just the tip of her cloak. But she would be gone, over the edge into a strange, black void, and he would wake up drenched in sweat, his chest heaving like a pair of bellows.

A bare hour after dawn that morning Max was on the road to Paris. He wanted to see Gabrielle with his own eyes and know she was all right.

The streets when he first entered the city seemed eerily deserted. The damp, still air was filled with an acrid smoke; the sky was the color of pewter, threatening more rain. He had just turned onto the Quai d'Orsay when a mass of men, armed with pikes and staves, spilled out of one of the cross streets, coming toward him. They were chanting, "We want gunpowder!" and "To the Bastille!" Max jerked his horse's head hard around and headed back over the bridge. The last thing he wanted was to get caught up in the mob.

As he galloped through the streets, Max felt fear grow within him with every sparking strike of his horse's hooves on the cobblestones. By the time he turned onto the Rue de Lille, he was almost frantic with worry. He leaped from his horse, flinging the reins at a groom, and raced up the steps to the *hôtel* two at time. The door swung open beneath his hand and he looked up into Aumont's dumbstruck face.

"Monsieur!" the majordomo exclaimed. "We were told you were stricken ill. Madame and *le petit* left for Versailles yesterday evening."

Max felt a piece of himself break off and die.

Simon Prion, with his wife's angry admonitions ringing in his ears, had set off that morning to join a demonstration in search of gunpower to be distributed to the people. The king, it was said, was sending mercenary troops to surround Paris and slaughter his subjects. His subjects wanted to be prepared.

They went first to Les Invalides, the veterans' hospital,

where rumor had it a huge cache of gunpowder was stored. They found a couple of muskets and a few old swords, but nothing else. Then someone said there was gunpowder at the Bastille.

"To the Bastille!" an old woman shouted, and the crowd begin to take up the chant, Simon's voice carrying loud and strong among them. "To the Bastille!"

They picked up more people along the way. But as they came within sight of the massive blackened stone quadrangle with its eight round towers, as tall as a seven-story building, the seething mass of chanting rioters suddenly quieted, until the only thing Simon could hear was the whining cry of a child and the rustling shuffle of hundreds of feet.

This, Simon Prion thought as he stared at the fortress, this is the invincible Bastille. His chest ached with the awe of it. The Bastille. The symbol of arbitrary power, where people were sent without knowing why or for how long, on a simple order of the king. Suddenly he no longer cared about the gunpowder; it was the Bastille he wanted. If the Bastille could be taken, destroyed, then the people of Paris would have wrested their freedom from the monarchy. They would have liberty.

Simon looked around him. He was at the very forefront of the crowd, pressed against the shuttered entrance to a perfumer's shop that was tucked right up against one of the fortress's mighty outer ramparts. The varied floral and spicy scents emanating from the shop filled Simon's head, making him feel slightly drunk. He saw a drainpipe and used it to pull himself up onto the awning over the door, climbing from there onto the roof.

"Down with the Bastille!" he shouted, and his voice boomed out over the silent crowd.

"We want the Bastille!" someone shouted back at him, and then everyone was shouting, waving their pikes and cudgels in the air.

A man with a massive belly and arms shaped like hams climbed onto the roof next to Simon. He grinned, showing a gap of missing front teeth. "To the Bastille," he said, and then jumped from the roof into the outside courtyard below. Simon looked down, muttered a prayer, and jumped after him.

They were followed by others, armed with axes and maces, who severed the drawbridge chains. With a mighty groan, the drawbridge crashed down, spanning the moat, and the rioters began to swarm across. Within seconds the gates to the fortress were hacked open and the mob streamed into the outer courtyard.

The guards on the towers opened fire.

Like Gabrielle, Max's first thought was that the duc de Nevers was behind the abduction.

He saddled a fresh horse and galloped the ten miles back to Versailles as if a pack of wolves bayed and snarled at his heels. He had never been more frightened in all his life, or more filled with self-disgust. He could hear his own voice, cocky and confident, saying *Dominique is my son now, and I will protect him*. Instead he had failed her, Gabrielle, his wife, his love, his life. Again.

The palace was a pink and gold confection, glittering even beneath the overcast skies. Max didn't see its beauty; he saw only a bloodred haze of rage. He asked the first person he came upon—a woman who could have been Marie Antoinette for all the attention he paid to her—where he could find the duc de Nevers. He followed her pointing finger toward a pair of doors that opened into the Oeil-de-Boeuf.

The Oeil-de-Boeuf was a reception room adjoining the king's state apartments, a waiting room for high-ranking court dignitaries. It took its name from the two distinctive bull's-eye-shaped windows in the domed ceiling. Max paused in the doorway to scan the faces in the room. The duc wasn't there.

Ignoring the startled gasps of the lounging nobles and the shocked looks on the faces of the king's bodyguards, he barged directly into the king's apartments without permission and without waiting to be announced.

The first sight that met Max's eyes was a pair of broad buttocks straining the seat of vivid blue satin breeches. The king of France was bent over a telescope that pointed out the window, focused onto the courtyard below. The duc de Nevers and a handful of other fawning sycophants were standing beside him.

The king straightened, turning, and actually smiled. "Well, it is my astronomer, the vicomte de Saint-Just. Have you come again to see my laboratory?"

Max ignored him. He didn't even make a perfunctory bow. It was more than ever a sign of how France had changed in the last several months that, although mouths fell agape with shock, no one made a move toward him or insisted he pay proper subservience to his king.

Max crossed the room in three strides and seized the duc de Nevers by the lapels of his velvet coat, lifting him off his feet.

"I say!" one of the nobles exclaimed.

Max shoved his face into the duc's, and his voice was deceptively soft. "Where are they?"

"What?" the duc squeaked.

Max flexed his arms, and the duc rose higher off the ground. "My wife and the boy. What have you done with them?"

A hand fell on Max's arm and he jerked his head around, snarling like a rabid beast. The nobleman, who hadn't really wanted to interfere anyway, backed off. The duc's eyes fluttered and started to roll up in his head, showing the whites, and his jaw sagged. Max shook him roughly. "My wife!"

"*Ma foi,* spare me. I don't know . . ."

Max relaxed his grip and the old man sank all the way to his knees. His head was bowed and he was breathing heavily, his hand pressed to his chest.

"The lawyer, Louvois," Max demanded. "Where is he?"

Two seconds ticked off and Max took a step toward the panting, bent figure. The duc painfully lifted his head. "I don't know, monsieur. I swear it. I don't know."

Again Max drove his flagging horse the ten miles back to Paris. Louvois had them, he was sure of it. The bastard had had them for over eighteen hours now. Max's mind recoiled at the thought of what could have been done to them during that length of time. By now they could be—

No! His mind slammed down on the thought. If she were dead he would know it. He would feel it in his gut, and then he would kill himself, because he didn't care about surviving anymore. He'd already learned that bitter lesson once—life was nothing without her.

One dark, wet night over a year ago Max had followed the lawyer Louvois from an abandoned slaughterhouse in the Faubourg Saint-Antoine to an apartment on the Place de l'École. Max had no trouble finding the apartment again. On that other night he had climbed silently through a window. Today he kicked down the front door.

Louvois's servant was witless with fright and Max had to rein in his temper in order to get the man to speak. Once started, the servant wouldn't stop. He hemmed and rambled, scratching his head, and finally said he thought he remembered Monsieur Louvois saying something about an appointment at the Bastille. He had thought monsieur to be joking at the time. Monsieur Louvois, the servant said, had a strange sense of humor.

Smoke seared Simon Prion's face and teared his eyes. He crouched behind a burning hay wagon in the outer courtyard of the Bastille. Between the rioters and the fortress was another wide moat. Although the mob repeatedly called on the defenders to capitulate, so far the wooden drawbridges remained up.

From time to time a musket ball whizzed past Simon's head as the soldiers fired sporadically from the crenels in the battlements. The man with the missing front teeth who had climbed onto the roof with him now lay dead at Simon's side, in a steam of muddy water, his chest torn open by a musket ball.

A stranger with a soot-blackened face ran up behind Simon and touched him on the shoulder. Two columns of French Guards with cannons, he said, were on the way to reinforce the soldiers in the Bastille. Some of the leaders were thinking about withdrawing, and he waited patiently for Simon's opinion. I'm going to die, Simon thought, and he could taste the fear in his mouth, salty and metallic, like blood.

Just then a loud cheer erupted from the rear of the mob and word was passed from mouth to mouth. The cannon were being pointed *at* the fortress. The French soldiers had joined the mob.

Then another cheer went up, this time from those in front. The drawbridges were being lowered. The Bastille had surrendered.

Max smelled the acrid scent of gunpowder and heard the roar of the mob long before he saw the tall crenelated towers of the Bastille. He was amazed to find the drawbridges lowered, the moats clogged with paper. From one of the towers overhead, men were dumping stacks of the fortress's archives into the water below. It was the only thing in the Bastille to loot.

Within the inner courtyard he saw soldiers, disarmed and facing the wall, and guarded by men with pikes and pitchforks. A small, ragged group of people were huddled together in one corner and Max urged his horse toward them. He scanned the pale, frightened faces. They were all men.

"Are these the only prisoners released?" he said to the back of the man who guarded, or protected—it was hard to tell which—the ragged group.

The man turned and looked up.

"Monsieur Max!" Simon Prion exclaimed. "How did you get here? Did you ride with the French . . . Guard?" His voice trailed off as he got a good look at Max's face. "Gabrielle?"

"Louvois has her. And the boy. I thought he brought them here."

"*Sacre bleu . . .*" Simon paled and shook his head. "They weren't locked up with the other prisoners in the tower cells." He gestured over his shoulder. "Only these few pathetic wretches."

"The dungeons?"

"I don't know whether they were searched or not." Simon turned to shout a question at another man, but Max didn't wait for the answer.

Lighting a torch from one of the burning wagons, Max methodically searched the dungeons. He felt nothing as he went from cell to cell, for he had at last walled off all feeling. There would be time enough for grief and rage later. Now he had only one thought, and that was to find her.

He doubted these cells had been used in years. They smelled rancid, as if something had been shut up in here long ago and left to die. In the deepest, darkest part, at the end of a long, low-ceilinged tunnel that dripped water, he found a locked door.

He banged on it with his fist. "Gabrielle!"

Nothing.

He didn't want to take the time to search the entire fortress for the key; he doubted he would find it anyway for it was probably at the bottom of the moat by now. He stepped back and fired his pistol at the lock, then kicked the door open with his boot. Stepping inside, he raised the torch above his head.

She was in the corner, curled tight into a ball with her arms wrapped around her legs, and she was naked. In the dim light her small, slender body looked bruised and broken, and a sob tore at his chest.

He set the torch into a bracket on the wall and knelt beside her. As gently as possible, he touched her shoulder.

"Gabrielle . . ."

She raised her head and looked at him with blank, unseeing eyes.

Then, slowly, her gaze focused and he knew she saw him, and the feelings of failure that had been like a dull ache in his gut all morning became as sharp and twisting as a knife.

"Too late," she said to him. "You're too late."

Chapter 25

With the help of Simon and his friends, Max searched the dungeons and towers and then the entire fortress looking for Gabrielle's son. One of the guards, who had been taken prisoner and was now eager to be helpful, admitted that the boy had been there at one time, locked in a cell. Now he was gone. So was Louvois.

Max had found a blanket on one of the bunks in the guardhouse and, with hands that shook uncontrollably, he wrapped it around his wife's pale, dirty, and bruised body. Although he held her, stroked her, and crooned words of love and reassurance to her, he could not erase that stricken, tortured look from her face. She was no longer aware of him, nor did she recognize Simon or anything around her. She seemed to be reliving some unimaginable terror over and over in her mind. But except for the bruises and a few minor cuts he could find nothing seriously wrong with her. On the outside.

Too late, she had said. *You're too late.* God, Max wondered, what had the bastard done to her?

There was a particularly terrible purple mark on her cheek and he pressed his lips to it, shuddering as a violent rage consumed him. If it took him the rest of his days, he would hunt down the man who had done this and he would kill him, slowly, so that he died in agony.

Lifting her in his arms, Max carried her out to the court-yard, where Simon had appropriated a cart.

"I'll take her back to the shop," Simon said. "To Agnes. She'll need a woman's care in case she was . . ." He couldn't finish, but the words hung in the air. *In case she was raped.*

Max's lips were bloodless, his eyes the color of flint. "I'm going to question those guards further in case Louvois let something slip about where he was going. Then I'll check all the *barrières.* He's sure to have left Paris by now. If he has, it was by coach and it was through one of the gates.

"Dominique?"

"The last anyone saw of him he was still alive. We'll have to believe he still is."

It was early the next morning before Max led his weary horse up to the pawnshop on the Palais Royal. He found Simon and Agnes in the kitchen.

"She's upstairs," Simon said immediately before Max could ask. "Sleeping."

"Has she . . . ?"

"Nothing. If only she would cry, or scream, or I don't know, do anything, it might . . . help." He sighed and pushed his hand through his thinning hair. "Agnes doesn't think she was raped."

Max squeezed his eyes shut, hiding a sudden rush of tears. He felt a jumble of emotions—rage and pity and relief for Gabrielle that she had at least been spared rape, but also, to his shame, a relief for his own sake. He was a man, with all of a man's possessive pride, and he couldn't bear the thought of *his* woman being violated by another.

Wordless for once, Agnes pressed a cup of steaming coffee into his hand. He sank down slowly onto the oaken settle before the hearth. "I found a man—it was one of the last *barrières* I had left to check, the one on the road to Reims— who remembered seeing someone late last night matching Louvois's description riding in a heavy black berlin and ac-companied by a small blond-haired child. The man said he thought the child was asleep because it was wrapped up tight in a cloak. It was why he couldn't tell the child's sex.'' Max's lips twisted bitterly. "They let Louvois through because he was so obviously a bourgeois and a friend to the revolution.''

"Jesu . . .'' Agnes muttered, and glared at her revolutionary husband.

"I'm guessing Louvois is making for the border,'' Max went on. "Right now the roads are packed with people leaving Paris—it's almost impossible just to get out of the city. He's way ahead of us, and once he crosses into the German states we may never find him.'' Or Dominique, they all thought, although no one said it.

The streets were clogged with barricades made of anything that came to hand—bits of fences, church pews, paving stones. The barricades were manned by armed guards who refused to let anyone, particularly those suspected of having royalist sympathies, pass. Shops were closed, and many of the great houses shuttered, as noblemen and rich bourgeois tried to flee what had become a city of terror and violence.

"I'm going after him with the aerostat,'' Max said.

"What!'' Simon exclaimed.

"It's possible,'' Max said, thinking out loud. "It just might be possible.''

During the past year Max had made considerable progress with his hydrogen-filled balloons. For one thing, he had found a much quicker way to produce the gas, isolating the hydrogen content of water by passing steam continuously over hot iron particles set in a brick furnace. He had also perfected a flexible varnish containing india rubber with which to coat the envelope, thereby reducing leakage. One of Max's new aerostats could remain inflated for as long as three months, and there was one tethered and waiting for him now in the field at the Jardin des Plantes.

"The aerostat's my only hope,'' Max said. He stood up, rejuvenated with a rush of energy. "He's got at least a six-hour head start, and with the roads jammed as they are I'll never be able to catch him any other way, even on horseback. But the sky is empty. Look . . .''

Max paced the small room in his excitement, working the plan out in his own mind as he spoke out loud, explaining it to the others. "We know he's taken the Reims road, traveling east, right in the direction this rainstorm is moving. If it weren't for these strong westerly winds it would be impossible. Even with the winds on our side it's going to be damnably difficult to follow that road with the aerostat. But I think I've come up with a way to control its lateral movement somewhat, and so . . ."

He had named them risers—a series of pulleys around the balloon capable of collapsing a small portion of the envelope at a time, thereby allowing him to control the aerostat's movement from side to side, as well as vertically. Of course, he would still need the wind in his favor, but he *had* the wind in his favor and it was going to stay in his favor if he had to make it so by sheer willpower alone. He couldn't, wouldn't, fail Gabrielle another time.

"I'm going after Louvois in the aerostat," Max declared. "It's our only chance—"

"I'm going with you."

They all turned at once. Gabrielle stood at the bottom of the stairs. She wore one of Agnes's nightgowns, which was several inches too short for her, showing a pair of impossibly frail-looking white legs. Her eyes were as purple as a bruise, and they stared at Max from a face that was drawn and pale, except for the livid mark on one cheek.

Slowly, tentatively, Max went to her. He stood before her, searching her eyes to see if she still hated him for failing her. It was only a moment, he might even have imagined it, but he thought he saw a spark of love flaring quick and bright within those violet depths, before they turned cold and blank again.

He gathered her into his arms and buried his face in her hair. Agnes must have washed it for her, because it was clean and silky, and he rubbed his cheek back and forth across the top of her head. "Gabrielle . . ."

"Louvois has our son," she said.

Our son. For the second time that morning, Maximilien de Saint-Just almost wept from relief.

He brushed the curls off her face, kissed her forehead. "I'll get him back, *ma mie.*" Even if it costs me my life, he added silently.

"I'm going with you," she said again.

Max looked over the top of her head to Simon and Agnes, and they both nodded mutely.

Agnes stepped forward and took Gabrielle's hand. "Come, *chérie.* You can't go wearing my nightgown. I'll lend you some clothes."

"Make it something warm," Max said. "Bundle her up with lots of petticoats and lend her a cloak, the heaviest one you've got, and a fur hat if you've got one, and gloves."

As they prepared to leave the pawnshop in the Palais Royal, Simon pinned a red and blue cockade on Max's hat and one to the lapel of Gabrielle's cloak.

"It's the new symbol of the revolution," he said. "This way they won't stop you at the barricades." And it worked, for it took them less than an hour to make their way on foot to the Jardin des Plantes.

Throughout that time, Gabrielle spoke not another word. She was wrapped in her own silent world of fear and pain, and Max couldn't even begin to break through to her. He could only hope that she would recover after Dominique was found. He prayed he was doing the right thing to bring her along, but both Simon and Agnes seemed to think that if he didn't, something inside her would snap completely, perhaps leaving her mind permanently damaged.

His plan was to take the balloon up as high as he dared, at least ten thousand feet, to catch the fast stream of westerly air that circled the globe. At that height the wind would push them along at a good pace, at least three or four times that of carriage speed, and they could make up a lot of time on Louvois. When they got within probable range of him, they would descend to just over treetop level and start searching the road for the black berlin.

This early in the morning and with the excitement of the

day before, there was no one at the Jardin des Plantes but the caretaker. The skin of the new aerostat—red and white striped this time—sparkled with a sheen of morning dew. It was taut, still filled with just the right amount of gas, and even in the midst of his anxiety over Gabrielle and Dominique, Max felt a flash of pride in his new invention.

He had a little difficulty releasing the mooring ropes by himself, but then Gabrielle was suddenly at his side to help him. He gave instructions and she followed them precisely, although in a strange, tense silence.

He took the balloon up through blanketing clouds thick as rain that soaked their skin and clothes. Up until they burst out into an icy blue sky shimmering with sunshine. And higher still, until he began to feel the telltale sharp pains in his ear and jaw that told him if he went much higher he would run out of what he thought of as breathable air.

At this height what air there was was cold and dry, and his extremities quickly grew numb. He worried about Gabrielle and kept asking her if she was all right. She wouldn't answer him. Except for her eyes, which blazed now with a strange light, her white face could have been carved from marble, it was so expressionless.

He navigated using his mariner's compass, the sun, and those years of experience sailing a ship across a wide, flat ocean, praying all the while that the road to Reims would still be beneath them when they descended back through the clouds.

After a couple of hours, when he figured they had come far enough to be only an hour or so behind Louvois, Max decided to bring the balloon down. The cloud cover seemed to have thickened, and as they sank into it, the world became a suffocating white shroud. Max had visions of church steeples and trees waiting below for him like spikes in a wolf trap, and then suddenly they were free, skimming across the green and brown earth, and there below them was a road. *Let it be the right road*, Max prayed.

By alternately valving and throwing out ballast, and pulling on his risers, Max maneuvered amid the low-altitude winds, able to follow the twists and turns in the road as he searched for a black berlin. Gabrielle, who had stood unmoving the entire time, clutching the edge of the aerial car, suddenly leaned way over the side.

Alarmed, Max grabbed her arm. "Careful, *ma mie.*" He tried to smile. "Remember, it's a long way down there."

"He'll be in a black berlin," she said. They were the first words she had spoken since standing on the stairs in Simon's pawnshop.

"Would you recognize it?" he asked, careful to keep his voice neutral.

"Yes."

It seemed only moments later when she pointed. "There. There he is." There was no excitement in her voice, only a hard resolution.

Max aimed the balloon for a spot in the road beyond the approaching carriage. He controlled the speed and direction of his descent by carefully shedding ballast and pulling on the risers. He glided the balloon onto the downhill side of a wooded, sloping rise just as the berlin crested the top.

The team of horses reared in their traces, whinnying in terror, and the berlin slewed off the road into a gully. Max pulled on the rip panel—another of his inventions—venting gas rapidly and collapsing the balloon almost immediately, before it could rise again.

Max vaulted out of the car, hauling Gabrielle with him with the strength of his right arm. He held his pistol in his left hand, but he switched it to his right as he and Gabrielle ran toward the berlin. The coachman, terrified already at the sight of the balloon seeming to descend out of nowhere right on top of him, abandoned his master and took off running down the road.

It was so silent Max could hear the moisture dripping off the trees. Clouds of vapor billowed around the horses' heads and one stamped his foot nervously. The black berlin was tilted at an angle, one wheel in the ditch, and there was no sign of life behind the dark, curtained windows.

Max slowed down, grabbing Gabrielle's arm to hold her

back, and they approached the carriage warily. He pointed the pistol at the door.

"Louvois. Open the door and let the boy down. Slowly and carefully."

The door swung open. Dominique was dangled out over the side, held by invisible hands.

His face was dirty and smeared with dried tears. His eyes went immediately to his mother. "Maman," he croaked hoarsely, and Max heard a sob tear from Gabrielle's throat. He let out a slow, shaky breath, for the boy appeared to be all right, then caught it immediately when he noticed the big carving knife held tight to Dominique's throat.

"Throw the pistol on the ground, Saint-Just. This way," said a cold voice, "or I'll slit the boy's gullet."

Max didn't hesitate. He tossed the pistol toward the carriage door.

For a long moment nothing happened, and then Dominique was whisked back inside. Gabrielle cried out and took a step forward. Max flung out his hand, stopping her.

Clutching Dominique tight under the armpits, Louvois descended awkwardly from the berlin, still pressing the knife under the boy's chin. He backed up a step until he was leaning against the open carriage door. He hitched his hips onto the edge, balancing Dominique against his stomach. Shifting his arm, he clamped his hand across the boy's mouth and pulled his head back, gruesomely exposing the small, pale throat to the silver blade of the knife.

"Now, Gabrielle . . ." Louvois was panting hoarsely and his eyes bulged insanely behind the distorting spectacles. "You will pick up the pistol. Pick it up!" he snarled when she didn't move.

She stumbled over to where it lay and picked it up. Max made a tiny, reflexive movement, and the knife blade jerked. Dominique's eyes opened wide, and a muffled sob came from behind Louvois's hand. A tiny trickle of blood oozed down the boy's throat, and Max clenched his fists, forcing himself to stand still.

Louvois smiled. "Please do not move, Monsieur le Vicomte. I'm feeling rather nervous, as you can see . . . Do you love your husband, Gabrielle?''

"Oh, please don't . . . He'll do as you say." She turned pleading eyes to Max. "Won't you, Max?"

Louvois laughed. "Do you remember, Gabrielle, that first time we met in your mother's house?" Gabrielle stood unmoving, looking bewildered. "Do you remember?" he shouted.

"Y-yes," she said quickly.

"I promised that day I would find the price of your pride and that I would destroy you with it. I have found your price, Gabrielle. And you owe me. For the scar, for the years you made a fool of me, for thinking yourself so damned invincible. Well, you're not invincible now, are you, my fine and haughty aristocratic bitch?"

"I will give you whatever you want, anything. Only let my son go."

"Anything?"

"Yes, yes. Anything."

Louvois turned and looked full into Max's face. "Then you will give me *his* life."

"No!" Gabrielle cried. "You can't—"

"Not me, you. You will shoot him dead yourself, with that pistol. Before I count to five. If you don't, the boy dies by my knife. It's your choice, Gabrielle. Your man's life, or your son's. You, my dear, will do the killing, and then I will let you live with it." He laughed again. "That will be my revenge, and I will *own* you then, Gabrielle. Oh, yes."

Silent tears poured down Gabrielle's face. Slowly she shook her head back and forth. "No, no, no . . ."

"One."

"Do it," Max said softly and to her alone.

"Two."

She turned to him, her love, her life, and her face twisted with anguish. "I can't . . ."

Do it, my love. I am not afraid of death, he told her silently, with his eyes, with his heart. *I would die for you with no regrets.* "Do it. For our son."

"Three."

She raised the pistol and pointed it at his chest. It wavered a moment and was still.

"Four."

"I love you, Max."

"I know, *ma mie.*"

"Fi—"

She pulled the trigger. The sound of the shot echoed through the trees, and Louvois screamed.

For Dominique had bit down on the web of Louvois's hand, so hard his tiny teeth pierced the skin and flesh clear to the bone. Reflexively Louvois dropped the knife and flung the boy away from him, and Max launched himself through the air.

He hit the ground on a roll, scooping up the knife and coming up on his feet, smacking Louvois in the chest and sending him crashing against the side of the carriage. For a moment nothing happened, and then the heavy lids fell over Max's eyes and his lips tightened into a smile.

Slowly, silently, he slid the knife between Louvois's ribs, burrying it deep in the thin chest. He held it there, twisting until the blood gushed from the lawyer's mouth and his eyes stared unseeing at the gray sky overhead.

Max stepped back, letting Louvois's body fall to the ground. He walked away, without looking back, over to where Gabrielle knelt on the ground, hugging her son tightly to her chest. He knelt beside them, gathering them both into his arms.

"Papa," Dominique said, squirming out of their embrace. "Maman shot you again."

"No, I didn't," Gabrielle said, sitting back on her heels, laughing and crying at the same time. "I missed."

Max smiled, shaking his head. "Gabrielle . . . did you mean to miss?"

"Of course!"

He laughed and turned so that she could see the tear in the arm of his coat, and the slowly seeping stain of blood. "If you're going to continue firing weapons when I'm in the vicinity, *ma mie*, then I really must teach you how to take proper aim.''

''Oh, *mon Dieu* . . .'' She fell against him, burying her head in his chest. He hugged her tightly, as if he would never let her go.

They held each other for a long time, and then she raised her head and looked over his shoulder at the heavy black berlin and the body of the man lying beside it, and she shivered.

''Don't be frightened, Maman,'' Dominique said, wrapping his arms around her waist. ''That bad man is dead. Papa gutted him.''

Max shifted his shoulders, wanting to shield her from Louvois, even in death. ''It's all over,'' he said.

Turning back within his warm, strong embrace, she laid her palm against his lean cheek, and her lower lip trembled softly. ''Oh, my sweet love . . . it's only the beginning.''

Maximilien de Saint-Just looked down at her beloved face, and lost his heart, his soul, all over again, to a pair of violet eyes that beckoned, promised, fulfilled. I know everything about you, those eyes said. Everything. But I want you still . . .

And I will love you always.

Author's Note

Bastille Day, July 14, 1789—the day the Bastille was stormed by the people of Paris—has come to symbolize for France the triumph of liberty over tyranny. Since that day two hundred years ago, the French have celebrated Bastille Day much in the same manner as we celebrate our Fourth of July, with fireworks and picnics. This July—their bicentennial—they plan to throw the biggest party ever, and as only the French can do it.

In the two years after the great fortress was stormed by the mob, it was dismantled stone by stone. Parisians, always an enterprising lot, made pieces of the stone into bracelets, paperweights, and cockades and sold them as souvenirs for years to come. The day the Bastille fell was the beginning of the end for King Louis's reign, but it was not the end of tyranny, as so many had hoped. As various factions within the new republic fought for power, the revolution turned bloody. A new form of execution was put into use—the guillotine. Thousands of people, including Louis XVI and Marie Antoinette, lost their heads, and the early years of the 1790s went down in French history as the Reign of Terror.

Max and Gabrielle and the other characters in this book are all figments of my imagination. But I believe they do exist in some mysterious dimension where they live and grow old, argue and make love. And this is what happened to them:

Max—being a stubborn male with more courage than sense—wanted to stay in France and continue the fight for liberty and equality. Gabrielle, with the blood of Sébastien in her veins, cared only about survival. Gabrielle threatened to take their children (by now they had a new baby in addition to Dominique) and leave France without Max. He suspected it was all a bluff, but he wasn't interested in testing his theory. Hadn't he learned the hard way that his life was nothing without his Gabrielle?

So, in 1791, the vicomte de Saint-Just and his family emigrated to Le Mississippi, where they lived out their lives with much love and laughter, producing three more children and numerous grandchildren and great-grandchildren.

Simon Prion remained active in the revolution until he inadvertently chose the wrong side in one of the political power struggles. He and a grumbling, scolding Agnes had to flee Paris a bare step ahead of Madame Guillotine. They joined the Saint-Justs for a time in America, but when the Reign of Terror ended in France, they returned to the pawnshop in the Palais Royal.

For to the end of his days, Simon Prion remained convinced that the Palais Royal was the center of Paris, and Paris was the center of the world.